DANCING WITH CASSANDRA

Riley drew Cassandra to the terrace. The doors stood only slightly ajar. He pushed them farther apart so that they might pass, then left the doors that way so the music might drift through.

The night air was cool, but he had his desire to keep him warm and felt no breeze when it stirred. The only thing Riley felt was the stirring of his own heart.

She looked beautiful in moonlight.

Riley saw Cassandra lift an inquiring brow. "If I keep the door ajar slightly, we can hear the music and dance—and not be subject to prying eyes."

Stepping behind Cassandra, Riley took her hands in his and began to move in time to the music. She could feel the warmth of his chest against her back, and it ignited something kindred within her. "You are very considerate," she whispered.

As he moved slowly, Cassandra fell easily into step, letting the music course through her body. Just as his kiss had the other evening.

"No, I am very selfish," he corrected her.

As she swayed against him, the smell of her hair wafted to him in the breeze and he was filled with her scent. "I want you for a little while to myself, Cassandra. All to myself . . ."

BOOK YOUR PLACE ON OUR WEBSITE AND MAKE THE READING CONNECTION!

We've created a customized website just for our very special readers, where you can get the inside scoop on everything that's going on with Zebra, Pinnacle and Kensington books.

When you come online, you'll have the exciting opportunity to:

- View covers of upcoming books
- Read sample chapters
- Learn about our future publishing schedule (listed by publication month *and author*)
- Find out when your favorite authors will be visiting a city near you
- Search for and order backlist books from our online catalog
- Check out author bios and background information
- Send e-mail to your favorite authors
- Meet the Kensington staff online
- Join us in weekly chats with authors, readers and other guests
- Get writing guidelines
- AND MUCH MORE!

Visit our website at
http://www.pinnaclebooks.com

CASSANDRA

Marie Ferrarella

Pinnacle Books
Kensington Publishing Corp.

http://www.pinnaclebooks.com

PINNACLE BOOKS are published by

Kensington Publishing Corp.
850 Third Avenue
New York, NY 10022

First Printing: August, 1998
10   9   8   7   6   5   4   3   2   1

Printed in the United States of America

Chapter One

She was of medium height, with eyes such a clear blue it was as if the sky had come down and gently kissed her in a moment of weakness. Her hair was blond and long and as straight as the needle she plied so skillfully. It caught the morning sun and trapped it there, making the rays gleam amid the golden threads. She shunned a cap and was thought by some to be brazen for it.

But the opinion of others had never troubled her. Except once.

And though she was warm and compassionate and many were compelled to seek her out for her abilities, there was a distance to her. It was as if she moved in a different world from the people around her, as if she were privy to sounds they couldn't hear, sights they couldn't see, knowledge that they would never know.

Her name was Cassandra.

At twenty, Cassandra MacGregor was her father's eldest child. There had been two before her, but they were gone now. Her brothers Robert and Roy, three and five years her elder, had died bravely within hours of each other eight years ago in the Highlands of Scotland. Sacrificed to a feud whose origin none could clearly remember. But that was the way with blood feuds.

Cassandra had fought alongside them. When the time came, she mourned them and helped her father bury them. As she did her mother less than a scant two years later. Always thought of as the strong one, the one with an exceedingly potent sense of survival even when she was barely more than a child, Cassandra had buried all three more deeply than her father had. Her grief she kept to herself.

After their passing, there were moments when Bruce Mac-Gregor spoke to his deceased sons and wife, and times when he appeared to be walking with them.

The moments were happening more and more frequently as time began to leave its mark on the once strong, proud man, taking the light from his eyes and leaving behind only a haunted glow. For him, the tragedies did not lessen as the years went on, but grew, their hold tightening around him more firmly.

His behavior worried Cassandra.

She feared he was slipping irrevocably away, but held on to him as tightly as she could for Rose's and Brianne's sake. For his sake.

And for her own.

After a time, her father would return from his vapid journey and for a while he would be almost the way he'd once been. Each time, Cassandra would pray that it was the last trip, though she knew that it was not.

Misfortune cloaked in evil whispers had forced them to abruptly leave New York. Driven by urgency, they abandoned the bulk of their possessions, taking only her father's tools and a few mementos of past, happier days, as they slipped into the night. It had been Cassandra's choice to come to Morgan's Creek and begin anew.

The town's existence had made itself known to her in a dream.

Though only half the man he once was, the MacGregor knew better than to disregard a dream, for dreams were visions handed down from a higher power. His mother had had them. And his grandmother before her. Both had been blessed, and cursed, with the Sight. Bruce MacGregor knew the power of it and thought himself humbled to be in its presence, humbled to be the guardian of the vessel containing the power. His daughter was now that vessel.

For longer than time had cast its shadow over the moors, there had been those in the Highlands who were gifted, different, kissed by fairy queens. Theirs, from the beginning, was a different path, and common mortals had no knowledge of it.

His firstborn daughter was a seer.

She had seen the outcome of the battle that gray morning that was to claim both of his sons and his two brothers. And many more things before and since. A day before they had fled, she had seen this small Virginia town and known that it would be good to come here. Good to leave the chaotic shambles of New York, where, six years before, he had buried the remainder of his heart.

It was the same city that had once held such promise for him. The same city where he had forged his mark as a furniture maker, sought out by the well-to-do. A city where they had enjoyed a measure of prosperity before the war's end had begun to reverse the fortunes of many.

Yet they were forced to leave not by pending economic hard times but by a man. A man who wanted to bring ruin to Cassandra and her family because she refused his bed. Simeon Radcliffe was a very handsome, charming man skilled in the art of manipulating people to his way of thinking. He was both rich and powerful and, as with all rich and powerful men, he was accustomed to getting his way. The charm had slipped from him when he met with Cassandra's stony resistance.

The very devil had been in his eyes when she had spurned him.

So they had fled, leaving behind the thriving furniture shop Bruce had painstakingly built, leaving behind most of what they had owned, and taking with them little more than their pride and their heritage.

All so that Cassandra might be spared. So that Cassandra might live.

And now they were here.

"In the middle of almost nowhere," Brianne fretted moodily as she stood back and studied, with a critical eye, the rickety building they had just that morning rented from the man who held the deed.

She spun on a heel that was sadly worn down and looked at her older sister, her lower lip protruding in a pout some had called comely.

"I don't understand why we couldn't have gone to someplace more exciting than this. A *real* city. Like Charleston or Richmond or even North Fork." She tossed her head. The long, honeyed ringlets bounced riotously against her back. She tucked a stray hair under her white cap. "Why did it have to be here?" Impatiently, she waved a hand around.

The shop was situated at the end of a small row of buildings that sagged together like four sorrowful spinsters seeking common warmth against a storm. There was a dressmaker shop, a mercantile store, and the widest building, on the opposite end, was the tavern. It was the tavern owner who held the deed to this property.

All in all, it was a very sorry collection of shops, Brianne decided as she thought back to the bustling city they had left behind.

Cassandra looked up from the rotted wood she was pulling up. Three broken boards marked the entrance to her father's new store, one more treacherous than the last. Together they formed a barrier that in her estimation would dissuade potential customers and cast doubts on her father's fine abilities.

She rested the hammer she held in the palm of her left hand and smiled patiently at her sister. She was used to Brianne's complaints, used to her chaffing. As the youngest, Brianne was accustomed to being spoiled and indulged. Coming to Morgan's Creek had been a huge disappointment to the seventeen-year-old girl.

"Because here is where we're supposed to be, Brianne." Cassandra's voice was calm, but there was no ignoring the quiet authority behind it. It had been Cassandra who had governed the family since her mother's passing. Governed it benevolently but firmly as she saw to her father's comfort and the girls' needs, both always above her own.

Brianne huffed as she frowned. With another toss of her head, more spiraling curls sought their way free of the cap she wore.

"I'm tired of these mysterious ways of yours, Cass." She thought of the dances she had just begun to attend. The dances that would be taking place without her now that she was marooned in this desolate place. "Why can't you ever think of us for a change?"

Cassandra resumed her work. Gripping the hammer in both hands, she hit the center of the board, making it crack straight across. Grasping an end, she began to wiggle it away from the others.

"I am. You'll be happy here. I promise."

Brianne had her doubts. In a rebellious mood, she kicked at the board Cassandra was attempting to loosen and caught the end of it with her toe. The board moved out farther.

"Thank you," Cassandra said mildly, never looking up. "But it might be doing us a sight more good if you used more conventional methods than your shoe. You're cracking the leather as well, and we've no money to pay the cobbler for another pair."

Brianne murmured something under her breath that Cassandra chose to let pass.

Rose stepped out to join them. She eased the door closed behind her. Inside, her father was busy readying the large room in order to prepare it for the various pieces of furniture he had plans to build. Above the store was a room large enough for all of them to live in.

When they had brought him there that morning, Bruce MacGregor had brightened at the sight of the store. All three sisters hoped that this was a sign of better times to come. There less than two days, with the wagon they had traveled in now housed behind the livery, Cassandra had been quick to complete the negotiations.

Enticed, intrigued, the tavern owner had readily rented the store to her.

Older than Brianne by a year, Rose had a subtler beauty than her sisters. Softer spoken than either one, she was also the most patient of the three. People had a tendency to overlook her for that very trait. She had emerged from the small shop in time to hear Brianne's complaints.

Even if she hadn't overheard, she would have guessed at the nature of Brianne's discontent. Brianne had complained the entire long, tedious journey from the borders of New York to Virginia. Rose could only shake her head at her sister's behavior. Brianne hadn't left behind her heart the way she had, Rose thought. But that was something she kept to herself. There was no use in adding to Cassandra's burdens.

Rose moved closer to Brianne, taking care that her voice was low and that no one passing them could overhear.

"If we hadn't left, Simeon would have attempted to have Cassandra burned at the stake as a witch." Her deep brown eyes were wide with repressed fear and compassion. Her heart was filled with the horror of her sister's near escape.

But if the thought filled Rose with horror, it only made Brianne laugh. She looked at Rose with a touch of superior smugness.

"For heaven's sake, Rose, this is 1783. They don't burn witches anymore. That's positively medieval." She sat down on the lone chair that was backed against the store. It tottered dangerously even under her meager weight. Brianne chose to quickly rise to her feet rather than be unceremoniously deposited on the dirty walkway. "Besides, Cass isn't a witch."

"Lower your voice," Cassandra ordered softly.

Brianne crossed her arms defiantly before her soft breasts, barely holding her tongue in check.

Rose joined Cassandra and added her hands to the effort. Cassandra smiled her thanks, then put her shoulder to the task. Rose glanced at Brianne and shook her head. "Simeon insisted she was, and he was rich. The rich can buy anything. He would have had her put to death for refusing him."

Selectively, Brianne heard only what she wanted to hear. She sighed as she leaned against the store's outer wall.

"Will we ever be rich, Cass?" Her eyes became eager as

she leaned forward, searching her elder sister's face. "Can you see it, Cass? Can you see that for us? Rich husbands? Luxuries? A goose-down bed as wide as the ocean?" The last was one of her fondest wishes as each night she went to sleep upon a bed filled with straw.

This wasn't the first time Brianne had asked Cassandra to divine their future, to tell her things that were to come. The younger girl never quite understood that it didn't work that way, Cassandra thought. The visions had her, not she them.

Cassandra shook her head as she glanced toward Brianne. "Sometimes it doesn't do well to know too much."

Brianne had expected as much, though it didn't hurt to try every now and again.

"That's what you always say." She smoothed the skirt of her dress with the flat of both her hands. The muslin was old and worn, but the pattern was her favorite. Perhaps Cassandra would make her another soon. Brianne smiled at her sister, attempting another tact. "I bet you don't know."

Brianne was as transparent as a glass of water, Cassandra thought fondly. "Perhaps I do, perhaps I don't. What I do know is that if we don't get to work on this, and quickly too, there'll be no customers crossing the threshold into Da's shop."

Rose peered into the shop through the one window facing the street. She'd left their father repairing the wooden table inside. But he had obviously stopped. As she looked into the near-barren store, she saw that he was standing by the other window, the one that looked out onto the alley. Hands clasped behind his back, he was staring out. Rose didn't have to see his face to know that the stare was blank and that his mind was not on matters of this world.

She sighed quietly as she looked away. "I don't think he feels much like working again."

Brianne laid a hand on Rose's shoulder as she peered into the store herself. "He's drifting." She swung around to look at Cassandra. Complain though she might, it was to Cassandra she always looked for guidance. "Oh, Cass, what are we going to do?"

Cassandra squared her shoulders. "We'll manage," she said cheerfully for her sisters' sake. "We always have before."

But Brianne was afraid and in no mood for simple words. She hadn't properly dealt with her resentment at having to leave New York. She was too young to remember the Highlands. New York was all she knew.

And all she wanted to know.

"If we'd have stayed, I would have had a husband by now. Jonathan Chamber—"

Cassandra thought of the handsome fop and curbed her urge to laugh. He had attempted to catch her alone on the terrace at a ball, but she had thwarted his efforts. Cassandra had never told her sister about her experience with Jonathan of the thousand hands.

"—would not have married you," she concluded now. Soft brows drew together as she looked at Brianne. "He had other plans for you, chit."

Angry, wounded at the coarse implication about her beloved's intentions, Brianne fisted a hand at her waist and lifted her small chin up defiantly as she glared at Cassandra.

"I think you're making it up. I don't think you know as much as you pretend to."

"Bri—" Rose said sharply.

Brianne's wrath swelled to include Rose in its path. "Well, I think it's just an excuse she uses to keep us in line."

Cassandra let the hammer fall. It bounced down the single step and landed in the street a foot away. She crossed to her youngest sister.

"Perhaps sometimes," Cassandra agreed as she draped a hand over her sister's shoulders. "But not this time. The man wanted you warming his sheets, not wearing his name." She let her hand drop as she stepped back. "And spoiled goods—"

"Can't be bartered," Brianne intoned with a bored voice as she rolled her eyes heavenward. She turned toward Cassandra. "If I don't use my 'goods' soon, they won't be any good at all," she wailed. "They'll be curdled."

"Bri!" Rose hushed her, looking around to see if anyone

had overheard her outspoken sister. A huge wave of pink rose up both cheeks, coloring them.

But Cassandra only laughed as she stepped down from the walkway to retrieve the fallen hammer. "They'll be good for a long time to come, I guarantee it, Bri. Now, help me with these boards."

Long, dark lashes dusted her cheeks as Brianne looked down at the board and then back up again at Cassandra. "I'll get splinters." She held up both hands, palms out, as if that pleaded her case.

But Cassandra was getting low on patience as she bent to pick up the hammer. The street, such as it was, was a drying river of mud. It had rained for three days, making their journey here particularly arduous.

The hammer's handle was muddied, and Cassandra frowned as she curled her fingers around it. "You'll be getting a lot more than that if you don't stop pouting and be of some use to us."

"Cass, look out!"

Cassandra turned at Rose's warning, knowing what was about to happen a moment before it did. But it was too late to do anything about it.

Besides, it was part of the design.

Chapter Two

Riley O'Roarke was late.

That was what he got for forgetting himself, for grabbing a bit of leisure and behaving like the gentry for the space of three days.

Two and a half, if you took away the time it took to ride to and from Jason's plantation, he amended.

Ah, but it had been a grand two and a half days. With Rachel gone, Riley found himself hungry for the company of a good, quick mind with which to spar and to peer around both sides of an opinion with. There weren't many around who would go toe-to-toe with him without resorting to fisticuffs. That was why Jason McKinley and his wife, Krystyna were like unmined treasures for him. Learned, in possession of a wide variety of opinions without being opinionated, Jason and Krystyna had stayed up half the night with Riley, talking.

It had been that way both nights of his stay at the plantation.

Riley found himself almost insatiable. There was much to discuss, to explore, for the world they all suddenly found themselves in was continually redefining itself, reinventing itself. Neither fish nor fowl, it was searching for its own place, its own identity.

And the search was marred. The prosperity that had been born of the needs of war had suddenly been deflated, like a filled water pouch whose side had been punctured by an arrow.

Aaron had joined them the second evening. Jason's elder brother, once a stout Tory who had been made to see the error of his thinking, had brought up the thought that the town council should be resurrected now that the war was over. They had all agreed on the point that the town needed a loving but strong hand to guide it if it was not only to survive, but grow.

But Aaron thought that the council's power should be extensive, while Jason believed that what was required was only the lightest of touches. The argument had continued for a while, until Krystyna had reminded them not to count chickens from eggs that hadn't even been laid yet. It would take more than just a discussion in the night to bring back the council.

Riley recalled now that Jason had turned his dark eyes on him when he talked about electing new officials to the long-vacated seats. Him. Sitting on a town council. He had laughed out loud, but secretly it had made Riley's chest swell.

Or perhaps that had merely been the effects of the wine.

Riley grinned to himself as he remembered the evening, the conversation, heated at times, and the feeling it generated. The varying degrees of pleasure he had experienced both because of the food and the company was priceless.

But now there was a price to pay. And by no means was it the dull ache that sometimes followed a night of liberal libation. That carried no greater repercussion with it than a passing desire to die and a thunderous headache that took a wee bit longer to abate. No, the price was higher and bore a greater consequence with it. One that rankled his sense of responsibility, dormant at times, but nonetheless alive and strong when it counted

The Virginia Gazette was due out by Wednesday afternoon and he hadn't finished the typesetting by a half. It was his own deadline, elected of his own choosing, but binding to him as if it were written in stone.

A man was only as good as his word. It was true in Ireland and just as true here.

Riley had ridden his horse hard and quickly since he had left Jason's home before the first creases of dawn had stretched pink, probing fingers across the sky. Muttering now under his breath, Riley urged Devil Wind toward Morgan's Creek.

If he concentrated, he could just faintly discern the small cluster of homes and buildings that huddled together a shade beyond the outskirts of the woods. It wasn't much compared to Philadelphia, but it it looked like a metropolis compared to where he had come from. And compared, he knew, to what it had once been.

The monotonous rain that had assaulted the land for three endless days had left its mark. The grass, where it grew, was a brilliant green. The trees all looked as if they had been freshly washed and were now wearing their Sunday best.

That was the good side.

The bad side was the mud.

It seemed to be everywhere, sucking at the horse's hooves, waiting for tribute it could swallow up into its brown belly. Devil Wind had nearly lost his footing twice in the ride home. Both times had made Riley's heart stop. He was far from an accomplished horseman and didn't relish the thought of sliding from the horse's back into the oozing mud below.

Both in Ireland and Philadelphia, he and horses had always maintained a wide path away from one another. What did he know of horses as a boy, save for the one sorry sorrel attached to his father's plow?

But here in Morgan's Creek there was need of four-legged transportation if a man had ambitions of eventually amounting to something.

The thought made Riley grin again just as he ducked his head to avoid being unhorsed by a low-hanging branch. Devil Wind seemed completely unmindful of the passenger he carried on his back. The horse's goal was apparently the feedbag filled with oats that was waiting for him at the stable.

Amount to something.

Riley repeated the simple phrase again in his head. Who would have ever thought a ragtag, scraggly boyo from County Cork, Ireland, who had nearly died thrice at the hands of British overlords would be running his own newspaper halfway around the world?

His own.

Well, perhaps not quite that. He laughed as he thought of what Rachel would say to his thinking of *The Virginia Gazette* as his own. If truth be known, the newspaper was just as much hers as his. Before she had sailed on the ship bound for France on the arm of Benjamin Franklin, ready to bear witness to the august goings-on of the peace treaty negotiations, Rachel had worked just as hard as he to produce the newspaper.

Harder. And she would be the first to point out that fact. As outspoken as she was pretty, his sister gave vent to her fierce opinions within the editorials as frequently as he did. They had their initials in common and thus many in Morgan's Creek were none the wiser that a good deal of the inflammatory words set down by "R.O'R." belonged to Rachel and not to him.

But Riley was certain that many others suspected as much, having come to know Rachel the way they did.

Riley ducked out of the way of another branch and laughed out loud as he thought of Rachel and her rapier tongue. If Sin-Jin had set his heart on her, as Riley felt sure he had, then the man was certainly going to have his hands full.

And just as certainly he had all of Riley's heartfelt sympathy in the bargain.

It was the first and perhaps the only time Riley had ever felt even the smallest bit of sorrow for anyone remotely British.

Saint John Lawrence was born on British soil, a little more than a day's ride from London. A second son with no claim to his father's fortune, Sin-Jin had wielded the British sword in combat against the Americans before his conscience, and his judgment, had gotten the better of him.

Now, eight years after he had turned his back on his mother country, Sin-Jin was a landowner, same as Jason and bound to him, Aaron, and Morgan McKinley, the town's founder, by blood, for Sin-Jin had married Morgan's only daughter, Savannah. The marriage lasted less than half a decade, for Savannah had died of the fever.

Her death had left the ever-optimistic and resourceful Sin-

Jin feeling alone and lonely for perhaps the first time in his life. Until Rachel had entered it. Their first meeting had been auspicious enough. She had pointed a musket at his heart.

Cupid had pierced it nearly around the same time.

"Sin-Jin can't say he wasn't warned," Riley said aloud to Devil Wind.

God, but he missed his sister. Riley fervently hoped that the treaty would be signed soon so that she would sail back. He needed her for her quick mind and quicker fingers, if not for her company.

But negotiators, he knew, had a love of their own voices, and he was certain that it would be many months before he saw his sister again.

And meanwhile, there was work to do.

Mud flew along the normally dusty road as Riley urged his horse on faster. The horse snorted his protest but continued the fast pace.

If he ever became rich, a fine carriage would be his first purchase, Riley silently vowed to himself. And a livery man to drive it.

But not a slave, Riley thought. He wouldn't have a slave. Instead, he'd employ someone. A willing freeman. Riley didn't believe in slavery. He abhorred the whole concept. It was a heinous institution not far removed from what the British felt compelled to exercise over their Irish brethren. There it was called servitude, but the concept was the same at heart. They owned you until you died beneath their boot. That had been the way of it for his own mother.

His face grew grim just from the mere memory of it, of the years he had spent in Ireland, toiling beside his father on land that would never be theirs, having nothing to show for it but sweat. Riley was of the same mind as some of the citizens of Pennsylvania and Maryland, who had outlawed slavery within their borders.

But Riley knew that it would be a long way down the road before Virginians would follow suit and give up the claim to their own slaves. The economic climate of the state made it almost an impossibility to contemplate. Men like Jason and

Sin-Jin had freed their slaves and paid them wages, but there were more men like Aaron and Morgan than Jason and Sin-Jin.

Far more.

Riley chewed over the thought for a moment as Devil Wind finally gained the perimeter of the town. A call to abolish slavery would make an interesting editorial, though it would rankle many.

He'd never been above rattling a few cages.

It certainly wouldn't be the first time his views met with disfavor and harsh criticism. Rather than be wary of adversity, Riley thrived on it. More, he felt as if he owed it to the people who paid the halfpenny for his gazette to give them the benefit of his conscience as well as the sweat of his brow.

Now, if only—

The surprised gasp Riley heard as he rounded the corner startled him out of his thoughts. Holding tightly on to Devil Wind's reins, he pulled back. The horse pranced impatiently as he skidded to a halt. Riley tugged on the reins as he turned the horse around and looked about to see who had cried out and why.

He turned toward the row of four buildings.

The woman in the street bewitched him the first moment he looked upon her.

Though there was mud outlining the bottom of her dress and more splattered on portions of her torso where a man's eyes were not supposed to linger, the young woman was the most beautiful creature Riley had ever seen in his life.

At the last moment Cassandra had averted her head and been spared the embarrassment of having mud on her face. But there was some on her arms. She looked down at them now, and then at the man on the horse.

Her mouth curved in a smile. "Your mouth is hanging open, sir. I suggest that you'll be closing it quickly before someone else comes riding by, chased by the devil as you were, and awards you with a mouth full of mud."

Her voice was low and throaty, and there was humor in it. It was shining in her eyes as well. Eyes so blue that they pulled in his very soul.

Riley didn't quite remember sliding from the back of his horse and into the mud. But he knew he must have, because the next moment, when he looked down, he saw the mud sliding brown fingers along his newly polished boots.

It didn't matter.

Habit had Riley wrapping the reins around his hands to keep the horse from escaping. No conscious thought was necessary; it was instinctive.

His eyes were on the woman before him. "A thousand pardons, Madam."

Cassandra wiped the mud from her arms and was already turning her attention to the final board. " 'Tis Mistress, sir, not Madam, and one pardon will do very well if it's sincere."

Still holding the reins, Riley was quick to rip the board completely out for her. He tossed it on top of the others. He was vaguely aware that there were others occupying the same space as he and the blond-haired angel, but if they were women or creatures from another world, he had no idea.

All he could see was her.

Chapter Three

Riley stood there, transfixed like a man captured within a bubble where time had ceased moving forward. The world around Riley filtered by without him taking note. He struggled to blink his eyes. The naturally reflexive action required effort on his part.

Gradually, his surroundings came into focus. He felt as if he were being roused from a deep, dream-filled sleep and was having difficulty separating the real world from the dream world. He took a deep breath.

The dream continued.

He became aware of the fact that the beautiful rose before him had two almost equally lovely buds on either side of her.

But it was she who took his breath away and left him speechless. Not an easy feat, considering that he was a man who was accustomed to talking almost as much as he was accustomed to doing.

For one of the very few times in his life, Riley felt awkward. As if to wipe away the feeling, he rubbed his hands on the sides of his britches. He flashed an appealing grin. "I'm sorry, where are my manners?"

Cassandra smiled, amused. She saw the momentarily discomfort that flickered through his eyes before it faded away again. Here was a man, she thought, who was generally at ease with himself. A man who knew his limits and when to push past them.

She nodded toward the muddied path that stretched out behind his horse. "Perhaps they're still galloping down the street."

Her answer, said without malice, made him smile all the more. Riley admired wit almost as much as he admired beauty. Perhaps, at times, even more, since of the two it was the rarer.

"No doubt," he agreed, and her smile widened in response. "I'm Riley O'Roarke." Riley waited for her to give him her name in exchange, but there was only silence that greeted him. Well, he was not unaccustomed to prodding, he mused. "And you are—?"

She knew it wasn't seemly to be exchanging names and pleasantries with a stranger, and while she was not one to be governed, much less shackled by mindless conventions, she did have work to attend to if they were to settle in reasonably well before the evening.

"Busy, it would seem." With determination, she turned her back on Riley, prepared to grasp the end of the board she'd been working on with both hands.

When she turned away, Riley noted, much to his chagrin, the full extent of what he had done. The mud trailed the length of her dress as well. The splatterings formed almost a straight arrow upward, pointing toward a waist that would have reduced a corset maker to tears for its slenderness.

He had long ago learned to face up to his guilt no matter how large or small it was. Franklin had taught him, while he and Rachel had lived in the statesman's house as his wards, that the mark of a man was not in his offenses so much as in how he faced them and the manner in which he rectified them.

"Your dress—" Riley began to apologize hesitantly.

Cassandra stopped and glanced over her shoulder. More mud. She held out the skirt and saw the ugly streak. She sighed, but it was the sound of resignation, not annoyance. Dropping her hand, she let the material settle against her once more.

"Most of it'll wash out, I suspect."

He'd also learned a thing or two about clothing, at his sister's insistent behest. The dress was ruined. "And the rest won't. I take my responsibilities seriously. It is my duty to replace your dress."

For just the barest instant there was a flash of a thought through his mind. It involved removing the soiled garment from the young woman's supple torso and replacing it with another, but not too quickly. The thought made him warm.

Lucky he was, he thought, to have enough control to prevent the idea from clearly registering upon his face. It was the kind of thing that got a man's face slapped, and justifiably so.

Cassandra took her measure of the man before her and felt a warm glow filtering through her as she did. It was the glow a woman experienced when she had made intimate contact with a man. She saw things in his eyes that Riley had no idea he was revealing. And it made her blush even while, in a secret part of her soul, it pleased her.

He was a man, Cassandra saw, who took pleasure in knowing the fairer sex. Knowing them in the biblical sense. A charmer with a tongue of silver, she'd wager. She'd never known of an Irishman who couldn't succeed, at some point, in charming the leaves from the trees.

Well, there were no leaves coming from her trees. At least, not at the moment.

"It's been my experience, Mr. O'Roarke, that men who buy women dresses on occasion feel the need to ask for them back. Usually at the most inopportune times. Therefore, I free you of any obligation you might feel you have toward me."

She was about to return to her work, when she saw Rose's hands fly to her mouth. The girl's eyes were huge as she looked at her older sister in disbelief.

"Cassandra, I can't believe you said that." Pink flames rose to claim both cheeks and then some.

"I can," Brianne said, attempting to appear very blasé and worldly before this male audience.

The youngest of the sisters turned to take her own, none too subtle appraisal of the man who stood before them. He was wide of shoulder and narrow of hip. And though his clothing was rougher than that of the men she had hoped would squire her in New York, the detraction they afforded was far outweighed by the fine, chiseled features of his handsome face. A man could be forgiven a great deal if he were handsome.

More if he were handsome and rich.

Brianne nodded toward her older sister, a touch of disdain in her voice. But only a touch, lest he think her too contrary. These were wiles both her sisters refused to learn. Wiles a woman needed, Brianne thought, to marry well.

"Cassandra always speaks her mind."

"Cassandra," Riley repeated, rolling the name around on his tongue like a fine whiskey. It was rich and melodious and suited her perfectly. "Is there a surname that would be going with that?"

His question was directed to Cassandra, but once again it was not she who gave him his answer.

"We're the MacGregors." Brianne could move swiftly when she desired, and she did so now, placing herself between Cassandra and the handsome stranger.

Her vivid blue eyes flirted with him as she told him her name. "I'm Brianne, and that's Rose." She barely nodded toward her other sister. She searched Riley's face, eager for a sign that she had captured his fancy. "And you already know Cassandra's name."

This one was young, Riley thought as he nodded to each sister in turn, younger than her years would warrant. Brianne looked like a paler copy of Cassandra, but that would undoubtedly change in a year or so. At least on the surface.

But there was something within the clear blue eyes of the elder that set her apart. A distant worldliness that he doubted Brianne would ever attain.

Few did.

To see it embodied within Cassandra fascinated him as an editor, and as a man. For Cassandra was as comely as any woman he had ever seen.

More.

"I'm pleased to meet you all," he said, smiling first at Brianne and then at Rose. The latter curtsied politely. But his eyes came to rest on Cassandra, as if drawn there by a force he had no control over. "Are you three ladies planning on remaining in Morgan's Creek?"

"Yes," Brianne answered before either of the others could. There was still a slight pout in her reply, but it was growing less so as she smiled up into Riley's face. "We're originally from New York," she added importantly. "Just."

He doubted that. At least, in Cassandra's case. There was a burr to her words that didn't have its origins in the northern state. It was plain that she, at least, was an immigrant, same as he. It gave them something in common.

"New York." He gathered the information like a miner working a vein. His eyes, like soft velvet, passed over Cassandra's face. "And what brings you here, Mistress MacGregor?"

Why was he looking at her sister, when she was the one who was talking? Brianne drew herself up. "Cassandra and her—"

"Bri!" Cassandra cried sharply.

The chiding tone both shamed Brianne and caused her to grow sullen and quiet. Knowing she was guilty of almost having given away a family secret, Brianne looked grudgingly down at the ground.

She passionately wished there were no secrets to give. Then they could have remained in New York. And she would have had her fill of parties instead of standing on a muddied street, having a conversation with probably the only good-looking man for miles.

The sharp reprimand aroused Riley's curiosity. What was the girl about to say? And why was it met with such rebuke?

It was obvious that there would be no answer to his questions. At least, not in the immediate future. But he could be patient when necessary. Patient to a degree that surprised even him at times. There were secrets here. Secrets he intended to uncover.

"I thought the change would do my father good," Cassandra

said smoothly, weaving her reply into the tapestry of the fabric Brianne had laid out.

Another piece of information. "Your father?" Riley echoed. "Then, he has come here with you?"

It had seemed rather odd to him that three women would venture anywhere unaccompanied. Even Rachel did not go about unescorted, and she was as close to a hellion as he ever wanted to meet.

Then he remembered that Krystyna had made her way alone, for the most part, on these shores. Riley looked at Cassandra with greater interest. Had his path crossed yet another independent woman? For it was clear that of the three, she was the one in charge.

"Yes." Cassandra glanced toward the remaining rotten board. She was wasting too much time, standing there and talking. So much remained to be done. A tiny thread of her patience began to unravel. "Sir, are you always in the habit of conducting inquisitions on people who arrive in your town?"

Riley spread his hands wide, a smile curving his generous mouth. He hoped to nudge a kindred one from Cassandra.

"Asking questions is part of my work." He saw that his reply had sufficiently aroused her curiosity. "I'm the editor of the town newspaper. *The Virginia Gazette,*" he added with no undue pride, the kind a father felt for his child.

Gossip.

The word leapt to her mind without thought. It was gossip, and the threat of worse, that had caused them to leave their home of eight years in the first place. She abhorred it.

Cassandra pressed her lips together, struggling to maintain her manners in the face of this new turn. "Be assured that we've no wish to see our name spread across the pages of your periodical, Mr. O'Roarke."

Brianne looked aghast at her older sister. She could think of nothing grander than to have her arrival announced for all to see.

"Speak for yourself." Brianne made no effort to hide her

annoyance. Her sister was always thinking only of herself, never them. Never how they were affected by her actions. "How are we to meet people if no one knows we're here?"

Cassandra shook her head. Brianne never saw beyond her nose. "We needn't be announcing our presence from a rooftop to meet people, Bri."

Riley saw the way Cassandra's brows drew together, and he wondered exactly what she thought of periodicals. And why. Some people thought them a waste of time, but no one took umbrage with them the way she seemed to. The mystery surrounding her deepened and piqued his interest all the more.

He sought to reassure Cassandra of the caliber of his work. "It won't be from a rooftop, I guarantee you, unless, of course, the wind blows it there."

Light entered her soft, deep brown eyes as Rose thought of the possibilities. She laid an imploring hand on her older sister's arm.

"Cassandra, think of what it might do for Da's business," Rose urged gently. It wasn't in her nature to be loud or unduly willful. But neither did she falter when her mind was made up. She glanced at Riley and felt at ease. There was something about his smile that caused her to trust him. "Letting people know we've settled here might do him some good."

Cassandra nodded, secretly contrite at her omission. It should have been she, not Rose, who had thought of that. She was the one in charge of their welfare now that Da had his spells. It had to have been the appearance of the stranger, galloping full bore into her life, that had caused her to be momentarily remiss.

She smiled now and nodded in agreement. "Yes, it very well might."

Intrigued, seeing a crack opening up before him through which he might gain entrance, Riley crossed his arms before him and leaned against the post. "And what business might that be?"

Before any of the girls had a chance to answer, an ominous creak warned him that he should shift his weight, and quickly.

The post groaned like an old man rising from a sunken bed of straw.

Riley straightened and eyed the post critically. "That needs repairing."

Cassandra nodded. Her eyes followed the length of the crack along the post. The cleft traveled from the very top to the bottom, and ran deep. It didn't need repairing, it needed replacing.

"As does everything else, to be sure." Cassandra raised her eyes to his. He was going to offer to help in the next breath. "My father can take care of that," she told him before he had the chance to form his words.

She wasn't defensive, he noted, so much as distant, despite the warm smile that curved lips the color of ripe raspberries. He wondered if she was afraid of him for some reason. He had never struck fear into anyone's heart, not even Rachel's, though he had tried mightily when he was younger. Rachel had always said he couldn't scare away dust from a table.

He attempted not to stare at her, but he had a feeling that Cassandra somehow knew that he wanted to. "Handy, is he?"

"More than handy," Brianne was quick to put in, not wanting to be left out of the conversation with this man for more than a moment or two. "Our father's an artist." She lifted her chin proudly. "People would come from all over just to see his work and purchase it."

Riley refrained from smiling indulgently at Brianne's boast, but he did raise a brow at the title of artist that the young girl bestowed on her father. He took it to be no more than the childish prattle of a foolish, prideful daughter.

Cassandra did not need the mantle of seer to read what was so plainly on Riley's mind. She knew that Brianne had laid the words a little thickly about them, but still, there was an urgent need to ride to Brianne's defense, as well as her father's, that piqued Cassandra. She sought to dissolve the smile Riley was endeavoring to suppress. And failing in his attempt.

"He isn't an artist the way most would be thinking the term to mean. He puts no brush to canvas, nor unearths any secret forms from within clay. Yet in his own way my father is as gifted as any who'll be wearing the lofty title." She spoke the words calmly, and they had all the more weight for that. "And 'tis true that his talents were sought after by many, at least while they had the money to spend on luxuries."

He found himself willing to believe anything that she told him. "You have me at a disadvantage, Mistress. What is it that your father creates?"

"Furniture," Cassandra replied before Brianne could blurt out the word. She saw her sister bite her tongue in aggravation. Patience was something that had never suited Brianne to exercise or even experience.

"Furniture?" Riley glanced toward the store. The one lone, large window gave testimony to what appeared to be an empty shop. He wondered if the man had pieces stored somewhere.

"Furniture," Cassandra repeated. "My father is regarded as a craftsman."

A fond smile lifted the corners of her mouth as she remembered the pride her father had always placed into his work. Sweet Lord, she hoped that could be rekindled again. If it could, that would be what would save him. His work and his pride. And her, if she had any say in the matter, she thought with determination.

Cassandra saw that Riley was waiting for her to continue. Since she had already told him part, she saw no reason not to give him the rest.

"He had his own shop in New York, and a thriving business it was. But the end of the war brought other changes as well. Demand fell off as people looked to their necessities rather than to their desires for luxuries." She shrugged philosophically. She bore no grudges. At bottom, they were all attempting to survive in their own way. "Floors are good for sitting and lying as well as walking. It leaves a craftsman with nought to do."

Riley nodded in sympathy. "Pockets have been empty since the end of the war," he agreed.

He couldn't very well find it in his heart to grieve with her over the matter, since the misfortune of a deflated market had brought them all there. He dropped the solemn appearance he felt the situation had momentarily called for.

"Well, in any event, New York's loss is most assuredly our gain." He looked from one face to another and lingered on Cassandra's. "If it hasn't been said before, may I be the first to bid you welcome to Morgan's Creek."

Chapter Four

Cassandra acknowledged Riley's formal greeting of welcome with a nod of her head. But she had wasted far too much time as it was.

"Thank you. Now, if you will excuse me, Mr. O'Roarke, I truly have work to do." Once again, and hopefully for the last time, she turned her attention to the second rotting board in the walkway and her back to him.

She meant to take that out all by herself, he realized. Riley quickly came to life and moved to Cassandra's side. He attempted, unsuccessfully, to nudge Cassandra aside, but she stood her ground.

He saw the stubborn look enter her eyes. A stubborn look that belonged not to a sullen child, but to a woman who knew her own mind and her own capabilities. But when it came to the master of stubbornness, he had never been known to take second.

Riley held fast to the edge of the board. "You shouldn't be trying to pry off something like that by yourself."

Another man who thought her helpless just because she'd been given a woman's form. She had no time to argue with him as she put her back into it and strained to pull the board free.

"Well, spirits won't be lifting the boards for me," she grunted through clenched teeth, "and lifted they must be, and replaced, or else there'll be no way for anyone to come to the shop."

Riley had the distinct impression that arguing with Cassandra would be futile. Instead, he managed to edge her out of the way and, putting his brawn to it, succeeded in prying the rotted board away from its kin. The last board quickly followed behind the first two, and now there was a gaping hole staring down at the dark, damp ground beneath.

Sam should have taken care of this before he rented the place to the girls, Riley thought. He slid the back of his hand across his brow and stood back, surveying the empty store. It looked like a poor relation beside the other three.

"How much did he soak you for?"

Cassandra offered him her handkerchief, which he accepted gladly. "Who?"

The tiny bit of material had a sweet, airy scent that became her, he thought, attempting not to be too obvious as he inhaled the fragrance. Riley wiped his face with it and returned the handkerchief to her. His skin tingled as if she had touched it herself.

"Sam, the tavern owner." He nodded toward the end of the walkway. The tavern stood there like a benevolent overseer. Suspicion suddenly entered his eyes. "You did rent it from him, didn't you?"

She tucked the handkerchief into the sleeve of her dress, her eyes on his. What manner of fool did he take her for?

"Of course I rented it from him. The store 'tis his, isn't it?" Riley inclined his head in affirmation of her question. "Who else would I be renting it from?"

Apparently there were areas that she was naive in, he mused. "From someone who would lie and say that the store was his to rent. Someone who might want to unscrupulously take advantage of a pretty lady."

The words brought an indulgent smile to her lips. Flattery,

the empty variety, was something she was very well acquainted with. Men felt it was their duty to shower it on any woman with a pretty face.

She'd seen through them all, Simeon in particular, which was why they found themselves there in the first place.

But "there" seemed like a nice place to be, she thought, despite Brianne's protests. Morgan's Creek was a young, thriving town, and it would grow until it rivaled larger cities. This she knew to be true.

Her smile made her eyes sparkle like warm blue crystals. He had to struggle not to allow himself to drift, lost in their spell.

"Not like yourself, I take it?" Cassandra asked, amused.

She had him all but hypnotized with her eyes. It took everything he had to keep his wits about him. He dug deep into his reserve of inner strength. It wouldn't do to stutter like some milk-faced boy. What sort of power did she possess, he wondered, even as he felt himself losing to it.

"I never take advantage." He winked, and Cassandra had to admit that she felt something stir within her as he did so. "'Tis the ladies who take advantage of me."

There was a lilt to his voice, a melody that came from her part of the world but not from her isle. And his words assured her of his origin more than his surname did.

"You're Irish, aren't you?" It wasn't a question so much as a statement.

His heritage was something Riley was very proud of, even when it had not been popular to be so. His eyes remained on her face to see if it was touched with disdain at his answer. "Yes."

Cassandra nodded knowingly. "That would explain the

Riley thought. He
genuine

And as they are,'' he added, knowing she understood his meaning.

"So does Cassandra,'' Brianne said a bit too vehemently. She was rewarded with a sharp jab in the ribs by Rose for her trouble. Brianne stifled a yap and glared at Rose. She crossed to Riley. "What is the town like, Mr. O'Roarke?''

"It has . . .''

His voice trailed off as Riley searched for the word that would most aptly describe the tiny, struggling town that wanted so badly to grow to be as important as some of the older cities. He knew it was only a matter of time. But time, for some, moved too slowly. As it probably did, he judged, for Brianne.

". . . a great deal of potential,'' Riley finally concluded.

Brianne's face fell. "Oh.'' She sighed. She knew what that meant. It meant that Morgan's Creek was nothing at all like New York and had little chance of ever being so in the near future. "I see.''

She looked far too young to seem so disappointed, Riley thought. He quickly added, "And a great many more men than women.'' Brianne suddenly came to life before his eyes. He had to hold back his laugh. "You'll be a welcome addition to the population.''

He glanced over his shoulder and saw that Cassandra was attempting to stack the boards one on top of the other. The dress he had offered to replace was now in definite need of retirement. Sighing impatiently, he joined her, gently moving Rose out of the way.

Cassandra took his silent offer of help in stride. For a man, he did not get that much underfoot.

Brianne was eager to corner him about his statement. The information he had casually tossed her did a great deal to change her initial reaction to him as she stood directly behind at her back as she

boards where they were piled. He'd managed to accomplish what would have taken them much longer to do. Cassandra always gave everyone their due. "Well, it's beholden to you we are."

He liked the sound of that. There was a promise to be garnered, to be explored upon another day. "I'll find some way for repayment."

She had no doubt that he would, and what that repayment might involve. Rather than take offense, she smiled, sweeping the matter away.

"Don't trouble yourself, Mr. O'Roarke. We'll have you to dinner some night when we can set a proper table for a proper printer." Her mouth curved even more. "And the debt shall be repaid."

The amusement in Cassandra's eyes aroused his own. She was a rare one, he thought.

"Cassandra's a wonderful cook," Rose was quick to boast.

The unexpected endorsement from such a quiet corner had Cassandra looking at her sister in surprise. She felt slightly uncomfortable at the unsolicited praise.

She lifted a shoulder, then let it fall. "At least no one's ever died at my table," Cassandra added, wondering why her sister felt compelled to announce her virtues to this stranger.

In a rare moment of courage Rose summoned hers to her and added, "She's being modest, as usual."

What had gotten *into* Rose? "And you are being very vocal, which is decidedly very *un*usual for you." She turned her face toward Riley. "We mustn't keep Mr. O'Roarke any longer."

He was disappointed at the dismissal. Riley found himself wanting to remain in Cassandra's company a little longer. "Oh, you're not keeping me."

Cassandra lifted a brow. There was something intuitive and knowing about the slight gesture, Riley thought, as if she were looking into his very soul. As if she had already *looked* into his soul while he had stared at her, as dumbstruck as an adolescent.

"Shouldn't a proper kind of printer be putting out a newspaper?"

The reminder was like having a pan of cold water spilled

upon his head from high above. He came to attention. The newspaper and all the work that lay waiting for him had completely slipped his mind the moment he had gotten his first look at her. Her words jarred his memory.

Quickly, he caught up the reins of his horse and rounded to the side of the animal.

"Why, yes, I—" Riley stopped just before his boot slid into the stirrup. He lowered his foot to the ground once more and looked at Cassandra, puzzled. "How did you know that?"

He hadn't mentioned when the newspaper came out. He took pride in the fact that it made its appearance every Wednesday, without fail, since he had begun the task a year ago.

But she had no way of knowing that.

Cassandra smiled easily, though she could tell without looking that Rose was shifting helplessly from side to side.

Poor Rose, Cassandra thought. This ability of hers had caused her sister much anguish. Rose was always afraid someone would discover Cassandra's abilities and put the wrong meaning to it.

The way Simeon had in New York.

But some things were just arrived at through natural intuition, as this had. Cassandra smiled at Riley, making her answer seem perfectly plausible. "You said you were the editor of the *Gazette*."

Riley shook his head. "Yes, but I never said when it came out."

Her smile never wavered. "I made an assumption," she told him innocently. "Was it incorrect?"

He sighed, flustered. And shackled by his responsibilities. "No, no, it was very correct indeed, and I'm behind as it is. You'll have to excuse me for now."

"You've already been excused," she told Riley softly.

And with that Cassandra lifted her skirts. The muddied hem rose above the ground. She turned on her heel and opened the door to the empty store. Within a moment she was gone.

Nodding to her sisters, Riley quickly made his way to the newspaper office.

Chapter Five

Rose eased the door closed behind herself and the others. She was the last to enter the store and the first to speak.

"I can't believe you were so forward with a man," Rose chided in a soft, hushed whisper as she shook her head at Brianne. Her sister was always forward, but this was outrageous, even for Brianne.

Criticism of any sort was not something Brianne accepted graciously. "I was being sociable," Brianne objected, daring Rose to contradict her. Her hands fisted at her waist as her eyes narrowed. "And why shouldn't I be?" Brianne demanded with a toss of her head. The man was good-looking and showed promise. "If Cassandra doesn't want him—"

Cassandra looked at Brianne reprovingly. Brianne was carrying on, which in itself was not unusual. However, the tenacity of her conduct possessed a depth and breadth that concerned Cassandra. She saw a potential problem in the making. Both girls were being extremely difficult today. As if she didn't have enough on her mind.

But then, she relented, she supposed they were entitled to a little leeway. After all, they had been uprooted from the only home they had ever known. They were reacting to the uncertainties, the fears they were experiencing. It was different for her. She had already been forced to leave what she considered her home once. She had known then, at the end of that long journey, that New York was but a temporary stop. Temporary no matter how many years lapsed. They were not meant to stay there.

"We're talking about a man, Brianne," Cassandra reminded her sister patiently. "Not some article of clothing or a serving of soup."

The look on Brianne's face told her that her words were floating from one ear to the other, unheeded in their passage. Her expression spoke of a deep-rooted stubbornness. What Cassandra said had no more effect than if she had been addressing a granite cliff.

Cassandra threw up her hands in frustration. "It isn't a matter of my wanting or not wanting—"

Brianne seized on the words. Wanting was something she understood, something that governed her life.

"It is with me. For pity's sake, Cassandra, I am seventeen." Brianne said the last as if being that age meant that one foot was already in the grave.

Cassandra sighed and closed her eyes for a moment. When she opened them again, she was calmer and in control once more. She laid a hand on her sister's arm. "There's time, Bri."

Brianne jerked her arm away. She didn't want to be placated or talked to as if she were a child. She wasn't a child. She was a woman. With a woman's yearnings. And a woman's needs. She wanted comforts, all that money could buy.

"Time? For what? To be an old maid?" Brianne had almost said "Like you," but bit her tongue in time. Instead, she reminded Cassandra of something they all knew. "Mother was married at my age."

"Aye," Cassandra agreed sadly. She thought of their mother, of the waste that had resulted. "And used up before her time."

Brianne hadn't had to say the words "Like you" to her. Cassandra had read them in the younger girl's eyes. And heard them in her heart. Was she? she wondered. Was she an old maid? Her own future was a mystery to her, and there were times when she was just impatient enough to wish to know.

But those times passed swiftly. The power had not been bestowed upon her for her personal indulgence, but for servitude.

Brianne tossed her head, tired of tiresome words. "Well, *that* won't happen to me. I'll set my cap for the richest man here and live a good life."

"Good comes from the inside," Rose reminded Brianne, and so saying, aligning herself with Cassandra.

"And comfort"—Brianne's voice rose, angry at the reprimand—"comes from without." She pursed her lips as she glared at Rose. "You're always taking her side," she accused hotly. "Why don't you ever side with me?"

"Because, Bri, you're never right," Rose pointed out simply.

Brianne opened her mouth, a scathing retort on her tongue, but Cassandra placed a cautioning hand on either girl's arm. Both turned to look at her.

"Girls" was all she said to her sisters. The warning was clear. They were to cease immediately. Her eyes silently indicated their father.

The squabble, in danger of exploding only a moment earlier, ended aruptly. Both younger girls saw that their father, far from gazing vacantly out through the window, was actually working. There was a single dusty table in the middle of the room, left there by the last occupant of the store. It was in sad condition, with one leg obviously lame. Bruce had spread out his tools upon the badly scarred wooden floor and was busy taking measurements so that he might replace the leg.

"Da?" Cassandra said softly as she approached. Her skirt, stiffened with mud, rapped along the wooden boards like scratchy fingers being dragged against the grain as she walked. "What are you doing?"

Her father was on his knees, preoccupied with his task, oblivious of everything else, including the argument that had flared. He looked up at her, his eyes clear, and she saw that his mind was with them.

He would be better for a time, she thought, her heart filled with joy at the prospect. It was a good thing that they had come here.

Her vision had been true.

"I would have thought that obvious." Bruce sat back on his heels and gestured at the wobbly table leg. He was taking precise measurements and intended to create a sturdier duplicate of it by evening. "I certainly cannot work very well on a table that lists to one side like a drunken stable boy, now, can I? What sort of impression would that make on patrons who would come in and see that the furniture maker cannot even make himself a decent table?"

"Not a very good one," Cassandra agreed, the corners of her mouth dimpling with the smile that was brimming within her.

Their heated argument temporarily forgotten, Brianne and Rose gathered around their father. They were united in their delight at seeing him thus occupied.

"Beds," he announced suddenly as he looked at the ring of love that encircled him. "I'll be making beds for my girls next. Cannot have my beauties sleeping on pallets forever, now, can I?"

There was a mill not more than a mile from the town. He'd place his order for the wood in the morning, he thought with mounting pleasure.

She would have slept on rocks to see him like this. "It'll do for now, Da," Cassandra told him.

Bruce laughed and patted his eldest's cheek fondly. He knew exactly what she had endured for his sake. Like a soldier she had been, even as a child. He was supremely blessed.

"Not for my girls."

Her sister's selflessness annoyed Brianne. She edged her out to gain her father's eye. "Can I have a goose-down mattress when you're done, Da?" Brianne asked eagerly. "I do so want one."

It pleased his heart that he could indulge Brianne so easily. Bruce stroked his youngest's honey-blond hair, thinking how much she resembled her mother. They all did in different ways. Brianne had her mother's eyes and her love for fine things. Rose had her sweet nature, and Cassandra had Molly's golden hair and her tenacity.

"You'll have it," he promised. "With the very first sale that I'll be making." He turned toward his middle daughter. "Rose?"

She knew her father was asking her for her request. It wasn't hard. She didn't care where she slept or on what. And her clothes were of only marginal concern as long as they were clean. But adventures of the mind was something she dearly loved.

"A book, Da. Any book." Rose thought of the small library she had, still packed away in the wagon. The books had pages that were all well worn from many loving readings. "I would love something new to read."

Bruce pressed his lips together. He would have rather that she had asked for something pretty.

"Ah, you read too much, my Rose. Not that reading's a bad thing, mind you. But you do not give yourself sufficient chance to bloom." He saw the disappointment begin to form. Rose would never give voice to it, but he knew her well. He laid a hand across her narrow shoulders and hugged her to him. "But if it makes you happy, then a book you shall have. Two. Three, perhaps," he added expansively.

He turned to Cassandra as naturally as if she were the parent and he the child. "Do they have a place that sells books here?"

She wondered if O'Roarke had books to sell as well as a newspaper to create. "I'll be looking into it on the morrow, Da."

It was as good as done, then. Cassandra never failed him, even in the slightest requests. She was his comfort and his rock. A pity to do this to his own child, he thought, but, oh, at the same time, what a comfort it was to him.

"And what of you, Cassandra? What is it that you would want?"

Cassandra had only one wish, one request that filled her day and night. "Only your happiness, Da, and your good health."

He knew she spoke the words from her heart and not merely to appeal to his vanity. His eldest was too selfless. He wished her a little less so for her own good.

With a sigh he took both her hands into his. "There has to be more, Cass," he insisted.

"If there is," Cassandra replied, glancing almost unconsciously toward the window that looked out on the muddied street. "It will be coming in time."

Bruce paused, his hands still enveloping his daughter's. He knew better than to ask Cassandra to explain herself. There were times she didn't know how to, even to herself. Words would come to her that she had no knowledge of forming. But that did not make her words any the less true.

"All right, then know this and be happy. I am a very joyful man. I have my work and my girls. I have everything." Withdrawing his hands from hers, he returned to his work.

For the time being, his soul was free.

Too much time had been allowed to slip through his fingers, Riley thought, upbraiding himself silently as he now labored to make up for that loss. Swiftly, he arranged the letters on the platen that were to form the words on the first page of his newspaper.

Women would surely be his downfall, Rachel had often chided. Perhaps she was right.

There was certainly no getting away from the fact that he wouldn't mind falling down beside the very lovely Cassandra MacGregor. Perferrably in a green meadow, with no prying eyes for miles in any direction.

His blood quickened at the thought.

Cassandra.

Her name floated through his mind again, as it had more than a dozen times since he had flown into the newspaper office and thrown himself into his overdue task. If he wasn't mistaken, that was the name of the princess in Greek legend. The one who could only make prophesies of doom. It was certainly a gloomy legacy to have attached to one's name. Especially someone like her.

Riley grinned to himself as he tightened the platen down to imprint the letters on the fresh page he had spread out. One had only to look at her to see that there was certainly nothing gloomy about Cassandra MacGregor.

No, not gloomy. Only distant. He wished that she were as eager to further their acquaintance as her younger sister obviously was.

To be sure, Brianne was appealing. But she was only a sunbeam.

He was after the sun.

And he meant to capture it. He meant to get to know Cassandra as soon as he was able.

He frowned now as he watched a bit of ink being squeezed out at the side of the platen. Though it was his trade first, having learned it at Ben Franklin's elbow, Riley was admittedly more untidy at the task than Rachel was.

With a sigh he grabbed the darkly soaked rag he had flung to the side earlier and quickly cleaned away the oozing ink. As he did so, he could almost hear Rachel's voice echoing in his head.

"Ink's expensive enough as it is without wasting it on the floor."

You'd have thought she was the older one instead of he, Riley mused. He glanced down. Ink stained his fingers. He rubbed them on the leather apron he wore when working on the press. Of the two of them, Rachel had always been the more serious one. Life, Riley had come to believe early on, was a lark. At times a difficult one and one assuredly that needed to be tamed and mastered, but a lark nonetheless.

The test of that was that no matter what anyone did, they would never get out of it alive. So why not make the best of it while they had the chance?

His muscles tensing, he pulled hard, then eased the platens away from one another gently, so as not to mar the print. He carefully peeled the page off. Giving it only a cursory glance to make certain that all was as it should be, Riley hung the page on the rope that was strung out across the length of the back wall. At first glance it appeared as if heavily inked laundry had been hung there.

Why not enjoy it indeed, he mused.

In a process that he could do in his sleep, Riley quickly reinked the tightly arranged letters and gingerly placed another snow-white sheet of paper across them. Grasping the handle, he brought the two halves together once more and held on tightly.

And the way he was going to enjoy himself, he decided then and there, was to get to know Mistress Cassandra MacGregor on a far more intimate basis than she undoubtedly foresaw.

Riley released the handle and sighed as he glanced down at the platen. That is, if he ever got the time. There were times, he was beginning to believe, when responsibilities were not only the measure of a man, but the measure of his coffin as well.

Coffin.

Furniture.

Riley's mind swung wide as it made its own rhyme and reasons, its own odd collection of connections.

He smiled.

Why not?

An idea had struck him, and he began to create a paragraph in his mind concerning the newest neighbors to have entered the boundaries of Morgan's Creek. After all, if a man did not use the tools that God had given him, he deserved to have them taken from him. And what woman could resist, no matter what she might say to the contrary, seeing herself favorably mentioned in print, for all the town to read?

He released the handle on the press and quickly crossed to his desk. He picked up his quill and, dipping it into the well, began to compose.

Chapter Six

Sam's Tavern was a wide, two-story building that stood squatting comfortably at the end of the walkway. It had been there, on the very same spot, for nigh on to fifteen years. Sixteen if one counted the year that Sam had conducted his business beneath a rotting pitched tent.

It had taken Sam that full year to save the money to purchase the wood and the labor to build his establishment, but Sam had husbanded his money well and prospered steadily. He now boasted ownershipp of the other buildings on the walkway, indeed had provided the money to have them built in the first place.

Because of the proximity of the harbor, a tavern had been the logical first place of business to grace what had now become Morgan's Creek.

Thriving in one form or the other since Sam had opened his very first keg of beer and pushed a spigot into it, the tavern was a place where the town's male citizens could gather to exchange pleasantries, information, and, most important, to seek respite from the hard labors of their lives.

And in more than a few cases to escape the sharp tongues of their wives while they gazed at wenches who were comely in their own unique ways. Wenches who asked nothing more than two bits for the pleasure of their undivided attention and the comfort of their warm flesh.

Bruce MacGregor was beyond the white-hot passion of his youth. It had been literally years since he had sought that sort of diversion to ease his troubled soul. But he hoped that he would be dead before he abandoned the pleasure of looking and flirting with soft-skinned girls who possessed wide, tempting hips, scarlet, smiling mouths, and sparkling, wicked eyes.

He enjoyed watching the barmaids as they flirted with him and the other men in the tavern. Bruce had always appreciated fine lines and curves in any form, be it in a well-executed statue or a finely crafted piece of furniture.

Or a divinely shaped woman.

This was his first visit to Sam's. Bruce had found it easily enough, since it resided on the opposite end of the street that he now called home. He liked it the moment he opened the door.

Sam was an affable bear of a man who enjoyed scowling as much as some enjoyed talking. It was just his way. Though it had been Cassandra who had met Sam's acquaintance and arranged for the renting of the store Bruce was now to fill with his furniture, he felt it was his obligation, as the patriach of his tiny, woefully diminished clan, to meet the man as quickly as could be arranged.

The fact that their new landlord also served liquid refreshment that went a long way to easing a man's pain and clearing the dust from his throat was but an added boon.

Bruce MacGregor had walked in feeling almost every one of his fifty-seven years. Little by little they had slipped away, eased along on their path by the sips of ale he took. Sips that depleted whole tankards one at a time.

He wrapped his long, delicate fingers about the tankard now as if it were an old, trusted friend, and sighed deeply. The joy he felt was nudged aside a bit by a small kernel of sorrow.

He hated the fact that there were times when he slipped away. It had begun that first night, after he had buried his bonny boys and his fine young brothers. Gone, the lot of them, with so many promises unfulfilled. The ache in his heart had been so grievous that night, he couldn't bear it.

So he hadn't. He had just slipped away.

But responsbilities to his bairns and his wife pulled him back from that formless, misty region. Plans had to be made. Changes begun.

And so they had come to America. To New York, where he had put his skill to work and built them a life by building other people's furniture.

All in all, it was a good life. But his beloved Molly would have none of it. She had buried her mother's heart with Robert and Roy, back in the Highlands. She died but a short two years later, grieving. And leaving him without her.

After that he'd slipped away again. And again and again. It was a shameful, weak thing to do with young ones depending on him. So through sheer grit, he had managed to hold himself in check. To hold himself together for their sake.

But as they grew to womanhood and his sorrow refused to fade, he found himself slipping away once more. And more than once. Just before they had left New York, it had been happening with more frequency.

He fervently hoped, nay, prayed, that it would abate once again now that they were in Morgan's Creek. The girls still needed someone to protect them, to take care of them. It wasn't fair to leave the burden on shoulders so slender, even though Cassandra had always been equal to any task placed before her.

No, he thought, draining his tankard again, it wasn't fair. Not fair at all.

Cassandra should be looking to care for her own bairns, not waiting hand and foot on an old man whose mind wandered and tumbled away freely, like a leaf in the wind.

Bruce smiled his thanks as Annie, the generously endowed barmaid, exchanged his empty tankard for a freshly filled one. He tossed her a coin which she dropped down into her low, clinging blouse and then jiggled, catching the coin and pillowing it in an eminently soft resting place.

He felt an itch he hadn't felt in a long while. Maybe he

wasn't so old after all. Or maybe it was the ale that felt young, he mused with a soft laugh.

Better, he would do better, he vowed, tipping the tankard back. He would do better by Cassandra and by the girls.

A little of the ale spilled down and melded into the short, well-trimmed beard. A little managed to slide down his throat. It felt cool. Contentment slid through him in its wake.

He could have easily swum in a vat of ale, he thought hazily, his eyes taking in the merriment about the long, scarred bar. One of the men was whispering something in Annie's ear, and she laughed, moving her hip against the man's thigh in a seductive promise.

Oh, to be young again, without the sorrows of age, he thought.

And then he chided himself for his lament. He'd had a good life, a full one, with more blessings than a man had a right to expect from the almighty. If the blessings were mixed in with a cup filled deep with sorrow, well, there were many who had the latter without ever experiencing the former. He need not cry into his cups for what was and what was not.

It had been a good life up until then, and he owed it to his girls to try to make it the best that it could possibly be.

His eyes, a little blearier now from the ale than they had been a mere moment before, swept about the large room once more, as if taking stock for the first time. It was dark without, almost ten o'clock. The darkness here within was held at bay by lanterns that hung about the walls and the warm glow that spilled out from the hearth.

Bruce MacGregor felt good here. He felt as if he belonged.

Slowly, as if attempting to read a page of writing that was held down beneath the water, he became aware of someone standing over him. He looked up and saw that a tall, brawny man had approached his table and now stood there in silence, waiting for him to turn his attention upward.

As he did, Bruce MacGregor's head felt very heavy, as if the ale had caused it to gain weight. To ease the burden for his neck, he leaned his head to one side.

The man who stood at his table was young. A handsome

buck with an easy, kindly smile. He looked to be a man who enjoyed a drink or two. Bruce liked that.

He returned the young man's smile, though it was suddenly an effort to do so. Bruce was beginning to feel very tired. Old age was a shrewish mistress, he thought, who stole things from a man when he wasn't looking. 'Twas a time he could drink young bucks like this one under the table and have enough stamina to go a full day more, and do his work besides.

He looked down at his hands and saw that they were lax around the tankard's smooth sides. This when he thought they were gripping it firmly. His senses were going too quickly.

He exhaled loudly.

"Would you be minding if I joined you?" Riley asked, one hand on the back of the chair. The other held his drink.

Bruce began to shake his head, then thought better of it. Any undue motion would be a mistake at this time. Even now the tavern was tilting, threatening to spin uncontrollably at any moment.

"No, have yourself a seat." He gestured toward the empty chair that the man had already claimed.

Turning it around with a flick of his wrist, Riley straddled the chair.

His visit to the tavern was a reward to himself for a job well done. Even though he had arrived at the newspaper office late, he had succeeded in getting all four of the newspaper's sides completely printed in an astonishingly short amount of time. Especially considering the fact that he was working without Rachel's nimble fingers to aid him. The *Gazette* sat now in the office, its pages neatly arranged and folded, ready for distribution.

The *Gazette*'s readership, he smiled to himself, was growing. Even those who did not read bought a copy just to boast that they possessed it and were as knowledgeable as their neighbor about the goings-on in town. Since it was his editorial that the people read and discussed, it filled Riley with pride. The son of an illiterate tenant farmer from Ireland had come a long way on these shores of opportunity.

And he intended on going a lot further.

Feeling good about himself, Riley had put the newspaper to bed and took himself out. He had earned it, he mused. Besides, he was a newspaperman. It was his duty to gather the news. What better place than the tavern, where all converged sooner or later?

Ever on the lookout for new faces, Riley had noticed the older man almost as soon as he entered the tavern. The man, neatly dressed though his clothes were far from new, didn't have the look of a peddler about him. Since he knew of no other new families settling in Morgan's Creek, Riley easily deduced that the man had to be Cassandra's father.

"I'm Riley O'Roarke." With a wide smile Riley extended his hand to the older man. "Do I have the pleasure of addressing Mr. MacGregor?"

"I'm Bruce MacGregor all right." He took the extended hand and, Riley noted the long and slender hand had the grip of a young man. "Whether 'tis a pleasure or not is up to you to decide." MacGregor's eyes narrowed just the way Cassandra's had earlier as he pondered the puzzle before him. "How is it that you've come to know my name? Have we met before, sir?"

There were times, when he slipped away, that MacGregor knew that others saw him. Even spoke to him, though he answered not. Had his path crossed O'Roarke's at one such time?

There was suspicion but no hostility in MacGregor's question. Riley dispelled any concern with his reply. "I met your daughters earlier today. Brianne and Rose. And Cassandra."

Though he was more than a little in his cups by now, Bruce was certain that he detected a change of tone in the man's voice as he said his eldest's name. Well, well, well, another one struck by her beauty and her distance. He vaguely wondered if O'Roarke would suffer the fate of the others.

She cast one and all aside, ignoring them as if they were no more than troublesome insects. She claimed they got in the way of things. Things, he thought, like caring for a father who was given to drifting.

MacGregor smiled now with all the pride of fatherhood, made that much more sentimental by the ale he had downed. "They make a lovely bouquet, all three of them, if I must say so myself."

Riley sipped the single shot of whiskey he had purchased at the bar before crossing to MacGregor. "You won't have to once the town gets a look at them."

The ale, while making him mellow, intensified the shadows of his life as well. MacGregor leaned in closer as he frowned. His eyes, the color of leaves in the fall, searched Riley's face.

"Is there danger here, boy?"

"None the way you might mean." Riley was quick to set the man's mind at ease. "But eligible young ladies are in short supply and handsome ones with the look of your daughters will easily gladden the hearts of many men around here."

MacGregor drew his shoulders back, relaxed once more. "Then it's a very good thing we've come to this place. They need good husbands, my lasses."

On the heels of this pronouncement, Bruce MacGregor paled slightly, his color shifting from rose to milky white. His hand snaked out and grasped Riley's sleeves as if the sound of his voice would not garner his attention sufficiently.

"Mr. O'Roarke, is it?"

"Riley."

He looked with concern at the man sitting opposite him. Riley downed his whiskey quickly, then placed the glass on the table and turned his attention fully to Bruce MacGregor. The man had definiely grown sallow of face.

"Is anything the matter?"

"Riley." Bruce MacGregor breathed his name as if it were a secret. "Would you be doing an old man a favor?"

"If I can."

"This you can, I assure you." The smile he attempted to produce would not come. "Would you be telling Cassandra that I'm sorry?"

Now it was Riley's turn to be confused. "Sorry? About what?"

But Bruce MacGregor wasn't able to answer, though he

sorely wanted to. It was just as he had feared. The very next moment, as his mouth opened with a reply, his face met the surface of the table, narrowly missing his half-empty tankard.

He was utterly and peacefully unconscious.

Chapter Seven

Rose looked out the window that faced the heart of the small town. The crescent moon was a poor provider of light, barely illuminating the houses that stood across the way. There might have been nought but themselves for miles around for all that Rose saw.

It created an eerie feeling.

A surge of loneliness, of desolation, pervaded her soul.

Rose looked at Cassandra as she ran her hands along her arms more for comfort than for warmth. "Do you think anything's happened to Da?"

Brianne moved restlessly about the large communal room that they now called their home.

"He seemed fine earlier," she pointed out, though her fingers were as knotted as her stomach was when she turned toward Cassandra.

Their differences and bickering now aside, it was always to Cassandra that everyone turned.

Of the three, Cassandra alone remained calm, plying her needle now by the light of the hearth, fashioning a dress for Brianne as the girl had requested of her more times than there were full moons in a year.

It had been a day filled with work, and much headway had been made. The small shop had begun to take on a look of its own. They had unloaded the wagon that had taken them these many miles, positioning several fine pieces of handiwork that were examples of their father's craftsmanship about the shop. They were few and small of stature, but little could be accommodated in the wagon.

Throughout it all, their father had been at their side, doing more than his share, his enthusiasm a heartening sight to behold when each girl in turn thought back to other, more recent times.

Indeed, it had been rather like old times, when they were small and helping out any way they could in his shop in New York. He'd sung refrains of songs he'd remembered from his boyhood today, as he had done then. As the day wore on, the girls felt an inner peace rising up within them.

Even Brianne had been forced to admit, though it had taken a sharp jab in the ribs from Rose to bring it forth, that perhaps coming here was a good thing after all. Though it was Simeon's threat that had forced them to leave New York and not the decline of business, as Cassandra had told Riley, their father had, over the last few months, lost more than a little of his spirit and that in turn had brought a loss of business with it.

Dennis, the apprentice who had worked for their father, had done much to offset that end of it. But there was nothing to alleviate their growing concern. To the girls' increased sorrow and alarm, Bruce MacGregor had been given to wandering away from them in his mind more and more.

But now he seemed at home here. Each sister had eagerly seized the hope that this aroused.

None of them had noticed, between unloading the wagon and turning both the store and the room above it into something respectable in appearance, just when their father had slipped away.

"Seemed," Rose echoed now, putting a fine point on it as she glanced toward Cassandra. "He'd *seemed* fine."

Their father had seemed fine, but appearances were not always what they seemed.

Rose crossed to Cassandra. Her sister sat on the rocker where their mother had sat years before, lulling each of her five children in turn to sleep. In her heart, Rose wished her mother were with them still, and especially now. She knelt beside the rocker, her hands clutched the arm, her eyes supplicating Cassandra.

"What if he's—" Rose licked her lips, afraid even to give voice to her fears. "You know, wandering again? He doesn't know his way around here, Cass. What if he's gotten lost, or worse?"

"He hasn't," Cassandra assured her softly. She raised her eyes to take in Brianne as well. Though spoiled and selfish at times, the girl had a good heart. And they all loved one another and their father, even if at times that love was difficult to discern.

Rose laid a hand on Cassandra's arm, stilling her needle. She wished she had a little of what the angels had granted to her older sister.

"Are you sure?" Rose's voice begged for the answer to be yes.

Cassandra nodded and then laid aside her work on the floor. The knowledge had come to her, as it always did, quietly, with no ceremony, no lightning bolts streaking through her. It was just there.

Cassandra smiled at Rose, trying to ease her concern. "I'm sure. He's fine, just as Bri said." She glanced in her youngest sister's direction.

"Well, then, where *is* he?" Brianne whirled on Cassandra in her impatience, anger in her eyes.

Why was it that Cassandra always spoke in half statements when there was a rush to know things? Did she enjoy lording it over them? Did she enjoy rubbing their noses in the fact that she was kissed by heaven when they were not?

Knowledge of where their father was had come to Cassandra an instant later. A clear image of her father, sitting at a table, with noise surrounding him and a welcome tankard of ale held tightly in his hands. There was only one place he could be.

"Enjoying himself," Cassandra answered Brianne, "as well he should."

Brianne stuck out her lower lip. In the last month she had traveled what seemed an endless amount of miles through horrid country, giving up her home, her friends, and her promise of the future just to settle in this no-man's-land. To make matters worse, Cassandra exacted work from her at every opportunity. If anyone deserved to enjoy themselves, it should have been she, who'd suffered so much.

"What about us?" Brianne asked, wanting to say "me" but knowing that would only earn her a lecture from Rose, if not Cassandra herself.

Cassandra stood up. Brianne's dress would keep. She ran a hand over the young girl's cheek. "You're looking none the worse for your ordeal, Bri."

Brianne tossed her head, her curls flying through the air and bouncing about her shoulders.

"I don't like work," she bit off.

Cassandra pressed her lips together in order not to laugh. "Ah, and how well we all know that, my love."

She crossed to the door and reached for her shawl. It hung from the ornamental rack her father had carved so patiently. Tomorrow the rack would be placed downstairs, by the entrance. It was sure to catch someone's attention there and find a new home soon enough.

She would miss it, Cassandra thought. It was almost as old as Brianne was and Cassandra had a vague recollection of sitting by her father's feet as he had worked on it, hour after hour.

Cassandra wrapped the shawl around her shoulders. "See to dinner for us, will you, Rose? I'll be bringing him home by and by."

"You still haven't told us where he is," Rose pointed out quietly, her tone more patient than Brianne's. But her curiosity was none the smaller for that.

Cassandra had one hand on the doorknob. There were times when she forgot they did not know things the way she did.

"At the tavern, taking a bit of comfort in the sound of male voices and the taste of brew." She pulled open the heavy door.

It stuck badly. Da would have to see to this soon, she thought, making a list for him in her mind.

"The tavern?" Rose's eyes widened as she cried out the words. "You're going there?" She made it sound as if Cassandra were about to venture through the open gates of hell.

Cassandra turned and gave her sister a reassuring look. She had always been able to look out for herself.

"Well, it won't very well come to me now, will it, lass?" She shook her head, her mouth creased with affection. Rose was always making things worse than they were. "Do not spend so much of your time worrying, Rose, there'll be wrinkles on that lovely face of yours all too soon if you don't stop."

Rose didn't care a fig about wrinkles. It was her sister's welfare that caused her concern. Seer or not, Cassandra was a woman first. And didn't Mr. O'Roarke say that the men far outnumbered the women here?

She crossed quickly to Cassandra. "But what if someone becomes brazenly forward and attempts to exact favors from you?"

Cassandra smiled. She already sensed that wasn't going to happen, at least not tonight. "There are ways of dealing with that if it comes to pass. And besides, Da will be there. As will he."

"He?" Brianne and Rose chorused together. Brianne's eyes gleamed in anticipation, for she had already guessed at Cassandra's answer.

"Riley," Cassandra told them.

Brianne's pout had transformed into a wide smile. "He's there too?"

Cassandra nodded. "I've a feeling."

Which was, the girls knew, as good as saying yes. Cassandra, when she gave voice to things she felt were true, was never wrong. It was not whimsy or wishfulness that made her say things, it was knowledge.

Brianne reached for her own shawl on the rack. "Then maybe I should—"

Cassandra stayed Brianne's hand with her own. "—help

Rose with the dinner," she concluded firmly. "I can take care of bringing Da home."

It wasn't her father whom Brianne was thinking of, and that was all too obvious by the expression on her face.

Cassandra could only shake her head as she opened the door once more. "Patience, lass, patience."

Brianne glared, stepping back to do as she was bidden. "Easy for you to say," she mumbled under her breath. "You're already old."

Cassandra said nothing as she left. But she had heard.

Though she had the Sight, Cassandra knew that it did not protect her in any way. Nor did it supply her with an immunity to dangers that might arise. For this reason, she did not want either of her sisters with her. It would only give her someone else to look out for, someone else to be in charge of, and at times it was difficult enough being in charge of herself.

And besides, she was always leery that the time might come when one of her visions would prove untrue. She would risk no one else if that should come to pass.

Cassandra hurried through the street, or what passed for one here. In New York it would be regarded a muddied rut.

The darkness soothed her. It was like a cloak that had been slipped about the shoulders of the small town. There was a scattering of tiny buildings here and there, housing people who were endeavoring to make a living from the land and from their own talents.

Morgan's Creek had a good feeling to it, Cassandra mused.

In a few moments she reached Sam's Tavern, where she had struck the bargain that had given them their store and their living space.

The glow from the tavern welcomed her as she pushed open the swinging doors. The noise was loud and it took a moment for her to untangle the skein of sounds and determine that it was all due to raised, friendly voices and nothing more. A moment later, and she could discern conversations here and there as she entered.

Eyes turned in her direction.

Women entering the tavern were a rarity. Like as not, if one appeared, it was usually a distraught wife looking for a husband who was long overdue on his way home. When that occurred, anger and embarrassment would crease the brows of women made old before their time. If, perchance when a woman walked in, a tolerant smile curved her lips, then she was an entirely different sort of a woman, one who sought to make a living from the weaknesses of the citizens who patronized the tavern.

It was obvious to one and all that Cassandra was of neither variety. Her appearance in the tavern aroused everyone's interest. By the time she had taken ten steps into the establishment, every pair of eyes, both those seeing clearly and those blurred, were turned in her direction.

Sam had looked up almost from the moment her foot touched the uneven floor. He recognized her immediately. Cassandra's was not a face a man forgot easily, if at all. Her slender, haunted features had carved themselves upon his mind the minute he had first set eyes on her.

He instantly ceased polishing his beloved counter and dropped the rag in his hand.

Moving more agilely than a man his size would be thought to, he eased his considerable bulk around the bar's opening and crossed to Cassandra, his very presence warning others away. Already he had seen two men begin taking steps toward her. They ceased abruptly and returned to their drinks, content to seek oblivion in a glass rather than meet it at the end of a beefy fist.

Looking at her, he was reminded of a lamb that had gone astray, wandering away from its flock. Clearly it was in danger of being eaten by wolves. Wolves with tankards of ale in their grimy hands.

Well, not while he ran the establishment.

Sam seemed to tower over Cassandra as he looked down into her face. "Mistress MacGregor, I believe you've lost your way."

Chapter Eight

Cassandra raised her eyes to Sam's florid face. He wasn't a
religious man, but he had entered a place of worship once or
twice when he had made his home in Charleston years ago.
When he looked into the girl's eyes, it created within him the
kind of impression a man felt when he first stepped inside a
church. It made him feel that the very tone of his voice should
reflect the reverence that being within such a holy place exacted.

She saw concern crease the generous folds about his face,
though she instinctively knew expression of that emotion was
a foreign thing to Sam.

"No, I've not lost my way," she assured him.

The next moment they were no longer standing alone, just
as Sam had feared. But when he turned, he saw that it was
Riley who joined them, and not one of the rowdier men who
frequented his establishment.

"It's looking for her father she's come, if I'm not mistaken."
Riley saw the answer in her eyes as he stood beside her.

Sam looked from the girl to Riley. He might have known.
Riley made it his business to be everywhere. Still, he asked,
"You know Mistress MacGregor?"

"I know everyone," he answered simply as he looked down

into Cassandra's face. Was it his imagination, or did she grow more beautiful with each encounter? "At least, everyone in Morgan's Creek."

Yes, Sam thought with a touch of envy, and some, such as those of the female persuasion, Riley knew better than others. He was a stallion, that one, but one with manners. A lady would always be safe with him, no matter what. Sam had witnessed the way Riley handled himself in a brawl. It would take a man of mighty size to beat him.

Sam saw two men attempting to reach over the counter and help themselves to his brew. Duty called. He slapped Riley once on the back, his eyes narrowing in on the activity at his bar.

"Then I'll leave her in your care." The end of his sentence floated behind him as he hurried back to the bar. And to the men whose ears needed cuffing.

"Thank you for your concern, but I don't need depositing into anyone's care," Cassandra called after Sam's back. Her words were eaten up by the swell of the din around them.

Cassandra turned toward Riley to see if he had heard her.

He had. It was just as he had suspected earlier. The woman was as independent, as headstrong as his sister was. It was his lot in life, apparently, to encounter women who refused to be domesticated.

But then, spirit was something he both admired and required.

"Then I'm the sorrier for that knowledge," he told her with a grin. "For if you were deposited with me, I would lock you away for safekeeping."

Her eyes met his and held for a moment. They were deeper, Riley thought, than the wide ocean he had crossed years before.

"No doubt," she murmured. She looked around the crowded room. Cassandra's eyes rested on her father almost immediately.

He would have expected a startled gasp to follow recognition. Riley was intrigued that none such reaction was forthcoming from Cassandra. She merely crossed to the table swiftly.

Riley was quick on her heels. "He's all right," he assured

her hastily, lest she begin a tirade on how he could have allowed her father to do such a thing to himself.

Cassandra lightly glossed her fingers over his graying hair. Affection shone in her eyes as she looked down at her father.

"Yes, I know."

The simple assertion dried up the words that Riley was about to offer in his own defense on the subject.

Riley could only stare at Cassandra as if she were not quite real. Indeed, she did not behave as if she were real. He rounded the table to get a full view of her face. Was she in shock?

"You do?"

She nodded, still regarding her father's inert form. "By the looks of it, he's had a little too much liquid libation." Gently, she removed the half-empty tankard from his fingers and wondered how many he had had. "It's been a while since Da's indulged himself this way. I fear the headache he'll have on the morrow will be a grand and inglorious one."

Riley straightened and gazed at her. "I must say, you're taking this all very well."

Cassandra raised her head, then, to look at him, amused by his words and his surprise. "Tell me, how should I be taking this?"

Riley could think only of the innumerable lectures on the pitfalls of the demon rum that flowed from Rachel's lips whenever he had the occasion to entertain a tankard or two. Or three.

He grinned at her. Cassandra obviously was of a different school. "Caterwauling comes to mind."

She scented a touch of ale on his breath. It was warm and pungent. She knew without being told that he was acquainted with the very behavior he had found absent in her. She lifted her shoulders and let them fall once more, to show the futility of what he was suggesting.

"What good would it do?"

Now, there she had him. He'd never known why Rachel took such pleasure in seeming to be miserable about pointing out his failing.

"It might make you feel better," Riley suggested, guessing. It wasn't as if her father made a habit of losing himself within the waves of a bottle. There was no harm in an occasional lapse or two. It certainly didn't disturb her.

"For your information, Mr. O'Roarke"—she measured the distance from the table to the door and thought of the road beyond that—"I feel fine as it is."

Her eyes swept back to Riley, and he felt himself drowning. It wouldn't have helped him one whit if he did know how to swim. He knew he would have drowned in her eyes anyway.

Without thinking, he laid his hand on her arm. "If I help you bring your father home, do you think that there would be a possibility of you finding it in your heart to call me Riley?"

He was a bargainer, a man who had never gotten anything easily in his life, she thought. A man accustomed to living by his wits, who felt he had to trade to get what he wanted. She laughed and shook her head.

"There's a possibility of my calling you that even if you didn't help me bring my father home." Certainty filled her eyes as she looked at him. "But you will."

Of course he would, but she didn't know him well enough to be so confident of his behavior. And she didn't have the look of a naive fool who took too much for granted. He studied her face, wondering what thoughts went on inside her head.

"Oh?"

She could almost see his mind working. She could certainly feel it. Odd, what an instant affinity she seemed to have for Riley. There were many whom she could not read. Riley she had connected with immediately. She smiled now to set his mind at rest.

"You're a gentleman, aren't you?"

Riley's grin grew larger as he remembered one recent, hastily ended assignation. "There is some dispute about that."

His face had been slapped more than once, she knew. There were women who pushed much too quickly and were not ready for the consequences they generated. Brianne was one of those, Cassandra thought sadly.

But her face betrayed none of her thoughts. "All without merit, I'm sure."

Riley wasn't certain if she was just being polite because she needed his help, or if she truly believed what she was saying.

As if it would help clear the mystery, he looked closer into her eyes. The same thing happened now as had happened before. He felt himself being drawn into a pool of crystal-blue water at the base of a cave that seemed to have no end. No bottom.

It felt somehow almost spiritual.

For just a moment he felt as if he were in the presence of someone who had been kissed by powers that most assuredly were not of this world.

Riley shook off the feeling. She had just given him a compliment and he had yet to respond.

He grinned at her now. "It's refreshing being in the presence of someone so intuitive."

It was a grin, Cassandra had no doubts, that had set many a young girl's heart pounding quickly. There was something endearing, yet wickedly stirring about the slightly off-center expression. She had to concentrate in order not to succumb herself.

"Yes, I'm sure it is." She stepped back, away from her father's chair. Da had slept peacefully throughout this entire exchange. As she knew he would throughout the whole of the night to come. "Now, if you'll be helping me with him, I'll be grateful."

Riley was already lifting MacGregor to his feet. Securing one arm around the man's not-too-slender waist, Riley draped MacGregor's arm about his shoulder. When this did not readily lend itself to his making any headway, Riley slung the man over his shoulder, his very knees almost buckling from the weight. It would not be an easy matter going home with him, but it could be managed. Especially with the right incentive.

He looked at her now, peering around her father's form. "Another debt, Mistress MacGregor?"

She smiled as she led the way to the door. He was quick, this one was. But then, Cassandra had known he would be.

"Another dinner, Mr. O'Roarke." She held the door open for him, aware that they had an escort of eyes as they left the tavern.

"Riley," he reminded her as he made his way out onto the street.

Thank God the man didn't live far away, he thought. Since his home was so close by, he had brought no horse to the tavern, and though he prided himself on his strength, carrying Bruce MacGregor any long distance was out of the question. He tried not to pant as he kept up with Cassandra.

"Riley," Cassandra echoed. The sound of her voice wrapped about his name brought a shiver to him that the night air could not have accomplished.

He struggled not to let the man fall to the ground.

"I haven't had the first yet," he reminded her, although dinner was not foremost on his mind when he looked at Cassandra.

"That'll be arranged by and by," she promised, slowing her pace so as not to tire Riley out.

She was tempted to offer giving him a hand. With an arm draped around each of their necks, they could carry her father home between them. But she knew that it would offend Riley's manliness if she suggested anything of the sort. No matter that she was a strong woman for her size. Men took pride in flexing their muscles. Even men as intelligent as Riley obviously was.

Cassandra looked up at her father's face. The bit of moonlight that guided their steps highlighted his features. In repose, there was a smile frozen on it.

He'd had a good time tonight, she thought, pleased. He had so few good times of late, he deserved to enjoy himself whenever he could.

She clung to the feeling that things *might* be better here.

Riley craned his neck to get another look at her. She seemed preoccupied. Even so, her expression was nothing short of sweet.

"You're a rare woman, Mistress Macgregor."

Ah, the flattery began afresh. "How so?" she asked, intrigued.

Her treatment of her father's unconscious condition in so public a place still held him in awe. "Most that I know would be angry to find their father drunk and passed out on a table in a tavern.''

She shrugged and pulled her shawl a little tighter around her shoulders. ''Public opinion matters not a fig to me.''

It wasn't quite true. It mattered when they wanted to destroy her for what they thought she was. She wanted to keep away from public opinion as far as possible.

Riley paused to get a better grip on MacGregor's waist. He tugged the arm around his neck a little tighter. ''As I said, a rare woman.''

She glanced down the street toward the store. It wasn't so far off now.

'' 'Tis my father's welfare and happiness I am interested in. He spends his days in the company of women. He needs to hear the sound of male voices sometime.'' She gestured toward the tavern that lay behind them some good distance now. ''What better place than the tavern?''

Her opinions matched Krystyna's, and he would have sworn that Jason's wife was one of a kind. Obviously not. ''Rarer and rarer.''

Cassandra shook her head. ''There's no need to flatter me.''

And flatter her he was certain that men had. Endlessly. For reasons not yet completely formed, Riley did not want to be regarded in the same realm as they.

''I wasn't trying to flatter, merely observe.'' God, but this man was getting heavier by the moment.

Cassandra laughed, the sound echoing into the night air and rivaling, in his opinion, the song of the nightingale.

''And so you flatter all the more.''

Hers was not a head that was easily turned. He liked that. ''You've discovered my secret.''

Ten more steps and they were before her father's store. She stopped then and turned to look at Riley.

''Your secret, Riley,'' she said with all the seriousness that was at her disposal, ''is that you never give up until you've attained that which you seek.''

It was a rare, intuitive remark for one who knew next to

nothing about him. For a moment it gave him pause. But he found his tongue after a beat.

"Now you flatter."

But she merely shook her head. The smile was implied. "No, now I know."

He had the feeling that she was right. That somehow she knew him, knew the secrets of his soul, though he knew not how.

But before he could ask her any more questions, her sisters came hurrying down the stairs that led up to their new living quarters, and the moment for private conversation was gone.

Rose stared, horrified, at the lax body that Riley was holding up. Her hands flew to her mouth to hold back a gasp. "Da! Is he—?"

"Resting comfortably," Riley assured her. He stifled a moan as he contemplated the length of the stairs before him with no joy.

"You won't have to be carrying him up. There's a pallet in the rear of the store," Cassandra told him, easily reading his thoughts. "Bri." She looked up at her sister, who stood on the last step of the stairs. The young girl's eyes were fixed on Riley. "Bring the lantern this way."

Brianne's eyes shone as she pushed past Rose to reach Riley. "Gladly."

Chapter Nine

Though Bruce MacGregor was shorter than he by probably a good six inches, Riley judged that the man had to outweigh him by a good two stone, if not more. It had made carrying the older man to his doorstep no easy feat.

With a nod, Riley once again tightened his hold around the man's legs. His shoulder began to ache fiercely.

"Lead on," Riley murmured to Cassandra, not trusting himself to say too much more. He hoped that he did not sound as out of breath as he felt.

Cassandra opened the door to the store. " 'Tis just back here."

She gestured into the darkness, then turned to look at her sister. Rather than follow Cassandra, Brianne had aligned herself beside Riley. Just as Cassandra had known she would.

"Brianne, bring the light over here in front of Mr. O'Roarke."

Though her smile never faded, there was a stubborn glint in Brianne's eyes that her family was more than passingly familiar with. Brianne remained where she was, her steps measured to equal Riley's gait. Since it wasn't brisk because of the added weight he had to deal with, Brianne had no trouble keeping up.

"Mr. O'Roarke can see better if the light is beside him," Brianne retorted to Cassandra's admonishment.

Despite being otherwise occupied at the moment, Riley, ever mindful of the warfare that might erupt, sought for a way to defuse the situation. He paused for a moment to get his breath.

As he did so, he cast his glance around to encompass the three girls. His gaze was warm and approving on all counts. "I am, as it were, surrounded by lights."

Brianne blushed and preened, while Rose, behind her, merely blushed.

But Cassandra, who had bent to turn down the cover upon the pallet, looked up and smiled. She saw the intent behind his words. Maintaining the peace had always been an important objective to her.

"Nicely done, Mr. O'Roarke."

A half dozen steps farther and he would have reached his goal. None too soon, he thought as perspiration slid down his back. His shirt was stuck uncomfortably to him and chafed his skin.

"Our bargain was for you to call me Riley," he reminded Cassandra.

Exhaling a grateful breath, he gingerly lowered Bruce Mac-Gregor down onto the pallet.

Done, he thought with relief. Being a good Samaritan, he noted as he straightened, was decidedly hard on a man's back. He felt a twinge shoot up along his spine, traveling in the reverse direction taken by the perspiration only a moment before.

"What bargain is that?" Brianne asked, alerted, not letting not a word this man said pass by her unexamined. She looked from Riley to her sister and back again, waiting for an explanation.

It had been a long, hard day, and Cassandra felt her patience slowly unraveling. She was tired of Brianne's incessant poking and prodding about matters.

" 'Tis all very simple, lass," she replied a bit more tersely than was her custom. "Mr. O'Roarke offered to help me bring Da home if I would call him Riley."

It wasn't fair. That gave Cassandra an advantage over her, one Brianne knew she certainly wasn't grateful enough to even realize that she had.

"What must I do in order to be permitted to call you Riley?" Brianne turned her mouth up to him in an eager invitation she was not completely mindful of giving.

This one needed a brother to watch over her, Riley thought, grateful that Rachel hadn't been such a flirt while she was growing to womanhood. Now there was Sin-Jin to deal with her, and she was, Riley decided, more than likely out of the realm of his concern in that manner.

"Nothing," Riley informed Brianne brightly, adjusting his vest. The weight of MacGregor's body had caused it to bunch and gather against his skin. His look took in the two girls. "You may all call me whatever you choose." So saying, his eyes shifted toward Cassandra. "So long as you call me often."

The man was a hopeless charmer, Cassandra thought, enjoying the warmth of his words herself. But she at least knew that they were as empty as they were captivating. Brianne did not. She was going to have to keep a watchful eye on Brianne before the girl allowed herself delusions and caused them all a great deal of grief.

Cassandra stepped away from her father's sleeping form. Before Riley realized what she was about, she had slipped her arm through his.

As he looked at her in pleased surprise, Cassandra led Riley toward the front of the store.

"We've detained you long enough, Riley," Cassandra murmured softly.

She heard Brianne's moaned protest behind her, but with practiced ease Cassandra brought Riley to the door and then ushered him outside the shop.

He would have followed her through the gates of hell just as easily with no protest whatsoever, Riley thought. She so entranced him. It did not happen often.

In fact, he thought, it did not happen at all.

The air was for a change mercifully cool. The breeze rippled along her skin and feathered willowy fingers through her hair.

Just as he longed to. The moonlight gave a silver cast to her face, creating an impression that she was not quite real.

As if he had dreamed her.

And perhaps, when he woke on the morrow, he would find that he had. But for tonight, this divinely formed woman who had come from nowhere was real. As real as the yearning he felt for her.

He raised his hand, wanting to touch her hair, then dropped it once more to his side. She was like a butterfly, and he feared frightening her away.

"Nay, Cassandra, you haven't been detaining me at all." His mouth curved in a gentle smile. "But perhaps someday you will."

She understood the meaning of his words and what there was in his heart. It was as if the part of him that held his soul had been suddenly laid open for her to see. She knew what was on his mind before he did.

And she saw the kiss coming before he thought to give it.

Heat flared through him as the wanting grew too much to rein in. He needed but one taste of her mouth, one sweet sample, and then he would be on his way. Just one, he swore to himself. One to warm him tonight as he lay in his bed. And to set him dreaming.

As he lowered his mouth to hers, Cassandra touched Riley's lips with her fingertips, creating a barrier and aborting the kiss before it had an opportunity to flower between them.

"Perhaps," she agreed softly. Perhaps someday she would detain him of her own volition. Of her own needs. But not tonight. "For now I must bid you good night and leave you with my thanks."

He caught her hand and pressed it to his chest. She felt his heart beating hard just beneath her hand. Beating for her.

"Ah, but you also leave me with an emptiness."

Their eyes met and held. Very slowly Riley released her hand, and she slipped it out of his, her fingers gliding down the length of his hard chest.

She turned and began to walk away, but at the last moment she stopped and looked at him over her shoulder. He had not taken a single step in retreat. ''It'll be filled, Riley. By and by, the emptiness will be filled.''

It was a pledge that had been made to her for both of them.

To some it might have seemed like a harmless reply. Perhaps even a flirtation. To Riley it shimmered like a promise of the future.

He knew he had to content himself with that. And oddly enough, he could.

The door slowly closed behind her.

Riley looked toward the tavern at the end of the walkway. He thought of all the ales that stood there, still waiting for him. For a brief moment the temptation was strong.

Then he lightly skimmed a finger across his lips where she had touched them. A smile bloomed there, as if the very lightest contact from her hand had made the ground fertile.

Slowly, Riley turned on his heel and started to walk home. He'd had enough celebration for one night.

''He almost kissed you!'' Brianne accused Cassandra in a raspy whisper, pouncing upon her sister as soon as she walked in.

''Lower your voice, Bri, or the rest of the town will know it too,'' Rose chided.

Rose gripped her sister's arm as if that would silence her. But the eyes she turned toward Cassandra were wide because of what she had almost witnessed. It was shocking to kiss in public so, especially with a stranger. How could Cassandra have allowed such a thing to almost take place?

Brianne pulled her arm free and waved an impatient hand at Rose. Her attention was completely centered on Cassandra. What was wrong with her sister? Was she utterly devoid of a heart?

''He almost kissed you,'' she repeated. Determined to investigate this tonight and not be put off with vagaries, Brianne stepped around her so that Cassandra was forced to look at her.

It was difficult to speak when her heart was hammering in

her throat. But Cassandra managed to say, "Yes, he almost did."

"Why didn't you *let* him?" Brianne demanded, completely bewildered.

Though she was attracted to Riley, the man was very much fair game. She couldn't understand why her sister would allow such an opportunity to just slip away.

"Because such things just aren't done," Rose insisted, thinking she was coming to Cassandra's aid.

Brianne glared at the interruption. "I am talking to Cass," Brianne informed Rose, frustration throbbing in her voice. She turned her face back toward Cassandra. "Isn't he pleasing to you?"

It was a pale word to apply to the impression his attributes created. Pleasing was for porridge, not for a man. But Cassandra had a preference for understatements. "The man is very handsome," she readily agreed.

Brianne raised a fisted hand to each hip. The mystery was growing larger, not smaller. If she liked him, why hadn't Cassandra reacted as if she did?

"So?" she demanded impatiently.

Cassandra gently laid her hands on Brianne's arms. "Bri, a lady cannot kiss a man straightaway just because he inclines his mouth to hers."

It would seemed the simplest method to her. "How else can she kiss him?"

Cassandra was forced to laugh softly. "When the time is right."

Brianne threw up her hands at that. "You don't have to be a seer to know it was right a minute ago." She gestured toward the window. "You had the moonlight and the man. What more did you need?"

Cassandra turned and looked out the window. In the distance she could see Riley walking away, even though the moonlight was scant. She wasn't aware that she had sighed, but her sisters were.

"The moon isn't going anywhere, Rose. And neither are we."

"Then, you *do* like him," Brianne insisted. She wanted an answer one way or the other, and she wanted it immediately. Though she was eager to be married and set up a household of her own, Brianne wouldn't be so heartless as to try to steal the object of her oldest sister's affection if that truly was the way of it.

But if it wasn't, she needed to know that too, because from where she stood, Riley O'Roarke was a most appealing specimen of a man. So if Cassandra had no designs on him, she was free to try to snare him, and quickly, before another came to cast a line in the water.

Cassandra turned from the window, aware of two sets of eyes on her. And that her pulse was still racing from the fleeting touch she had pressed to his lips.

" 'Tis too early to tell." This she had no answers to. This she had to explore like any mortal woman, a hesitant step at a time. The sight did not aid her in all things, least of all in her personal dealings.

She felt her pulse quicken just from the mere thought of the exploration ahead.

Her reply far from satisfied Brianne. She knew, the girl thought. She knew and she just wasn't telling. It was so like Cassandra to remain close mouthed till the very end. Like telling them on the morning they had to go that they were to leave. She couldn't have given them a week so that proper arrangements might be made. No, it had to be then and there. Without so much as a by-your-leave.

And *she* gave her lectures about patience, Brianne huffed. Patience, her foot.

"Answer me straightaway," Brianne insisted, "or I swear I'll scream and wake Da."

Rose rolled her eyes. She knew as well as Cassandra that Brianne meant to carry out her threat. "If she screams, she'll not only wake Da, she'll wake the dead."

"I'll do it," Brianne warned. "I swear I'll do it. Now, do you like him or not?"

Cassandra's face took on the expression that Brianne abhorred. The patient one that made it seem as if she were the mother and Brianne the child, though only three years separated them.

Three years and more of life than Brianne had ever understood.

Something was going to have to done about the girl before terrible things came to befall her, Cassandra thought with real concern.

Finally, she replied, "Yes, I do."

This answer was more mystifying than if Cassandra had told her no, she didn't. If she cared for a man and that man had tried to kiss her, she certainly wouldn't have sent him on his way and then come in to chat with her sisters. Cassandra's actions made no sense to her whatsoever.

She stared at Cassandra in bewilderment. "Then why—"

"Because," Cassandra answered firmly, slamming the door on the subject for now.

It remained firmly closed though Brianne cajoled and pouted as she followed Cassandra upstairs to their room.

There was less than little rest for either sister that night. Both laid awake on their separate pallets, contemplating the pieces of a puzzle, though for different reasons.

Only Rose slept the peaceful sleep of the very just and the very tired.

Chapter Ten

With the undiluted, untainted pride of a child sharing an accomplishment created by his own hand, Riley arrived a little before noon the next morning at MacGregor's Furniture Shoppe, as the brand-new sign that hung before it declared, a copy of *The Virginia Gazette* under his arm.

Riley had spent the better part of the morning distributing and selling his newspaper. He thought it only fitting that the newest citizens of Morgan's Creek should receive their first copy free. Especially since they were mentioned in it.

His hand raised, ready to knock, Riley saw the door in front of him swing open before his knuckles could make contact with the weather-stained wood. Brianne stood in front of him the next moment, her wide smile welcoming him in. She had spied him approaching from across the street as she was gazing through the window she was supposed to have been washing.

It was as if her silent dreams had come true, she thought happily. Since Cassandra had really given her nothing but tangled vagaries on the subject of Riley last night, wavering in her answer, Brianne had decided that Mr. Riley O'Roarke, newspaper editor extraordinare, and handsome bachelor, was still very much there for the winning.

And she intended to win him.

"Good morning!" she cried with every bit of the enthusiasm she felt. Within the next moment, Brianne's hand was clapped upon his wrist, lest he change his mind and retreat.

Riley inclined his head, returning her greeting. "Good morning, Mistress MacGregor."

He quickly scanned the large rectangular room behind her. Rose was only a few feet away, sweeping the floor with a broom that had seen more than its share of wear. Unlike her father, she had stopped her work as soon as she had heard the sound of Riley's voice.

Bruce MacGregor seemed oblivious of sounds. He was bent over an inverted three-legged table that looked for all the world like a turtle flipped over on his shell. A large piece of wood destined to be the fourth leg lay on the floor next to him.

Riley absorbed all this while Brianne was drawing him into the room.

Riley could tell by the way the girl's eyes shone that he needed no excuse to be there. Still, he felt he should produce one.

"I brought you a copy of the *Gazette,* fresh off the press, as it were." He took it from under his arm and held it aloft like a shield of truce. Brianne was becoming entirely too enthusiastic for his liking.

He looked around but saw no one else. "Is Cassandra about?"

"No," Brianne tossed off, disappointed that even in her absence Cassandra was still with them. She laid the newspaper aside on a bureau. "She's gone out."

He'd been to all the shops and houses in town that morning and passed her at none of them. Where else could she be?

"Out?" He looked from one sister to the other. MacGregor, he noted, was still laboring over his task, as undisturbed by the sound of their voices as if he were completely alone.

"Gathering herbs and whatever else it is she finds," Brianne said vaguely in a bored tone.

Cassandra was always dabbling in those smelly things, swearing by their abilities to make people well. Brianne didn't wish to waste precious time discussing her sister with Riley.

Herbs, he thought. This was something he was acquainted with. Rachel set great store by her herbs and the poultices she fashioned from different roots and plants that grew in the glen. It was something she had been taught by her grandmother while she was still a slip of a thing in Ireland.

By then, Rose had joined them, much to Brianne's dismay. Riley turned toward her, nodding his greeting. "So your sister's a healer?"

The statement had been uttered conversationally. He had no idea why Rose looked at him so sharply. What had he said?

Testing the ground hesitantly, he continued. "My sister sets great store by her herbs."

"Sister?" Rose's voice went up, spiced by her intrigue. Though she loved her sisters dearly, she was hungry for companionship. "You have a sister?"

"Aye, that I do." A very keen-tongued wench, he thought fondly. Absence had blunted the sharpness of her instrument in his mind. It would take but a hour or less in her presence to bring it all back to him, of that he was certain. "But she's in France right now. With Ben Franklin."

MacGregor dropped the mallet he was holding. Riley's voice had finally penetrated the insulation the older man had surrounded himself with in order to concentrate on his work. He rose to his feet, taking care to hold not his aching back, but his aching head, the one he had acquired last night. His eyes narrowed as he drew closer to Riley.

"You *know* Ben Franklin?" Even Bruce MacGregor had heard of the man.

It was with no small amount of pride that Riley numbered Benjamin Franklin as a close friend. More. As a surrogate father.

"Yes, I do. Mr. Franklin took my sister and me in when we arrived from Ireland. We had landed, orphaned, in Philadelphia."

Of course, the circumstances of their first meeting were a

little less upstanding than his statement might lead the others to believe.

Riley smiled to himself, remembering. He had lifted Franklin's purse and had run like the wind, hoping to find a few pence in the pouch he clutched that might help to feed his starving sister. Their father had died on the journey over to these shores, as had their younger sister, Deirdra. The pox had taken them both.

There was none of their family left but he to care for Rachel, and she had fallen ill. In desperation he had housed her in a corner of a filthy alley and then gone to seek their fortunes.

No more than a boy, there was nothing Riley could do to help Rachel but steal. And steal he did.

Yanking loose the purse from Franklin's wide waist, Riley had flown on what he thought were winged feet, certain that the rounded old man he had been forced by circumstances to rob would be left far behind.

He had not reckoned on the stubbornness that had seen Benjamin Franklin through so many dire times. Franklin pursued the young rascal as he shouted after him with fury.

Riley ran for all he was worth, and finally darted into the alley where Rachel lay waiting for him. Darkness was beginning to fall, and he didn't want her there alone. Wild dogs roamed the streets at night.

Franklin followed, triumphant that he had cornered the young hooligan.

But the wrath of having his purse cut and stolen vanished abruptly as he looked down into the face of the sickly little girl. Franklin ceased his shouting and gently lifted the child into his arms, though Riley railed at him and beat at the man with fists made impotent by hunger.

The elder statesman took both children into his home and, subsequently, into his heart. Rachel and Riley lived with him until they were ready to strike out on their own, their lives greatly enriched by the contact they had with Franklin.

But all this was a story for another time, when friendship had deepened their acquaintance. For then, all Riley said was yes.

"Hopefully," he continued, thinking of how he missed her and her happy aptitude for work, "Rachel will be coming back before long."

Though Riley was eager to be on his way, eager to begin his search for Cassandra, he knew it wouldn't be polite to leave so abruptly. So he turned his attention to the man he had carried home last eventide.

The man's complexion had a thin, pasty cast to it, and by the way he was squinting, Riley could tell that MacGregor's head was giving him no small bit of pain. How well he could relate to that. Still, it wouldn't do to point the fact out, especially not before the man's daughters.

Instead, Riley smiled heartily at MacGregor. "You're well, I see, Mr. MacGregor."

MacGregor looked Riley over slowly, a memory nudging itself to the fore in his mind. The voice was familiar, as was the set of the shoulders. MacGregor tried to place the young man and failed.

But it would come to him, he thought. All he needed was a little help.

"We met last night, did we not?" MacGregor asked. He waited to hear more of the man's voice, hoping that would unlock his memory.

Riley grinned. So that man wasn't as ale-soaked as he had appeared. He remembered.

The first time he had made Sin-Jin's acquaintance had been at Sam's Tavern. Riley recalled none of it the day after, even though he had fallen into Sin-Jin's arms at the time.

"That we did," Riley told MacGregor.

"He carried you home, Da," Rose whispered as if it were a secret and not something they all knew to be true.

MacGregor was long past being flustered at such acts. That was for young boys who sought their mother's forgiveness for shameful behavior, not for grown men who had earned a little respite from their burden-filled lives.

MacGregor inclined his head toward Riley. "Then I am in your debt."

"Cassandra has already asked me to dinner," Riley volunteered, hoping to solidify one of these invitations. "Twice," he added for good measure.

MacGregor nodded. That was as it should be. A MacGregor stood in no one's debt for long.

"Then I shall make it a third. With a date pinned to it." He had no idea about the condition of their supplies, but that was for the girls to deal with. "Will tomorrow night be too soon?"

Riley's grin was wide. Success, he thought. "Not for me."

MacGregor clamped his wide hand over Riley's, sealing the bargain. The hearty action brought a wince to the older man as arrows of pain shot through his head. "Then tomorrow night it is."

Riley slowly freed himself of the bearlike grip. He was not unaware that Brianne was beaming over the invitation. Things were going to have to be set to rights here somehow. He wanted his intentions clear from the beginning. His interest, still forming nebulously, lay with Cassandra.

"By the way," Riley interjected, attempting not to appear too interested and, in his estimation, failing. At least the look in MacGregor's eyes seemed knowing. "Did Cassandra mention where it was she would be going?"

It occurred to Riley that since she was new in town, Cassandra would not know her way around and might easily become lost. It wasn't his place to chide the father, but he felt it his responsibility to add, "She really shouldn't have gone off on her own without someone to guide her about."

Like you, eh, bucko? MacGregor had all he could do to keep from chuckling. Instead, he assured the young man, "Cassandra always knows her way around." He leaned his head forward, as if imparting a secret. " 'Tis we who follow her."

"Cassandra never gets lost. She has a wonderful sense of direction," Rose chimed in quickly. Then she colored, as if she had mispoken. Rose cleared her throat self-consciously. "Or ability to find her way around as it were."

Again he had no idea what it was that had set Rose off this way. His intuition told him that something wasn't right here. What it was he had no notion. But at the moment his main concern was Cassandra. Her family might regard her to be some sort of great pathfinder, but even the best of those lost their way on occasion, and that was after knowing the area. How much easier would that be if one didn't know the area?

He looked at Rose patiently. "And where would this wonderful sense of direction, or ability to find her way around," he qualified, "be taking her?"

"To the side north of the town," Rose volunteered at the same instant that Brianne shrugged her shoulders.

The latter still nurtured the hope that Riley would abandon this conversation and turn his attention toward something more interesting. Such as asking to look around the shop.

Or taking a walk with her.

But Rose pressed on. "By the stream we passed on our way here."

He knew the area well that she spoke of. The stream ran by the Morgan plantation and made its way down to North Fork. Rachel frequented it. Odd that Cassandra would know just where to go to find the best herbs.

But then, Rose had said that they had passed it on their way there. Cassandra had probably taken note of it then. That would be her way.

He took the information as a signal to leave and backed away toward the door. "Well, I'm off."

Brianne's face fell notably. "Must you go?" she implored. She threaded her arms around his, anchoring him to her.

Carefully, he disengaged her hands from his arm. "I'm afraid I must. I've things to attend to and papers to distribute." The latter was a lie, but a safe one, he hoped.

Brianne, reluctant to release him from her sight, rocked on her heels. "Might I help you with any of those *things?*"

He took her hand and, bringing it to his lips, kissed it in parting. "That is very generous of you, but I believe for the moment your father would be having far more need of you than I."

Brianne cradled one hand in the other, the imprint of his lips tingling her skin. He needed her, she thought dreamily, hearing only what she wanted to hear. She looked over her shoulder toward her father and sighed. ''Obligations can be troublesome at times.''

Riley suppressed a grin as he took his leave of the girls and MacGregor. ''So I have been told.'' He indicated the newspaper on the bureau. ''Oh, I'd pay special attention to a paragraph on the second page if I were you. I mentioned you.''

Brianne fairly flew to the newspaper as Riley slipped away.

Chapter Eleven

It was Riley's inherent curiosity that had urged him on as a boy to learn how to read even though his father had insisted that it was all nonsense and that his time would be better spent in the field. But curiosity about the mysteries of the printed word had won out, and with the help of the village priest, Riley had learned.

Later, curiosity about life had served to drive him. Part of his work on the newspaper now depended upon his being curious about the dealings of the people who lived in and around Morgan's Creek. More, it was curiosity about where they were all headed in a time when the land he lived in was defining and redefining itself.

Always, it was curiosity that motivated him.

So it was no wonder that curiosity had his steps leading him from the center of town, in the direction of the glen where he surmised that Cassandra might be. Curiosity of a personal nature. About Cassandra. This though he knew that there was still work to see to in the newspaper office. And if there wasn't that, Lord knew there was more than enough work waiting for him at home after that.

But none of that mattered at the moment. Only his curiosity.

He wanted to see her alone, without the circle of her family wreathing about her. Alone. Just a man and a woman, with nothing but the forest animals for company. He wanted to see how she reacted to him then.

He stopped at the shop only long enough to avail himself of his powder and musket. The war might be over, but it was still not safe to travel without a weapon close at hand.

But before he had managed to reach the outskirts of town, he heard someone hailing him by name. Turning, he saw Jason striding toward him.

"Riley!" Jason called again as he hurried toward him. "Wait up."

Jason's nephew, Christopher, was at his side, matching him stride for stride. At nineteen, the young man had filled out considerably from the scrawny youth he had been when his uncle had married Krystyna.

With the years, Christopher had grown indispensable to Jason. He had become knowledgeable in all aspects of maintaining the plantation. His eye was keener than any overseer. Christopher had an instinct for knowing what needed to be done and when. So good was he that Jason had given him the responsibility of running Sin-Jin's plantation while Sin-Jin was away, accompanying Rachel and Ben Franklin to France.

Both men appeared pleased to have encountered Riley. Jason clamped a hand on Riley's shoulder.

"Krystyna's requested, actually, insisted is more like it, that I travel to town to get a copy of that rag you insist on putting out each week."

Riley took the good-natured joking in stride. Krystyna McKinley was his most avid reader, always thirsty for knowledge. Jason was not far behind his wife in that quest.

"I've saved a copy for you as well as for your father. They're in the office." He gestured toward it with his free hand. "You've but to help yourself."

Jason nodded his thanks. "I'll leave the price of them in your desk drawer." He glanced at the musket Riley held. "Going hunting?"

"In a manner of speaking." Riley's reply was purposely evasive. He was hunting answers, not game.

"Well, I wish you luck." He took a step, then abruptly turned. "Oh, I nearly forgot. A number of us are gathering at my father's the evening after tomorrow to discuss the possible resurrection of the town council." Jason exchanged a glance with his nephew. "We'd like you to be there."

They'd talked of this the other night, though only in passing "As the editor of the *Gazette?*"

"As a possible council member," Jason countered.

Jason was rewarded with a pleased look from his friend. So Jason had been serious after all, he thought. "I'll be there early," Riley promised. "And the *Gazette* is on the house Give it to Krystyna with my love."

Jason waved once as they parted. "I'll give it to her with your best wishes," Jason emphasized with a laugh. "Love she'll get from me."

With that, he and his nephew hurried on their way to the newspaper office.

Though he thought of himself as a free man and happy to be so, there were times when Riley truly envied Jason for what the man had with Krystyna. It would seem infinitely comforting he reflected, to know that that sort of love was in your life.

With a long, determined stride, Riley crossed to the outskirts and soon left the town behind him. He set out for the wood.

Damn, he thought as he tramped along, he was behaving like some sort of lovesick boyo sniffing after his first skirt. But it felt, he had to admit, as if there were a fever in his blood.

It had been a long time since he had sampled his first taste of a woman's kiss. Of a woman's body. A long time. And there had been a great many since then. Riley had always enjoyed the company of a willing woman with no real thought of permanency crossing his mind.

Marriage, children, the settled, responsible, dependable life—all that was for others. He was far too busy to think about that.

And yet, here he was, all but running off to find her. Running off as if he were hurrying to meet his destiny. Or get a glimpse of it at any rate.

He argued with himself that in actuality it was none of that. That what drove him to look for her was a concern that she might become lost.

Lord knew she wouldn't have been the first to have done it, not even since he had arrived in Morgan's Creek. The glen was a warm, sunny place, but the forest just beyond it was not always friendly, especially to someone who had lost their way.

No ill was going to befall Cassandra. Not if he had a say in the matter. That it was not his place to tell her what to do did not even begin to cross his mind.

The glen, as he approached it, was bathed in sunlight. Wide, lush, it was home to many plants and herbs as well as a large variety of wildflowers.

He looked around, searching for a sign of Cassandra in the field and amid the bushes that bordered the stream. Riley remembered accompanying Rachel here, to pick the herbs she felt were so important in mixing the potions and medicines she used to help heal.

It was knowledge from the Emerald Isle his sister had brought with her. Words that had been whispered from mother to daughter aided her in choosing which plants to use and which to discard.

Riley wondered if that was the way of it for Cassandra. Had her mother taught her? Or had there been another mentor who had guided her? A kindly grandmother or an old woman in the village? There was so much he wanted to know about Cassandra.

So much he needed to know.

He had a hunger, a thirst that far outdistanced his newsman's interest, to know about this ethereal, blond-haired woman who had all but drifted into his life.

He heard the dried grasses protest under the weight of his boots as he trampled through the glen, his eyes squinting against the sun.

Searching.

A blue jay flew by, loudly announcing his passage. Riley's attention was drawn to the faint glimmer of blue as it streaked across the sky.

He still owed Cassandra a dress, he thought, and he meant to make good on his promise, with no underhanded motives in mind. The dress would be hers to wear, not his to remove, as she had so knowingly pointed out. He'd never presume to do anything like that.

Although the thought of it brought a smile to his lips and a rich fantasy to his mind.

Another bit of blue caught his eye.

This time he saw it as he approached the stream. It was on a bush. But this was no blue jay perched in a limb. And it was far too low to belong to the sky. At the same time, it was far too striking to belong to the stream.

As he drew closer, instinctively taking care not to make too much noise, Riley realized that what he saw was the skirt of Cassandra's dress.

The dress had been very carefully spread out on the shrub. Beside it were undergarments he was more than passingly familiar with, though he would have never admitted that, or whose it was that he was familiar with. A gentleman, and he was one, never mentioned his trysts, even to his friends.

Or to his confessor, he thought with a smile. But there was no such man of the cloth to try to wangle his secrets from him in Morgan's Creek, only the dour reverend to whom he barely spoke. Riley kept his own council as to his amorous activities.

None of them were even a faint memory to him now. All had been erased as if they never were. The only one on his mind was Cassandra.

Slowly parting the bush for a better look at the stream, he saw her and felt his blood quicken in his veins.

She was a vision. A pure vision.

There was no other way to describe the scene as Cassandra slowly moved across the water. Her skin gleamed like porcelain.

Riley's heart caught in his throat and his grip upon the musket tightened.

Had the musket been a twig, he would have readily snapped it in two, so hard was he attempting to exercise control upon his feelings.

A gentleman would have undoubtedly turned his back and walked away.

Perhaps, Riley mused as he stood rooted to the spot, unable to shut his eyes or lower his gaze, he was not so much a gentleman as he had thought. Perhaps there was a great deal of the untamed heathen savage that still ran through his views. Whatever the reason, he could not move, could not even breathe.

God, but she was beautiful.

Sunbeams danced along her body as she swam, as if they were intimate confederates. No, more, as if they were worshipful servants. As her slender arms rose above the water, then leisurely sliced through it once more, the beams of light shone upon the water that caressed her body, turning the beads into jewels. They glistened along her sleek body each time she made a stroke.

The very breath stagnated in his lungs as he knelt, half in worship, half in desire for some practical cover behind the very same bush that held her clothing.

All he wanted to do was remain there to look upon her.

It was sinful and, at the very least, wrong, but he couldn't help himself. He had never been entranced by such a sight.

Her body was perfect.

When she shifted and moved closer to the stream bank, he found himself envious of the very water that was allowed the joy of caressing her breasts, her thighs, her belly, so intimately.

Would that it were he.

He knew he should leave. He remained where he was. His tongue turned to dust within his mouth as he continued gazing.

It had been a hot morning. Unseasonably so.

It was the last of the warm weather before it retreated from the land to regions unknown, where it would again await the first call of spring. Today it made the land simmer beneath its hand.

Leaving her sisters and father at the shop, Cassandra ha thought it necessary to replenish her supplies. She had com with her basket, intent on filling it high with such things a chamomile and rosemary. And a legion of other herbs she migh use for the simple pleasure of cooking.

Or the task of healing, if it came to that.

But the heat had hung oppressively about her. Soon he clothes had felt too heavy to bear.

Since she was alone and it appeared that she would remai so, Cassandra had whimsically decided to shed her clothin and indulge in a swim. Whimsy was not a thing that cam often to her. When it did, she usually hesitated in followin its lead.

But not today.

And she was glad she had. The water had been delicious cool from the first. Submerging herself in it had gone a lon way in rejuvenating her spirits.

When she had shed her garments, it was as if she had, albei temporarily, shed her concerns and her responsibilities as well For a brief, isolated moment, she felt like a child again, playin along the shore of Loch Ness, without a single care to troubl her.

It seemed as if even her sight had drifted from her at a tim like this.

But the Sight returned now, and with it the power. And th knowledge that she was not alone. Though she couldn't se him, she knew that he was there. Had been there for more tha a fleeting moment.

Riley.

Embarrassment washed over her, hard and humbling. But i gave way to acceptance as she turned in a circle and looke toward the bank. She knew things arranged themselves withi life in a pattern, and he was part of hers, though what part sh was yet unable to see.

That would come to her too, she told herself. She had bu to be patient.

At times, being patient was not an easy matter for her. A a child, she had never been patient. Very much like Brianne she had wanted everything to happen then, not later. Patience was a skill she had had to learn, and she had worked at it just as diligently as she had at learning to ply her needle.

Still, be Riley part of that pattern or not, this did present an awkward situation for her. She was, after all, naked. And he was standing where her clothing had been laid aside.

Biting her lip, she debated the best possible way to approach the matter.

Then, suddenly, a scream echoed, like that of a terrified woman, and Cassandra knew there was no time left for the luxury of a debate.

Riley was in danger, whether he knew it or not.

Chapter Twelve

His heart hammering, Riley jumped away from the bush as the shriek rent the late morning air. It was a sound that made his blood run cold.

Riley did not have to be told what made the unearthly noise. He knew. He had heard it twice before and had once seen its gruesome handiwork after it was done with its unwitting victim.

The shriek belonged to a mountain lion. One that was on the hunt.

And from what he could detect, the mountain lion was not very far from there. Riley blessed the forethought that had him bring his musket with him. The very next heartbeat had Riley raising the weapon to his eye, prepared to fire as he nervously scanned the grounds.

The mountain lion could leap out of the wood at any moment.

Within a flash, Cassandra saw it, and knew she had to stop him before it was too late.

"No, Riley, you'll miss," Cassandra called out to him with the certainly of one who knew.

Startled, he swung around to look toward her. There was no time to apologize at having been caught this way. No time for explanations. There was only the danger.

He lowered the musket a fraction, his fingers still tensed on the trigger. "I'm a good shot," he assured her.

Cassandra knew he was not bragging, but it made no difference.

"You'll miss," she repeated with authority. She swam a little toward him, her eyes urgent for what they had just seen. What would be if he didn't listen to her and heed her words. He would miss and the animal would tear him to ribbons.

"There's no time. She's coming this way. You'll have to jump into the water."

He would have laughed at the suggestion had the situation not been so dire and his throat not so dry. As it were, his eyes widened at the very thought of what she proposed.

"Then it's my end I'll meet, one way or the other." He glanced over his shoulder toward the woods, then at Cassandra again. "I cannot swim."

She didn't look surprised at the revelation, Riley noted, but merely nodded in response. She raised her arms from the water and toward him in a manner he would have welcomed but a minute sooner.

"I'll hold you up," she promised.

There was no time for debate.

The next moment, another shriek echoed around them. As Riley's head jerked in that direction, he saw what he would have easily seen earlier had he not been so preoccupied with finding Cassandra. Two young cubs. The mountain lion was protecting her own.

With graceful stride she cleared the trees and was heading straight toward him.

Riley knew that all animals, save him, swam. He fervently hoped that the mountain lion was not so inclined today.

"All right," Riley shouted to her, his feet moving quickly, "I'll place my faith in you and the Almighty. Not necessarily in that order."

Casting his musket to one side and the powder horn he had slung over his shoulder to the other, Riley ran with the speed of a stallion at full gallop into the stream.

He had always hated the water.

As a boy in County Cork, no more than about three his father had told him, Riley had tumbled from a makeshift footbridge into the river that ran through their landlord's property. He had very nearly drowned. His father had jumped in after him and pulled him out, but not before Riley had drunk more than his share of the River Lee.

Ever since then, Riley had had a healthy respect and more than a little fear of water. He always gave it a wide path whenever he came within the vicinity of more water than could be held in a barrel.

So it went against everything he believed in to run full bore into the water now.

But it was also against his belief to allow himself to be torn limb from limb, as Paddy Wilson had been. The portly man had gone berrying with his wife and children the previous year and somehow gotten separated from them during the course of the day. When the search party finally found him, it hadn't been a sight for a weak-stomached man to behold.

Riley had no intention of something like that befalling him.

Of course, drowning was not very enticing either.

The water was up to his hips now, and rising ever higher. Within a moment or two, Riley knew he wouldn't be able to feel the bottom of the bed with his boots any longer. The thought alarmed him.

As the realization took hold and panic began to spin a web around his rational thoughts, his mind was in danger of being swept away, just as surely as his body was.

And then he felt her arms, slender and strong around him.

Riley forced himself to steady his breath. Blinking back his terror until he could manage it, Riley focused his eyes and saw her. Cassandra's face, slick with water, was level with his. She was holding him up in the stream, just as she had promised.

Slowly, Riley's mind cleared. And he knew that he was safe.

"I have you," Cassandra said.

It was the third time she was repeating the words. This time they seemed to have penetrated the wall of terror she had seen in his eyes. Fear abated rapidly as his dark lashes blinked to clear his eyes and fan away the drops of water on them.

Holding him so, the past made itself known to her, and with it, the incident Riley had suffered in the water. She understood his terror now and managed, just by being there, to drain it from him.

"Aye, that you do." He tried not to notice that his breathing had quickened once more, but for a different reason.

Because of her.

Riley turned his head, looking toward the bank. There, sleek and golden, the mountain lion paced about the water's edge. For some reason, the big cat was unwilling to go forward, though she could easily swim to them. She seemed content to stand on the bank, a living, breathing threat, warning him off from her young.

She would not enter the stream today, Cassandra thought with a great deal of relief. Sometimes the confidence with which she sensed things held her in awe. And unnerved her just a little.

" 'Tis rather a magnificent beast, is it not?" The admiration was plain in her voice as she gazed at it. They had no such animals in Scotland, and she thought the mountain lion almost a mythical thing, a beast spun from the pages of folklore.

Except that its claws were deadly.

"When it's not tearing a man apart with the swipe of its outstretched paw." There was no admiration in Riley's voice, only guarded respect.

Riley suddenly became aware that Cassandra was moving. Not just bobbing up and down, but actually moving farther from the bank.

Unease sliced through him afresh. Riley clung to her, his arms around Cassandra's neck like a newborn babe holding on to its mother. He was not proud of this, but there was naught he could do. If he let go of her, he would drown.

And there were worse things than cleaving to a nude woman.

Riley glanced back to the shore. "Do you think this is necessary?" He nodded as best he could toward the direction they were taking. "Swimming farther?"

"To be safe," she answered vaguely. In case her vision had failed her. She could not afford to be reckless with his life.

Her own was a different matter, but she wanted no one's life on her conscience.

He tried to maintain a rein on the panic that was renewing itself. At all costs, he endeavored to keep it from his voice.

"I can't touch the bottom."

Cassandra smiled, and it managed to calm him a little. "There's no need. My father always called me a strong swimmer. I can swim for two."

Slowly, Riley felt his fear unraveling. In its stead, he became aware of her. Acutely so. Aware of the fact that her nude body was but a heartbeat away from his. That he had but to hold fast to her to feel every inch of her supple form against his.

That it brushed along his own as she swam for them both.

His thoughts were not on his face, but she was aware of them nonetheless. They were there in his eyes.

"I see that you are not afraid anymore, Riley," she told him.

The sun bounced from the water's surface, obstructing a clear view of her, but he thought he could see anyway, at least in his mind's eye. And just knowing she was there had his blood pounding hot through his veins.

His voice felt almost hoarse in his throat as he answered. "At this very moment I'm thinking of dropping a line of thanks to the mountain lion."

She ceased swimming for the opposite bank and remained still now, treading water. She, too, was aware. Aware that she was nude. Aware of the yearning within her own body. And within his.

"She won't be able to read it," Cassandra heard herself whispering, though the words seemed somehow more dry than amused.

Her entire body was tingling.

"I'll still be meaning it. The thanks," Riley clarified.

He swallowed, aching for her despite the danger that was receding from them even now. Despite the dictates of mores that shackled him to a behavior he had no wish to adhere to.

But adhere he was bound to.

Still, he felt he had to tell her what was on his mind. " know that this isn't the proper thing for a man to say to woman who hardly knows him, but God, you are most divine woman I have ever seen.''

With one hand still around her neck, he slid the other along her back, his fingers spread as if each had a mind of its own. As if each were eager to touch her and assure itself that she was real.

Her movement in the water aroused him as her body came in contact with his over and over again. He felt pulses throbbing in his loins, and knew that he would have no relief.

Gently, his eyes on hers, his hand dipped lower until it reached her waist. It lingered there, fascinated at its diminutive size. Then, ever so slowly, he trailed his fingers upward along her ribs until, hesitantly, he filled his hand with her breast. He heard her sharp intake of breath. It echoed his own.

Flames licked through her as desires ricocheted, begging her for things she was as of yet unfamiliar with. The mountain lion that had disappeared into the wood with her young from whence she had come was forgotten as completely as if she had never existed.

Everything was forgotten except Riley.

But only for a moment.

Cassandra knew she could not allow herself to forget. She could not allow herself to be lost in the sights and sensations created by a man like any normal woman. She was not a normal woman, not allowed to experience things that shimmered like forbidden fruit before her.

A burden came with her gift. A responsibility that she could not shirk. One that would always keep her separated from him.

'' 'Tis right, you are,'' she agreed, though she had no idea where she found the breath to speak. '' 'Tis not proper.''

Because there was no air in her lungs, Cassandra was forced to draw in a deep breath. With determination, she moved his hand from where it was and once again placed it around her neck.

"But this is a situation that is far from ordinary." As was she, she thought silently, and for perhaps the first time, with regret.

Riley hardly heard what she was saying. It was as if it were some distant music swirling about his head. He heard only the symphony that was generated within him the moment he had touched her. The skin on his hand still hummed from it.

He knew he would never be satisfied until he had had her.

And perhaps not even then.

"Cassandra?" he whispered softly, his fear of the mountain lion and the water distant from him now.

She could not tear her eyes away from his. It was as if he were holding her prisoner. She was unaccustomed to feeling this way, and it troubled her even as it fascinated her. "Yes?"

The very sound of her voice skimmed seductively along his skin. "Are you quite certain that you can continue to hold me up?"

The mountain lion was gone. They would be swimming back to the bank in a moment. Why was he questioning her about that now? The danger had passed.

Or had it? she suddenly wondered, anticipating.

"Aye."

Riley grinned his satisfaction. " 'Tis all I wanted to know."

He placed his faith in her once again. So doing, he gave in to the urgings of his body and his mind. Urgings that had haunted him since the night before, when she had kept him from kissing her.

This time her hands were around his waist and forced to remain so. They would not be getting in the way as they had done last night, forming a barrier between them and pushing him away.

So he was free to follow his inclination. And his heart.

Drawing her closer, Riley brought his mouth down on hers. And very quickly slipped, unarmed and unprepared, into paradise.

Chapter Thirteen

It became crystal clear to her the instant his mouth touched hers. Cassandra knew immediately, as if the message had always been there, waiting for her, what her weakness was.

It was he.

Cassandra felt herself both being buoyed up and sinking under the water at the same moment. Her arms, still around Riley's waist, tightened without any thought on her part as the heat surged through her, snatching her breath away. Making her head spin.

Images clashed like lightning creasing the summer sky and rumbled through her. There was heat and there was passion.

His. Hers.

She'd never really known passion before, not anywhere close to this degree. Not where it inflamed her, encircled her, and fought her for the very ownership of her soul. Her passion had always been for her family, for forging a path for them. For guarding the power of her sight so that she might be of help to others.

It had never involved her as a woman before.

It did now.

And she knew not how to begin to deal with it.

Sweet Lord, he was drowning, Riley thought. Drowning just as surely as if he had lost his grip and slid beneath the stream's surface.

Drowning in her.

What matter of sorceress was she that she could rob him of his thoughts like this? That she could rob him of his very mind? All he could think of was wanting her.

Wanting to have her, to possess this body that was so close to his.

With his arms around her neck, Riley slanted his mouth over hers as he sampled and resampled her lips.

It was more than sweet, more than compelling. One taste urged him to take more, and more again. And still there was no satisfaction forthcoming. No end. Only desire as he held her to him.

Desire consumed him.

He burned with it far hotter than any torch giving light to the dark.

It was Cassandra who drew away first. Shaken, she pulled back her mouth from his. Riley thought he caught a glimmer of fear in her eyes for just a moment. Fear of what had erupted so mightily.

Fear of what was to come.

He didn't want her afraid of him. Ever. But he had to admit to himself that even he felt a shimmer of uncertainty at what had transpired between them.

"You've bewitched me, Cassandra," he murmured, keenly aware that her body was rubbing against his even as she tried to wedge a space between them.

He saw something flare in her eyes at his words. Instantly, it was as if a wall had been thrown up between them.

There was that word again, she thought in dismayed alarm. *Bewitched.* So close to *witch.* So close to the truth and yet so far away.

"I have no powers with which to bewitch people," Cassandra replied, her manner stoic, so different from a moment ago.

"Perhaps not people," he countered. His voice was soothing, gentle, as he searched for a way to remove that line of consternation from between her eyes. "But certainly me. From the very first moment I stumbled down from my horse at your feet, you bewitched me like no other woman ever had."

He was speaking figuratively. She was being too skittish, she chided herself. But once burned . . .

She smiled sadly at her own choice of words.

Regaining her composure, reining in her unease, she smiled at him tolerantly now. "The bewitching 'tis but your imagination."

Though he still feared sinking beneath the water, he hazarded freeing one hand. Ever so lightly, as delicately as the kiss of a butterfly, he traced his fingertips along the hollow of her cheek. It was as soft, as pure as the first snows.

" 'Tis not my imagination that makes me burn so, Cassandra."

His very look made the breath stop in her throat. She knew it could not be so. It was too dangerous. For him as well as for her. She could never forget who she was. And who she could not be.

The specter of suspicion and doubt would always rise up to haunt her and those she loved.

With effort, she attempted to seem unfazed. "If you burn, then the water should have surely served to cool you off."

The grin that spread across his face was slow, lazy, and all the more sensually appealing for it. "Aye, but what if it is what is *in* the water that strikes the flint to my wick and sets me aflame."

He could not help himself. His eyes dipped down, eager for but a glimpse of her. But once again the sun reflected its rays from the water so that he could not see.

Her sight once more deserted her as an unease slipped over Cassandra. She trusted him instinctively, yet was she being foolish to do so? After all, she was at his mercy, without a stitch of clothing on her body. There were many men who would be driven to take advantage of the situation.

Would he be one of them?

As was her way when she found all paths blocked to her, she sought to brazen the situation out.

Cassandra's eyes grew dark as she regarded Riley's face. "I've saved your life. Is this how you think to repay me? By mocking me?"

He had no idea how she could have misunderstood and reached that conclusion. There was nothing in his manner to suggest derision.

"I do not mock you, Cassandra. I desire you." *So much that it would surprise you. It does me.* " 'Tis myself I mock, for not doing what men in my position would most assuredly do."

She felt compelled to draw in a breath before she asked, "And that is?" Her voice was as still as the very air that drifted around them.

His eyes held hers. And made love to her where they were, though he touched her not at all. "Take you."

There was no anger swelling in her voice, only disappointment. "Then you would be as savage as the mountain lion you sought to escape."

"I know." Riley nodded, his eyes still on her face alone. They might have been the only two people left in the world for all he was aware of at the moment. "Instead," he sighed, "I shall be a fool and touch you not, though I burn to."

His declaration, and the yearning in it, brought a smile to her lips and relief to her soul. She had been right about him.

"Fools are stupid," Cassandra pointed out softly.

Her blood was just now beginning to cool. And only a little at that. Though only disaster would result, she knew in her heart that she desired the same thing he did.

"And you are not." She looked toward the bank. The mountain lion had long since retreated into the woods once more with her cubs. "I believe it's safe for you to come out."

Though he had silently vowed not to touch her, Riley was unwilling to give up his proximity to Cassandra so soon.

"What if the mountain lion returns?" he inquired innocently, hoping to prolong their time together.

She saw right through his effort and laughed softly. "She won't."

Cassandra's tone puzzled Riley. "You say that as if you know."

She shrugged as best she could, then stopped, realizing that she was once more moving against him. "Some things you can sense."

A smile curved his mouth, but he did not laugh. "You are a mystery, Cassandra."

The smile did not reach her eyes, for she did not feel it, though she offered it to him. "And will continue to remain so."

But Riley shook his head as he grazed at her lips. There was no part of her that he could look upon and not find himself wanting her.

"I hope not."

Cassandra chose not to reply. Instead, she began to swim again, taking Riley back toward the bank until his boots touched the bottom. Her hands were already releasing him. "You can walk from here."

Nodding, Riley began to do so, then turned to look at her. She had remained just where she was, behind him. "And you?"

She was not about to walk out of the water by his side. There was just so much temptation either one of them could successfully resist.

"I shall wait until you are gone."

"Why?" Her answer more than wounded him. He realized that it offended him as well. He wanted her trust. "I give you my word, I shall not look." Even though doing so would have made him everlastingly contented to the end of his days.

Cassandra hesitated as a quivering sensation slid all through her. She recognized it to be nervous anticipation. "No, I—"

Riley had reached the bank. As he slowly walked out, it felt as if there were an oppressive hand making him steadily heavier. His clothes, weighed down with the water, felt as if they were a stone or more.

He turned to look at her once again, refusing to let the matter go. It was a point of honor now.

His honor.

"Trust me, Cassandra, just as I trusted you to hold me up."

She shook her head. "It is not the same."

"Isn't it?" he countered, his eyes challenging her. To him it was exactly the same.

Cassandra gave her trust guardedly, and then only after a long time had lapsed. This was asking a great deal of her. She wavered now, searching for a feeling to guide her. There was none. None to aid her decision. It was to her own instincts she had to resort. There was no other way open to her.

After a moment she pressed her lips together and nodded, "All right, I will."

Riley smiled as he turned around.

"You'll have to be moving from the bush," she instructed his back. "My clothes are there." As he well knew, she thought.

Without a word Riley stepped away from the bush where her clothing lay in the sun. He felt both pleased and frustrated at the same moment.

The burden of trust, he thought as his eyes scanned the woods warily for a sign of the mountain lion's return, was great. While it bestowed a princely mantle about his shoulders, it also robbed him of the privilege, and most assuredly the pleasure, of swinging around and taking his fill of her lovely body in the sunlight.

At all times the waters had distorted her image for him and showed him only enough to tantalize and to tempt. Riley wanted more. He wanted to see and to touch.

He wanted what he could not have.

For to satisfy himself now would be to lose Cassandra forever.

So he stood, restlessly contemplating the wood just beyond and listening, in frustration, to the sound of Cassandra clothing herself.

Like a man in a trance, Riley closed his eyes and envisioned the wondrous sight. He could all but see the white undergarments clinging to her wet skin as she slipped them on one by one. His throat tightened at the thought of the chemise sliding along her breasts like a second skin, molding itself to her ripened nipples.

Riley felt his loins pulsing in response to his thoughts and chided himself for engaging in such mental torture. But he could neither refrain from it nor help himself. He had become, in this short while, her prisoner.

Watching his back cautiously, Cassandra had quickly hurried into her clothes. Too much temptation was difficult for anyone but a saint to resist, and she knew from the way he had kissed her that Riley O'Roarke would never be a candidate for that holy position.

The garments had an uncomfortable feel to them as they clung to her body, but at least she was properly dressed once more. She was certain that she had never gotten dressed so swiftly in her life.

" 'Tis done, I am," she told him, releasing a large sigh as well.

He turned and saw that her clothing, damp with the sheen of water that still remained on her body, did indeed adhere to her just as he had envisioned. He pressed his lips together to stifle a groan, but swallowed it instead.

She smiled when he said nothing in reply. He appeared a little dazed. "You kept your word."

Was that surprise he detected? Or pleasure? "Did you think I wouldn't?"

Cassandra did not answer immediately. Instead, she looked into his eyes. And then his soul. "No, I knew you would."

Then she knew more than he, for there had been a moment of decided wavering when temptation wrestled with common sense and honor.

He dragged one hand through his wet hair. Droplets rained down onto the grass. Riley nodded toward her filled basket.

"Can I help you gather any more herbs? My sister took great pains to train me."

There was no need of his aid. Cassandra shook her head as he bent down to pick the basket up.

"No, I'm finished." She hooked the basket onto her arm. "The swim was but a small respite for me before I began to return home."

Riley bent down and retrieved his musket and powder horn. He slung the latter over one shoulder and the musket over the other. The muzzle pointed down behind his back. Since she was on her way into town, he had no further business out here.

"Then may I accompany you to town?"

"Yes," she assented, and her eyes sparkled. "You can keep me safe from mountain lions."

He laughed. "And you, me."

Riley took the basket from her, though what he truly yearned to do was take her into his arms once more. But he knew that the path to a goal was slow and not reached within a day.

He would have to wait, he told himself.

God willing, it would not be too long.

Chapter Fourteen

It was not until the next day that Riley remembered his promise to Cassandra. The one he had made that first morning. The one she had summarily rejected.

Rejection or not, he owed her a dress.

Profits from the *Gazette* were finally beginning to materialize. Since there was just himself to look after now and not Rachel, and his needs were easily met, Riley had managed to put aside money for the very first time in his life.

There was certainly enough for a dress to repay a young woman who had not only borne his cloddish staining of her garment with grace and humor, but then went on to save his life into the bargain.

Even if this were not the case, Riley would have felt inclined to give her some sort of present. The ruined dress provided him with the perfect excuse to do so. He knew that once the very fetching Cassandra MacGregor made her presence known about the town, she would not lack for suitors. He wanted to find a way to stand out. A gift would give him that way.

Whistling in anticipation of Cassandra's thanks when she received her new dress, Riley left his office and crossed the sun-baked dirt street to the dress shop.

He was quite aware that her father's store was right next door. As he passed the fledgling shop, Riley looked in but saw only Bruce MacGregor. The man was busy conversing with Morgan McKinley and using a great many hand gestures. Morgan, Jason's father, seemed to be nodding in reply.

He was sure to hear about the discussion by and by, Riley thought. All conversations eventually came to his ear in one form or another. Usually at the tavern, if not before.

Like as not, politics were being discussed between the two men, he mused. It was on everyone's mind these days. Now that the revolution was finally over, far lesser schisms were taking place between people. Unrest seemed to the very order of the day.

Riley entered the dressmaker's shop. A tiny tin bell just above the door tinkled, announcing him. He felt a little foolish, but forged on. This was for Cassandra, not his sense of well-being.

That, hopefully, would come later.

The dressmaker's shop was owned by the Widow Watkins. At fifty-one, the widow was a tall, willowy woman with iron-gray hair and a body that was reminiscent of an elm in winter. Her cheerful disposition belied her rather stern appearance, and small, thin-lipped mouth.

When Riley entered, there was but one other person in the shop, and her back was to him. He knew instantly that he was not looking upon the widow.

The back he was gazing upon was strong and young, tapering to a slender waist and then down to hips daintily hidden beneath the folds of a simple gingham dress. But they were as visible to Riley as if there were no fabric in the way at all.

"Cassandra."

Riley hadn't realized that he had said her name aloud until Cassandra turned to look at him. She raised her brow in surprise to see him standing within the shop, as surprised as he to see her. The proprietress was nowhere about. Cassandra was behind the counter, adjusting the bolts of cloth. Obviously she had not come in to make a purchase.

He was quick to approach her, though the counter separated them. "What are you doing here?"

Cassandra returned another bolt to its place. Here only an hour and already she knew where everything belonged. Neatness was very much a necessity to her. She could not function without it.

"I'm the dressmaker's new assistant." She turned and looked at Riley. "The question that would be begging for an answer is what *you* are doing here?"

Two women had entered behind Riley. Their laughter was bissected by the tinkle of the bell. Both sounds died away as, Riley knew, the women took stock of Cassandra as only established citizens could of a newcomer.

Riley stepped to the side, lowering his voice for Cassandra's benefit. He knew she would not appreciate her business making the rounds so soon. It was enough that she would be examined and reexamined by the sainted matrons of Morgan's Creek.

"I came to keep my word and repay a debt."

He was talking about the dress. It had been ruined, but no matter, it was as much her fault as his. She could easily make another when she found the time.

Cassandra shook her head, contradicting him. "That debt, if you recall, was repaid the first night."

She was referring to his helping to bring her father home. Riley noticed that the two women, their heads supposedly bent over a rather bland bolt of cloth, had perked up their ears.

He knew that they had come to the shop as much to view Cassandra as they did to peruse the fabrics that the Widow Watkins imported into her shop.

Gossip among women spread faster than a fire across a dry meadow, he thought. Thank God their husbands were slower, or there would have been no need for his *Gazette*. Look at the way they had known she was working at the dressmaker's shop.

Riley sorely missed Rachel. *She* would have known that Cassandra was here, even if he did not.

But Riley would not be dissuaded from his intent by Cassandra's modest protest.

"Not nearly enough," he insisted.

When she moved away, Riley followed Cassandra to the long table that held an array of dolls that showed off the latest French fashions. Two had just been set out that morning. He knew this was the way in which women from the plantations chose their clothing.

"And then there is the matter of you saving my life." He eased the doll she was arranging from her hand to draw her attention to him. "Surely that is worth a dress in repayment."

Cassandra took the doll back and, adjusting its dress, placed it on the table once more. "If I have need of one, I can make it for myself."

He nodded. This was a development he had obviously not foreseen. "Aye, as it seems you will in any event. But at least allow me the pleasure of purchasing it for you."

His persistence was wearing. She licked her lips and nodded toward the women who were regarding the entire exchange in pleased silence.

Riley recognized both. The older was the Reverend Edwards's sister, Prudence, who had come to care for the older man, and her daughter, Alma. Both women had strong tongues that wagged tirelessly.

Cassandra turned her back to them so the women might not hear as easily. "Are your pleasures so limited," she inquired of Riley in a hushed whisper, "that you must resort to buying them?"

Riley enjoyed the flash of light that entered her eyes. They turned from an almost clear blue to something darker. And lovelier.

He ran a fingertip over his lips as he looked at her. His meaning was clear. "My pleasures, of late, have been multiplied a thousandfold."

The tiny bell above the door sounded again, signaling the entrance of yet more customers.

It was going to be a busy morning, he thought. Obviously it appeared as if the entire limited female population of Morgan's Creek had taken it upon themselves to visit the dressmaker's shop today to pass judgment. This time the would-be customers were Madame Beaulieu and one of her four daughters. The eldest, he believed, Elizabeth.

Riley was surprised that Krystyna hadn't come in. Though she lived far from town, by then she had read about the newcomers, and she was never one to sit back and let things pass by without her participation.

"It is becoming crowded here," he noted almost helplessly, abandoning, for then, the notion of discussing the dress with her. This occurrence was not entirely without merit. It did afford him with an excuse to return another time.

He saw the widow emerge from the rear of the store, where all the fittings were done. The tall woman pulled closed the dark green velvet curtains that separated her work area from the front of the shop. She looked pleased at this sudden hopeful surge of business.

Riley took Cassandra's arm and drew her to a small, tight corner.

"The space is far too small for me now. I shall see you tonight," he promised. "And we shall discuss the matter further."

Though he tried to keep his voice low, he knew he did not succeed entirely in keeping his words from the ears of others.

Cassandra looked at Riley, confused by his statement. "Tonight?"

He nodded. The reverend's sister was attempting to elbow him out of the way, accompanied by a sternly murmured "Excuse me." It seemed that he was blocking the table where the dolls were displayed. Riley moved toward the door. Perforce, he had to raise his voice. Just as the others had hoped.

"Your father has made good one of your invitations. I'm to come to dinner tonight."

Her father had neglected to inform her of that. But then, she had been in a hurry to leave that morning. It would not do to be late her very first day, and there were things to see to at home before she left the house.

She nodded now, understanding. "So that was why Brianne was humming."

Amusement shone in Cassandra's eyes. If Riley wished to

wheedle his way into her home, this was the price he was going to have to pay. He was going to have to suffer the adulation of her youngest sister.

He had no wish to discuss Brianne, especially not in front of the matrons.

''And you, Mistress''—he used the formal title since he knew the others were well within hearing, others whose tongues were far looser than the stays of their corsets—''do you hum?''

Cassandra understood his implied question, but chose, because of the company around them, to answer in as nebulous a form as the question had been phrased.

She shook her head. ''No. I sing, and then only when I know the words.''

Clever, he thought. There was something very irresistible about a clever mind. When it was coupled, as it was, with a comely form, the combination was something to behold.

He smiled as he laid a hand on the door, aware that all cursory conversation had ceased around them. All were silently regarding him and Cassandra with more than a little interest. So be it, he thought.

''Then I shall teach you the words, Mistress MacGregor, and the sooner the better.'' He inclined his head as he took his leave. ''Until tonight.''

The promise was like an arrow shot straight to her heart. Cassandra felt a blush rising to her cheeks. It was something entirely foreign to her, for there had never been cause to blush before. She had always remained unaffected by a man's words.

Until then.

Cassandra averted her eyes from the door as Riley left. Instead, she met the widow's interested gaze. The widow, like the others in the shop, was eagerly absorbing the exchange.

The widow cleared her throat. The sound signaled a return to noise within her store. She placed a motherly arm around Cassandra's slim shoulders.

''I read O'Roarke's words of welcome in the *Gazette* yesterday. I must say, I had no idea they were so personally intended, my dear,'' she said kindly.

The observation begged for an explanation. Cassandra did

not hesitate to give it. "We met when his horse spattered mud on my dress."

"I see," the woman murmured with a knowing nod of her head.

The other women in the store exchanged knowing glances. The reverend's sister smirked.

Cassandra raised her eyes and slowly regarded the cluster of women. They represented an inner circle she was not intended to penetrate. But she meant to. This time she meant to. She would work hard be accepted, she thought, and succeed. This she felt certain of. In so doing, she would thereby cease to be the one they all harbored their suspicions about.

When they came to her, and they would, it would be with faith and hope, not distrust.

She knew she could not endure the whispers again. If not for her own sake, then for her father's and her sisters'. It was difficult for them, she knew, being the family of one who was regarded as different.

It barred them from acceptance, and acceptance was what she meant to secure for them. It was part of the reason she had approached the widow yesterday about working for her, selling her abilities with an eagerness that Cassandra was entirely unaccustomed to. But there was a need for her to mingle among these people. And a need of the money. They needed money until her father had an opportunity to establish himself. She was the only one with the skills that would earn it.

There was no payment for her other skills. And like as not, at times there were recriminations. As there were the last time.

But this time, she vowed silently, it would not be like the last time. Like the other times. This time it would be different. Even if she had to bend over backward and pretend to be what she was not.

Now, she thought as she looked at the faces that surrounded her, she had to begin to lay those foundations. She had to win the friendship of the women here. If not the friendship, then at least the acceptance.

Each journey began, she knew, with the first tiny step. She took it.

Turning a bright face toward the curious group as yet another woman entered the shop, Cassandra smiled broadly.

"Good morrow to you ladies. As you must already have surmised, I am Cassandra MacGregor. The Widow Watkins has kindly allowed me to work for her. 'Tis here I am to help you with your choices today."

Her eyes narrowed slightly as she looked at the pinched-faced woman who hovered over the girl beside her. The younger woman was a replica of her mother. The reverend's sister, Cassandra knew, carried a great deal of weight with her opinions, standing in the shadow of the reverend the way she did.

Cassandra moved toward Prudence Collins. "You were the first in," she noted. "Are you looking for a dress to accent that lovely complexion of yours?"

Cassandra's question was rewarded with a smile of welcome.

Chapter Fifteen

The room above the store had been transformed into a home in the girls' very capable hands, Bruce MacGregor thought as he looked around.

He had provided the scant pieces of furniture that decorated the single large open room, but the girls had made it into a home. The paintings Rose had created, vividly capturing the heather and moors that she had never seen, were now hung over the fireplace. The multicolored rug that Cassandra spent so many nights plaiting lay before the long wooden bench where they would take their comfort in the evenings. And even Brianne had contributed. She had tatted the delicate covers on the bench. The final touch, his beloved wife's dishes, were being spread out, even now, on the table.

It was a home, MacGregor thought, not just a room anymore.

"Riley'll sit next to me," Brianne announced as she placed her mother's delicate china plates upon the table one by one.

While her sisters had cooked, Brianne had busied herself with her own toilette. When she was finally satisfied, she turned her attention to setting the table. It was the only contribution she could make to the evening. Brianne was admittedly inept at cooking and had absolutely no desire to learn. It was something, she had retorted to Rose when the latter had chided her for her laxness, that the servants would do for her.

Brianne had high hopes. Her father saw nothing wrong with that. It was high hopes, along with his skill, that had brought him to this country originally and enabled him to set up his shop.

MacGregor raised his eyes from the hearth, where he had been gazing into the fire, and regarded his youngest daughter. He had gotten the faint impression, though Cassandra never made her private thoughts plain, that his oldest was interested in the man who was coming to dinner as well.

It hadn't been anything she said, of course. That would have been too simple. But there was something altered in her manner, though MacGregor was unable to say exactly what. She seemed a little unsettled, restless, as it were.

Different.

Since there didn't seem to be anything else at hand to blame it on, MacGregor thought it had to do with their dinner guest.

The notion of Cassandra being attracted to a man made him smile. 'Twas time, he thought. 'Twas definitely high time.

His eyes narrowed as he approached the table. Brianne had elaborately arranged one setting. She meant to have Riley to herself as much as she could possibly manage, he wagered.

His eyes met Brianne's. An elfin smile curving his mouth, MacGregor laid his hands on either side of the setting. With elaborate care, he moved the arrangement to the foot of the table.

"He'll sit at the end, opposite me," he declared firmly. He shifted the glass that would hold a bit of red wine tonight. His mouth watered in anticipation of the tangy taste. MacGregor did like his liquid refreshment now and again .

"With you on the one side and Cassandra on the other, as is fitting." He straightened and moved away from the table, eyeing Brianne expectantly. "Any objections?"

Brianne tossed her head. This wasn't what she had planned. But as long as she had one side of Riley, she supposed that was enough. After all, she thought as she looked at her sisters working by the hearth, she was the most flamboyant of the three. If it were up to Cassandra, the woman would put would-be suitors to sleep as they sat watching her ply her needle or spin yarn from flax, all the while saying little.

How different Rose and Cassandra were from her, Brianne mused. She knew when to laugh at a man's words and when to remain silent and gaze up adoringly. All these were practiced skills, as surely as cooking and sewing were, and far more enriching. Her best friend, Sallianne, had taught her the way of it. She would have taught her more as well, had Brianne not been so rudely forced to relocate.

Always it was Cassandra who got in her way. Someday, Brianne mused, there would be no Cassandra to obey, no Cassandra to censure her behavior, and then she would be free to enjoy life as she pleased,

"None, Da," Brianne replied prettily, just as a well-brought-up, obedient daughter should when her father spoke. Her cheeks dimpled as she smiled up at him.

MacGregor hid an amused expression while Rose and Cassandra exchanged incredulous looks. Brianne was usually as docile as a polecat defending its terrain. She was most assuredly up to something.

And that something, Cassandra thought as she turned the main course upon a spit, was named Riley O'Roarke. Her younger sister had bedecked herself in her finest dress. The toilet water they had brought from New York had found its way to her body. All of it, she judged by the strong scent.

Even now it interfered with the scent of roasting meat.

This had the makings of an interesting evening, Cassandra thought, trying not to think on the anxious fluttering within her own stomach. She was entirely unaccustomed to this sensation, and she liked it not.

Well, they were taking care of everything, MacGregor thought as he settled into his chair. He dug his pipe out from his vest pocket, his eyes on Cassandra rather than on his task.

"You didn't tell me how it went today." He took out a pouch out filled with tobacco and began methodically packing his pipe with it. "At the dressmaker's shop," he prodded when

Cassandra made no reply. "Did the Widow Watkins treat you well?"

The air over the spit was warm and uncomfortable. Cassandra wiped the back of her wrist across her forehead.

"Yes, why?"

Wide shoulders rose and fell, indicating his helplessness at pinpointing an explanation for her behavior. "You have a different look about you, as if there were something on your mind."

Cassandra succeeded in taking on a more cheerful appearance. She had not thought that her unease was visible. "There is."

He sat forward on the hard seat, alert. "Another vision?"

"Dinner" was the mild reply.

Cassandra glanced at the piglet roasting on the spit in the hearth. She turned it once more. There were some, especially in New York, who trained their terriers to run so that they turned the spit while wearing a harness. But the poor animals were of necessity in a cage and she could not see doing that to a living creature just to make her own life easier. So she stood and turned and told herself that she did not feel hot.

MacGregor sucked deeply on the stem of the pipe and then blew out a cloud of smoke. He watched it swirl above him with vague interest.

"Nothing to worry about there. The farmer who sold me our dinner said that his were the tastiest pigs around for fifty miles in all directions." MacGregor knew a boast when he heard one, of course, but there was always some truth to a rumor. "And even if it weren't, your apple pie would make everyone forget the pig's shortcomings, Cassandra."

MacGregor turned his head and smiled broadly at the one inanimate object within the room that he took great pride in. The cast iron stove. He had managed to secure it for his girls, had to pay double what the man said he had paid for it because they were so scarce. MacGregor wanted to make his children's lives easier.

Cassandra's pie was in the stove even then, baking for their enjoyment. Earlier, Rose had made the bread that was to grace the table.

"And, of course," MacGregor added hastily, lest Rose felt left out. He was always forgetting about the girl, but it was partly her own fault. She never called any attention to herself and tended to be easily obscured by her sisters. "There is the bread.

"I snitched a piece of it," he confessed, placing his hand to his chest. He saw that Rose had stopped what she was doing and was now listening eagerly. "And thought I had crossed over to heaven without benefit of dying, just at the taste of it." He smiled benevolently at Rose, and the girl fairly beamed back. "You've a knack for making bread, just like your mother."

Rose's small smile had broadened at his compliment, and it did his father's heart good to see it.

"What of me, Da?"

As he turned toward the plaintive question, Brianne flounced down beside him. She had on her best dress. It was a little tight about her bust, but the fact did not displease her. She had grown some since last year when Cassandra fashioned the dress for her, and in places a man noticed. The tightness now was all to the good, she thought. Sallianne had whispered that men's fancies led them to gaze there in appreciation when others thought they observed them not.

Bruce MacGregor stroked her head. "What about you, lass?" he prodded.

She raised her face to him and tried not to wrinkle her nose at the scent of the tobacco, while he in turn tried not to wince at the heavy fragrance that fairly reeked from her.

"What was it that I contributed to this?" She was hungry never to be left out. If one of her sisters received words of praise, she wanted to share in them whether she'd done a thing or not.

"You've set the table," Rose pointed out cheerfully as she placed long pussy willows into a tall, clear vase. She earned a pout in response.

MacGregor raised Brianne's chin with the crook of his finger until her eyes met his. He said the exact words she was hunting for.

"Your beauty, of course, lass. 'Tis gracing any table you would with your loveliness." He looked around at his other daughters, working diligently to set as fine a feast as they could upon the table he had carved as a wedding present for his wife so many years earlier. "Ah, I'm thrice blessed, I am, to have such beauty in my house, both of the flesh and of the soul."

His eyes narrowed ever so slightly as he looked into Brianne's eyes. "Remember that, my pet. For the outer fades. 'Tis the inner that leaves the lasting impression."

Brianne doubted that Riley would be looking into anyone's soul tonight. That dreary matter was best left to people like Cassandra. A man of Riley's worldliness would have his eye on more easily seen things. Such as a comely face and shape.

One like hers.

A gentle smile gracing her rosebud mouth, Brianne rose to slip into the tiny room she shared with her sisters. It was curtained off from the large, common room by a dark drape, just as her father's was on the other end. She wanted to pinch her cheeks once again to bring more color to them. She thought it cruel that her father expressly forbade any other methods of enhancing her features, but there was not time enough to make him change his mind tonight. So pinch she was bound.

"Yes, Da," she remembered to murmur in a voice that was well practiced, then turned to make her way to the rear of the room. She would leave Rose and Cassandra to complete the meal. She wanted to look fresh and at her best for Riley when he arrived.

MacGregor merely chuckled to himself as he took another puff upon his pipe. He knew that his words had not found a home in her mind. But someday, he felt certain, they would. She was a good girl, just a little vain and shallow. But youth was the time for that. Changes would come to her soon enough.

The knock on the door had MacGregor sighing. His pipe clenched in his teeth, he rose, holding firmly to the arms of the chair to aid him to his feet.

"I'll get it, Da," Brianne called from behind the curtain.

She had barely enough time to reexamine herself. Her heart beat fast as she hurried out. Riley was there. Early. It meant, of course, that he couldn't wait to be with her. She almost laughed aloud with glee.

But her father had reached the door before she could manage it. His hand was on the latch and his look stopped her in her steps.

" 'Tis up to a man to greet visitors at his door," Bruce MacGregor informed Brianne patiently. He was aware that both his younger daughters had gathered at his back as he turned toward the door.

Cassandra chided herself on her reaction. 'Twas but a guest coming. And there had been many guests at their table in New York. Why did her heart feel called upon to pound this way now? Her fingers fumbled as she tore the apron from her waist and flung it to the side just before she approached the door.

Yes, she thought, there had been many guests, but she had never floated naked in a stream with any of them, and there was the difference.

"Am I too early?" Riley inquired when the door was opened.

He stood in the doorway, dressed in his best suit of clothing. He'd even remembered to polish the buckles on his shoes, something he had not done since the cobbler had sold the pair to him. Uncertainty, an uncustomary companion, gnawed at him all the way there.

In his hand he held a huge bouquet of wildflowers he'd picked in the glen less than an hour earlier. He would have to say, of course, that it was intended for all three of the young women. But there was only one whom he had thought of as he picked the flowers.

"For me? Oh, they're absolutely beautiful!" Brianne cried, pushing herself in front of her sisters and snatching up the bouquet.

"Brianne," her da chided.

She swung around, too happy to be upset at Bruce's tone. "I'll just set them in a vase, Da. It'll give us all something to look at during dinner."

Brianne hurried off to find the vase she had carefully wrapped when they left. The one that she dreamed would hold flowers from her true love one day.

Riley turned toward Cassandra. "I picked them in the glen." The smile on his face coaxed one in kind from her. "There were no mountain lions there this time."

"How fortunate for both you and the flowers." Cassandra turned to lead the way into the room.

MacGregor wondered what manner of communication was humming between the two, for there was definitely something there. And it went beyond the words, which was a mystery to him. Brianne might be the one snatching Riley's flowers from him, but it was Cassandra, MacGregor could see, who had snatched his attention.

Chapter Sixteen

The meal was excellent. At least Riley felt that it was so for the first two helpings. By the third, his taste had waned considerably. But Rose continued to urge food on him until he was certain he would burst.

The conversation at the table was almost exclusively dominated by Brianne. She probed Riley with scores of questions about his life, both in Ireland and, more important to her, in Philadelphia. She seemed to hang, suspended, upon each word as if her very existence depended on his replies.

Riley found her amusing, but his interest was intent on Cassandra.

Throughout the dinner Cassandra made little attempt to speak. She was content to let Brianne take center stage. It provided her with the opportunity to study Riley, to observe him in a detached fashion.

Though she spoke little, her eyes, whenever they turned toward him, seemed to speak volumes.

Or was that merely his wishful thinking, Riley wondered, afraid of what the answer might be. He was as bent on culling her favor as Brianne seemed to be on culling his.

Cassandra had not been out of his mind since the blood-heating incident at the stream the day before. All night long, whenever he managed to fall asleep, he had dreamed of her, her nude body gleaming before him invitingly, until he thought he'd go mad.

This time he saw her, unconcealed by conspiratorial waters and sunbeams that flashed to her aid. He saw her as nude as the day she had been born. A unwitting temptress if ever there had been one created.

With a heart that was pure.

Four times he had started from his dream. And four times he had returned to it the moment he had shut his eyes and sleep claimed him.

He knew as well as he knew his own name that he would have no peace until he had her.

But until that time came, he had to find a way to go about his life and pretend that his mind was not almost exclusively consumed with thoughts of her.

"More pie, Mr. O'Roarke?" Rose asked, already slicing another piece to slide onto his plate.

"No, thank you." He raised both hands to create a barrier between his plate and the oncoming piece of pie. "I'm afraid I will explode if I sample any more."

Rose looked crestfallen. "But—"

Cassandra came to Riley's rescue. "Stop trying to fatten him up, Rose. 'Tis full the poor man is." To reinforce her statement, Cassandra took her father's plate and presented it to Rose. Her sister slid the piece she had cut onto it. Cassandra moved the plate closer to her father. "Here another piece would be more than appreciated."

"Aye, that's true," MacGregor laughed, patting his expanding waist.

"It isn't that the pie was not appreciated," Riley was quick to correct Cassandra. "The dinner was excellent, the best I've had since Rachel left. But there can be too much of a good thing." His eyes held Cassandra's for a moment. "Although that may not always be the case," he murmured.

Cassandra lowered her eyes, not quite knowing what to do with herself. This was entirely too new to her. This was a foreign place she found herself in. She knew how to handle her visions, how to cure simple illnesses. But this—this was something she knew not what to do with.

The same could be said for the uneasy feelings she was experiencing. The uncertainty involved in both the situation and her feelings troubled her greatly. She was not accustomed to being uncertain.

"I said, Mr. O'Roarke," Bruce MacGregor repeated, raising his voice this time to penetrate the fog that had obviously encroached upon the boy's mind since he had exchanged looks with Cassandra, "have you been in Morgan's Creek for very long?"

Riley blinked, realizing that this was not the first time the man was asking the question. The other girls were looking at him, Brianne with rather a sullen pout and Rose with bemusement. The small tinge of embarrassment he felt at being caught preoccupied served only to intensify the devil-may-care curve of his mouth.

"Forgive me, Mr. MacGregor. In the face of all this loveliness"—he gestured around the table—"a man is apt to lose his train of thought."

Brianne and Rose absorbed Riley's glib compliment gleefully. Cassandra merely looked away, as if her interest lay elsewhere. But MacGregor could have sworn there was a blush just skimming over her cheeks, as if she knew that the compliment was hers alone.

Riley leaned back upon the bench. "But to answer your question, we've been in this town, my sister and I, a little over a year. We came here directly from our home in Philadelphia with the hope of establishing our own newspaper. And so we have."

"Yes, indeed, a fine piece of work." MacGregor nodded. "I enjoyed it greatly. I meant to thank you for that paragraph you included on us. Already today I've had the pleasure of meeting three of your leading citizens, all of whom were moved to visit because of your kind words. Mr. McKinley commissioned a chest of drawers."

"Morgan McKinley?" he asked with interest.

"Jason, the younger," MacGregor corrected Riley. "He said it was to be a gift for his wife." He smiled, well pleased. "And I owe all that to you."

" 'Tis what neighbors are for, Mr. MacGregor." Riley shrugged off the thanks.

"Many forget that," MacGregor pointed out. "They forget neighborliness when faced with strangers."

When Riley raised an inquiring brow at him, MacGregor cleared his throat, as if that would clear the memory of the sentiment he had just expressed as well.

"Do you smoke, Mr. O'Roarke?" he asked, producing his pipe .

"Riley, please," Riley urged his host. "And no, I fear I have never had the occasion to develop the habit. Ashes and ink do not mix well." He thought of the disaster that would befall him if he allowed a lit ember to fall on the wood casings. "And I spend most of my time with ink."

MacGregor was already lighting the pipe. He had few habits he enjoyed, and none as much as smoking.

"Ah, you don't know what you're missing, Riley." Mac-Gregor sighed as he blew out a smoke ring that was almost perfect in its circular shape. "A calming smoke after dinner, while the girls clear away the table. 'Tis almost like having heaven here on earth. And 'tis the only time I get to relax."

MacGregor leaned forward and winked broadly. "We'll have to find another way for you to relax, Riley."

Riley had his own ideas on that score. He watched as Cassandra carried away the huge platter, now nearly empty, and once more his thought drifted to yesterday and the opportunity he had been forced to let slip away because of honor.

Would there be another?

There had to be, he vowed. He would make his own opportunity if need be

MacGregor was silent, as if debating something as he slowly stroked his chin. He was not oblivious of the looks that had been exchanged over the table.

"Cassandra," he addressed his daughter abruptly. "Why don't you leave that for your sisters to see to?" He patiently ignored Brianne's moan of protest. "And take in a breath of air with Riley? You've been working entirely too hard."

He turned toward Riley and said in a loud aside, "She does, you know." MacGregor shook his head fondly as he looked at his daughter once more. "She never knows when to stop."

Neither, apparently, do you, Da. "When it's done, Da, when it's done," Cassandra said in a rare display of stubbornness.

She piled the plates on top of one another, looking at her father defiantly. She didn't quite understand why he felt it his duty to thrust them together. She'd been thrust enough against Riley. More than enough in her opinion. She'd had too little sleep the last two nights, all from remembering.

This was an entirely different episode in her life, not at all like any she had ever experienced before. There was no certainty as to what path to take, or what to do. Things did not fall into place for her as they did at other times. As they did when they involved visions.

It was as if she were negotiating her way blindly upon a narrow wall in the mists of the moors, in danger of falling to her death at any moment.

"I'll go, Da," Brianne volunteered, more than ready to take her sister's place at Riley's side. Especially since Cassandra displayed such, in her opinion, foolish reluctance.

MacGregor removed the pipe from his teeth. "I said Cassandra," he told his daughter softly, but all the more firmly for it. "Will you take her out for some air, Riley?" he asked the younger man. "For her own good, even if she doesn't realize it."

As if that were a hardship, Riley thought, not attempting to hide his pleased expression. He inclined his head. "Gladly." Then, turning toward Cassandra, Riley offered her his arm. "I am at your service."

Cassandra gave her father a reproving look. In all matters he had always deferred to her, to her judgment, feeling it only just, since she had the Sight. Why, then, had he changed so, the one time she did not feel confident of her way?

Cassandra purposely ignored Riley's arm. Instead, she turned and took her shawl from the rack her father had decided to leave in their living quarters. It always gave her pleasure to look upon the rack.

She hardly noticed it as she moved past it out the door. With her hand on the railing, she made her way down the stairs.

"It's steep," Riley pointed out, right behind her.

She kept her face forward. "Yes, I know."

Riley attempted to make his way to her side. There was just enough room for two on the steps. "Perhaps you'd better let me hold your hand."

She would have none of it, attempting, as she was, to come to terms with a temper that rarely showed itself. "I've negotiated these very same stairs before without the benefit of your hand in mine, Riley. I think I am capable of doing it again."

Her tone was almost waspish. Again he was reminded of his sister. And, as with Rachel, perhaps there was something troubling her as well. Rachel never snipped to him unless there was something gnawing at her.

Riley presented himself before Cassandra as she reached the last step, blocking her way. "Have I offended you somehow, Cassandra?"

She shook her head, but refused to look at him just then. His eyes, she thought, were her undoing. They were a light spring green, and she thought of the Highlands when she saw them. And of her childhood that had been so innocent until she had come to understand that she was different. Different from others, and, so, excluded.

"Then why are you so distant with me tonight? You act as if I'm a stranger who is unwelcome in your house."

She took a deep breath, still gazing off. "My father welcomes you."

"And you?" he prodded. He took her aside so that others might not be able to look upon them from above, or from across the street. "Do you welcome me as well?"

She did. And she could not. That was the very nature of the problem that lay between them.

Restless, Cassandra began to walk away into the darkness. He was quick to follow her.

"Riley," she began to say slowly. The crunching sound

beneath her feet of dried pine needles was a comforting sound. "There are things you do not understand."

She'd heard, he thought suddenly, annoyed at the rapier tongues of gossips who spread rumors so quickly. She'd heard and it had embarrassed her. He prayed that the damage they had done was not unmendable. "Oh, then you've heard the talk."

She stopped walking to look at him, confused. Had some word reached Morgan's Creek about her? Simeon had threatened to hunt her down if she ever left.

"Talk?"

He nodded grimly. "About us."

Her mouth curved almost unconsciously. Relief flooded through her. "No, what about us?"

Then she *hadn't* heard. Riley was heartily sorry he had brought it up, and shifted uncomfortably as he made the revelation to her.

"It seems," he said, a touch of indignation in his tone for her sake, "that some have taken the words we exchanged at the dressmaker's shop earlier and fashioned them to mean something they did not. They think we've kept company together. If it has an effect on your reputation, I shall do my best to clear it up, though in my experience, protest only reinforces rather than erases."

In her experience too, she thought sadly.

Rather than be shocked or upset, Cassandra merely shook her head. "Do not trouble yourself. I am accustomed to people whispering about me."

"Whispering about you?" he repeated. Now it was his turn to be confused. "You mean other than about your beauty?"

She laughed softly, lacing her fingers together as she gazed out into the darkness. "That is the last of what they whisper about."

"Then all the people you have known were blind, Cassandra, for that was the first that had struck me." His very words seemed to glide along her skin, undoing her.

She attempted to look away again, but his words brought her back.

"What is it that they whisper about you, Cassandra?"

She merely shrugged, wishing that he would let the matter go, wishing that her tongue had not been so loose as to let a hint drop.

He turned her face toward his. Though it was dark, he could see her plainly. "Tell me."

It was not hers to share. She could not draw him in. "I cannot. It's best if you know little about me."

Her answer annoyed him. "Best for whom, Cassandra?" he demanded softly. He placed his hands on her shoulders. "Not for me. I mean to learn everything there is to know about you."

He did, she thought. And he shouldn't. "You might get more than you bargained for."

"Not if I plan on getting more than I bargain for." His eyes teased her.

Cassandra frowned. "That is a riddle," she pointed out.

"Aye," he nodded. As was she. "And one I am looking forward to unraveling."

It was a promise, and she feared it.

Chapter Seventeen

Cassandra felt it once more. That wild, pulsating sensation that poured through her, drawing her to him. And as the sensation uncurled, her sight receded from her. It was as if it could not cross into this region with her when she reached for it.

She could feel her heart beating wildly. Turning from Riley, Cassandra looked toward the stairs, half hidden in the shadows.

"I think perhaps we should go in."

The night air was a little chilly. She ran her hands along her arms. But it was more from wanting something to do with them than from the cold.

Inside, she was not cold. Inside, she burned and vainly attempted not to.

"Not yet," he told her.

She both heard and felt the whispered words as they skimmed along her hair, tingling her scalp. Tingling her soul.

Slowly he turned her until she faced him. "Not just yet." He smiled down into her eyes. "This time I have two hands."

"As do I." In an act of nervous defiance, she folded her arms before her.

If she meant to form a barricade with them, she was sadly

mistaken. He bent just a hint of a breath closer. Yet it was enough. "Let me show you what I wish to do with mine."

Riley framed her face and inclined his head until his mouth was only inches from hers.

She meant to use her hands to block the closeness, to lock it out. But Cassandra could no more do that than she could take her father's tools and build a palace in a single day.

Her hands betrayed her. Instead of keeping him away, they went about Riley's neck as he kissed her. It was as much to anchor herself in place as it was to hold him to her. For hold him she dearly wanted to, even though she knew she should not.

The sensation of warmth and comfort, mingled with yearning and unease, swam all through her body as if it were a hot, liquid thing.

His kiss was even more exciting than the last. And because of that, so much more foreboding.

She was sinking and didn't care. And yet she knew she must. For only she could control this. Only she knew the dangers if they were to continue upon this route. He was innocent of the grief entanglement with her would bring to him.

A tiny bit longer. Oh, please, just a tiny bit longer, Cassandra thought desperately as she twined her hands through his hair. Her body cleaved to his as if she were a leaf caught in the high winds and blown against the bark of a tree.

Riley felt her resistance just as he felt her desire and her hunger. It was all there in her kiss. That and so much more.

His hands absorbed the outline of her back as they roamed the length of it. He could not get enough of her.

Lord help him, but he wanted to take her there, then, upon that caked piece of earth within a stone's throw of her home.

With supreme effort he reined himself back. But the very taste of her lips made it difficult for him to hold on to the shreds of decent behavior. As a consolation, he rained kisses upon her face, then forced himself to draw away. Her skin was soft, like rose petals. He dropped his hands. They felt large and clumsy touching her.

It took a moment before he could find his voice. "Now we can go back."

She looked up into his eyes and saw. Just for an instant, she saw. And then the Sight was shut away again. But it was enough for her to understand.

"No, now we cannot," she whispered. She had taken that first dangerous step forward. There was no going back.

He was sure he had misheard. Riley looked at her, confused. "What?"

Cassandra shook her head, ashamed that she had let the words slip out. If she didn't tell him what was ahead for them, perhaps it would not come to pass and he could yet be spared.

"Nothing." She pulled the shawl tighter, though she hardly felt its warmth at all. "Come. Brianne will have my head for monopolizing you for so long." She raised a cheerful face to his as she linked her arm in his. "And I know that Da wishes to discuss politics with you a little more." The thought that her father's mind had taken on such scope pleased her greatly. It was a sign that, at least for a time, things would be better. "It makes him feel as if he's a part of things."

Riley shortened his stride to keep in step with her. "But talk of politics will only bore you."

There was much about her he didn't now. Things that were safe to reveal. She smiled at his assumption. He was not the first to think so.

"Events that occur around me never bore me," Cassandra replied. She looked up at the moon and thought that it was, after all, a glorious night. "I have never liked pulling the covers over my head and pretending that the rest of the world does not exist." Although, she had to admit, there had been times when she was sorely tempted. Such as when her mother died.

Such as the first time she had heard the word *witch* spat at her.

Her statement surprised Riley. And pleased him. She was like his sister and Krystyna, he thought. He was truly blessed to have discovered another woman like them.

A man's mind, he mused, had to have something to work with. After all, lust went only so far in occupying his time.

Although, Riley amended thoughtfully as he followed Cassandra up the stairs, his eyes skimming over the slender sway of her hips, lust certainly had its place.

Especially just then.

It was, Riley thought the next evening as he held a very fine glass of brandy in his hand, a time for rebirth and upheaval. Especially with the revolution behind them. This was a time to sweep away the chaos and organize things so that they were in order rather than disarray.

But what sort of order?

It wouldn't do, Riley felt certain, to merely sit back and do nothing. The country needed restraints placed on it until it knew where it could run and where it could not. But what sort of restraints? Dictated by whom? And would it accept them peacefully? Guidance was needed, as was a stabilizing hand, but held out by whom?

It was something to be determined one step at a time.

But perhaps not as slowly as it was being done, he mused, looking at the gathering of faces at Morgan McKinley's table.

Here they sat, a collection of rudely educated men whose main claim to governing was that they had either position, or plantations, or both. And a good deal of wind, for they had been talking now for over three hours.

Riley looked at his watch and wondered if time had somehow stopped, sealing him in this room filled with rhetoric forever.

An apt sentence for a newspaper editor, he thought, still able to cling to a shred of humor.

He felt a little like a poor relation, sitting there beside money-eyed men like the McKinleys and Dr. Beaulieu. And then, of course, there was the Reverend Edwards. The elderly, unsmiling man had not followed the way of the cloth and renounced all his worldly goods.

Reverend Edwards had more than his share of worldly goods, Riley thought with a smile, though his good sister was trying earnestly to help him share that wealth. Unable, obviously, to live up to her name, Prudence Collins spent the reverend's money on whatever she was able whenever she was able.

There were several others at the table as well. Harrison and Johnson and Andrews. Plantation owners all. Were they the only ones who felt themselves fit to govern, he wondered.

With a suppressed sigh he sat back and listened to the words as they flew back and forth like blackbirds without a sense of direction.

He caught Jason's eye and knew that while perhaps Jason's brother, Aaron, might be of the opinion that only the rich and well-placed could make the laws for them all, Jason was not. Thank God for that. There was humor in his friend's eye, as if he viewed this entire proceeding with more than a touch of amusement.

It did, in a way, seem like a collection of grown men playing at being gods.

Was that always going to be the way of it, Riley wondered. The winners becoming like the very rulers they had vanquished? He sincerely hoped that they, Americans all now, had not shed one yoke only to come under the burden of another.

Morgan held up a hand gnarled by age and work as a point had finally been made.

"Then it is agreed." His voice boomed loud, echoing from a wide barrel chest. "We shall bring back the town council. The town needs rules now that the armies have gone their separate ways."

Edwards coughed loudly. It was his way of securing attention. "But not all of the old members," the man protested.

Morgan glared at the reverend as if he had lost his mind.

"Some of the old members," Jason reminded the man politely, thinking it best to intercede now before his father said something rude that would offend the reverend, "are either dead or have fled, having chosen the wrong side to back in this war."

A low titter met his statement. It swelled into a loud guffaw, then abruptly vanished in the face of Morgan's serious expression.

The hour was late and Morgan desired to bring the discussion to a close. They had been wrangling over points, minute and great, for the better part of the night. Nothing was actually being settled. He had a horror that all the sessions would be as ponderous, as pompous and as unfruitful as this one.

In the old days he would have swiftly dismissed the notion of a council and found a way to govern by himself. But he was not young anymore. And he abhorred all dictators save himself.

"Of course not the same members," he snapped at the reverend. "We shall have elections."

Riley raised his hand and waited until Aaron nodded toward him. "Who'll vote in these elections?" He noted that interest was keen on the reply.

"Why, we will, of course," Morgan growled, irritable and eager to call it an evening.

But Riley was a dog with a bone now. A hungry dog. "Only we?"

"And any man with property," Andrews injected importantly. He nodded his bald head at his compatriot, Johnson, who openly agreed with him. "Same as always."

"But, gentlemen, is this what we have fought for?" Dr. Philippe Beaulieu inquired, his French accent lyrically jarring the air.

The others exchanged looks. They might have expected something like this from a foreigner.

Riley knew that the dashing-looking man had journeyed here years before from his native Paris to find opportunity in the colonies. As a doctor, he had fought and healed these last long years on the side of the rebels. He appeared quite disappointed at the turn that the conversation had taken now. He obviously had envisioned, as Riley had, a country where all might take part and vote for the laws that were to govern them.

This merely smacked of the rich taking power again, Beaulieu thought, and while he was of that gentry, his heart was not.

"Surely you do not mean those words. We fought for the right of representation," Beaulieu insisted.

"And you'll have it," Harrison pointed out, his reedy voice grating on the frayed nerves in the room.

Behind them, the fire crackled just as tempers did.

We fought to rid ourselves of the British,'' Aaron reminded the physician.

But, ever polite and in control of his temper, Beaulieu nonetheless pressed on. ''We fought to rid ourselves of oppression.''

Aaron didn't see a contradiction. ''And?'' he asked impatiently.

Riley felt it his duty to come to the doctor's rescue. Unpopular stands were his daily fare. His newspaper office had almost been burned down because of an editorial a Tory had taken exception to.

''And we can't be setting up our rules and commanding everyone to obey just because *we* say so.'' He toyed with the stem of his glass. He'd had only a single taste of it, wanting to to keep his head clear for the arguing that he had known lay ahead of him. ''That would make us no better than Fat George ever was.''

The reverend pressed his lips together, and they disappeared entirely. The man was a heathen and a papist to boot, he thought, annoyed to be forced to share the same table with Riley.

''It isn't the same,'' he insisted imperially, thinking that was an end to it.

''But it is, Reverend,'' Riley replied in a patient voice. He looked toward Jason and Beaulieu and saw he had support in that quarter at least. ''It most definitely is.''

Chapter Eighteen

Voices rose hotly in protest following Riley's statement, most notably those belonging to the reverend and to Andrews, who had never cared for the tone of many of Riley's editorials. A heated debate appeared imminent.

Finally, unable to take the din any longer, Morgan raised his hands in the air. There would be no resolution in here tonight. After all these hours, they were further away from agreement than when they had first sat down. It was time for quiet contemplation of the issues.

When his gesture did not receive the proper response, he stood up in an attempt to win silence once more.

Slowly, self-consciously, the voices melted away. Morgan looked at the ring of men gathered around his table. Most he had known for years. Some, like Riley, he had known only a short period of time. He found himself agreeing with all or none of them only sporadically.

Now, he would have readily found himself agreeing with the very devil if it would have given him the peace he desired. He was getting too old for this, he thought. Too old.

He looked at Riley and thought that in agreeing with him, he *was* most likely agreeing with the devil. The Irishman was cocky and brash. And reminded Morgan of himself forty years ago.

"Mr. O'Roarke has a point. We cannot appear to be like our previous overlords."

His mouth curved down as he sat once more. It was the word *previous* that he liked. Nothing had pleased him more than sending the British fleeing from his land. As they had once sent him fleeing from theirs.

"Hence, in the interest of being fair, perhaps we should allow every able-bodied white male over the age of twenty and five to cast a vote." Morgan's look took them all in at once. "What say you?"

Dissent and agreement was immediate.

He longed to place his hands over his ears. It was just as he had surmised. These could not agree on anything. He glanced at his younger son and saw Jason's amusement as he kept his tongue still.

"I thought as much." In disgust, Morgan waved his hand, silencing them all once more. "We'll speak of this again at another time."

He looked at the grandfather clock that stood just beyond the door, in the hall. It was set to chime the hour in another moment. Eleven.

"It is late and I am not the man I once was. I need my sleep even though the rest of you seem to revitalize yourselves with bickering."

His remark served to shame some and secretly annoy others at his high-handed ways. But his position and his name allowed him privileges where they had not.

Riley observed it all and took note. And was amused.

"I should like to conclude on a more genial note."

Morgan waited until all eyes were turned toward him before continuing. He rather liked holding court, though if any accused him of this in those exact words, he would have readily called them a liar.

"This Saturday next I shall like to officially celebrate the hesitant step we are all attempting to make together. The reformation of the town council," he said when the reverend looked at him blankly. "You are all invited to my house for a party. The proper invitations, to satisfy your wives, will, of course, be going out on the morrow."

Morgan looked at Jason. "Tell Krystyna her services are required."

It was an old battleground and one they continually found themselves upon, turning and twisting for position. Usually, it was Morgan and Krystyna who were the opponents, but in her absence, Jason felt honor bound to take up the lance for her.

"I shall ask Krystyna if she would like to volunteer," Jason replied, changing the critical words that his father had employed.

There was a moment of silence as the others looked on to see if the younger or older would win this round of the eternal conflict.

Morgan was truly tired and in no mood for rounds. He let this one pass.

" 'Tis lucky that I like the countess," Morgan informed his son. "For the airs she gives herself are too much at times to bear."

"No airs, Father," Jason added patiently, though this ground had been crossed and recrossed countless times. He suspected his father did it for the sport and mental exercise as much as for his dislike of royalty in any form. "She just wants the sort of respect you might accord to a man."

A man. That was definitely one thing that the former countess from Poland was not, Morgan thought.

"I am old, Jason. I give everyone the same amount of respect." Which they all knew was minimal. "I expect them all to listen to me when I speak." He punctuated his statement with a mild chuckle.

But the men at the table knew that it was not really a jest.

A party, when all their lives were so filled with the drudgery and the scramble of forging a living, was something very precious indeed. Everyone had taken their invitation with a sigh of happiness and glee.

Morgan, who might have narrow thoughts when it came to the privilege of voting, was an egalitarian when it came to the people who might attend his social gatherings.

Here, at his vast home, newspaper editors rubbed elbows with self-made men of vast property. Reverends mingled with furniture makers, and dressmakers were placed next to second-generation gentry.

If Morgan hadn't demanded it, his daughter-in-law Krystyna would have surely seen to it. It was in her nature, despite the title she had been born to, to view everyone as the same. It was only their merit that differentiated one from another in her eyes.

When Riley arrived at the appointed hour, he saw that there were already several carriages ahead of his. All were eager to forget the strife-filled times, he thought as he climbed down.

He handed the reins of his carriage to a keen-looking stable boy. Riley recognized him, or thought he did. The boy seemed to have grown a full six inches since he had last visited Morgan's home for a celebration a few months earlier. Then it had been to honor Benjamin Franklin and the end of the war.

"Seth, is that you?"

"Sure is, Mast' Riley." The tall youth sat down in the driver's seat, careful not to disturb anything in the carriage even though it was old. Riley had purchased the vehicle second-hand from the blacksmith.

He looked up at the youth and smiled. "What have they been feeding you? You're growing like a weed."

Seth's response was to laugh. "Must be these new shoes Mast' Jase had them give me." He pointed one toe for Riley's benefit before he gently snapped the reins and urged the horse on his way.

Riley watched Seth drive away. With the carriage gone, Riley had a clear view of the front of the magnificent mansion. Instantly, he came to life and hurried across the cobbled walk.

Cassandra and her father, as well as her sisters, were just now about to enter the mansion.

Theirs had to have been the last carriage, he thought absently as he quickly crossed to them.

Taking the wide steps two at a time, Riley managed to catch up to them just at the front door. Winded from his run, he leaned a hand against one of the Doric columns to catch his breath.

They had all turned in unison at the sound of his approach.

"Cassandra. Mr. MacGregor," Riley added hastily, lest he be thought to overstep his place. "Mistresses." He nodded his greeting at the other two girls.

Though he knew of Morgan's penchant to invite the great and the small, he had not considered the fact that an invitation would be tendered to MacGregor and his family.

The evening before him brightened considerably.

"You look surprised to see us," Cassandra observed. She knew he was.

"I am," he admitted.

His glance took in MacGregor. It was only proper that he address the patriarch, though he found what was proper tiresome at times. He would have much rather taken Cassandra off and spoken to her in private. Topics did not matter. He wanted merely to absorb her presence.

No doubt about it, he thought, he was smitten, and deeply so.

"I had no idea that you would be here as well," Riley confessed.

"And why is that?" MacGregor asked genially. "Can furniture makers not break bread with plantation owners in Virginia?"

Riley realized the error of his choice of words. He bowed, concerned that he might have caused MacGregor, or more important, Cassandra distress. "I meant no offense."

MacGregor was quick to set Riley's mind at ease. "None was taken, lad. It was a harmless enough question on your part. I was only being rhetorical in mine. Mr. Morgan McKinley's hospitality is well known, even to newcomers." His smile included his daughters.

Brianne had remained demure, in her opinion, long enough. "Will you dance with me tonight, Riley?" she asked. "I don't know anyone here, and I don't wish to be a wallflower.'' Her words were sincere enough, reflecting a young girl's insecurity.

''You could never be a wallflower, Brianne,'' Riley assured her.

His statement was not meant to flatter, merely to set her at her ease. And he spoke the truth. She was far too pretty a woman to leave by the wayside. Especially since the men did outnumber the women here. She would not lack for attention and company were she twice less comely than she was.

There were others gathering behind them now. Riley became aware that they were impeding progress with their conversation.

He knocked on the ornately carved front door, and it opened instantly. A tall, stately house slave stood there, dressed in black livery. Recognition flickered through the man's eyes, though Jeremiah was far too well suited to his position to acknowledge the fact in so formal a gathering as this.

MacGregor, clearly impressed by the entrance of the opulent mansion, looked around like a man who had stepped into the pages of a fairy tale. Awestruck, he handed his hat to Jeremiah.

''MacGregor,'' he whispered. ''Bruce and his daughters Cassandra, Rose, and Brianne.'' He wondered if the man would be confounded with all these names.

To his pleased surprise, Jeremiah enunciated each name perfectly as he announced them to the hall. Then he announced Riley without being told. He solemnly stood his place, awaiting for the next arrivals to cross the threshold.

''We've none of that where we come from,'' MacGregor confided to Riley as they walked into the grandly lit ballroom.

MacGregor was not certain if he was impressed or just a little appalled by the black people who moved amid the shadows, doing their best to seem as unobtrusive as possible as they served the gaily dressed crowd attending Morgan's party.

''Perhaps,'' Riley replied quietly, ''someday we will not either.''

''We?'' Brianne was quick to pick up the word and just as quick to thread her arm through Riley's now that they had walked into the ballroom. ''Does that mean you have slaves, Riley?''

The very notion brought a shiver to his spine.

"Not I. To me the idea of owning another human being is nothing short of odious."

Though the opinion he held was a passionate one, Riley kept his voice low. There were many there who would be offended by his beliefs. A party was not the time to arouse tempers. There would be other, more opportune occasions to raise such matters and deal with them. He knew that Jason and Sin-Jin agreed with him and that both had already freed their slaves, as had Washington before them. The blacks who remained worked for pay.

"It is too much like servitude and bondage in Ireland," he concluded.

He spoke with such venom on the subject, Rose felt compelled to inquire, "Were you bonded to someone, Mr. O'Roarke?"

He noted that she alone of her family did not address him by his given name. Her shyness was pervasive. "No, but my father was a tenant farmer for a man whose heart was carved from stone and whose morals were lower than a mongrel's."

A man who had assaulted his mother. Rachel, almost a child at the time, had come running in to try to save her. She had stabbed Lancaster's leg with a poker. The man, enraged, had fled, only to return late that night to exact vengeance by burning the house down. They—he, his father and two sisters—had fled to sanctuary and then to America soon after.

His mother and the unborn child she carried had died in the fire.

Cassandra saw all this in his eyes. He had not to say a word. She had suddenly grown very still and the vision had come to her. So still that Brianne looked at her in alarm, knowing the signs.

She laid an imploring hand on Cassandra's arm, trying to draw her back. "Not here, Cass," she whispered urgently into Cassandra's ear. "Please, not here."

The next moment, the vision had fled, leaving behind an ache in Cassandra's heart for the man who stood next to her father.

Cassandra flushed when she saw that Riley was regarding her with keen interest.

"Hush, girls. Riley did not come here to endure an inquisition," she chided in a light voice. With ease, she linked her arm with his and turned a face that was entirely too innocent up to Riley's. "Will you be introducing us to our host?"

He was taken aback by her sudden shift in mood and wondered if she was hiding something. But he smiled and covered her hand upon his arm. "With great pleasure."

He looked around and spied Morgan, as always, standing in the center of a cluster of people. Krystyna was nearby. As usual, she was attending to everything in Morgan's stead.

Morgan's wife had died many years before, and his other daughter-in-law, Lucinda, a sweet-tempered, mousy thing who had brought property but not much life into his family tree, was unequal to the task of arranging even the simplest of things, much less something of this nature. Her heart was in the right place, as Krystyna was oft to say, but her head, sadly, was not.

So Morgan left all preparations in Krystyna's capable hands, as he had been doing for the last seven years.

"Fortunately," Riley said to Cassandra, "they all seem to be together, so I will be able to make the introductions at one time." A thought struck him. "How did you come to receive your invitations?"

"A tall, blond-haired god came riding up to our door," MacGregor answered. He slyly cast his eye toward his younger daughters. Both Rose and Brianne had appeared to be smitten instantly with the young man when he had entered the shop to tender the invitations.

Riley nodded knowingly. "That would have been Christopher."

"You know him?" Rose asked, her tone breathless. She blushed instantly.

"Why, yes. He's Morgan's grandson."

Riley had the distinct feeling that his words caused much anticipation and pleasure for the younger Mistresses Macgregor. He welcomed the thought that Brianne's attention would finally be shifted to someone closer to her own age. In any event, it would be shifted away from him.

Which was good, for he wanted to be free to concentrate his attention on Cassandra.

Chapter Nineteen

Morgan had his back to Riley as the latter approached him flanked by the MacGregors. Conversation had abruptly stilled. Morgan turned to see what had caught everyone's attention.

As he did so, Morgan smiled broadly.

Though there was gray now where once there was a far more robust color in his hair, and he was far into the winter of his years, in certain ways Morgan McKinley was as young as the next man. He and Benjamin Franklin shared a fondness for looking upon the pleasing face and comely form of the fairer sex.

And here he was, presented with three such ladies, each one lovelier than the last. Franklin would have surely envied him, Morgan thought.

"Well, well, well, Mr. O'Roarke, it would seem that your nose is not always buried in your work." Morgan edged his way passed the men he had been conversing with. His glance was long as it swept over each girl in turn. "What treasures have you brought to me tonight?"

Riley was not fooled by the display of southern courtliness. Morgan McKinley knew very well who these young women were. He knew the name of each and every person who set foot in town for any length of time. He made a point of it.

But Riley knew when to play along. He bowed before the older man, then turned to his companions. "Mr. McKinley, Christopher." He noted that the young man had made an effort to join his grandfather. "I'd like to introduce Mr. Bruce Mac-Gregor to—"

"Yes," Morgan interrupted with a wave of his hand, "I've had the pleasure of making Mr. MacGregor's acquaintance earlier this week."

Shaking MacGregor's hand now, he gave the man a cursory glance. The whole of his attention was given to the three young women who were standing beside their father.

" 'Tis the ladies I have yet to be introduced to. Are these your daughters, Mr. MacGregor?"

Appreciation permeated his voice. There were times when he yearned to be twenty years younger, if not more. It was not just because he knew he was facing the last of his life, but that he wished once more, however briefly, to have a young woman smile up at him and cleave to him with pleasure in her eyes rather than a hint of resignation. The girls in the tavern were all willing enough, but it was because silver crossed their palms, not because desire flowed in their veins.

To see desire for him bud in a young woman's eyes but once more would have sent him to his eternal rest a happy man. He sighed inwardly, resigned, at least in this, to what could not be.

MacGregor visibly preened, as he always did when he introduced his daughters. Of all the things he had accomplished in his life, all the things he had fashioned, they represented the very best.

"Aye, that they are, every last one a beauty too." The two younger ones blushed, but Cassandra gave her father a mildly reproving look, which only made him laugh the more. "Mr. McKinley, I should like to present my daughters, Brianne, Rose, and, my eldest, Cassandra."

Each girl curtsied in turn to Morgan as her name was spoken. Cassandra merely bent her knee. She would have preferred a clasp of a hand to acknowledge the meeting rather than to bow like a subservient maid before her master.

Morgan recognized the proud streak within the girl immediately. While the other two girls had a pleasing look about them, Morgan was quick to see the spark of intelligence that flashed in Cassandra's eyes. Though all three were beauties, there was something compellingly captivating about the last.

It had to be a sign of old age, Morgan mused, to regard a mind a pleasure when it was combined with a fair face. There was a time when the girl could have had the mental capabilities of a potato and it would have mattered not to him. He would have preferred it that way. Now he enjoyed having someone to talk to as well as look at. Yes, he was getting old.

Morgan noted that his grandson seemed to be captivated by Cassandra as well. He knew that he had not misunderstood the sudden, alert look that came into Christopher's face.

A match.

He turned the thought over in his mind. Yes, it pleased him. The boy was of age, of course, and it was time to begin thinking along those lines. Jason had taken too long to make up his mind, though he had been fortunate in his selection when he had ultimately made it.

Be that as it may, Morgan did not wish to see Christopher tarry as long as his uncle had. Morgan was not getting any younger and wished to see his first grandchild married before he died.

Morgan moved obligingly to the side as Christopher stepped forward. "I didn't have the opportunity to make your aquaintance earlier." Taking Cassandra's hand in his, he pressed a kiss to it. Brianne and Rose looked on, envy highlighting their cheeks. "When I came to your father's store to give you my grandfather's invitation, you were not there."

Very delicately, she slipped her hand from his. "I was at the dressmaker's shop."

Her eyes were so blue, Christopher thought. He could easily lose his way. He almost lost his tongue. "Selecting a pattern from one of the new dolls?" he finally managed to ask.

She smiled and noted that Riley was moving restlessly at her side.

" 'Sewing one. I am the dressmaker's new assistant.'' Cassandra paused, waiting for the information to bring forth some comment from the others.

She heard several whispers behind her. Though she told herself that others' opinions bothered her not a whit, her chin rose instinctively, as it did whenever she felt challenged.

But she saw no flicker of censure in either Christopher's eyes nor in his grandfather's for that matter. Her own shifted to Morgan's. As she did so, his history became known to her. Morgan McKinley had arrived in this country, a British outcast, with merely the shirt on his back. He was barely thirteen years old. The struggle to make himself into the man he was today— the owner of the largest plantation in Virginia and a man well respected among his peers—had been a long one. Along the way, he had lost his wife and his daughter, and the signs of sorrow had etched themselves into his leathery face.

He knew, she thought, what it was like to be deprived. To sweat and toil for what you dreamed of owning. To struggle toward a goal loftier than just earning bread for the table.

Though he was gruff and opinionated, in the final analysis Morgan McKinley was a fair man, and she liked him instantly.

Their hands were no longer linked, but Christopher did not look inclined to release Cassandra. ''Are you able to sew men's shirts as well as dresses, Mistress MacGregor?''

It was her father who answered for her. ''Aye, that she can, and with stitches so small, they seem not to be there at all.''

Christopher smiled, and his young, untried features took Brianne's breath from her. But it was Cassandra who had his attention, she thought rebelliously, promising herself to do something about it.

''Then I must come to the Widow Watkins's shop, and soon, to place my requests,'' Christopher vowed.

And Riley had a keen feeling he knew just what manner of requests Christopher was entertaining.

''I've one now,'' Riley spoke up. He took hold of Cassandra's arm before any more could pass between her and Christopher

Mildly surprised, Cassandra raised her eyes to Riley's questioningly. The other two girls took the opportunity to tighten their ranks about Christopher, one to each flank. Morgan and MacGregor exchanged looks and merely smiled at the foibles of youth.

Riley inclined his head slightly, as if he were bowing to Cassandra. "Would you do me the honor of having the next dance with me?"

Krystyna had brought together a group of musicians from the surrounding area. They were to play, with a few intermissions, throughout the whole evening. A few couples were taking advantage of the music and had formed a line to dance a minuet.

Cassandra pressed her lips together as she surveyed the group. "I fear I'm not good at that," she demurred.

He was willing to bet his soul that she was good at everything. He stopped just short of the line formed by the dancers.

"You don't dance?"

She shook her head and smiled in reply to his surprise. "Only the Highland fling, and there's doubts I have that the fine musicians Mr. McKinley has hired will be playing that rendition anytime soon."

He rolled the thought over in his mind. "They might if I asked. If you promised to dance it for me."

He was serious, she thought, and was flattered and perhaps a little flustered at the thought of dancing just for him. She waved away his suggestion. "Without bagpipes, the sound is thin."

Riley nodded. He had something far better in mind. He took her hand and held it tightly to keep her from returning to her father. "Then there's nothing for me to do but teach you."

"Now?"

He smiled, enjoying the way surprise bloomed in her eyes. "Now."

Cassandra looked about the vast hall and shook her head. "I don't want to attempt my first dance here, in front of everyone."

She had no desire to appear awkward amid these people whom she was endeavoring to mingle with, and it had truly been a long time since she had danced the minuet.

Startled, she turned to face him once more. "The terrace will be fine."

Riley was completely taken aback. "I hadn't suggested it yet."

Too late Cassandra realized that the words she had heard had not been on his tongue. She lifted a shoulder, then let it fall again carelessly, to cover her error. "But you were going to."

"Yes." Stubbornly, he refused to let the matter go. "How did you know?"

She looked away, afraid that he would see things in her eyes she had no desire to let him know. And no power, for some reason, to keep from him. " 'Twas only a calculated guess."

"You calculate well." He linked her fingers with his own. "As, I am sure, you do everything well."

So saying, he drew her to the terrace. The doors stood only slightly ajar. He pushed them farther apart so that they might pass, then left the doors that way so the music might drift through.

The night air was cool, but he had his desire to keep him warm and felt no breeze when it stirred. The only thing Riley felt was the stirring of his own heart.

She looked beautiful in moonlight.

When he was much younger, in Ireland, his sister used to tease him that he became smitten with a boring regularity. Indeed, his young heart had managed to fall for one pretty face after another.

But as he grew to manhood, though attractions for him multiplied and he followed their lead when he could, none had ever aroused him to this height.

Not like Cassandra.

It was as if all that came before was but a prelude to what was to come now.

Riley was both in awe of it and more than a little uneasy as well. For he was now faced with a path that he had never tread before.

But fear was not a bedfellow that he allowed to be harbored.

The only way, he had learned long ago, to cease to be afraid of the dark was to enter it and explore.

He meant to do just that.

Riley saw Cassandra lift an inquiring brow. "If I keep the door ajar slightly, we can hear the music and dance—and not be subjected to prying eyes."

Stepping behind her, he took her hands in his and began to move in time with the music.

She could feel the warmth of his chest against her back, and it ignited something kindred within her. "You are very considerate."

As he moved slowly, Cassandra fell easily into step, letting the music course through her body. Just as his kiss had the other evening.

"No, I am very selfish," he corrected her.

As she swayed against him, in time, he felt himself becoming steadily more aroused. The smell of her hair wafted to him in the breeze, and he was filled with her scent.

"I want you for a little while to myself, Cassandra." He turned her and then took her hand, holding it high overhead as he stepped forward, then back. Riley silently blessed Rachel for taking the time to teach him the steps. "There are too many who wish to gain your attention."

Their eyes met and held as she drew close to him, then stepped away again, mimicking his steps. " 'Tis the custom with new people."

That might be true, but not in Cassandra's case. "If you had been born in this town, it would make no difference. You attract attention and dreams, Cassandra, wherever you go." As he said this, a question rose in his mind. He took care to continue with the dance, even as he pondered it. "How is it that you have not married, Cassandra?"

He felt her stiffen slightly. Even her fingertips grew tense, although there was no change in her expression.

"I've not had the time for marriage and bairns."

The reply was too vague for him. Too unsatisfying. "A beautiful woman like you?" He turned her once and then brought her to him. They were but a heartbeat from each other when he paused. "I would have thought that some determined man would have made you find the time."

It was she who resumed dancing and he the one who followed her now. "I'm not easily led from the path I choose to take, Riley."

She was not telling him anything he did not already sense. "No, I thought as much."

His words made her smile. "How so?"

The music had stopped and he leaned against the railing, watching her. "I am well acquainted with that stubborn set of a chin. My sister has it as well." He called up a memory of Rachel in his mind. "Though in her, the stubbornness is at times perverse."

Cassandra settled beside him. She looked out on the lawn, buried in darkness, while he faced the house and the light. She liked the fondness she heard in his voice. "I look forward to meeting her someday."

Riley turned, but faced her so that he could look upon her face rather than the landscape beyond. "As I hope you will soon."

Cassandra did not move when he drew closer. "You miss her."

He laughed. "Like the devil. We have shared much together. There are times," he said philosophically, "that I feel as if she is the other half of my mind."

"And your soul?" Cassandra whispered, though she knew the answer to that already.

He looked at her, his eyes sweeping along her face, caressing her in his mind since he could not with his hands. "No, my soul lies elsewhere and I am in search of it." With all his heart he wanted to kiss her again. "Though I suspect I am already in its presence."

Chapter Twenty

Desire pulsed through him like an urgent, persistent itch just under his skin. There was just so long a man could continue to resist and still remain sane.

Riley suspected that he had already crossed that line. In one form or another, Cassandra had preyed on his mind, haunting him. Tempting him.

Now, here on the terrace, with only the night to see them and a tall fern to shield them from preying eyes, he thought to alleviate that persistent itch just a fraction.

He lowered his head to hers and saw by the look in her eyes that the reception he would meet would not be a cold one.

But his lips had just barely skimmed along hers when the double doors behind them were boldly thrown open to admit the warmth spilling out from the ballroom as well as the noise.

And Christopher.

Riley and Cassandra moved apart quickly.

If he realized that he had intruded on something vastly more personal than a minuet, Christopher gave no indication of it. His eyes looked bright for finally finding Cassandra.

"Ah, you did steal her away. I might have suspected as much." Christopher shook his head at Riley, but then immediately his attention turned to Cassandra. "I searched the whole ballroom for you."

Smoothly, in the ways that had been passed down from uncle to nephew, Christopher moved to place himself between Riley and Cassandra. "But what are you doing, dancing here? Surely it is too cold for one with skin as delicate as yours."

Christopher was tempted to trail his fingers along her skin to sample just how delicate it was, but knew that he would be overstepping himself if he did. He reined in his eagerness.

Riley, at least for the moment, felt more amused by Christopher than threatened.

"You've been apprenticing Jason, haven't you?" he asked the younger man.

Riley had heard tales concerning Jason's ways before Krystyna had crossed his path. The man's life had been a little, he reflected, like his own had been up until then. Enjoying the company of all women alike, wanting none to permanently grace his hearth.

He looked at Christopher now as Christopher preened before Cassandra. Riley made a point of holding on to his humor. He liked Christopher and wanted no rivalry to spoil that. Besides, he reminded himself, Christopher was a boy, while he was very much a man.

But it seemed obvious to Riley that they were two hounds on the scent of the same deer.

Riley wondered how Christopher had managed to disentangle himself from Rose and Brianne. He was sorely disappointed in their abilities, especially Brianne.

Christopher laughed at Riley's comparison. "Why would I take lessons from him? My uncle is an old man, hopelessly in love with his wife."

Cassandra had caught a glimpse of the two together, just as Riley had ushered her to the terrace. She had felt envious just to see the love that was so apparent. She found the way the two interacted beautiful.

"I see no harm in that," Cassandra noted.

Christopher was quick to correct his words lest they cost

him her company. "Neither do I. Fidelity has a strong attraction for me."

As he moved to place an arm about her shoulders, Cassandra was quick to step aside. And into Riley's protection.

"My sisters will be well pleased to hear that," she told the young man. "You have created a very good impression on them."

But Christopher was a McKinley and, as such, persistent. "As you have on me." He took her hand in his, then raised his eyes to Riley. "May I steal her for a dance, Riley?"

"Of course." Riley took a step aside. "She is not mine to monopolize."

"Yes, I know." Christopher turned his eyes to her. "Mistress, would you do me the honor?"

Before she could give her assent, Christopher had swept her away.

Resigned to the temporary separation, telling himself that it was foolish to be jealous of a man ten years his junior, Riley made his way into the ballroom. He crossed to the punch bowl. His eyes remained on the couple.

He frowned deeply as he helped himself to the punch. He was unaware that Jason had joined him until the taller man spoke. "I see that Christopher has found the most attractive woman here, barring Krystyna, of course."

Knowing he wasn't doing himself any good watching the two, Riley turned to look at his friend.

"When did he become so grown?" Riley grumbled, taking a long sip. The punch had rum in it and it hit his tangled stomach hard before it burst upon his senses. At the moment, it was what he needed. Riley was quick to refill his cup. "I seem to remember this tall, lanky boy following you about—"

He sighed heavily as he drained another cup.

Jason raised his cup in a toast. A little of the red liquid spilled along the side. "All boys are men in their hearts."

"I have always believed the opposite to be true," Krystyna said as she joined her husband. Both men looked at her questioningly. "That all men, no matter how old, are boys in their hearts."

Jason did not miss the opportunity to press a kiss to her cheek. It amazed him that each day he loved her more. He never ceased to be grateful that he had resisted his father's constant entreaties to marry any wench and held out until Krystyna came into his life. He was eternally thankful for his reluctance. And his subsequent good fortune.

"Only when lust keeps them young," Jason assured her, offering her his cup.

She took it from him and sipped once before returning it to his hand. "Then you, my love, will remain young forever."

He threaded his arm around her waist and drained the remainder of the punch. His eyes skimmed over her face. "God willing."

Riley shook his head good-naturedly as his fingers curved about his own half-emptied cup. "All this connubial happiness is making my Irish heart feel very envious and empty."

Krystyna shifted her eyes to Riley and looked at him knowingly. He had intoned his words in a jest, but he was serious. She glanced toward Jason's nephew and Cassandra. They were still dancing. A very lovely woman, Krystyna thought. She and Riley were well matched.

Krystyna rested a hand on her husband's shoulder as she regarded Riley thoughtfully. "Then why do you not do something about it, my friend?"

He shrugged, attempting to appear careless. "Your nephew has beaten me to it."

It was easy to hide behind words and do nothing. Krystyna had witnessed it often enough. But it was action that won a woman's heart, not repose.

Krystyna suspected that Riley was aware of that. He did not strike her as a man who gave up easily. "For the moment, perhaps. But it is evident that she does not want to hurt his feelings. Though Christopher has grown, that does not make him a man for her."

She inclined her head closer to Riley's, though what she said was no secret. Krystyna merely wanted to emphasize her point.

"Deeds count." She smiled as she looked into his eyes. "But you already know that."

Krystyna glanced about the room and satisfied herself that all was going well. Good. It was yet an hour before dinner was to be served. She had time to enjoy herself.

"What have you heard, my friend?" she asked of Riley, trusting him to be the first to know. "What is the latest news?"

Jason rested a hand on Krystyna's shoulder. "She devours the news."

We must always keep abreast so that we might be prepared. Had I not," Krystyna pointed out with a casualness brought on by years of distancing herself from the event, "I would have remained in Poland and, perhaps, died there."

She might have distanced herself from the events of their first meeting, but Jason had not. He still vividly recalled the first moment he laid eyes on her, the so-called property of a bondsman who had killed her father and kidnapped her. Jason had ransomed her "contract" and sold himself to her instead.

He drew her close to him, as if to melt away the memory of all she had suffered. "And I should have lived out the remainder of my days a dour, saddened man."

Her eyes laughed at him. She knew of his past reputation. "With your head pillowed in the lap of some tart."

He spread his hands wide, innocent. "A man must rest somewhere," he teased.

Krystyna pretended to cuff Jason's ear, but her laughing eyes gave her away. "So, what say you?" she asked Riley again. "What news?"

There was not that much to tell her that had not already been said.

"Things have not changed," he assured her. With a sigh, Riley reiterated facts that brought him no pleasure. "The government still owes its own people well over sixty-five million dollars as well as being eleven million in debt overseas."

He thought of the merchants who would have to do without and wondered how badly this would effect MacGregor. The man had already abandoned one shop in New York because of hard times. Would it be any better for him here?

"Times will get harder before they get easier," he told Krystyna.

She nodded as she refilled his cup. "It will be hardest on the tradesmen, I suspect." She glanced toward MacGregor as Riley accepted the cup from her hand. "Jason, perhaps I could have a new desk for my writing room?"

The request was casually stated. As if she needed permission to do anything, Jason thought with a smile. Whatever she desired, she obtained.

The scope of her heart did him proud. "Always thinking of others."

She lifted her shoulder carelessly, wanting no praise. It was each of their responsibility to watch out for one another. It was a philosophy her beloved father had taught her. "I am thinking of myself. It is I who will be using the desk."

He wasn't about to let her shrug this off. "Yes, but it is MacGregor's purse that will hold the money for purchasing one." He did not tell her that he had already commissioned a chest of drawers for her as a gift.

She spread her hands wide, as if dismissing the notion he presented. "Details."

He laughed and kissed her lightly on the lips, content to think of what would transpire in their rooms tonight once this accursed party of his father's was over. Unless, of course, he managed to draw her into some darkened room.

The thought brought a light to his eyes.

Jason straightened and took his wife's hand, suddenly inspired.

"Pardon," he excused himself to Riley. "But I have just thought of another detail that I would like to attend to."

She knew that light in his eyes well. "Jason," Krystyna cautioned, but without too much fervor in her tone. "There are guests."

"And guests and more guests," he agreed, leading her off. "They will continue to keep arriving for some time to come. Dinner is still more than two hours off."

"One hour," she corrected him.

He shrugged. "One hour, then. Still enough time. Just barely. Come," he coaxed. "I've something to share with you that only you can help with."

Krystyna lowered her eyes demurely, though the soft laugh that echoed was knowing and lusty. "Mingle," she urged Riley as Jason took her away. "And do not bide your time too long."

Riley toasted her with the cup she had filled for him. "Thank you, Krystyna."

Left alone, Riley looked back at the floor where Cassandra had been dancing with Christopher. To his surprise, Riley saw that she now had a new partner. A tall, distinguished man with reddish hair. There was a warmth about his gaunt appearance.

Riley recognized him instantly. The tension that had laced his body up tightly abated. He was slipping, he thought. He had no idea that Thomas Jefferson was in the immediate vicinity.

She was beginning to interfere with the workings of his mind, he thought. It wasn't a good sign. Nonetheless, he made his way closer to her.

Thomas Jefferson had come to the gathering at the behest of his friend, George Washington. Jefferson thought it might be good for Martha to mingle once again. She had been too long shut away at Monticello. She always looked her brightest at parties.

Spying Cassandra, Jefferson had left Martha in the company of some old friends and Dylan who was always solicitous of her well-being. He himself made his way over to Cassandra, delighted to see her.

He whirled about the floor with her now as yet another version of the minuet was being played. He wondered if the fiddler knew a good reel.

"Cassandra, I'd heard rumors from friends that you and your family were here." He smiled into the sympathetic eyes that looked up at him. There was a great comfort just speaking to her. "It has been a long time."

Cassandra nodded her head. "Yes, it has." She thought for a moment to their last meeting. "Almost two years." She glanced over toward where she had noticed the other woman. Martha looked well in her estimation. "How is Mrs. Jefferson?"

He nodded. "Martha is fine. We're both grateful for what you did for her."

While in New York on a visit, Martha Jefferson had consulted with Cassandra several times. Through the use of herbs, Cassandra had been able to alleviate the more severe symptoms of the malady Martha had been suffering from. She had also been able to help heal Mrs. Jefferson's small daughter, Polly.

But this was nothing she wished to discuss. "I did nothing."

Jefferson wondered why she was so reluctant to accept thanks and praise. He knew of many who pounded their chests where no regard was merited. "Martha swears by you."

Cassandra laughed lightly. She thought of Simeon. And the reason for her departure. "While others just swear at me."

He knew a little of her trouble, though not enough of it to help.

"That is," he said seriously, "unfortunate."

She looked up at him, annoyed with herself for saying anything to stir his pity. "It comes with the ability to help. People believe you can do everything. That God works through your fingers when it is only knowledge, and little of it at that, that guides them."

He allowed her to hide behind words. For some reason, her unusual ability made her uncomfortable. "God, magic, wisdom, whatever, my wife is well and we both thank you for it."

Cassandra merely smiled in reply. At that moment she knew, though her back was turned, that Riley had heard Jefferson's words. With all her heart, she would have rather that he had not.

It made her secret that much harder to conceal from him.

Chapter Twenty-One

Riley reached up and tapped Jefferson's broad shoulder. When the statesman turned, pleasantly resigned to losing his partner, Riley asked, "May I cut in?"

"But of course." Jefferson took a step away from Cassandra. "I have taken up too much of the lady's time as it is." Before he withdrew, Jefferson bowed to Cassandra. "It was wonderful seeing you once more. Martha would love a word with you before the night is over."

Cassandra saw by the look in Jefferson's eyes that it would be perhaps more than just a word of greeting that would be required of her. He wanted her to set his wife's mind at ease about something.

She inclined her head. "It would be my pleasure, Mr. Jefferson."

Riley readily took the place that Jefferson had vacated beside Cassandra. He glanced fleetingly after the tall, departing figure.

"How is it that you know Thomas Jefferson?" Riley hoped that he sounded sufficiently conversational and that his curiosity would not be too evident.

She thought of the tearful woman who had come to her, pleading for help in healing her child. Little more than a babe, the doctor was bleeding the little girl to cure her. Cassandra had put a stop to it and found a more effective manner in which to eradicate the child's fever. A few simple herbs combined with a nourishing broth and, compresses, and the child was well.

But all this was best left unsaid. "Our paths crossed a few times in New York."

She was deliberately being evasive, he thought. Why? "That sounds very mysterious."

"No mystery," she answered lightly. Cassandra seized upon the reason for the first encounter. Martha Jefferson had needed a new gown for a ball. It was later, after several fittings and rumors of Cassandra's "other skills" had reached her ears that Martha had begged Cassandra to help cure Polly.

"I am a dressmaker. Mrs. Jefferson had needed a new gown for a ball and someone recommended me to her. Hence, our paths crossed."

Cassandra felt his eyes on her, and that same nervousness threaded through her again. Why did he make her feel so unsure of herself when certainty had been her almost constant companion?

"She sought you out?" he repeated, impressed.

She nodded. "I am very good at my trade."

Of that he had no doubt. The dress she wore was exquisite and Rose had confided to him that Cassandra made all their clothes.

But there was more to this woman than just a needle and thread. "And what of the other?"

"Other?" Cassandra echoed the word innocently.

Why couldn't he just be satisfied with simple conversation and be done with it? Why did he insist on delving? The truth would only have him hurrying from her and she did enjoy his company.

That was the danger, she reminded herself. She enjoyed his company far too much and knew that she couldn't. Shouldn't.

The minuet ended, but Riley retained his hold upon her hand, unwilling to release her. They stood about with several other couples, giving the pretence that he was waiting for the music to begin again. But what he was waiting for was an answer.

Riley nodded toward Jefferson, now conversing with their host. "Jefferson said you returned his wife to her health."

Cassandra shrugged, vainly trying to stave off the inevitable. She knew Riley was destined to know her secret. *But not soon*, she hoped. *Not soon.*

"A few potions," she murmured vaguely, "no more. You are acquainted with what your sister can do."

Yes, he knew what Rachel could do. And no one had ever thanked her for saving a life with those talents. "Settle a stomach and clean a wound." His eyes remained on her face, searching for answers to his questions. He knew she would not offer them easily. "There is not that much more that she can manage."

Cassandra looked away just as the music began again. "Neither can I."

Somehow, he very much doubted that. Riley positioned himself for the next dance. The music's tempo was livelier. He lowered his lips to her ear so that only she might hear. "That was not the gist of what I heard."

She would not lie any more than she already had. Instead, she took the offensive.

"Then perhaps, sir, you should not have been eavesdropping."

He stood closer to her than the music warranted and custom allowed. It undermined her defenses.

"How else am I to know about you, Cassandra?"

Her unease gave way to a desperation. Cassandra truly didn't want Riley to know everything yet. When the time came, he would look at her oddly, the way so many had. She knew he would. Why would it be any other way with him? It was only need that made people come to her. Once that need was done, like as not, they feared her or reviled her. They gave her attributes she did not possess, and invoked God to protect them from her.

The same God she prayed to each night.

She looked up at him with determination. "I already answered that question for you."

She had told him that it was better for him not to know. He didn't see it that way. "Yes, but not to my satisfaction."

The look she gave him was meant to cut the discussion short. "Then, I am sorry, but—"

Riley raised her chin until their eyes met again. "Your lips say one thing, but your eyes another."

Cassandra drew her head back and smiled at the couple that was next to them. At all costs, this time she wanted to keep up the appearances of a normal life.

"Do not delve into things you do not understand, Riley," she whispered between lips that barely moved.

"Then help me to understand." When she said nothing at his urging, he continued, his mind working at the knot before him patiently. "I understand that since Martha Jefferson has lost so many children at birth, she places great store by healers and seers who can tell her if the next one will live. According to Jefferson's own words, she places great store by you. Putting the two pieces of information side by side, I deduce that—"

Cassandra looked up at him sharply as they were drawn together by the music. " 'Tis too much thinking you do, Riley."

His mouth curved at her words. "Yes, I do, and 'tis always of you." She filled his head the way air filled a room, taking up every space.

Don't. You'll be sorry and so shall I. "Then, again I say that 'tis too much thinking you're doing."

Her eyes warned him off even as he saw a glimmer of something else there. Sorrow. It was a strange combination. And as always there seemed to be no bottom, no end. It was like looking into a chasm that went on eternally.

"It cannot go well for you."

Was she telling him that she could never care for him? He felt he knew otherwise, but perhaps that was only delusion on his part. "Am I so displeasing to you?"

No, it was the opposite that was the matter. Still, it was a way out of her dilemma for her. "If I said yes, would you believe me?"

He saw Christopher approaching them again, and Riley shook his head firmly. Christopher backed away. For now.

"No," Riley answered her.

Cassandra laughed. He was tenacious if nothing else. And she knew that would be her downfall. She could not hold out against him indefinitely. "Then what is the point of my saying anything?"

Again his arm tightened around her waist. Riley saw others regarding them with open curiosity, but he did not care. "To hear you say the truth."

To hear her say that she did care.

Words had always come easily to him, all manner of words, written and on his tongue. But now he would have sold his soul to hear the right ones. From her. It was almost, he thought, as if she had cast some sort of spell over him. A spell he could not break free of.

She tried once more. "The truth is that you cannot know the truth about me."

It sounded like a riddle. He wondered if it was actually some dark secret she harbored. He knew the one Rachel carried with her had given her no end of despair. Was it that Cassandra blamed herself for someone's death, as Rachel had blamed herself for her mother's?

"Why? Have you killed someone, Cassandra?"

The question, mildly asked, had her looking at him in wonder. "No."

His mouth curved. "Have you buried husbands who have died suddenly of no obvious cause?"

He was laughing at her now, she thought. He thought her reluctance as merely mulishness on her part. He had no idea of the reason for it. "No."

The humor about his mouth softened into something tender. "Then the truth will not bother me." He looked into her eyes. "It would not have bothered me if any of the rest of it were true either." The humor returned to his eyes. "I would just sleep with a musket by my side."

For a moment Cassandra allowed herself to be amused. "It would do you no good."

He looked resigned to his fate. "Then I am completely unarmed around you." There was more than a little truth in the statement.

Cassandra played on his words. "If you sense danger, then you should leave."

He felt a longing to sweep her into his arms and kiss her then and there. It seemed to him unfair torture for a man to be allowed to touch a woman like this and then not be truly able to hold her.

She passed from his hands and went to another partner, and then another, as women drifted through his hands as well. Riley waited patiently as Cassandra made full circle and returned to him.

"Nay," he said as if there had been no pause in their conversation, " 'tis more exciting that way. And you are by far the most exciting woman I have ever met, Cassandra MacGregor Exciting and mysterious. But make no mistake about it, I mean to find out your secrets."

"It would be better if you did not."

Why was she so reluctant to tell him? What was there in her past that she hid so diligently? And what part did Jefferson and his wife play in it? Riley made up his mind to talk to Jefferson before the man departed that evening.

"There we have a disagreement." His eyes caressed her face as he gave her fair warning. "And I have always gotten what I set out to get."

Cassandra paused for a moment before she replied. "Yes, I know."

She said it not the way Brianne would have, flirtatiously attempting to win his favor. Cassandra said it as if she really knew.

The thought made him almost breathless. "How? How do you know?"

She looked away from him, searching out her father from the sea of faces in the ballroom. When their eyes met, hers had a mute appeal in them.

To her relief, she saw her father disengage himself from the people he was speaking with. He began to cross to her.

"A woman knows these things, Riley." She made the reply without looking at him.

Riley had considerable doubts that a woman would know any such thing. There was more to Cassandra, far more than was seen on first glance. He could see it in her eyes. Her deep, fathomless eyes. He meant to discover just how much more.

"Might I have a dance with my daughter, Riley?"

Riley tried not to appear overly impatient with MacGregor's request.

"Of course." He stepped back, wondering how Cassandra had managed to avail herself of reinforcements. It seemed an odd coincidence that her father would come just in the knick of time to spare her being asked any more questions.

For now he would bide his time. Riley looked over and saw that Jefferson was leaving the room. He hurried after him.

Cassandra watched him go. And knew what he was about to do.

"You look troubled."

Her father's comment brought her attention back to the ballroom. Yes, she was troubled, very, very troubled.

The music made MacGregor recall years gone by. When he was a much younger man. When it was his young bride he held in his arms and danced with until the rooster announced the new day. The memory made him smile for a moment. But then he looked at his daughter and the smile faded.

"Is it Riley?"

She nodded and pressed her lips together. "He's becoming too inquisitive."

He had watched the two of them dancing. Like two halves of a whole, they were, in his estimation. Like he had been when he had danced with his bonny bride. "I don't think it's idle curiosity that moves him."

She looked toward the doorway, hoping to see Riley return. But he did not. He had found Jefferson, and the two were speaking. Of her.

"I know 'tis not."

MacGregor saw no problem. "Then why don't you tell him?

It'd be better coming from your own lips than from another's.''
He did not need to say what. They both knew.

"I cannot." She attempted to keep the bubble of despair from bursting within her.

MacGregor carefully examined his eldest daughter's face. As always, she was unreadable and he had to ask. "You feel nothing for him?"

"I feel, Da. 'Tis just the trouble." It was then he saw a glimmer of her unhappiness. "I feel."

But he still didn't understand the nature of it. Riley seemed to be a fine man. All that he had heard in the last few days told him so. And Cassandra could never care for someone who was not worthy of her. That was for others, who could not peer into a man's soul.

"Then?" He was at a complete loss.

Cassandra ceased dancing and moved to the side, her hand locked in her father's.

"I cannot pull him into my world. You and the girls suffer enough. You saw how Rose looked when the vision took me. I would not do that to Riley. To live with the constant fear of discovery, of being reviled and run from a town." And that, she added silently, was only if he didn't turn from her at the start. That, she knew, would hurt even more.

"Your grandmother married," MacGregor pointed out patiently.

But she merely shook her head. She had gone over this ground in her head before. "It was different there. Seers were not thought to be the spawn of the devil."

The description brought a short laugh to Macgregor's lips. "Anyone looking at you would not say such a thing."

But she knew better. Had heard differently. She did what she could to shield her family. But not herself. She remembered Simeon's words to her.

"There is more fear here than in our homeland. Fear of things not understood."

He understood, and as a father he grieved for her. But as a believer there were other things required of him. He had to point out the truth to her, though he felt she knew.

"You cannot keep your power hidden, lass. That wasn't why it was granted to you."

She closed her eyes, wishing the burden, just for a moment, away. But it was not to be. Ever.

"I know. I know." She opened her eyes to look at her father. "But in accepting it, I also accept that I cannot have the life a normal woman could. Not here. Not with him." With a sigh she stepped away to the table where the punch bowl was.

MacGregor heard the yearning in her voice. "I think you underestimate him, Cassandra. Riley O'Roarke looks equal to the burden."

She turned and poured herself a little punch. She raised the cup to her lips but did not taste of it.

"Well, he will never have to be tested, so we shall never know."

But she did not say it with certainty, and Macgregor guessed that perhaps she knew more than she said.

As always.

Chapter Twenty-two

MacGregor looked up from the bureau he was working on when he heard the door to his shop open behind him. This would be his first customer of the week. Good. He could always use the work, and as of yet his business was a long way from becoming established.

He smiled broadly as he watched Christopher cross the threshold. A moment later MacGregor heard a hurried thumping noise just outside the shop, in the vicinity of the stairs leading from their living quarters. It was the sound of feet flying down the steps.

MacGregor set down his chisel and stifled a chuckle. Oh, they were bold, these girls of his. It was not difficult to guess that Brianne had seen the young Mr. McKinley crossing to enter the shop and intended to do something about that sighting.

He silently wished the young man luck. He did not seem to be a match for Brianne once she set her mind to something.

MacGregor came forward to greet the boy. "What is it I can do for you, Master Christopher?"

He quickly surveyed the entire shop. His glance did not take in the shelves of decorations fashioned from dried flowers that Rose had added, nor the fine articles of workmanship that were scattered about, carved by MacGregor on cold, blustery nights while he told his daughters stories of the homeland.

Though they were there and in plain sight, Christopher didn't see any of them. His interest lay in the human inhabitants that might be about the store.

And, to his everlasting disappointment, were not.

Christopher had hoped that in running an errand for his uncle, he would also be able to satisfy his desire to see Cassandra. He was thoroughly, completely, and hopelessly bewitched with her as only a young man could be with the first woman who had stolen his heart.

He nodded pleasantly at the square-shouldered man before him. Bruce MacGregor reminded him a little of what he imagined an elf would look like, except much larger. He wondered if the Scots had elves, or was that just the Irish?

"I have come to inquire on your progress on Krystyna's bureau."

"Ah, yes, the gift." MacGregor was well pleased with the work he had done so far. And there was talk, once this was done, of a desk as well. Thus far, the McKinleys were his best customers.

He wiped the wood dust from his hands, then beckoned Christopher forward to him. "See for yourself." He gestured grandly to the piece which was well on its way to completion.

For just a moment Christopher forgot the other reason he had come, the reason closest to his heart. He was not so incredibly smitten that he was blinded to the excellent craftsmanship that had gone into creating the bureau. The surface of each drawer, which would eventually be stained with the light polish MacGregor liked to employ, was dusted with dainty hand-carved flowers. Flowers like the ones that were found in the meadow.

Hesitantly, Christopher reached out a hand and ran his fingertips over the design. He looked up at MacGregor, who saw the awe in the young man's eyes. "It's beautiful."

"Aye, that it is," MacGregor agreed.

There was no false or pompous pride in his voice. Rather, it was the tone a father used to praise a child when he had managed a task that was particularly clever. As with his children, MacGregor took credit only in siring the piece, not in producing its beauty. That was a thing unto itself.

MacGregor stood back and folded his arms before him, a contented look upon his face. He was never happier than when he was working with his hands. It was, he knew, what he was born to do.

Just as Cassandra had been born to the Sight.

He tried to view the bureau with a dispassionate eye and found that he truly could not. It was too much a part of him. Still, he thought it one of his best pieces by far. He turned and looked at Christopher.

"Do you think your aunt will like it?" He knew that it was a secret and that Jason intended to give it to his wife as a birthday gift.

"She'll love it." The promise was given without reservation.

Christopher heard the door opening behind him. He swung around, anticipation quickening his very breath until it was all but gone. His hopeful smile faded marginally when he saw that it was Brianne who entered the store and not Cassandra.

Only MacGregor could detect it from his vantage point. The disappointment was hidden from Brianne.

There would be trouble here soon, MacGregor mused. Trouble between his daughters, for the one wanted no attention from this quarter and was doomed to receive it all, while the other desired it ravenously and was forced to stand in her sister's shadow.

He could all but hear the accusations flying from Brianne to be suffered in silence and patience by Cassandra.

Sometimes, MacGregor thought as he watched Brianne approach, laughter in her eyes, he imagined that it would have been easier being the father of all boys.

But then he remembered the two he had sired. The two who were now gone. And the ache seized him afresh, as it always did when he thought of his boys, wasted so young for a cause that was to die. Would that they had been born female and were alive still, MacGregor thought. He would have put up

4 BESTSELLING HISTORICAL ROMANCES BY YOUR FAVORITE AUTHORS CAN BE YOURS, FREE!

Kensington Choice brings you historical romances by your favorite bestselling authors including Janelle Taylor, Shannon Drake, Rosan▶ Bittner, Jo Beverley, and Georgina Gentry, just to name a few! Each book is filled with passion, adventure and the excitement of bygone times!

To introduce you to this great club which is part of Zebra Home Subscription Service, we'd like to send you your first 4 bestselling historical romances, absolutely free! And once you get these 4 free books to savor at home, we'll rush you the next 4 brand-new books a the lowest prices available, as soon as they are published.

The way the club works is that after your initial FREE shipment, yo will get our 4 newest bestselling historical romances delivered to yo

doorstep each month at the preferred subscriber's rate only $4.20 per book, a savings of up to $8.16 month (since these titles sell in bookstores for $4.9 $6.99)! All books are sent on a 10-day free examination basis and the is no minimum number o books to buy. (And no charge for shipping.) Plus as a regular subscriber, you'll receive our FREE monthly newsletter, *Zebra/Pinnacle Romance News*, which features author profiles, subscriber benefits, book previews and more!

So start today by returning the FREE BOOK CERTIFICATE provided. We'll send you 4 FREE BOOKS with no further obligation: A FREE gift offering you hours of reading pleasure with no obligation...how can you lose?

*We have 4 FREE BOOKS for you
as your introduction to
KENSINGTON CHOICE!
To get your FREE BOOKS, worth
up to $24.96, mail the card below.*

FREE BOOK CERTIFICATE

Yes! Please send me 4 Kensington Choice (the best of Zebra and Pinnacle Books) Historical Romances without cost or obligation (worth up to $24.96). As a Kensington Choice subscriber, I will then receive 4 brand-new romances to preview each month for 10 days FREE. I can return any books I decide not to keep and owe nothing. The publisher's prices for Kensington Choice romances range from $4.99-$6.99, but as a preferred subscriber I will get these books for only $4.20 per book or $16.80 for all four titles. There is no minimum number of books to buy and I may cancel my subscription at any time, plus there is no additional charge for postage and handling. No matter what I decide to do, my first 4 books are mine to keep, absolutely FREE!

Name _____

Address _____ Apt. _____

City _____ State _____ Zip _____

Telephone ( ) _____

Signature _____

(If under 18, parent or guardian must sign)

Subscription subject to acceptance. Terms and prices subject to change.

KF0898

with the bickering and the moods, and gladly so, so long as they remained both alive and well.

Since he knew the lines that were drawn in this silent battle, MacGregor moved forward to give his aid in the fray. No one, he knew, wanted Brianne to succeed in winning Christopher's affection as much as Cassandra did.

"Ah, Brianne." He smiled at his youngest benevolently. At the same time, his manner urged Christopher forward to greet her. "You've arrived just in time to welcome our guest." He turned to look at Christopher solicitously. "I was just thinking of taking a short respite. Would you care to join me in having some tea?"

But Christopher was already taking a step toward the door. "No, but thank you. I've still errands to run for Jason." Since Brianne was regarding him with such adoring eyes, he couldn't resist adding with just the smallest touch of importance, "I'm helping him manage the Lawrence plantation until Sin-Jin returns."

He was rewarded with an awed smile from Brianne.

Brianne had seen the mansion he was to inherit from his grandfather, and it had made her girlish heart sigh with joy. Seeing as how he was a handsome youth with a wondrous aptitude for dancing and more than a sufficient amount of intelligence, she had decided then and there that Cassandra could have Riley. *She* wanted Christopher.

"Ah, yes." MacGregor nodded, thinking back to a previous conversation he had had with Riley. "The man who went to Paris with Riley's sister and Franklin."

MacGregor was pleased that the different names he had absorbed were still making sense to him. At times, sadly, they drifted together into a tangle and he could discern them not at all. Those were the times he slipped into the haze that completely swallowed him up. God willing, those times had passed.

When Christopher took another step toward the doorway, Brianne was quick to bar the way.

"Oh, but you will not stay?" She underscored her question with a pretty pout. She'd practiced it in the looking glass to assure herself that she looked properly fetching and not like a crybaby, the way Rose had accused her. "I've just now made some shortening bread. It's fresh from the oven, just barely a quarter of an hour old. Won't you have some with us?"

"Shortening bread? You?" The incredulous words tumbled from Bruce MacGregor's mouth without thought. He quickly closed it.

If his youngest had truly made it, the shortening bread was either hopelessly burned or flat. More likely than not, Brianne had not made it at all. Rose was the one who enjoyed baking.

"Yes, I," Brianne replied. "Da, you act as if I never baked shortening bread before."

MacGregor pulled his lips from the smile that begged to be released.

"My error. 'Tis the dust that is making me forgetful." For Christopher's benefit, he nodded toward the bureau he had been laboring over.

Christopher was torn. There *were* errands to see to, just as he had said. And Cassandra was not there as he had hoped. But the youngest of the MacGregor sisters was quite an appealing bit of work in her own right. A man could do worse than tarry awhile in her company. Especially since she seemed so amiable to be with.

"Well," he hesitated, stretching out the word as he debated with himself. "Perhaps for just a little while."

"Splendid." MacGregor clapped his hands together. He could see triumph flash in Brianne's eyes. "I always welcome the company of younger people. They seem to know so much more these days than I did at their age."

"I'll be just a moment," Brianne promised. "I'll pop right upstairs and get the shortening bread. You won't regret staying, Mr. McKinley. It'll melt in your mouth, even if I do say so myself."

She could easily make that guarantee, MacGregor thought, knowing of her sister's talents. He smiled at Christopher as the door shut behind Brianne. "She's not well acquainted with modesty."

"She's charming," Christopher murmured.

"Aye, that would be one word for it," MacGregor agreed

studying Christopher more closely. "Charming. Charm the shoes right off your feet when she's a mind to it."

"Then it's lucky I'm wearing boots," Christopher laughed.

Christopher looked about once last time, his eyes drifting toward the curtained area in the rear of the store. He had no way of knowing that the small space behind the curtain housed but a few more tools and odds and ends. He thought, hoped, there was another room beyond. Another room where someone might, even now, be working.

He glanced toward MacGregor, hope written across his young features. The words tumbled from his lips. "Will Cassandra be joining us, perhaps?"

"No, I fear not. There is no chance of Cassandra joining us this afternoon. Her work at the dressmaker's shop keeps her well occupied for most of the day." The look of disappointment on Christopher's face forced him to amend his words a little. "At least that has been the case thus far."

"Oh."

Christopher could have kicked himself for forgetting. The dressmaker's shop. Of course. Cassandra had mentioned as much at the party.

He looked over his shoulder toward the eastern wall, where the dressmaker's shop lay. He debated paying a visit there, for a bonnet for his mother or on some similar pretext. It would garner him a few minutes in Cassandra's company. He debated taking his leave now, though it might seem rude to change his mind so abruptly.

The next moment the mental debate was tabled as Brianne hurriedly returned to the shop. She held a platter of fresh bread and clutched a knife in her hand. There was a kettle on the small stove in the corner. It would take little to brew the tea.

MacGregor took the platter from Brianne and set it upon the table he had placed against one wall. There was just room enough around it for four.

Brianne flashed a smile at Christopher. "It'll be but a moment."

"And what," MacGregor asked his daughter in a whisper,

amusement lifting the corners of his mouth, "did you tell Rose?"

He knew her all too well, Brianne thought. She maintained a tone as low as his as she answered. "That you were hungry."

MacGregor looked over his shoulder toward Christopher, then arched his brow as his gaze returned to Brianne. "And only I?"

She looked uncomfortable at his question, then shrugged carelessly. "She did not ask if there was anyone here in the shop."

It was just as he had surmised. Brianne was guilty of the sin of omission.

"And you did not tell her." It was not a guess on his part.

Brianne beckoned Christopher over. "Sit, please, sir," she requested. When he did, Brianne sliced a large section for him. Brianne offered it to Christopher with her smile. "I saw no reason to trouble her, Da," she replied, her sparkling eyes fixed on their guest. And her future intended.

Yes, MacGregor mused as he sat down at the table opposite Christopher. There was going to be trouble indeed. Perhaps amid all the sisters.

And all due to the same hapless young man.

Chapter Twenty-three

Riley looked at the Widow Watkins's straight, prim back as she elaborately replaced the bolt of fabric she'd been handling on the shelf before turning around to answer the question he'd asked.

Some said that the widow's mother had entertained her guests by giving long dramatic readings from Shakespeare and that as a little girl the Widow Watkins had spent hours avidly listening to these readings. Whether she did or not was uncertain. But she did have a flare, Riley thought, for the dramatic whenever it came to imparting any sought-after information.

When she finally turned around toward him, she gave Riley a long, sweeping look, as if she had not seen him two score times and more.

"No, I'm sorry, Mr. O'Roarke." The smile on her small, thin mouth contradicted her words. She was not sorry at all, but absolutely delighted to be in the center of all this activity and interest. It took away from the daily boredom of life. "It's just as I told young Master McKinley when he came looking for her."

The widow laid a delicate hand to her breast as she leaned

forward and confided in Riley. She lowered her voice, though there was not another soul in the store besides them.

"He said he wanted a bonnet for his mother, but I knew by the glint in his eye that it was Mistress MacGregor he was looking to see, not any bonnet."

Triumphant in her revelation, she cocked her head so that the hair piled high on her head listed a little to one side, giving her the appearance of someone just rising from bed.

"I've given her the afternoon off since there seems to be so little to do at the shop for the moment. She said she had some business of her own to tend to." Grandly, the widow swept a hand to her right in the direction of the furniture shop. "I expect that she's home."

"Yes, undoubtedly you are correct," Riley agreed readily.

There was nothing the widow liked better than being right about things, unless, of course, it was more gossip. She looked inclined to retain him so that she might gently prod a little more information from him to fuel this scenario that involved Cassandra. The girl talked so little about herself that the widow had to resort to other means to satisfy her curiosity.

Riley sensed the widow's intent by the eager gleam in her eye. "Thank you for your time," he murmured. "And good day to you."

Quickly, he made his escape, all the while feeling amused eyes upon his back.

He suspected that the widow would not waste a moment in finding someone to tell the latest to. That there was not one man, but two, looking for Cassandra. He had no problem with the notion of his being paired off with Cassandra. He rather liked it.

Her being linked with Christopher, of course, was another thing entirely. He hoped that matter would be quickly resolved and that the boy would settle his attention on one of the other sisters. After all, they were closer to his age.

Furthermore, Riley fervently hoped that the boy's infatuation with Cassandra would not cause a rift to occur between him and Jason and Krystyna. They were partial to Christopher. It would be a sin to have trouble come of this. Riley truly valued their friendship. Especially in the wake of the council meetings. He and Jason would have to ally themselves against men like Johnson and Andrews. And the Reverend Edwards.

But whatever the outcome, both of the council meetings and of this infatuation of Christopher's, Riley knew he was bound to seek out Cassandra time and again. It was as if his soul had been fated for this. As if he had no choice in the matter.

He seemed to sense things about her. Even now he knew where to find her.

Knew, even as he passed MacGregor's Furniture Shoppe and waved in to MacGregor, that Cassandra was neither there nor upstairs. No, the business the widow had alluded to so cavalierly that Cassandra was tending to would take her to the glen.

He had no idea how he knew, he just knew.

Perhaps he was a little fey himself. The Irish called it fey. But fey, seer, or whatever, there was a bit of deep intuition to everyone, and it took no "little people" or visions to convince him of that.

His conversation with Jefferson at the party had been interesting to say the least. The man seemed a bit reluctant to speak to a stranger of his dealings with Cassandra. That only served to pique Riley's interest rather than to dissuade it.

He had sought out Martha Jefferson next.

Unlike her husband, Mrs. Jefferson had been far more willing to speak about Cassandra. Riley had bided his time and waited until the lady was alone before he introduced himself as the editor of the *Gazette* and a friend of Cassandra's.

By carefully feeling his way around and asking just enough, he managed to find out that Cassandra had not only made two of Mrs. Jefferson's dresses, but, more to the point, had healed her young daughter and given a brew to Martha to make her feel better. And foreseen that her next child would be born alive and healthy.

It was the latter that intrigued and at the same while troubled him somewhat. Perhaps Mrs. Jefferson had misunderstood his question, or Cassandra's assurances. Many said things to a friend to ease their mind. "Foreseen" was a word loaded with meanings that were not for the ordinary man to bandy about.

Foreseen.

He cast the word from his mind, unwilling to work the knot out now. He had something more important on his mind. It did not take a mystic to "foresee" the fact that Cassandra would run into trouble if she insisted on continuing to roam the woods unaccompanied.

Riley hurried to his office, stopping there only to get his musket. Armed, he went in search of Cassandra.

He went to the spot where he had discovered her the last time.

It was foolishness for her to wander about so, he thought, annoyed. She was too intelligent to be so oblivious of what might befall her. Someone obviously had to take her to task and point out the simple facts to her, if her father could not. A woman should not roam the wilderness, for whatever reason, without a man at her side.

Riley would have more than welcomed the chance to be there at her side. He hurried along, his long strides eating up the ground as he made his way to the stream. He remained alert for any signs of danger, human or otherwise, not allowing his preoccupation to interfere with his vigilance as it had the last time.

The first thing he saw as he stepped out of the wooded area into the clearing was the tempting flash of gold. It quickened his heart as he increased his pace and crossed swiftly toward her. Just as he suspected, she was picking herbs.

He was a little disappointed, at the same time, that she was not swimming, as she had been before. But the day had a slight chill to it, promising autumn not too far away. And lightning, Franklin had once pointed out to him, seldom struck in the same place twice.

"Cassandra."

She raised her head at the sound of his voice.

He'd come.

Just as he was supposed to, she realized suddenly. It hadn'

been known to her a moment before, but it was now. Riley O'Roarke was to be the one. And it would be today. Here.

It was the woman who trembled, not the seer, as she turned to the sound of his voice. She knew that she was smiling at him, though she could not feel the curve of her mouth.

"It seems that I cannot come here without you being somewhere close about." She raised her hand to shade her eyes as he strode forward. "Are you spying on me again?" She dropped her hand as he joined her. "You see, I've not gone swimming today."

Riley shook his head vehemently, denying her cheerful accusation. Not for the world did he want her to think of him in that light.

"Not spying. Instinct brought me here." He resisted the temptation to wrap his arm around her. To greet her with a familiar kiss, or, dropping all pretenses, to sweep her into his arms the way he wanted to. But there were roles to play and decorum to follow. "And it wasn't spying that I was about last time."

"Oh?" This time the amusement was genuine as it lit her eyes. "And what do you call peering around the bushes at a woman who is completely devoid of clothing?"

"Great fortune." He could see her that way now, even though he hadn't completely seen her that way then. His imagination had always been a wonderful, powerful tool. It burned through her clothing now. "Great fortune indeed."

Cassandra felt a blush rising and was intrigued by it. It was rare that she felt embarrassment at anything. In truth, it wasn't so much embarrassment now that colored her cheeks as— pleasure.

She wondered how many would call her wanton for that. To be flattered because he found her body tempting and pleasing.

Riley reined in his thoughts and took her basket from her arm as if the thing were too heavy for her to carry. He was barely aware of it as he slung it on his own arm. Riley fell into step with her as she moved around, searching for the right herbs to harvest.

There was a season for everything. Now was the season for

these. Soon autumn would come, sending the herbs she gathered on their way. In their wake, something else would come.

It always did.

She raised her eyes to his, knowing that something more between them was to come.

Goldenrod rained from her hands into her basket before she asked, "And what are you doing here now, pray tell, if not spying?"

His purpose returned to him, blotting out the fact that he found himself completely besotted with her. This couldn't continue. He wasn't some young, besotted fool. He was the editor of the newspaper and a representative of his people, if Jason had his say. This was no way for a man with either of those two responsibilities to behave.

Riley attempted to look at her sternly. "I've come to warn you."

She would feel his tension. Was there danger? If there was, why hadn't she sensed it? She looked around, then asked, "About what?"

"About being here alone," he retorted impatiently.

He watched her mouth curve again, and though the sight melted him, her reaction did just the opposite. It annoyed him. She was not taking him, or the situation he spoke of, seriously.

"A woman alone is not safe, wandering about." His tone grew harsh in hopes of bringing her to her senses. "She can never tell when someone of unsavory nature might happen upon her."

"I see." Her eyes danced as she looked at him. The breeze ruffled her hair. She dragged a hand through the strands of gold, pushing them back. "Such as now?"

The thought of someone taking advantage of her, of forcing himself on her, as had happened a time or two to others in the town, made his blood run cold.

" 'Tisn't funny, Cassandra." He had to make her understand. He followed her up a slope as she continued gathering. "Not every man can restrain himself the way I could that day I found you swimming here."

She bent over an ugly root and plucked it from the ground,

depositing it into the basket, then cocked her head to look up at him.

"Oh?"

He tried not to pay attention to the way the swell of her breasts strained against her dress when she bent over in that manner. His mouth felt completely dry as he pressed on.

"Yes, 'oh.' Another man would have dragged you from the water—"

Cassandra straightened, adding another specimen to the basket he still held for her.

"Provided that man could swim," she reminded him, her mouth curving so that it made him ache despite the humor at his expense.

"—or waited until you emerged," he continued doggedly, his voice lowering to a hoarse whisper as he remembered. "And then had his way with you."

Cassandra could hear every sound around her. The flap of the wings of the geese flying south overhead. The rustling of the grasses as the wind combed invisible fingers through it. A bee buzzed somewhere not far off. She heard it all. And the sound of her own heart hammering loudly.

It was time.

The words softly echoed through her brain, coming from a source outside herself, or was that only her mind?

"And what way is that?" Cassandra heard herself asking quietly, her eyes fixed on Riley's face.

As if his arms suddenly went lax, Riley let the musket and basket drop to either side of him. He was unable to resist the urge that raced over him when she turned her face up to his.

Lightly, he combed away the strands of gold that had been blown about her face by a mischievous breeze. One hand cupping the back of her head, Riley brought his mouth to hers.

It was as if he had been only half alive until his mouth touched hers. Only half awake to all the beauty there was in the world.

Riley kissed Cassandra over and over again. If, earlier, he had feared frightening her, his fears were swiftly assuaged, for she met him passion for passion.

He had never wanted anything as much as he did her. The
need exploded in him until he thought he'd die of it. And yet
he knew he couldn't act on it, couldn't merely take her in the
heat of the moment.

Not until she told him that it was well with her.

Completely shaken by the extent of the feelings that were
drumming through him, Riley drew back his head and looked
into Cassandra's eyes. The light blue crystals had darkened to
the color of the sea at night.

And, like the sea at night, they were fathomless and he feared,
quite accurately, that he would get lost there. That he was
drowning there, even then. The answer he sought was from her
lips, not her eyes, for they remained impossible for him to read.

His breath came in short supply, as if he had just run a great
distance, and he waited a moment until he could gather enough
together.

"Cassandra, I want you."

If she had never known the truth before, she knew it then.
And he had spoken it. But whether she understood as a woman
or something more was unclear to her.

"I know."

God, desire had never raged like this within him before.

"Now."

Cassandra could only nod. Her eyes on his, humbled by what
she saw there, she murmured, "Yes."

The intent of her reply was unclear. He didn't want to seize
it and make an unforgivable mistake. Riley wanted her to be
very, very sure. This was not a tryst he faced. This was eternity.
And his destiny.

"Yes, you know, or yes—"

She slipped her finger along his mouth, silencing him. "Just
yes, Riley." Her eyes caressed his face. "Just yes."

Chapter Twenty-four

Somehow she had known that when it would happen, it would come to pass in a place like this. On a soft bed of grass with a stream running by not too far away and the sun shining brightly overhead.

What she had not known was that there was to be passion—splendid, overwhelming passion. She had not begun to conceive of that fact, nor the extent of it.

Some things remained hidden from her, even then.

Such as her own vulnerability, her weakness for this man. And her own eagerness to travel to this unknown place she could not, with all her Sight, even begin to glimpse. Not without Riley.

The passion grew, mushrooming and engulfing her. And grew bigger still. It had no beginning, no end.

A reverence had slipped over Riley even in the height of his agitation. When she had said yes to him, she had not given just her assent, but handed him a huge responsibility as well. He had her whole trust in his hand.

More than anything, he wanted to make this the most glorious occurrence of her life, for he knew without being told that it would be her first. That *he* would be her first.

For a fraction of a moment he wavered, afraid that he would fail her. Afraid that it would not be for her what it would be for him. A deed completely wondrous.

He needed to be gentle when his body urged him to be forceful, slow and languid when he desired nothing more than to be quick. There was much required of him for this joy that lay ahead.

And what if someone came? He could not have her humiliated.

He glanced around one last time. But she touched his cheek, bringing his eyes back to her.

She knew part of what troubled him. ''There is no one else,'' she assured him softly. ''And there will be no one.''

He looked at her. There was something in her tone that told him she was not speaking of just now, but of longer.

For the moment, though, he took her assurance, knowing that she knew. It was her gift. Just as Martha Jefferson had told him it was.

He pressed his lips to hers and was instantly caught up in the whirlpool again. It was all he could do to hold fast to his mind.

His fingers expertly undid the laces at her back. As he pulled them apart, he felt her smile beneath his lips. Riley drew his head back and studied her expression. Beyond the haze of passion there was amusement. He wanted to understand.

''What?''

''You are used to this.'' It was not an accusation. Only an observation.

He feigned innocence, though there was no real attempt to lie. Neither was there a desire to cite past lovers who had drifted through his life. They all paled in comparison. ''Rachel often asks for my assistance. The laces snarl. 'Tis where I gained my expertise.''

Cassandra's smile broadened. ''There, and at the backs of girls you took.''

Still there was no accusation. She was a rare woman, he thought. And for now she was his.

"There were no girls," he assured her softly, his eyes on hers. A shiver threatened to consume his body as the dress slipped from her shoulders. It pooled at her waist. He tugged it down farther, then sighed as it touched the grass. "No others before. Only you."

And he meant it.

And she knew his words to be true in the most absolute sense. Though the dangers were no less and the sorrows still shimmered on the horizon, his words made her heart glad.

Cassandra trembled as his warm hands traveled the length of her arms, caressing them gently before he slipped her chemise from her as well. It joined her dress upon the grass.

She stood, ripe and waiting before him. With a groan that he did not bother to stifle, that he *could* not stifle, Riley cupped his hands gently around the silken skin of her breasts.

Ever so slowly he rubbed his thumbs along the rosy peaks until they hardened against his touch and she cried out his name.

When she did, he could not help but cleave to her, wanting to absorb the rose-petal feel of her skin. Cassandra buried her face in his neck as she fanned her fingers into his hair.

Her body throbbed for him and it, not her mind, led her.

It was the first time she undertook a journey without her mind first clearing the path. Her mind was not there at all, except to note, in a vague haze, the things that were befalling her—delicious, wonderful things that took her breath away and made her want to laugh and cry at the same time.

Cassandra yearned to feel him, to touch him as he touched her. Impatient, she tugged on his vest, then pulled it from his shoulders, the energy behind the act taking him by surprise.

As it did her.

Cassandra pulled Riley's coarse linen shirt from his britches. Her eyes on his, she splayed her cool hands beneath it, along his bare chest.

The smooth skin she found turned hot beneath her fervent touch.

He felt as if all strength were abandoning him, as if he had only the energy to stand, and that only if he held on to her shoulders. His breathing grew heavy as she pressed a kiss to his throat.

"Oh, God, Cassandra, what have you done to me? You're bewitching me."

The words echoed like a curse in her brain. She stiffened against him, instantly withdrawing as if cold water had been thrown on her.

Cassandra pulled back. She would have gathered up her clothes and fled had he not grasped her arms and held her fast. His eyes searched vainly for an answer. "What, what have I said?"

She told herself that she was reacting to the past. He had not meant the words the way others had before him. Cassandra drew in a breath to steady herself.

"I want one thing clear between us, Riley. What is happening—and *will* happen—is because you desire it, not because of anything else."

What else could there be? He had not a clue. He strove to reassure her with his touch, soft and gentle, upon her body.

"I desire it," he whispered with fervor. "Just as I desire you. With every fiber of my being. There is no question of that in my mind."

But there would be, Cassandra thought, tears gathering in her soul even as he held her again. Later there would be.

In the next instant Riley burned her tears away with the heat of his mouth as it assaulted hers, taking, giving, pleasuring.

He trailed his kisses everywhere, on each part of her body as he peeled away her garments one by one with hands that belonged to an adolescent rather than the man he had become. His eagerness, his craving for her, had somehow stripped him of his experience. It was now, as it once had been, the first time.

As ardently as he had proceeded, so did she, matching him movement for movement. She pulled off his clothing as cleanly as he did hers. Finally, with the last garments cast aside, their bodies cleaved to each other as if some force greater than they were bringing them together thus.

Riley could feel the heat, overwhelming, almost violent heat, searing from him like tongues of fire. It matched what was emanating from her.

He was both her master and her slave, showing her the way, then following her, awestruck, as if he had never come down this road before. He both led and followed, taught and learned.

She evoked all things from him.

Rather than the experience being wondrous for just her, she had swept him up in the wonder of it himself. *She* was the wonder, like elusive starlight caught, but for a brief moment, in his hand.

Awe poured through him.

Cassandra's head spun as she felt herself falling, then rising again. He was doing such strange things to her body, making it hum. Making it play a melody she had never heard before. Eagerly, she pursued the path that he uncovered for her.

Never had she expected anything near the scope of what she felt.

At that moment she would have forsaken everything else for this wondrous sensation that battered her body as his mouth heated further that which was already burning out of control.

Her skin was like butter, soft and creamy beneath his hand. Over and over he caressed her, let his hand travel the length and breadth of her body as if he were committing it to memory.

He thrilled to the passion that glowed in her eyes.

He could have gone on this way forever, exploring her, feeling her hands along his body. But the demands, the hunger that surged through him, wouldn't let him. Wanting her was beginning to completely undo him.

Control felt as if it were slipping swiftly from his fingers.

Slowly, preparing her as best he could, Riley struggled to hold himself in check until he thought her ready for him. Just as the reins he held threatened to snap, Riley raised himself over her body.

Instinct more than knowledge had her parting for him. She was eager to become one with him. Eager to feel him within her.

Eager to give herself to him the way she never had to any other.

He looked down at her, her hair fanned out like spun gold upon the ground. He had never seen anything, anyone so beautiful before. His very heart ached within his chest from just looking at her. From the sensation she created within him.

"I love you, Cassandra."

Still she felt blindly about, without a light to guide her in this unknown land she found herself in. Cassandra shook her head, her fingers over his lips. Was this what was said before a man and woman became one? Was this what a man felt required to utter?

If this was form, she wanted none of it. "You needn't tell me."

Again her reaction was a mystery to him. Another woman would have begged for these words he had never uttered before. Why did she deny them?

"Why, Cassandra? Why needn't I? When I feel them throbbing inside."

Even then, with the hint of his weight just above her body, she smiled.

"That might be something else throbbing in its stead." Her expression grew serious. "Hold your words until you mean them."

"But I do," Riley insisted, gathering her to him. "So help me, Cassandra, as God is a witness to this, I do mean them."

She wanted to believe. Truly she did. But whether she believed or not, it would not change what was to eventually be.

Balancing himself carefully on his elbows, Riley slipped into her. He saw the shock of pain burst into her eyes and grieved that it would mar the experience. But the next moment, as he brought his mouth to hers, he saw that the pain had faded from her. As his lips captured hers, she arched her hips to sheath him further.

Excitement roared through his veins.

Just as he had shown her the steps to the minuet, he showed

her another dance now. A timeless one that needed no music save the melody that played so ardently in their heads.

He rocked against her, heightening the rhythm until she rushed to meet him. Together they reached the summit. As they plummeted over it, they were as one before God and nature.

Chapter Twenty-five

If she were to shut everything else out, she could have remained with him like this forever.

But it wasn't possible.

Not for forever, not even for a few minutes longer. As the feeling of contentment and well-being slipped from her, all that remained was emptiness.

And the memory of who and what she was. And who and what she couldn't be, even for him.

Cassandra sat up abruptly, forsaking the shelter of his arms, startling him.

She looked so alert, he thought. Sitting up as well, he reached out to touch Cassandra's hair, but she pulled away nervously. Instead, she leaned forward and hurriedly gathered her clothes into her arms.

"What is it?" Now he was concerned. She appeared upset.

"I have to go." She spoke the words breathlessly, as if there were something chasing her.

Only a moment before she'd seemed so peaceful, so content. He didn't understand this sudden urgency that had seized her. He knew they couldn't remain here for long. But while they were wrapped within the warm blanket of euphoria, he'd thought they could tarry just a little longer.

"But—"

"Please." The single word was a plea for him not to argue or, worse, to question. "I have to."

Cassandra, her back to Riley, dressed hastily. She felt as if she were all thumbs. This clumsiness that governed her hands was something she was unaccustomed to. She seemed to be struggling with every garment.

Riley hurried into his britches and quickly pushed his arms through the sleeves of his shirt. It hung down untidily as he approached Cassandra. She was just reaching around her back, awkwardly attempting to secure the laces that continued to elude her.

"Here," he offered, "let me." Riley struggled not to be irritated when she stiffened.

She didn't want him touching her again. She felt as unsettled inside at the mere thought. When he touched her, her very thoughts dissolved.

"No, I—"

"—can manage," he concluded for her between his teeth. He continued to lace her up. "I'm sure you can, but it'll go a good deal faster for you if you'll be letting me work the laces."

Her protest died upon her tongue. Cassandra felt his fingers skim along her skin as he worked, and something heated within her even when she knew it shouldn't. She closed her eyes as she swallowed and worked at containing the emotion that dearly wanted to erupt again. He truly was her undoing, for all her resolutions to the contrary.

"I don't know about that."

He heard her dilemma, and her desire, in her voice. The irritation and frustrated hurt he felt receded in its wake.

"Ah, a compliment," he said softly as he worked on the last of the laces. "You bolted up so quickly, I thought perhaps you didn't like it."

She turned and looked over her shoulder. Riley's expression was partially serious. "How could you even be saying something like that?"

He dropped his hands from her back as he finished. Cassandra turned to face him. "A man's ego is a frail thing."

She studied his face. Yes, she believed it was, she thought. Even his. "So I have been told."

He realized that perhaps he had given away a little too much. And not received anything back in trade. "As are a woman's feelings," he countered.

She inclined her head, giving him that. "Agreed."

The defensiveness drained from him. He touched her shoulder lightly, needing the contact, however slight. "When can I see you again?"

Cassandra averted her eyes as she bent down to pick up her basket. Her voice was as devoid of emotion as her heart was full of it when she answered.

"It wouldn't be wise."

Her reply stunned him. How could she talk like that after they had lain together? It was almost as if she had not been part of what came before. "I don't want to be wise, I want to be with you."

She looked at him then, and her eyes were tortured. "You can't, not this way."

Pride would have dictated that he let the matter go, that he step away from her just as she was from him. But he couldn't. Not without answers.

"Why?" he demanded. "This wasn't just a passing dalliance with me, Cassandra. I don't want to sample you once and forget. I *can't* forget."

Didn't he realize how hard he was making it for her? "I'm sorry."

"Sorry?" He repeated the word as if it made no sense to him. Riley looked at Cassandra and slowly began to understand. Or thought he did. "Do you mean that you're sorry for what happened?"

It would have been easier to allow him to believe the lie and be done with it. But she couldn't let him.

"No. I'm not sorry that you made love to me." Her eyes entreated him, asking for his understanding even though she couldn't explain. "I'm just—sorry."

And with that she turned and ran from him, clutching the basket close to her breast. She ran as if the very demons of hell were after her.

She ran so that he wouldn't see her tears.

Riley wanted to go after her. He wanted to give chase as she disappeared into the wood.

But all he could do was stand there and watch her go, and wonder what had happened to change her so quickly. To make her turn her back on what he knew she wanted. By her own admission.

It wasn't just maidenly pride that made her act this way. It was something else, he felt certain.

He had no idea what.

In not knowing what to think, he attempted not to think of her at all.

For a whole week he attempted not to think of her. There was certainly enough work for him to do so that his thoughts were sufficiently occupied. And enough matters now that required his attention to keep Riley's mind immersed in details that had nothing at all to do with the dressmaker's comely assistant.

And yet it was to her that his thoughts strayed time and again. To the wood where he had taken her. To the lyrical melding of their bodies, if not their souls, though if asked, Riley would have sworn that that had happened as well.

But her behavior had indicated otherwise. And no matter what he pretended to himself, it wounded him.

Thoughts of Cassandra followed him everywhere. To the newspaper office where he toiled long hours. To his lonely bed at night as he lay, watching the fire die out on the hearth without even the comforting company of Rachel's voice to fill the void.

It followed him like a haunt to the long-abandoned meeting hall, where the men who had weeks before sat at Morgan McKinley's table now gathered once more.

Thoughts of Cassandra and puzzling over her abrupt departure from him kept Riley silent and preoccupied as others argued over laws and rules that were to govern the townspeople. It had kept his voice from joining Jason's and Beaulieu's when the two men protested the fact that the council had not been duly elected as it had promised, yet sought to enforce laws they were not asked to make.

Morgan frowned at his son's suggestions. It was one matter entirely to rout the British from their lives and their soil because they sought to bend the Americans to their will. But resisting the will of a McKinley when it only involved the town's own good was quite another.

There wasn't time for elections, Morgan had snapped back in reply.

"Waste of time the first go-round anyway," he had added with a snort.

He preferred that their disagreements were in private, not public, but his younger son was as stubborn, as pigheaded as he, so they were doomed to wash some of their dirty laundry where other eyes would see.

"Besides, I've known what was best for Morgan's Creek ever since I was the first citizen in it." Morgan all but turned his back on the source of the suggestion. "Let's see to what needs doing first and then worry about elections later."

To Jason as well as to Beaulieu it seemed like a matter of placing the wagon before the mare. Both men had initially refused to have any part of the decision and the council. But then, as if one, they reconsidered. If they dropped out of the reformed council, who would speak for reason?

Not Riley, it appeared, Jason thought with more than a touch of annoyance. But the looks he shot Riley all during the meeting went singularly unheeded.

Jason could barely contain his temper until his father rapped the gavel, calling the first session to an end.

As the men slowly trickled out from the rickety one-room structure, Jason hurried over to Riley and grasped him by the arm.

"What the hell happened to you in there?" Jason demanded in an uncustomary temper.

Once, before Krystyna had come into his life, Jason's philosphy had been one of laissez-faire. He interfered with no one so ong as they did not interfere with him. It had taken Krystyna's assionate involvement with the politics of the world to make im see that he could not refuse to make a stand where his ountry was concerned. Where people's rights were concerned. Ie still felt that way.

Riley looked at him, expressionless. "What do you mean?"

Jason wanted to take Riley by the shoulders and shake him, emanding to know what had come over him to make him act is way, so passive, so disinterested. Riley had always been ie most vocal opponent of restrictions.

Instead, Jason took him by the arm and ushered him toward ie old oak, out of the way of the others, so they might not be verheard.

"Why did you bother showing up at all if you were going) make as much noise as the boots that are standing in my loset?"

Riley could only stare at him. He'd never seen Jason so gitated before. "What?"

"Where the hell's your tongue, man?" he demanded, curbing is tone. He saw Andrews looking their way and knew the tter would like nothing better than to see dissent between iem. That would strengthen Andrews's side. "Where's that oice of yours that takes such joy in opposing reigning author-y? Have you suddenly become afraid of my father and the ols who sit on this so-called council of the people?"

The sound of Jason's tone, harsh and humorless, roused iley's ire, and he took offense at it. He pulled himself free f Jason's grasp.

"No."

Jason was relieved to see something besides resignation in iley's eyes. Still, the question wasn't answered. "Then where ere you? You certainly weren't here."

Riley's natural inclination when shouted at was to snap back. ut he knew that he deserved Jason's upbraiding. "I'm sorry."

Some of Jason's anger cooled. He frowned. "And well you hould be."

Riley turned to face Jason, and for the first time in several

days felt an actual interest stirring within him. "So you'r
dropping out of the council?"

Jason was strongly tempted to do just that, but there wer
reasons not to.

"No. Who's to temper them if I go?" He sighed, reluctantl
agreeing with a point that had been made tonight. "And rule
are needed. As are tax dollars to help do something about th
streets."

He looked down at the mud that was sucking at his boots
It had rained again that day and the streets had suffered for i
The streets of Richmond didn't look like this, nor did Charles
ton's.

"We can't continue having nothing but mud each time i
rains."

"Taxes," Riley repeated. The word was the eternal bane c
all men. "I thought we just finished fighting not to have unjus
taxes."

Jason held up a finger to correct his friend. "We fought nc
to have *British* taxes. These"—he smiled a little at the iron
of it—"are American taxes. Virginia taxes." He pared it dow
a bit more. "Morgan's Creek taxes, meant to help Morgan'
Creek. That *should* make the difference here."

Riley exchanged looks with his friend, the disagreeme
forgotten. "Not to an empty pocket," Riley said philosophi
cally.

Jason laughed shortly. "You're right there. The pocke
doesn't care who has picked it. It knows only that it's empty."
He threw an arm around his friend's shoulders in an eterna
show of camaraderie. "It's up to us to educate them." H
turned toward Sam's Tavern and began to guide Riley towar
the large establishment.

Riley looked at him, gladly matching his steps to Jason's a
they headed toward the tavern. "Meaning the *Gazette*."

"Meaning the *Gazette*," Jason affirmed.

Riley ran a hand thoughtfully over his chin. For the momen
thoughts of Cassandra and unrequited feelings were pushed t
the background. He grinned at Jason.

"I'll be needing a tankard of ale to help me think as I compose."

Jason returned his grin. "I had a feeling that you might."

"Are you buying?"

Jason spread his free hand magnanimously. "I'm buying." He gave Riley's shoulder a pleased quick squeeze. "Welcome back to the living."

Riley laughed as they parted the doors of the tavern and the warm air of closely pressed bodies and stale ale assaulted them.

"It's good to be back."

Chapter Twenty-six

The Widow Watkins's smile quickly disappeared as she closed the door behind the departing Mistresses Andrews.

The skin about her thin mouth felt as if it were stretched to the breaking point. Not that she didn't have anything to smile about. She did. There was a great deal to smile about. Business had never been this brisk before. And, she was certain, it was all due to her new assistant's excellent abilities. Women came to the shop urged on by idle curiosity and remained to place an order for a dress or two once they saw an example of her handiwork.

The widow stopped to fuss with the dress she had hung on the back wall. Cassandra had made it. Things were going splendidly.

"You know, my dear," the widow said cheerfully as she straightened the dolls that the youngest of the Andrews girl had insisted on playing with, "I think you have brought me luck. Indeed, I am sure of it."

The Widow Watkins paused as she righted a doll in a mint green dress. Richard Henry Lee's wife had been in just the past week to order this very pattern. My, my, wasn't *she* coming up in the world, the older woman though with glee.

She turned in Cassandra's direction and picked up a bolt of fabric she had taken out to show Mrs. Andrews. "I never would have imagined that Mrs. Henry Lee would actually place an order for a dress from my shop, what with all those other shops so much more elegant that mine."

A very satisfied smile lifted the corners of her mouth. Coming into one's own was sweet, even if it meant relying upon the abilities of others. Cassandra worked for her. It could be argued that since she paid for them, that made the girl's abilities part her own. So whatever success Cassandra had was hers as well.

"Of course, my shop is closer to her mansion, but then, proximity doesn't do it alone." She lay the bolt aside, then looked at Cassandra. The younger woman was working on a new dress. "But when she told me that Mrs. Jefferson encouraged her to come, why, I . . ."

The widow's words drifted away as she looked at Cassandra's face. Concern nudged triumph aside. "Cassandra dear, are you all right?"

Cassandra thought that she heard a voice calling her by name. It was coming from somewhere far away, as if from the other end of a long tunnel or deep cave. But she could not be sure and, in any event, she was unable to respond.

She was elsewhere.

Her hands had stilled. Her clever fingers had ceased working on the fine green satin dress that was in her lap. Mrs. Lee's dress, which had caused the widow such excitement. As the widow listened closely, it sounded to her as if Cassandra's breathing had become labored, as if she had been running. And her eyes had a strange sheen to them that made the widow feel somewhat uneasy.

"Cassandra, Cassandra dear, are you all right?" she repeated when she received no answer.

The widow placed her hand on Cassandra's shoulder and then shook her ever so slightly, trying to jar the younger woman's attention. It was almost as if it had completely flown from Cassandra's head.

The touch anchored Cassandra and brought her back.

Cassandra blinked and looked up, aware, as she always was

when these moments finally passed, that for however long the vision had overtaken her, she had not been in the present at all.

Her heart was hammering violently, stirred by what she had just witnessed. Cassandra did not have to look into a mirror to know that the color had drained from her face. She was a ghostly pale.

Flustered, the widow tried to think of what to do. "Do you want some water?" She thought of the teakettle on the stove in the back room. There was a little hot water left, she was certain. "Or some tea perhaps? Or would you rather just lie down for a little while?" she suggested hurriedly. A thought struck her in horror. "You aren't ill, are you?"

Rather than acquiesce to any of the suggestions, Cassandra abruptly rose to her feet. At the last moment she caught the dress she'd been working on before it tumbled to the floor.

"No," she answered, paying scant attention to what the widow was saying. "But I need to go to see someone. Quickly."

Then, without waiting for the widow to give her leave or permitting her to ask any more questions, Cassandra swiftly hurried to the door. She stopped only to pick up her shawl from the chair in the corner.

All this was happening too quickly. The widow was slow to react. Belatedly, she followed Cassandra to the door. "Wait, where are you going?"

"I'll be back presently," Cassandra promised. She had no time for idle conversation. Not now. She had to tell Riley before it was too late.

She didn't relish what she was about to do. What she had to do.

The vision had come, as all visions did, unannounced, unexpected. It unfolded vividly before her eyes, blocking out everything else, all sounds, all sights. And what she saw had frightened her. She did not know the exact hour when this would all come to pass, only that it would.

And that Riley needed to be warned.

The thought of Riley had her heart pounding wildly. For a moment Cassandra almost hesitated, fearing the welcome, or lack thereof, that she would receive from him after the way they had parted. But she forced herself on, never missing a step as she hurried across the street.

A carriage rumbled by her, and she moved out of the way before the horse managed to splash her dress. The way Riley had that first morning.

Riley.

Cassandra had not exchanged a word with him since the fateful afternoon by the stream. She had vainly attempted to put that whole experience behind her, regarding it as a misstep. She vowed to forget that it had ever happened.

But she could not forget.

Neither her heart nor her body would let her, even though she knew it would be ultimately better for Riley if she did.

Finally forsaking all endeavor to forget, she selfishly husbanded the memory as if it were some fine, treasured jewel to be retrieved time and again and examined fondly. Examined with love.

Perhaps she would have done things differently. Doubts plagued her as she made her way to the newspaper office, but she had had nothing to guide her, nothing to show her the way. And no experience upon which to draw. Not even a woman she could turn to with questions. One could not ask just anyone about things like this.

There was only her heart.

And now was no time to try to make apologies or excuses. There was not even time to attempt to smooth things over, if her actions had indeed hurt him.

A real and imminent danger involved Riley. Cassandra knew she couldn't hide from her abilities any longer. She couldn't pretend to be an ordinary woman whose only skills lay in her fingers.

The time for pretense was over.

Taking a deep breath, Cassandra knocked once upon the deeply scarred, weathered door and then entered the small newspaper office.

As always, Riley was in the midst of a flurry of activity. There were twenty-one more copies of side four remaining to be printed. His ink-stained hands were wrapped around the lever he was in the act of pulling. Beneath the platen was a sheet of white paper waiting to receive the imprint of the letters he had just freshly inked.

Riley looked over his shoulder when he heard the door, a ready greeting on his lips. It disappeared without a trace. He felt as if his stomach had dropped out as he looked at her.

Sweet God, but she appeared on his doorstep even more beautiful than the last time he had seen her. Her hair had been freshly blown by the wind and there was a slightly wild look in her eyes.

She looked as if she were the product of his imagination, a figment of his dreams, not a flesh-and-blood woman.

But she was. And that flesh was what called to him even then. There was no denying the strong physical attraction that remained between them.

Then his pride swelled, blocking the doorway to his heart as he reminded himself how she had fled from him without a word of explanation. Fled without even once looking back. And in the days that followed, she had not made any attempt to see him.

It was certainly enough to make a man turn his back on a woman.

But in the next instant he saw the concern that was etched so plainly on her face, and all thought of pride and injured feelings turned to dust. This was no time to think of himself. Something was definitely troubling Cassandra. He was not going to discover what by tending to his own wounds.

Riley released the lever and crossed to her quickly. "Cassandra, what's wrong? What's happened? Is it your father?"

She shook her head, fervently wishing there were some other way to warn him. But there was no time. "No, it's you."

Riley stared at her, unable to comprehend what she was telling him. There was no reason for her to look that concerned about him.

"What about me?" And then a smile slid into place as he thought he understood her meaning. "Is it that you've missed me? Is that what you're trying to say?"

Was her tongue tied this way because she couldn't apologize? Was that what had kept her from him these last few weeks? He could understand not being able to apologize. He wasn't very good at doing that himself.

Riley drew closer to her and wiped his hands upon the leather apron tied to his waist. Ever so lightly, he toyed with the end of a stray tendril. She still didn't wear a cap the way so many other young women did. He liked the look of her hair.

"Are you trying to say," he asked in a whisper that trailed along her face, "that I've haunted your mind just the way you've haunted mine?"

"No." When he looked at her like that, she found it difficult to remember why she had come. He had a way of undoing her the way no other ever had. "Although all of that might be true—"

He took the hesitancy in her voice to indicate nervousness. Was she afraid that he would turn his back on her? If so, he would give her reassurances.

"It is for me, Cassandra."

Though his confession touched her and made her feel guilty for the way she had attempted to evade him, she had to press on. His very life might be in jeopardy. That part had been unclear to her. She'd seen the fire.

"Riley, you're in grave danger."

"Danger?" The words were so far from what he had expected her to say that he looked around like a fool, as if that could give him a clue to her meaning. "What danger? What are you talking about?"

She backtracked, realizing that in her agitation she was going too quickly for him to follow.

"That last editorial you wrote." Cassandra stopped to recall the wording. "The one that was critical of men who were too taken up with their own interests to see the common good and so were protesting the intended levy of taxes the council was considering—"

Riley leaned his hip against his desk and crossed his arms before him. He had especially liked the wording he had used in writing that.

He had come to his senses after his talk with Jason and had felt rather inspired. When he had paid attention at the next meeting, he came to understand how necessary certain evils were for the growth of the town. Listening to the talk at the tavern had shown him another side to the problem. Another obstacle, as it were. He felt obligated to show the men in the bar the error of their ways, just as he had erred.

She like the way pride colored his eyes, but now was no time to reflect on that or on the physical attraction that hummed to life each time she looked at him. "Well, it's irritated some."

A good editorial always inflamed a sector of the people. And inspired another. He was used to that. Expected that. "As it should."

He didn't understand, she thought. "It was the final straw. And now they want to do somthing about teaching you a lesson." She pressed her lips together. "They're going to burn the newspaper office."

His eyes narrowed as her words sank in. "Burn the— When?"

Cassandra felt herself tottering on the edge. She was going to have to tell him everything in another moment. "Tonight, I think."

Riley placed his hands on her shoulders, peering into her eyes. He knew there were disgruntled people in the town, people who complained they hadn't fought in the war only to serve another master now. But all that was just talk, angry words over a tankard or two of ale. Who would want to do something so heinous?

"What have you heard?" And how had she gotten access to this kind of information? "For that matter, *who* have you heard?"

Cassandra felt his fingers tightening on her shoulders. She should have waited to compose a lie. But she had been so upset, so frightened for him, she had felt compelled to seek him out immediately to warn him before her courage flagged.

Her eyes met his. "I've heard no one," she answered quietly. Her throat had grown so dry, she could not even swallow.

This he didn't understand at all. He folded his arms before him again, studying her face. "Then how do you know—"

Cassandra took a deep breath, realizing that once she said this, there would be no turning back. She braced herself for the look that she knew would come once this confession was finished.

"Because I saw it. In a vision."

Chapter Twenty-seven

A laugh bubbled up in Riley's throat. Cassandra's simple statement seemed far too fantastic to be true. She was jesting, of course.

The laughter stilled when he looked at her face. She was serious. This was no strange joke she was playing on him. Instead, it bore out what Mrs. Jefferson had alluded to at the party. That Cassandra could "see" things that other people couldn't.

"You're serious, aren't you?"

Cassandra nodded. "Perfectly."

Riley had always tried to keep an open mind about everything. He struggled now to understand what she was saying. More, he struggled to understand *her*. He was Irish and knew such things were possible, but he had never known anyone who was fey and thought it all just talk.

He studied her for a moment. "Cassandra, you've had visions like this before?"

Though she felt it damned her in his eyes, Cassandra was bound to admit the truth.

"Yes." Cassandra turned to look into his face. It was

important that he believe, for his own sake. "And they've always come true."

"Always?" He gave her no clue to what he felt, what he thought of this, as he asked the question.

Her eyes held his. Her heart was still as she waited for a reaction. *Any* sort of reaction. There was absolutely no indication what he thought, what he felt, nothing.

It was as if she were looking at a blank slate.

"Always," she repeated. "Unless prevented."

Another man might have laughed off her claim, even then, calling it a poor jest. But another man hadn't experienced the full depth of her passion. Another man hadn't looked deeply into her eyes and not seen an end. He knew she was incapable of lying.

"I see." He nodded slowly.

She stared at him, unable to fathom that it could be just this simple. "You believe me?"

Riley met her question with another. "Why would you lie?"

It was to his soul she spoke rather than to him. "I wouldn't. Ever."

Yes, instinctively he had known that even before his conversation with Mrs. Jefferson. Riley moved restlessly about the small room, making plans. He thought of the ugliness Cassandra had told him was coming and felt agitation rising within him.

But there was another matter to address first.

"Mrs. Jefferson told me a little about your 'abilities' the night of the party. How you 'saw' that her next child would be born healthy and strong. I thought at the time that you were just being kind to a friend."

Riley paused, knowing that if he watched her eyes when he spoke he would understand things better. "But you really foresaw that happening, didn't you?"

"Yes." Cassandra knotted her hands together before her. "Sometimes I can foresee what people ask of me." She stopped, waiting for the censure to occur, for the disdain to take shape or for the fear to cross his face.

None of it did.

"Have you no names to call me?" she finally asked, unable to stand the tension any longer.

Riley shrugged, his expression completely innocent. "Cassandra."

She regarded him warily, unwilling to rejoice so quickly. Surely he had to have *some* reaction to all this. "No others?"

A smile slowly lifted the corners of his mouth until it was a teasing grin. "Yes, but you'd run if I called you darlin'."

Cassandra let out a breath. He wasn't taking this seriously. He thought she was some addle-brained woman with delusions of grandeur.

"You're making sport of me."

He pushed back of lock of her hair and caressed her face. "No, Cassandra, I would never make sport of you. Especially not after what we shared in the wood." Riley stopped abruptly and studied her. His smile vanished as understanding unfurled within him like a runaway carpet that had been tightly rolled up. "Is that why you ran from me? Because you thought that I would call you names if I learned about your visions?"

He had stepped too close to the truth. Cassandra shook her head. "There's no time to talk of that now." She looked about the small office. The window that looked out on the back needed to be shuttered. "You have to prepare—"

Though he wouldn't run from a fight, the thought of facing his neighbors with a musket did not please him. "I could tell the constable—"

Cassandra's eyes widened. "Tell him what?" she challenged. "That one of the MacGregor women came to you and foretold the future? And you believed her?" Her very tone told him how ludicrous that sounded. "He'd tell you to go home to sleep off the effects of all the ale that you'd imbibed."

She made sense. "All right, I'll spend the night here, then, and defend what's mine."

Riley looked around. The office was spartan in comforts. But he could fix up a pallet for himself with a few blankets from the house.

Defending the office was the only course open to him. But

he would be one against several. Cassandra laid her hand on his arm and arrested his attention. "I'll stay with you."

That was impossible. There was no way he would let her remain with him that night. "Not that I wouldn't like the company, mind you, but if things are to get as heated as you say—"

"There is no *if*," she interrupted. "They *are*." It wasn't as she said, it was as she *knew*.

Her words only reinforced his point. "Then you'd be in danger as well." If anything happened to her, especially on his account, he couldn't bear it. "I really can't allow you to—"

Her expression cut him dead. "Begging your pardon, Riley, but there seems to be some misunderstanding here. I am not a possession that is bound by your command. You cannot allow or not allow me to do anything."

The words rankled him, but they were probably no less than he deserved. Striving for patience. Riley attempted another tact.

"All right, then, what would your father say to your spending the night away from home? And with a man, no less. It just isn't done, Cassandra."

His protests were flimsy. She knew he meant to protect her, but he had no power over her. At least, not insofar as to be able to order her about. His power over her was of a different nature, one she hoped he didn't understand the true extent of.

Cassandra raised her chin. "My father doesn't question what do. He understands that I must go about some things differently than would be normally expected of a daughter."

Even so, Riley didn't want to jeopardize her reputation. Her father might be understanding, but others weren't nearly so generous.

"And if someone were to see you staying the night with me?" he challenged. The gossip, he knew, would stain her permanently.

His concern touched her even as it made her impatient for other reasons.

" 'Tis interested in helping you save the newspaper I am, not in what people will say of me. I told you once, I've heard talk of me before. All manner of talk." She was not aware that her tone had changed, but Riley was. He heard the slight shift, the pain she tried to hide from him. And perhaps even herself.

"And been hurt by it."

Cassandra looked away from his probing eyes. "That is neither here nor there." Her being hurt by slurs was not important. Saving his newspaper was.

He took her hand to make her look at him. "But I am. Here I mean." Didn't she understand that if she remained with him, he'd be too preoccupied with her safety to do anything to save the newspaper office? "And I don't want to worry about you being hurt."

Cassandra laid her hand along his cheek, cupping it fondly. "Then don't worry. I fought beside my brothers in the Highland wars when I was but twelve. I know well how to use a musket."

Another piece of the puzzle she had given him unintentionally. He looked at her in surprise. "I didn't know you have brothers."

She took a breath before she answered, as if that could protect her from the hurt. But it couldn't. It never really could.

"I don't. Not anymore." If she closed her eyes, she could still see Robert and Roy vividly. The way they were when they fell. She kept her eyes open. "They died within hours of each other. I helped my father bury them both."

Riley didn't want her to dwell on anything so painful. There were tears shimmering in her eyes. "Then there's no talking you out of this?"

She slowly moved her head from side to side, her eyes remaining on his. "No."

Seeing the stubborn set of her mouth and knowing he had no power to dissuade her, Riley resigned himself to Cassandra remaining with him that night. Now he had two reasons to defend the newspaper office.

"Stubborn."

She smiled, relieved that he had given in. It wouldn't have mattered if he hadn't. She still would have arrived to help. But this made it easier. "Aye, my father says as the day is long."

He lifted his shoulders and then let them fall dramatically in a movement the widow would have been quite proud of had she executed it herself. Perhaps the raiders wouldn't come and then he'd have her to himself. It had possibilities. "I suppose, then, that it's my misfortune."

"That it is." She allowed herself to laugh at the expression on his face. She wondered if he really understood the full extent of what she had told him. Not about the anger that cause men to whisper about taking up torches, but about herself. She decided that he didn't, but the very fact that he did not look at her as if she were some evil, unnatural creature made her heart glad.

"I'll be back after dusk," she promised on her way out. "Now I've a dress to work on. The Widow Watkins seemed quite agitated that I left her so abruptly."

Cassandra began to weave a plausible excuse to tender to the woman as to why she hurried away. The widow was kind-hearted and would understand if the sudden memory of a deed left undone for her father had made her run off so swiftly, without a word of explanation.

Riley was left to stare at her back and wonder. After a moment he shook his head to clear ir. Had he imagined what he had just told him? Perhaps she wasn't quite real after all, he mused, but someone the angels had kissed.

As he himself had done and longed to do again.

Riley roused himself. If indeed her words were true, then there were preparations to be made.

Cassandra waited until the first long plumes of darkness had feathered along the land. Dressed in the clothing her father had worn when he had cut a more slender form, her hair stuffed into his tricorne hat, Cassandra quickly crossed the street and made her way to the door of the newspaper office. She carried a long, well-bundled item tucked under her arm. There were none about to pay her any mind.

She rapped once and waited. "Riley, 'tis me," she whispered.

The door opened instantly. Riley stared at the young person on the walkway before his office, bemused. He'd thought he'd heard Cassandra calling him.

"I'm afraid I don't—"

Cassandra pushed past him quickly. "I gave your concern more thought. If anyone looked, they saw a boy entering you office, not me."

"A boy bearing gifts?" He eyed the blanket-wrapped article she carried. "If I didn't know any better, I'd say that was a musket."

"Then you'd be right." She laid it down on the table and unwrapped it. " 'Tis my father's."

"We've muskets enough here."

Cassandra turned at the sound of the other voice. Jason stepped out of the shadows. She looked toward Riley in surprise

"I thought we might need the company. And the help."

For a moment she said nothing, wondering if Riley had told Jason everything.

Even with faint moonlight being the only source of illumination within the room, Riley was still able to read her expression

"I told Jason that I had received an anonymous warning that the paper might be attacked tonight because of my very visible connection with the town council." He glanced toward Jason "Seeing as how he's the one who talked me into joining, he feels responsible. He's offered to stand watch with me tonight."

Jason surveyed Cassandra's appearance. It reminded him of the first time he had ever seen Krystyna. She'd been dressed as a boy then, too, for the same reason. To avoid detection. In her case, it had not helped.

Jason moved closer to Cassandra, his voice low. "It's not safe for you to remain here with us, Mistress MacGregor."

"Aye," she agreed. "For the men who will attack." She picked up her father's musket and held it in her hands, her attention turned toward the window that looked out on the street.

"Here, perhaps I'd better take that from you now." Jason reached for the weapon. "You don't want it going off accidentally."

Cassandra retained her hold on the musket. "There'll be no accidents happening, I assure you, Mr. McKinley. It goes off only when I mean it to go off. I've known the way of these weapons since I was ten.'' Her eyes met him, and she saw humor there. But not at her expense. ''And I can shoot it as well as either of you.'' She considered her words a moment. ''Better perhaps.''

Jason laughed softly. After living with Krystyna, nothing about women surprised him. He shook his head and glanced at Riley. ''It seems that you're going to have your hands as full as I, my friend.''

It seemed that to his friend, he and Cassandra were already a set. Too bad Cassandra didn't see things that way, Riley mused. But she would eventually. He'd make sure of it.

Cassandra was no longer listening to either man. She urgently waved for Jason to be still. Though neither man heard a sound, Cassandra had. It was a soft rumble outside the building.

And it was moving ever closer.

Eyes alert, she turned to the men. ''They're coming,'' she whispered.

Chapter Twenty-eight

As he listened, Riley thought he heard something as well. He signaled for Cassandra and Jason to get down. He pulled his musket to him from the table where it lay.

Crouching, all three made their way the window. Riley had purposely left it open in case there was need to fire through it. He wanted there to be no reason to break the panes of glass that were so costly to replace.

He raised his head just enough to see out. Coming straight toward them was a man on horseback, a flaming torch lifted high overhead. Despite the added light, there was no way to see the man's face. It was hidden from view by the sack he wore over his head, the kind that might have been used to transport a small amount of flour from the mill.

The sack matched that on the heads of the two other men running toward the newspaper office, the flames on their torches rising even higher in the wind.

If there were more men, Riley couldn't see them. "Rotten cowards, all," he muttered angrily as he pulled back the firing pin. "Haven't even the courage of their convictions, hiding their faces like common thieves."

Jason measured and fired first, hitting the rider in the shoulder. The man dropped his torch. It fell impotently to the ground. The man screamed in pain and surprise, the sound shredding the night air. With one arm handing limply at his side, he reined in his horse. After a beat, he fled.

The retreat caused his companions to falter for a moment.

"Wonderful shot!" Riley brought his own musket into position as Jason reloaded. He glanced toward Cassandra. "Now you see why I asked him to join me when he stopped by earlier."

"I was aiming for his damned leg," Jason grumbled, unwilling to accept praise under false pretenses. "Not the damned torch."

"Whatever you were aiming at," Riley cried, "I think it accomplished our goal. You've managed to frighten them away."

No sooner had he said that than a torch was flung toward the office. It stopped just short of the door and fell to the ground outside. The flames were almost close enough to catch the walls of the wooden building.

A third torch was on its way, flung by the last man. It was arcing through the air, its aim truer. Cassandra quickly discharged the weapon. The musket ball hit the stem of the torch, altering the trajectory. The torch fell well short of its mark, its flight cut in half.

Riley scrambled out the door. The torch that had fallen before the office had to be smothered before the wind whipped the flames any higher and accomplished for these scoundrels what they themselves could not.

With no time to reload her own weapon, Cassandra grabbed Riley's unfired musket and hurried out after him. Her eyes keen as she looked around, she stood guard as Riley stamped out the fire. A moment later Jason had reloaded and was out beside them.

Faced with imminent defeat, the thwarted arsonists fled into the cover of night, following their wounded comrade rather than risking exposure.

"God damn them, but I wish I had gotten a look at their

faces,'' Riley swore. His boots were blackened with smoldering soot.

Doors around them were suddenly opening as people, roused by the noise, looked out to see what was happening. A few came out belatedly to help. But there was no need for that. Riley had managed to get everything under control.

It could have been a lot worse, he thought, if not for Cassandra. In more ways than one.

It was over much faster than it would have taken time to tell. The whole of it couldn't have taken but five minutes. Five minutes being the difference, Riley realized, between his establishment being turned to cinders or being saved.

Neighbors approached now and questions were coming at Riley from all sides as he and Jason exchanged relieved looks.

Unnoticed, Cassandra quickly slipped into the newspaper office, careful to remain out of sight of the others. She wanted to answer no questions as to why she was dressed in this manner, or what she was doing, standing beside Riley and holding a musket.

Questions always led to other questions, and the fewer asked, the safer her secret.

She pressed herself to the shadows and waited. Eventually, she heard the voices just outside the window slowly begin to fade away. Riley thanked everyone for their concern. Cassandra had heard the deep voice of Constable Browne asking what had happened. Riley gave the man a very abbreviated accounting of the event, with Jason adding in a few words.

As if by mutual silent agreement, neither man mentioned Cassandra's part in any of this.

She smiled to herself, relieved. Then, standing there in the cool darkness, Cassandra sensed things. And came to know more.

Riley had no idea what had become of Cassandra. He hadn't seen her leave. As he spoke to Constable Browne, a tall, powerful bull of a man who had taken up the job of protecting the citizens of Morgan's Creek less than four months earlier, Riley scanned the darkened streets for a sign of her. She had not stepped down to mix with the crowd, nor remained beside him and Jason.

When the crowd, convinced that the excitement was over, dissipated around him, Riley looked at Jason.

"Did you see where Cassandra went?" He retrieved his musket. Hers, he noted, was nowhere to be seen. She had taken it with her and vanished. An eerie feeling filtered down his shoulder blades.

"Not a clue." Rather than step over it, Jason picked up the extinguished torch and handed it to Riley, a souvenir of the thwarted attempt. "Perhaps she went home," he suggested, though with little conviction.

Riley doubted that as well. Cassandra wouldn't just leave without saying so. But for the sake of argument, he nodded.

"Perhaps." He looked around. The street was deserted. The only light of any significance was coming from Sam's Tavern. "As should you. It's my head Krystyna will have for keeping you so late and endangering your very life tonight."

Jason laughed. "The only way I would have been in danger was to have paid a visit to Sam's rooms above the tavern—with a pretty wench in tow. Then my life would surely have been in jeopardy. From Krystyna's wrath. Take care, Riley." Jason looked at the place on the walkway where the fire had managed to eat through before being put out. His expression sombered. "This may not be the end of it."

Riley nodded. "Aye, I know." But there was nothing they could do about it that night. He smiled at his friend. "Good night, and many thanks."

Jason waved away Riley's gratitude. "Anytime. Can't afford to lose the support of the *Gazette*, now, can we?" He grinned as he swung himself into the saddle. "Besides, you've given me a great deal to tell Krystyna tonight when I get home. It's I who should thank you. She loves to hear about adventure."

Riley waited for a moment until Jason had retreated, then walked into the office. He wanted to lock it securely before he left. Anyone with a mind to could easily break in, but it still made Riley feel better to do it nonetheless.

The moment he entered, Riley knew he wasn't alone. He

could hear breathing from the recesses of the room. Not knowing who was there, he raised his musket. It was useless in its present state, save as a club. But the intruder might not know that.

The soft laugh that greeted him had Riley lowering the weapon once more.

"You won't have need of that against me, Riley." Cassandra stepped forward out of the shadow.

Relieved, he let go of the breath he'd been holding. Setting the musket aside, he took hold of her shoulders. "Cassandra, why are you hiding?"

"I wanted to speak to you and I didn't want the others to see me the way I am. One glimpse of me this way and the widow would surely have enough fodder for tales for at least a month, if not more."

He laughed in agreement. "That's true." He thought of the way Cassandra had brought down the torch, and his admiration was renewed afresh. "You were magnificent tonight."

Moved by the moment and the immense relief he was experiencing, Riley allowed himself the luxury of placing his arm around her shoulders and pulling her close. She was soft and supple against him, in direct contrast to the coarse clothing she wore.

"I had no idea you could shoot that well." His eyes swept over her upturned face. What else was there about this woman that he didn't know? "But then, I am learning that you seem to do everything well when you put your mind to it."

A small smile curved the corners of her mouth at his ironic praise. If what he said were the case, she would have been able to maintain the barrier between them rather than let it melt down to nothing, she thought.

But at the moment they faced a more immediate concern than the disintegration of the walls she had erected.

"Riley, you won't be safe until the man who organized this attack on your *Gazette* is arrested and brought to trial."

She was right, but that didn't alter the situation. "There's little chance of that happening. They all escaped, and we didn't see their faces."

He stopped abruptly as he looked at the expression on her face. It told him that there was more to come.

"Or did we?" he prodded.

She didn't know if he was being serious or merely humoring her. In either case, the answer was yes, she had.

"I know who led it," she replied quietly. His face was what he had seen while waiting for Riley to enter. "He's at the tavern now, gone there to mingle with the others." The man was clever, she thought, and brazen to hide in plain sight.

Riley took a guess at who she meant. "The one Jason shot?"

She shook her head. It wasn't he she spoke of, but the other. The man who made her think of a grizzly. "I don't know where he is. But he isn't the one who organized it. Ned Curry is."

Riley could only stare at her in disbelief. "The blacksmith?"

"Aye."

It was true that he and Curry had never gotten along all that well. Their principles clashed whenever they exchanged more than a few words. But still, that was no reason to commit such an act of hate, even over an ideology. Riley could never understand destruction in the name of a belief.

"But why?"

She smiled and suddenly saw the goodness of his heart. He would have probably been affronted at her thoughts at the moment. A man felt threatened if his softer side showed, as if that made him any less a man. In her estimation, it made him more so, not less.

"Because you support new laws and he does not. And he believes that if you were out of the way, perhaps support for the ideas you put forth in your paper would disappear."

Cassandra thought back to what she had heard Curry say in her mind. The words had echoed through her brain like a painful tattoo. "He fought in the revolution and is not afraid to fight again in order to preserve what he thinks he's in danger of losing."

Riley had to admit it sounded like Ned Curry. The man was as loud and as brash as the hammer and anvil that was his stock and trade. And one of the men, the one who had tossed the torch that Cassandra had shot down, had been built like Curry.

Riley felt his blood heating in anger, and he worked hard to control it. If violence begat violence, nothing was gained by it except death. This was a matter to turn over to the constable rather than take it upon himself to exact vengeance.

But it was tempting, Riley thought as he eyed his musket. Very, very tempting.

After a moment his common sense won. He let his anger drain from him with a sigh and saw the worried look upon Cassandra's face recede.

"You know what I'm thinking, don't you?"

No, she could not read minds, not the way he thought. "Not exactly, but I can read your face. It isn't very difficult."

He nodded, accepting her words. He worried his lip a moment. "At the tavern, you say?"

She knew he was going to confront Curry. And knew there was nothing she could do to help. "Yes."

"All right," he made up his mind. "What are we waiting for?"

He took her hand in his and then turned toward the door.

But Cassandra resisted. She couldn't go with him, couldn't point the blacksmith out to the constable. There would be too much to explain.

"Wait, Riley, I can't go with you." He stopped to look at her. "And you can't tell anyone that I was the one who told you about this."

He wanted to protest, but instead nodded, understanding her reasons. This, of course, was going to make it harder for him. But not altogether impossible. Riley didn't pride himself for his wits for no reason.

"Agreed. I'll simply tell the constable I had an informant, one whose name I cannot reveal, but who stood me true."

She knew how that sounded.

"You won't be believed," Cassandra warned him, not as a seer, but as a woman who was intuitive about things that concerned the man she cared for.

He ran his hand along her cheek and smiled into her eyes.

"I'll handle it," he promised. He was reluctant to leave her, but he had to hurry. Time was important. "Wait for me here?"

She nodded. "I'll wait."

It was a promise he meant to hold her to. When this was over, he wanted to have words with her. And perhaps more than that.

Chapter Twenty-nine

Constable Amos B. Browne stood a full five inches ove
Riley. With his shoulders hunched forward, he looked ever
bit like someone's bad dream as he scowled at what Riley wa
telling him. He had had a particularly tiring day and was non
too happy about being asked to abandon his plans for gettin
to bed early.

Browne ran shovellike hands through his thick, waywar
silver hair and shook his head when Riley finished.

"I don't know, boy, this sounds like a lot of confusing tal
to me." He narrowed his eyes as if the gesture would squeez
the truth from Riley. "Why can't you tell me the name of wh
told you about this?"

Browne had never cared for secrets and taking things c
faith. He liked to know exactly what he was getting into eac
and every time. That meant no surprises. And no secrets.

Riley fell back on a common excuse. Where he came fror
informants were people who treasured their anonymity. To c
otherwise meant an early, untimely grave. "Because that perso
is afraid of retaliation."

Long words were not to Browne's liking. They tended t
confuse a man. Short and quick was the way he liked h

nversations. He had no idea what retaliation meant, but
uffed his way through. It wouldn't do to show his ignorance.
"I don't care what's scaring the cowardly devil, he should
me forward."

"He did," Riley answered patiently, hoping his manner
ould nudge the constable into action. "To me. Now, will you
me with me or not? It's precious time we're wasting by
lking here."

Browne placed his hand on Riley's shoulder. "Well, we'll
st have to waste a little more 'precious time' before I go
nning off with you. Or let you go running off by yourself."

The constable cocked his head and studied Riley's face,
tempting to learn the truth of it for himself. He was a fair
dge as far as men went. He'd thought O'Roarke a decent
rt, but you couldn't always tell.

"How do I know this ain't just some idea of yours to get
en with the smithy for some reason?"

Riley thought the constable acted more as if *he* were guilty
something than the men who had tried to set fire to his
fice. "Because," Riley said between gritted teeth, "until this
me to pass, I had no real quarrel with Curry. If you come
th me when I make the accusation, a lot of violence might
averted. I'll have the weight of the law behind me." He
ew well of Curry's quick, black temper. "But whether you
me with me or not, Constable, I'm going."

It was the sincerity in Riley's face that finally won the man
er. The constable removed his hand from Riley's shoulder
d looked at his considerable girth.

"The weight of the law, eh?" The next moment, he laughed.
e laugh was full and rich, echoing into the night. When he
ghed, the towering man sounded like the most affable crea-
re God had ever created. The joyous sound belied the quick
flexes of his hands and the cunning of his soul.

In his two score and ten years, Browne had had many trades.
'd been a sailor for a number of years, then a soldier when
tired of that, as well as a peddler. He had engaged in several
er professions to earn a living he would have just as soon

forget than tell. He had thought being a constable was t
easiest of them all.

Maybe he had been mistaken.

But Browne liked living in Morgan's Creek. The peop
were friendlier than most and Sam at the tavern was alwa
good for an ale or two in exchange for his keeping the peac

The constable hoped that whatever was afoot didn't invol
Sam. He hated when his loyalties were tested. The choice w
never a simple matter.

Browne sighed mightily. He'd rather go along with t
young whelp than be summoned later to pick up his remair
Browne took his hat from the rack as they walked out of t
jailhouse.

"All right, O'Roarke, lead the way." Browne jammed
hat onto his head and willed his tired body out into the nig
once more. "But I warn you, this had better be worth
trouble."

Riley refused to be intimidated by the deep, rumbling voic
"If upholding justice is worth your while, Constable, then t
will be worth your while."

They were at the tavern in a matter of minutes.

When he entered Sam's, an unusual feeling engulfed Rile
This had always been the place to come when he wanted
talk, to relax, to renew friendships and his own spirit. This w
the place to gather the information that was spread across
four pages of his weekly. This was not the place to look
one's enemies.

It was now.

With a guarded glance Riley looked about the large, noi
filled room. He saw one of the girls eyeing him. She lick
her lips provocatively and raised an inquisitive brow, but
shook his head. Undaunted, she turned to another man.

And then Riley saw him.

The blacksmith.

Curry was sitting on the far side of the tavern, a tankard
ale on the table before him. He was alone. Riley scanned

immediate area around the man and wondered who the others that had been with him were. The wounded man obviously could not come here, but that still left the third man unaccounted for.

He was going to have to watch his back, Riley thought. He made certain that the constable was behind him.

Ned Curry worked hard and drank harder. His opinions were loud and vocal and he had never cared who he offended so long as he made his point and got his way. By definition, since he was a blacksmith, he was a large, powerful man. As large in size as the constable was, and, if put to the test, more powerful, for he was younger than Browne by a score and one.

Curry raise shaggy black brows and glared ominously as Riley drew closer to the table. It was no secret how he regarded Riley of late. He raised his tankard in a mock toast, dislike curving his mouth into a snarl.

"Ah, the Tory's here. I guess I'd best be getting on my way. The air has a bad smell."

The din settled as the men around the room ceased their conversations and turned to listen and watch.

There was nothing Riley hated worse than being referred to as a Tory. "I'm Irish, Curry, and you'd be knowing that from the first. And if the air is bad, perhaps you'd be liking to take a bath yourself before making accusations."

The black scowl on Curry's face deepened to the color of storm clouds. "All I know is that we fought to get rid of one blood-sucking breed of men and now you and your like are pushing another on us."

There was no hope of arguing with the man and winning. Even Riley knew when to concede an argument. Curry was too prejudiced to admit that there were two sides to the coin. Besides, he hadn't come to debate. He'd come to point a finger.

"So you decided to burn down my newspaper to put a stop to it."

For a fraction of a moment there was surprise in the man's

small brown eyes. The next moment, mockery had replaced i
He fondled the sides of the tankard.

"I ain't the one, but I wish I were. It's something you deserv
to have happen." He tipped his chair and rocked slightly o
the back two legs, his expression cocky as well as menacing
"Maybe the next time, whoever tries will be luckier."

Browne had no time for this sort of dancing around. H
moved Riley aside with his hand and peered into the black
smith's belligerent face.

"Did you do it?" he demanded sharply. "Did you try t
burn down O'Roarke's place of business?"

It wasn't just the newspaper office Browne was thinking c
now. It was the rest of the town as well. Fires spread, and
took little to wipe an entire town out. He'd seen it before.

Curry righted his chair. "Hell, no, I've been here all along
just nursing this watered-down ale." He peered now aroun
Browne's bulk toward the bar. "Ain't that right, Hadley?"

Riley looked toward the man Curry was addressing. Bi
Hadley was a slight man with hands that seemed expressl
formed for the trade he had chosen, that of cobbler.

The other man, Riley thought suddenly as recognition struc
him. The third man had hung back, as if afraid to join in, afrai
not to. Hadley was a timid sort. And completely under Curry'
domination. He hadn't a thought to call his own.

Hadley glanced up, then looked deep into his tankard, hi
voice skimming along the surface of the untouched al
"Right."

Riley would have staked his life that both men were lying
He looked toward Sam. If anyone could keep ample track c
the ebb and flow of men within the tavern, Sam could. An
did.

"Is that true, Sam?" Riley asked. "Was Curry here a
along?"

"Are you calling me a lair?" Curry roared.

"No," Riley replied mildly. "Just someone unable to te
time. Sam?"

Sam had a business to run. But he also had a conscience t
live with, and customers or not, he lied for no man. He shoc

his head now, aware that all eyes, especially the constable's, were on him.

"Nope." He laid down the towel he'd been using. "Came in after the excitement died away."

Cornered, Curry became even more belligerent. "What does it matter when I came in?" He slammed down the tankard so that the ale splashed up the sides, spilling onto his hand.

They both knew that it was only a matter of time before Curry stood justly accused. Riley pointed to him. "The man who threw the last torch at the office was a big man. Wide. Powerful."

Curry snorted and took a long drink from his tankard. He refused to look at either of them, though they stood only a foot from him.

"Plenty of men who fit that description about." He raised his eyes and looked at Browne. "The constable, for one."

The comment raised Browne's considerable ire rather than his amusement. The matter became more personal. Of the two men, he tended to believe Riley far more readily than he did Curry.

"Do you have anyone to vouch for your whereabouts this last hour, now that it's been established that you weren't here at the time in question?" Browne demanded, irritable over his lack of respect.

"Yes," Riley chimed in as he leaned over Curry, his face inches from the blacksmith's. "The other men who were in the raid. He led it, I tell you," Riley insisted, not bothering to turn toward Browne. He knew his words rankled Curry.

The whites of the blacksmith's eyes all but glowed red as he glared at Riley. "There's no way you can make that kind of an accusation. The men wore hoods—"

Triumph creased Riley's face. "And just how would you be knowing that if you weren't there, as you said?"

"I heard," Curry snapped.

Riley had enough faith in Cassandra to be certain that she was right. The blacksmith was the man responsible for the attack. And more than likely the cobbler was in on it with him, since Hadley was the only one Curry had turned to to confirm his presence.

"Or perhaps you were there yourself?" Riley countered.

Both wide hands spread on the table, the blacksmith rose, his chair crashing to the floor behind him. Malice made his eyes almost disappear as he glared his contempt at Riley.

"If I were, my aim would have been better than just hitting the walkway," he hissed in a low, threatening voice.

"Very accurate description for a man who wasn't there." As far as Riley was concerned, the trap had sprung shut. "There were none about to have seen that but the men who were involved."

Curry wasted no more words. He took a full swing at Riley's jaw. Because the blacksmith's agility was impeded by his size, Riley was able to duck. He swung his doubled-up fists as hard as he could into Curry's jaw, then his wide midsection.

With a strangled curse the blacksmith doubled over. Riley, his hands locked together as one, came down hard upon Curry's neck. The blacksmith fell to his knees, where he remained howling in pain.

"I think if you question him further, Constable," Riley said as he rubbed one hand over his reddened, skinned knuckles, "and perhaps talk to his companion there" —he nodded toward Hadley, who was already backing away from the bar— "you'll get some answers."

The cobbler found his exit barred by Sam, who had stepped out from behind the counter and cornered him, clamping one hand on his collar.

"You'll find that there will be no more buildings burned around here in the name of so-called patriotism so long as they remain in your custody," Riley concluded.

"This wouldn't have happened if you hadn't used your filthy rag as a tool for the rich," Curry spat out as he finally lumbered up to his feet. "You're no better than a damned panderer."

"The just and fair-minded," Riley corrected him. "Not th rich. I'm not rich, and more than likely I never will be. But a least my conscience will be clear."

With that, he stepped aside as Browne collected his charges. "Good night to you, Constable. And many thanks." He nodded at Sam as he left.

The latter nodded at Riley, thrust Hadley toward the constable, and then wiped his hand on his dirty apron.

Chapter Thirty

Though she had given him her word, Riley still wasn't certain if Cassandra would be waiting for him at the *Gazette* when he returned. He still thought of her as elusive, something he had half conjured up in his dreams. There were moments, such as tonight, when she didn't seem real at all.

Just his luck to have fallen in love with a dream, he thought as he approached the darkened building. He held his breath when he raised the latch and opened the door.

Cassandra was there, sitting at his desk. Waiting, just as she had promised. She was bathed in moonlight, her golden hair turned silver as the beams wove through it. She looked like an angel, an angel in men's rumpled clothing.

She had turned toward the door when she heard it open. There was an odd expression on his face she couldn't fathom. Had something gone wrong?

"Riley?"

The sound of her voice was like a celestial melody and succeeded in rousing him so that he came to himself.

"Hmm?"

She was worried now, though there had been nothing to warn

her of things going awry. "What's the matter? Why are you just standing there?"

As if he were just then waking up from a deep sleep, Riley moved toward her, his stride eating up the distance between them slowly until he reached the desk. He smiled down into her face, her wonderful, captivating face.

"I was just looking at the most beautiful sight I've ever seen."

Relief and humor curved her mouth until she smiled. "An editorial with your name above it," she said with a soft laugh.

"No, a woman who is more like pure starlight in my hands."

Needing to touch her, he feathered his hands along her hair. It fell like silver rain from his hands. "Like pure starlight," Riley murmured again, completely fascinated by her.

Cassandra leaned into his hand, luxuriating in the comfort of the familiar touch. "Not quite starlight." She straightened, then looked up at him. "How did it go?"

He didn't want to talk of blacksmiths with hate in their souls or even of plans mercifully thwarted. He wanted only to be with her, absorb her, smell her. Touch her. He wanted to fill himself with her until he no longer existed and she had taken over the whole of his soul.

But he owed her an answer at the least.

He owed her a great deal more, he thought before replying, for she had woken up a portion of him he had not known existed.

"Curry and his companion, Hadley, are cooling their heels in the jail." He smiled at her. "Thanks to you. Browne has them under lock and key until such time as the magistrate comes through."

"Curry confessed?" She tried to keep her mind on his words and not give herself to the sensations building within her, the sensations that had nothing to do with a civilized conversation and everything to do with desire and fulfillment.

The blacksmith would have sooner roasted in hell than admit anything. "No, but Hadley did." He thought of the hate he had seen in Curry's eyes when Hadley had whimpered out his story. "I hope for his sake, Browne finds a way to keep them separated, or else Curry'll kill Hadley with his bare hands."

"And the third man?"

" 'Tis only a matter of time before Browne gets that from Hadley as well."

Riley grew impatient with the subject. He had no idea how much longer Cassandra could remain with him and he did not want to waste a moment of it talking about Curry or jails. "I owe you a great deal."

She lifted her shoulder and then let it drop. "It was nothing."

He placed his hands on those same shoulders, refusing to let her trivialize what she had done. "It was everything. As are you." He lowered his mouth to hers. "To me."

Cassandra turned her head, bringing a halt to the kiss before it flowered. She heard his frustration as Riley exhaled.

"I think," she began slowly, measuring her words carefully, "that it is time to tell you of many things, Riley. Of the way it is with me." She raised her eyes to look into his. "And mine."

Riley dropped his hands to his sides, releasing her. "All right. I'm listening."

Having his attention did not make what she was about to say any the easier for her. Cassandra searched for words that were not painful and found none.

She looked at him helplessly. "I don't know how to start."

He had never seen her like this before, so vulnerable, so unsure. His heart went out to her and he wished nothing more of life than to protect her from harm and the things that brought her sorrow.

Riley took her hand in his, giving her his strength and his patience. And with them, his heart.

"From the beginning, Cassandra. Begin at the beginning."

She smiled sadly, grateful for what he was attempting to do. The beginning took place years before she was even born.

"The very beginning would be boring to you." So saying she dismissed it. "I will tell you that it wasn't my father's declining trade that brought us here, although it had waned a little in the twilight of the war. But it was still healthy enough to keep us well housed, clothed, and fed. And an apprentice busy as well.''

With all her heart she wished she did not have to continue. She feared what was at journey's end for her. She feared Riley's rejection.

''Rather than a reversal of business, it was a man named Simeon who forced us to leave everything behind and flee as if we were but beggars into the night.''

Riley listened in silence, confusion and surprise drifting over his face.

Cassandra stared at the floor, remembering and not wanting to. ''Simeon wanted me to be his wife.''

''And you didn't want to be,'' he guessed.

MacGregor didn't strike him as a man who would force his daughter to marry against her will. This had to be about more than a rejected suitor.

''No, I didn't.'' She slowly shook her head.

Despite his wealth, marriage to Simeon would have been horrible. She had no need of her abilities to know that. Simeon was as cruel and ruthless as he was handsome. And unaccustomed to being refused. Ever. He had pursued her relentlessly for six months, showering her with attention and gifts, both for herself and her family. When he finally proposed, he was momentarily struck dumb when she said no. But he continued to ask.

''When I repeatedly rejected his proposal, he threatened me. He said if I did not marry him, he would say horrid things about me that people would believe because they were sowed in truth. That he would make things very ugly for my family as well as for me. I couldn't let that happen. I could bear it for me. I couldn't for them. It wouldn't be fair. I couldn't bear the shame for them.''

Riley didn't understand. ''How would he expose you? What would he say?'' It made no sense to him. ''What had you done?''

Even as he asked, he knew it did not matter. Not to him, even it if did to her. He cared for her, for the woman he had

held in his arms, and nothing she had to say would change
that.

"Done?" she echoed, an ironic smile curving her mouth.
She raised her eyes to his and he saw no humor there, no
amusement. There was only the sadness of the betrayed. "I'd
helped cure a few people and found a man lost in the hills so
that his wife would not be a widow and his children not be
bereft." She worked to still the anger within her breast. "Not
much of an offense, is it?"

He shook his head, waiting for the rest of it, for the heart
of the matter that plagued her so.

Cassandra lifted her chin. "As to what he would have said,
he was prepared to announce to one and all of my neighbors
that I was a witch, as a great many of them had come secretly
to believe. And fear. I had heard their whispers when I passed.
If Simeon had said it, it would have been so. My father ruined,
my sisters besmirched."

Riley could only stare at her. His heritage and upbringing
were rich in tales of druids and fairies, with an occasional witch
or two, but that was for children and the feebleminded. Not
for enlightened adults.

"A witch?" he whispered in disbelief.

She nodded. She could still hear Simeon's voice ringing in
her ears. *Marry me, Cassandra, or I swear I'll ruin your father
and you. They'll call you witch and burn crosses before your
home. Burn you if they're brave enough.*

"Aye."

He had never heard of anything so foolish. "But that's ridiculous."

The smile she wore had no humor behind it. "Not to those
who did not understand my ways. And there was a sickness
that came, an epidemic I had no way of curing. Twelve people
died. Simeon was prepared to say they died because of me."

Her smile became genuine as she looked at Riley. He was
pure of heart so he could not comprehend all this.

But there were others not so pure. "It is easier to believe in
evil, to have fear than to think." She moved about restlessly,
as if to escape the memory. "What people do not take the

trouble to understand, they often fear. As they had already begun fearing me.''

Riley struggled to understand, to separate fact from fiction about the woman before him. She was no witch, but though mortal, she was not ordinary either. ''But you do have a power.''

More accurately, it had her. Taking a breath, she began to explain. ''I am a seer. That means—''

He wanted to spare her at least a little of the agony she was so obviously going through. Riley raised his hand, stopping her words.

''I know what that means.'' Then, to prove it, he added, ''That visions come to you at times. Of both the past and future.'' It made things a great deal clearer now, he thought. It explained how she seemed to know things she had no way of knowing. ''As they did today about the blacksmith's planned attempt.''

Cassandra strained to hear a hint of revulsion or distancing in his voice. Even when Simeon had discovered her ability, there had been a certain look in his eyes, as if she were not quite human. It had not been enough to drive him off, but only because he had wanted to use her abilities in some way. As he used everything and everyone who crossed his path.

But she detected none of this in Riley.

Her eyes on him, she watched for some sign to reveal to her how he was really reacting to this information she gave him. Her sight was no help to her in this matter. It was far too personal. If insight came, it came on its own, not because she could summon it.

''Aye, as with the blacksmith.''

But that told him only half the story. ''And the healing?''

She shrugged. That was something else entirely. It was not part and parcel with the Sight.

''That you should know from Rachel. It's a matter of knowledge being passed on from mother to daughter over generations.'' Her voice grew tired, as if she had been defending this very thing for a long time. ''If I've skills, they, too, are inherited. Like the visions, I cannot deny them any more than I can deny my own family.''

He gathered her in his arms, though she tried to fend him off. But he sensed that she needed him more than she understood herself. He would not be pushed aside. "No one is asking that of you."

His voice was calming, his arms strong. The tension left her body. "But to use my skills—all of them—singles me out to be different." It was a dilemma she saw no resolution to.

Riley smiled at her choice of words. "You *are* different." He felt her stiffening, but would not release her. Instead, he pressed her closer. "A wonderful different. You would have been different, Cassandra, without all these trappings and skills you have been vested with."

She shrugged off his words, if not him. "You say that only because you . . ." Her voice tailed off.

So she knew, he thought. She had only to admit it. "Yes?"

Cassandra could not look into his eyes. Guilt was wafting through her. She had doomed him as she had doomed her family, just by being, to endure the disdain of others by association.

"Because you love me." She whispered the words so softly, he had to strain to hear.

But hear he did. "Aye, I do." He crooked his finger beneath her chin and lifted it until her eyes were level with his. "And you?"

She saw her own soul, trapped in his eyes, and knew her fate.

"I don't want to," she said hoarsely.

He smiled at that, knowing he had won. But she needed to say it aloud. He needed to hear it at least the one time. "I did not ask what you wanted or did not want. I asked what you felt."

She swallowed and took a deep breath. The words came out in an uncustomary rush. "Aye, I love you, Riley O'Roarke, and you shall rue the day I said so."

He tried not to laugh. "If that was a vision, Cassandra, I think, in this case, your vision is a wee bit obscured." He framed her face with his hands. Desire pulsed through his body. "Must I bring you home right away?"

She could feel her heart as it began to pound. "My father does not expect me back for a long while. I told him that you needed my help."

Her words amazed him. What manner of family were they? Seer or not, if she were his daughter, he would not let her out of his sight.

"And he accepted that?"

She heard the wonder in his voice, and smiled. "He knows what it means to have a seer in the family. His grandmother was one. As was his mother." She recalled the early days of her youth, before the world with its harsh realities had intruded so violently. "All the people of the village would come to them to ask for help."

He slipped his hands from her face and held her lightly in his arms, content to remain just so for hours to come. "Was it that way with you?"

"A little." It had begun with her, under her grandmother's tutelage. "But we left when I was twelve." Her voice became stoic. "Shortly after we'd put my two brothers into the ground. And two uncles as well."

Riley nodded. He knew what it was to flee one's own country and leave behind loved ones in graves. "You mentioned the Highland wars."

That was too pretty a name for them, she thought.

"Feuds were more like it," she said, cutting him off before he could ask any more. "Feuds that had a beginning lost in time. No one knew why they were. They just were." She strove to keep her bitterness in check. None of it should have been. "After losing Robert and Roy, my mother begged to leave before the bloodshed claimed my father as well."

"Was that when you came to New York?"

"Aye." She sighed. All that seemed so long ago. And yet it was removed only by the blink of an eye. "My father had a cousin there. We had to move once because I, in my innocence, thought that all would welcome my help. I was to learn differently. Witch, they called me. Some in jest, some in fear." Her mouth hardened. "All references were unwelcome. So we left, and settled in New York City proper. And I tried not to let too many know of what I could do. Only those that really needed help.''

It all became clear to him now. ''So that was why you looked at me so strangely when I said that you had bewitched me.''

She hated the very sound of that word. She always would. ''Aye.''

He looked down into her face. ''It still doesn't change the fact that you had. And have. And do.''

Before she could protest his words, he gathered her into his arms and kissed her.

Chapter Thirty-one

Just as before, she knew it would happen.

Just as before, she was unprepared. Not for the deed itself, but for what came before it. And in its wake.

The magnitude of not only the passion that Riley had for her, and she for him, but the tenderness as well overwhelmed Cassandra completely.

She had but to be with him to know that he was a rare man. Her comfort, her pleasure, her very happiness seemed to be his only concern.

As indeed it was.

Cassandra cleaved to Riley because of this. And because she could not stand another moment without being with him. Without tasting his mouth, hot and ripe upon hers. Without feeling his touch, by turns reverent and insistent, as it slid along her body. His fingers sought out places they already were familiar with, seeking to renew the joy of contact.

All this and more, she craved. Her body, like a temple where treasures had been hoarded all these many years, had its doors thrown open.

And he was at the gates.

The cry of sheer rapture that welled up within her throat was

muffled against Riley's mouth as she felt him begin to reliev
her of the confinement of her garments.

She could feel his smile against her mouth as the oversize
vest she had donned earlier fluttered to the wooden floor.

A smile to match his rose to her lips as she asked, "An
what is it that you're smiling at?"

He recalled the frustration of attempting to undress her b
the stream. "I have far better luck removing men's clothing.

Even as he spoke, the shirt she wore was being drawn fro
her shoulders. She stood in but her chemise, while Riley bega
to divest her of the britches she wore. She watched his hand
as amusement warred with the growing flames of desire.

"I can see that. Indeed, your speed seems to be great."

"As is my need for you, Cassandra," Riley assured her. H
stopped for a moment then, just to look at her face. And fa
in love all over again. "As is my need for you," he repeate
softly. "I can't begin to tell you how much you've haunte
me."

There was no need to tell.

"I know," she murmured.

With hands that were far more steady than the feeling tha
trembled within her, Cassandra began to mimic Riley's move
ments and remove his clothing from him.

She was woefully behind. When he had her down to he
undergarments, Cassandra was only now attempting to und
his britches.

"Here," he urged, his hands covering hers, "let me help.

"No," she breathed as she moved them aside. "I can manag
myself." Her eyes held his for a heartbeat, hers thundering
her chest. "But I can manage better if your hands did not roa
about my body so."

"Sorry." He shook his head, but the look upon his face sa
he was not sorry at all. "They seem to have a mind of the
own around you."

As if to prove it, Riley spread his palms ever so lightly ov
the delicate expanse just above her breasts. He felt the ve
breath within her stop, then resume, now more quick tha
before.

Excitement flared through him, just as the fire had threatened to flare through the room earlier. He could not take his eyes from her.

With renewed determination Cassandra slowly opened his britches. With them loosened, she placed her hands upon his hips to urge the clothing from him. Inch by torturous inch, it moved down until it finally found its way to the floor beside her own.

Restraint was shredded as Riley's breathing became more labored. Desire heated his blood as wanting her made it almost unbearable for him to remain where he was. What he really wanted to do was sweep her into his arms and take her, now, without a thought to anything else.

Cassandra smiled as she saw that he was as much in her power as she was in his. Equal, she thought, they were equal now. She wanted nothing more than to be equal with him, to please him as he did her, to create excitement within him as he created it within her.

It took every ounce of his restraint not to tear the remaining pieces of clothing from her supple, tempting body. A body warmed with passion and promise.

The chemise strap nearly snapped in two beneath his questing hands as he finally denuded her completely. The material sighed away from her skin. The next moment he covered the tempting swell with an array of kisses meant to keep her warm.

He succeeded all too well.

Cassandra felt herself on fire. She grasped for his shoulders, wanting to hold him tightly to her. Wanting to feel his body move along her skin.

Their lips feverishly slanting against one another, they sank down onto the pallet Riley had meant to use that night as he kept watch over his *Gazette*.

Now it had another use.

Cupping her head with his hand, he lowered her to the floor, his mouth never ceasing its assault. In one fluid movement his body covered hers. And she welcomed it.

As their bodies entwined, a madness overtook Cassandra. It

made her want to cry, to call out his name, to sob in shee
delight for the whirlwind she felt growing within her.

It consumed her as it enriched her.

She felt like a child being led, she felt like a woman wh
had captured the quarry she sought. A hundred sensations al
opposite to one another battered her body. She was both weal
and strong, humbled and proud. Cassandra felt herself to b
all things at once.

Because of him.

Because of the velvet mouth that stroked her body in kisse
both tender and passionate. She was almost wild with desire

And still he held off bringing her to the end. Tempting her
driving her. Making her hold on to to her sanity with bot
hands.

Making her let go.

This, she knew, she could not have foreseen, even thoug
she had known in her heart from the moment she had first see
Riley that he was her destiny.

And always would be.

Things that concerned her privately she had only hints of
It was as if she could see shadows upon the wall and coul
not see the faces of the people they belonged to.

Though it was cool both without the small office and withi
the small room, with no fire in the hearth, a fine sheen of swea
covered Riley's body. It mingled with Cassandra's.

His heart raced as he explored and reexplored her body
watching in fascination as she turned and twisted beneath hi
hand. He felt himself come ever closer to the brink.

When he could withstand the tantalizing call of ecstasy n
more, Riley raised himself on the palms of his hands and looke
down into Cassandra's face. Her hair was fanned out like
silvery halo upon the dark blanket, and her eyes were smok
from wanting him. She held his soul in the palm of her delicat
hand.

Yes, he could see why some would call her a witch, for ther
was magic about her. Magic and an ethereal aura that he ha
only begun to penetrate.

She had imprisoned his heart by doing no more than being. He knew he was no longer free and would never be so again.

Riley brushed away the wayward hair from her cheek. He thought of the last time. "I don't want you fleeing me again, Cassandra."

Slowly, she moved her head from side to side. The time for leaving him had passed. The time for leaving her might still be ahead for him, but she tried not to think of that. It would only make her grieve.

"Never again," she whispered, her words gliding seductively along his face. "I am yours for as long as you want me."

She meant it, he thought. He would have known if she lied. "Then you are mine forever, for I will never let you go. I will never tire of you." It was not an empty promise, but a vow.

Though she could not see the future in this instance, she could sense his sincerity and let that guide her. "Perhaps not, but it is not just me that you have gained in all this."

She was speaking of her family, he guessed. That went well with him. "It has been a long while since I had any more family than Rachel. I welcome your father and sisters into my life as well."

That wasn't what she had meant, though it was nice to know that he regarded them so well.

"And the ridicule when it comes? And the vilifications?" She shifted uncomfortably. "How will you welcome that?"

If she meant to frighten him away, she failed. "There might not be any."

Her smile was sad. He was wrong, she thought. "You have a happier view of people than I."

He considered her words. "Perhaps I have more reason to. But whatever happens, Cassandra"—he looked deeply into her fathomless eyes—"you are mine and I am yours. I shall never allow you to shut me out again."

Unable to resist him any longer, Cassandra twined her arms around his neck, bringing his mouth closer to hers. "You will regret this, Riley."

As she said it, she feared that it was a prophesy.

No matter what she believed, he refused to be shaken by it.

Refused to be driven away from her now that he had finally gotten her to admit her feelings for him.

"Only as I regret breathing."

Riley lowered himself a fraction, so as only to sample her mouth, not to take her just yet. This was something he held in abeyance, like a gift to be savored and looked upon before opening.

He skimmed his mouth over hers, at first a little, then more fully with each pass, until he lost himself in the joy of that.

Desire bloomed. Ecstasy danced just out of reach, tempting them to come just a little further, and then further still.

Riley resisted for as long as he could, for both their sakes. And when the last shred of willpower had ebbed from him, he entered her.

And felt himself being renewed once more. Felt himself being made whole again.

The same rhythm seized them. It was the same as the first time, yet new and different.

As it always would be, Cassandra realized as she rushed to take the precipice with him once more. Until he tired of her.

Until their life together became too difficult for him to bear.

But all that was for later.

Now there was only he, only the ecstasy that he produced. And the music that only he could create for her.

She danced to it until the thundering explosion came, racking them both, and they both fell back to earth. Sated, exhausted.

Contented beyond all manner of belief.

And in love.

Chapter Thirty-two

Though her mind told her a relationship of any sort with Riley would not be wise, Cassandra's heart told her differently. They had crossed a chasm together, she and Riley, and a relationship began to form and grow whether she believed it to be wise or not.

She loved him.

It was a simple enough matter, and there was no denying it, for it was true. She loved him for so many reasons, they were almost impossible to count. One of the foremost was that he accepted her the way she was, not the way he wished her to be.

She had bared her soul to him, and he had not flinched, not backed away. The true test, standing beside her while she faced public denouncement, still lay somewhere in her future and would be the deciding factor of his love for her. But for now she took comfort in the fact that he had not turned away from her.

He accepted her.

It came at a time when she needed it most. A time when she discovered that though she was strong, had always *been* strong, it comforted her to know she had someone upon whom to lean. Cassandra had never had that luxury before.

Her father's mind had begun to wander more frequently again. It took him down paths away from life, away from sorrow, to where he might visit and revisit with his dead sons and wife. And his brothers, all gone as well. Visit with them and not feel the pain of their loss.

At times he'd sit for hours, gazing into the distance while his hands remained idly wrapped about a tool. At other times, only minutes would pass before he was himself once more.

But the work fell behind, and with it, the money they would yield. The rent on the shop had come due, and there was not enough put away to pay Sam, even with Cassandra's earnings. The man accepted their excuses and said he would wait a little while more.

But Cassandra knew it would not be that much longer before Sam would have to make his demand more firmly, with consequences if there was no payment. And her father had slipped away again just yesterday. He didn't seem to know his daughters and merely smiled at the sound of their voices, giving no answer.

As with each time before, Cassandra, Brianne, and Rose could only pray that it would not last and that they would be given their father again. But each time it happened, the panic would grow a little faster, the worry become a little more intense.

Brianne and Rose had found their father this way when they woke up. There'd been no change. It was just as they had left him the night before. Sitting by the window, looking out into the sky above.

Upset, Brianne had pulled Cassandra over by the hand to look at their father, as if Cassandra were not already aware of the situation.

"Isn't there something you can do?" Brianne hissed, fear heightening her impatience with her sister, with the frustration of seeing her father this way and not being able to reach him. She fisted her hands at her waist, a sharp demand in her voice. "With all those powers of yours?"

"Hush," Rose chided. She glanced at her father, hoping the raised voices hadn't upset him. But there was no sign that he had even heard. It didn't diminish her annoyance with Brianne's insensitivity. "Don't you think if she could, she would?"

Brianne looked torn between shame and fear. "I know, it's just that . . ." Her voice trailed off, as she was unable to put her concern into words.

She didn't have to. Cassandra understood. "I know." She placed a comforting arm around Brianne's shoulders. "We all feel that way."

Brianne thought of the unfinished furniture below. Everything remained idle when her father was like this. Despair filled her.

"But what's to become of us, Cass? What if he doesn't come out of it this time? What if he remains this way? Who'll work the shop?"

Cassandra had already thought of that. She had no answers to what the future held for her father, no crack in the wall to give her even a glimpse of what was to be. So she had done the only thing she could think of. "I've sent for Dennis Cooper."

The other two girls looked at each other, completely taken by surprise.

"Dennis Cooper?" Rose echoed. "Da's apprentice at the old shop?"

Cassandra nodded. Rose's heart fluttered nervously in her young breast. She had nursed a secret crush for the man for the two years he had worked with her father. She tried not to smile at the news, but think of what it meant to the family.

"But I thought no one was to know where we've gone to. If Dennis knows—"

"Then Simeon will," Brianne concluded, her eyes on Cassandra. "Simeon has a way of finding out everything. He'll come here for you." Distress for her sister bloomed in her face.

Cassandra shook her head. "I've asked Dennis not to say anything to anyone. He has no family. It would be a very simple matter for him to come here and join us. He can work for Da like he used to." She attempted to feel as confident as she sounded. "At least, we can hope," she added quietly.

There was no time to discuss the subject any further. "I have to go. I'm late as it is. The widow isn't paying a good wage to stand and talk to my sisters, and we need every ha'penny I can earn."

So saying, she kissed her father's brow. He gave no sign he was even remotely aware of her nearness. With a heart that was heavy, she kissed each girl in turn and forced herself to smile, for their sakes.

"Don't worry, it'll all be well," she assured them briskly. "See if you can encourage him to come down to the shop with you later. Perhaps the sight of his work will move him as it did the other time."

But failed the time before that, she thought sadly.

Taking up her furred wrap, Cassandra left and hurried down the narrow wooden stairs. Her heels clattering on each step. The sun had yet to rise in the sky, but her day was already under way.

It was good to work with her hands, she thought. There was not the satisfaction that she felt when she managed to cure someone, but she was not drained either. Dressmaking required little more of her than a keen eye and a steady, neat hand. It did not take anything away from her soul.

But the rewards were not as rich either.

When she arrived at the widow's shop, the door was suddenly flung open. It was as if the widow had been standing in wait for her just behind it and had been alerted by the sound of her footsteps.

The woman looked all aflutter with news that dearly wanted to leave her busy tongue.

"Is something wrong?" Cassandra asked. For a moment she thought she saw concern in the small brown eyes, but then realized that it was merely the flicker of rampant curiosity.

"I am sure I do not know." The widow took hold of Cassandra's arm and all but dragged her into the shop. "I was almost going to come for you myself," the widow burbled. "There's a messenger waiting for you."

"Messenger?" Looking beyond the tall woman, Cassandra

aw an equally tall youth standing within the shop. There was
letter clutched in his hand.

"Mistress Cassandra MacGregor?" he asked as he stepped
orward.

"Of course it's Cassandra," the widow told him impatiently.
'Would I be pulling her toward you if it wasn't?"

"I'm Cassandra MacGregor," Cassandra assured the youth
oftly.

With a subservient smile the young messenger handed a
etter to her.

As Cassandra turned it around, she saw that the letter had
efferson's seal upon it.

A premonition flittered through her, and she felt as if she
ad just touched death. The way she had felt when she had
ouched each of her brothers. The day they were to die.

The widow hovered over Cassandra's shoulder, eager to
iscover what all this was about. She spoke of the youth as if
e were not even in the room.

"He said that Mrs. Jefferson directed him to the shop, for
he wasn't certain where it was you lived."

Cassandra hardly heard a word the woman was saying as
he opened the envelope. A shaky hand had written the words
a the short letter. Mrs. Jefferson was ill and entreating her to
ome.

"Well, then, you must go," the widow announced with
nality. She was too excited to even pretend to wait for Cassan-
ra to read the words aloud. She had already done so herself,
ooking over her shoulder.

Cassandra looked down at the letter in her hand, torn. How
ould she leave her father like this?

"But—"

The widow would brook no excuses. "My dear, when some-
ne as important as the Jeffersons summon you, you cannot
efuse to go." She frowned, confused. "Buy why would Martha
efferson require a new dress to be made if she is ill?"

Placing herself at the center of all this had confused the
idow, Cassandra thought with a touch of fondness. " 'Tis not
e dress she requires," Cassandra murmured. " 'Tis me."

The widow cocked her head as she peered at Cassandra studying her with no small measure of curiosity. There was still not that much she knew about Cassandra. Not nearly as much as she wanted to know. For all her ability and cheeriness the girl was maddeningly closemouthed.

"Why?"

Cassandra knew that tone. It was one that meant to pry into regions that Cassandra had no intention of letting the woman enter. She'd sooner take out an advertisement in Riley's paper announcing herself as a seer than tell the widow anything further about the matter.

She folded the letter and glanced at the youth, who stood waiting on her reply.

"You are right, madam. There's no time to waste. I shall pack immediately. I need to go tell my sisters where I'm bound." She paused only to consult with the messenger. "You are to come with me?"

The youth nodded. "Mr. Jefferson told me not to return without you."

"Then you won't," she told him simply. She motioned for him to follow. "Come, I live but a few steps away from here."

With no more thought to the widow, Cassandra hurried out the door. The widow stared after them, stunned at being abandoned in this manner.

"Well, I never," she murmured with a shake of her head. Disappointed, she closed the door.

Riley was just inserting the key into the lock of his door when he saw Cassandra hurrying from the dressmaker's shop to the stairs that led to her home. There was a youth following in her wake whom Riley didn't recognize at all. Pulling his key from the lock, Riley hurried down the walkway and across the street.

He caught up to Cassandra just as she gained the top of the stairs.

"Cassandra," he called up to her. When she turned to look

at him, he asked about the first person who came to mind. "Is it your father?"

She shook her head, unlocking the door. "No, it's Mrs. Jefferson."

Riley took the stairs two at a time. He glanced at the messenger when he reached the landing. "Mrs. Jefferson? Here?" He thought he had heard from Jason that the Jeffersons were spending the latter half of the year at their home.

The house was empty. Obviously the girls had succeeded in getting their father to go downstairs. Whether that meant he had come back to himself or had mutely followed them she did not know.

She hurried to the back, where she slept with her sisters and kept her few possessions.

"No, at Monticello."

Without turning to look at Riley, she took a battered saddlebag from beneath her bed. Tossing it on the bed, she opened the drawer she claimed as her own in the chest her father had made for the three of them. She withdrew a few articles and hastily folded them into one side of the saddlebag. The other side she left empty for her medicines.

"I'm to go to her."

He watched as she packed, confused. The messenger Jefferson had sent tactfully remained at the door. "But why?"

"She is gravely ill and wants me." As an afterthought, Cassandra handed Riley the letter she had let fall on the bed.

Riley scanned the letter quickly, then handed it back to her. "How long will you be gone?"

She looked up at him. Again the premonition swept over her even as she packed that she would be too late. But she tried not to dwell on it. Perhaps it was just her concern tainting the picture for her.

"I don't know."

He realized then that she had no way of knowing what she was facing. But he wasn't about to let her face it alone. "Then I'll go with you."

The declaration took her by surprise. "You've a paper to run."

Until two months earlier he would have said that the *Gazette* was the most important thing in his life. But no more.

He moved until he was standing before her. "I've my life to run as well, and you are a part of it. A very large part of it. I cannot allow you to go off like this by yourself."

She looked across the room at the lanky youth. He returned her smile shyly as he shifted from side to side.

"I won't be alone," Cassandra said to Riley. "I've company."

She was not about to talk him out of this. He had made up his mind. The youth looked hardly capable of taking care of himself, much less Cassandra, if anything were to befall them.

"Then you shall have more. The *Gazette* can wait." It might even make the people look forward to it all the more if it were to be a day or so late this one time. Or more.

She had no fear of traveling about with just the youth for protection, or even by herself for that matter. Cassandra had never been afraid to be on her own. It was her family she was concerned about. Riley could render her a better service remaining with them.

She frowned as she laced one side of the saddlebag closed. "I would rather that you look after my sisters, Riley."

He saw no reason to be concerned about the girls. "Your father—"

She cut him off, sorrow thick in her voice. "Is not well again." She shut the other side of the saddlebag.

He understood. Riley had seen the vacant look that came over Bruce MacGregor's face at times. At first he thought the man had visions, like Cassandra. But Cassandra had explained that it was an overpowering grief that took him away and made him drift to places where the pain could not find him.

Riley had a solution for the problem. "I shall send a note to Jason. Christopher would be more than willing to remain here at the *Gazette* and look in on your family." He smiled "He's become very taken with Brianne."

The mention of the pairing made Cassandra smile widely Brianne had worked long and hard to make the relationship evolve to this point. "Yes, I know."

That was one thing off his mind. He no longer had to worry about Christopher turning his attention to Cassandra and causing a possible rift in his friendship with Jason. "I have great hopes for that."

Cassandra laughed, thinking of her sister. "As does she."

He nodded, withdrawing. "It'll take me but a moment to pen the letter to Jason and be ready."

There were only a change of clothing and some supplies to take. Since Cassandra had packed a saddlebag and not anything else, he assumed they would be traveling on horseback. The thought did not fill him with cheer, but there was a great deal he was prepared to endure for Cassandra's sake.

Riley turned at the door. Cassandra, he realized, hadn't said a word to his statement. "You'll wait?"

She nodded. "I'll wait. You'll find me in Da's shop when you're done."

He hesitated at the door, then, on a whim, retraced his steps to her. As she raised a quizzical brow at his return, he brushed a kiss against her lips.

"I'll hurry," he promised, leaving.

Chapter Thirty-three

Though the letter to summon Cassandra had been sent bu
two days ago, and they rode quickly, by the time she and Riley
reached Monticello with the messenger, Martha Jefferson ha
died.

The sorrow that greeted them as they rode up to the beautifu
Roman-style mansion that Jefferson had fashioned and the deli
cate young matron had loved so dearly was all-encompassing
and overwhelming.

Everyone had loved the mistress. And now with her gone
everyone was deeply worried about "Mist' Thomas."

Cassandra looked around her as they approached the man
sion. She could feel the grief coming up in waves. The eye
in the faces she looked upon in the fields as they went by wer
swollen from weeping at their mistress's passing.

Riley was moved by what he saw. "I guess they're all worrie
about her."

Cassandra shook her head, correcting his impression. "No
She's gone."

Riley reined his horse up just shy of the mansion. "Are yo
sure?"

Cassandra gave no reply, but merely nodded as she stoppe

efore the sprawling house. Dismounting quickly, she handed
e reins of her horse to a small, dark attendant and hurried up
e stairs to the front door. Riley was but a step behind her,
ill dealing with what she had just told him. Martha had been
young, so full of the joy of life. It didn't seem fair.

A sense of urgency pricked at Cassandra's heart more now
an it did before. It was something she would not have been
le to explain to Riley. But it was important that she see
efferson.

There was no answer when Cassandra used the knocker. She
t the brass knocker against the door once more. And then
gain.

The door finally opened. A short, stocky black man with
in like twilight looked at her through deeply stricken eyes.

"I'm Cassandra MacGregor. Mr. Jefferson sent for me. I
ust speak with him. Now." She tried to pass, but the man
ood in her way.

Barely containing his sorrow, the man shook his graying
ead. "I'm sorry, but you can' go in. Mist' Thomas don' wanna
lk to nobody."

She knew that. Had felt Jefferson's despair even as they had
proached the house. That was what had spurred her on. She
ould not be put off. Cassandra knew that it was urgent that
e be allowed to see the newly widowed man.

Riley placed his hand on her shoulder. He knew what it
eant to be swallowed by grief, to want to do nothing but
ithdraw from everything around him until the pain was bear-
le. Riley understood Jefferson's desire to be left alone now.

He felt Cassandra grow rigid beneath his hand. "Cassandra,
erhaps we should go. We can leave our respects for him."
ley looked at the man in dark livery standing guard by the
oor. "The others will tell Mr. Jefferson that you were
re—"

But she shook her head, remaining steadfast. "No, I have
see him." She turned to look at Riley. "Now, before it's
o late."

Martha Jefferson was dead. They were already too late to

help her. What was Cassandra referring to? "Before what too late?"

Cassandra sighed as a premonition solidified within he "Before he slips away from life, like my father did." Sh turned toward the solemn-eyed man still blocking her patl "Please, I must see Mr. Jefferson. He won't blame you. If yo care about the man, please, let me talk to him before it's bo master and mistress you'll be losing, not just the one."

The dark man was visibly shaken by her words. He was man who respected the veracity of prophesies. "Mist' Thoma don' lay blame. He be so heartbroken now, I don' . . ."

The man's voice trailed off. His brown eyes looked int Cassandra's and then, with a sigh, he turned his wide back c her.

"This way. He be in the library."

He beckoned to them both and led the way. "He be ther for nigh onto the whole time," he confided. "Won' come o to see his child'un nor nobody."

The man stopped just short of the door, afraid to intrude c the mourning that was going on just beyond the wooden barrie

Cassandra knew that too. Felt it as it seeped into her bod The heartache, the oppressively overwhelming woe that cracke Jefferson's heart.

"If you don't mind," she said softly to Riley, "would yo wait for me here? Outside the room?"

Riley had no quarrel with that. He preferred it that wa though it was the coward's way out. There weren't any word he could find to express the proper feelings at a time like thi He was better setting down words of sympathy via his pre than he was with verbal condolences. Nothing ever seemed be enough at a time like this.

Cassandra knocked softly. There was no reply. The ne knock was more insistent. Still there was nothing. As she raise her hand again, Riley caught her wrist, stopping her. The stock man looked on in silence.

She looked at Riley, surprised at the interference. "Cassa dra, the man is grieving." Riley didn't feel comfortable abo intruding this way. "Perhaps—"

Her eyes were compassionate but determined. Riley didn't understand yet, she thought. But he would. "I know he's grieving. That's why I have to speak to him. If something doesn't make him come around quickly, the grief will consume him completely and then everything will be different."

"Everything?" he repeated, trying to make sense of what she was telling him. He felt like a man reading a sign written in a foreign language. "What do you mean, everything? What is it that you see, Cassandra?"

It was something that was not easy to put into words. She was not clear about it herself. It was more like seeing a scene through a haze. She attempted to explain as best she could.

"The course of history changing. I cannot quite tell you how, for I do not know myself, but if Thomas Jefferson is not made to realize his responsibilities, it will be hard not only on his daughters, but on everyone." Her eyes held Riley's. "Trust me."

"I do." Riley released her wrist and stepped to the side of the library door as she knocked again.

A voice resembling none that he had heard before churlishly snapped out, "Go away. Leave me in peace, whoever you are."

Riley thought he heard the sound of a glass shattering upon the hearth. Jefferson was drinking to numb himself to the pain, he suddenly realized.

Riley exchanged looks with Cassandra. The house slave quietly slipped away, unable to view his master's grief should the door be opened.

Cassandra tried the door. It was locked from within. She rattled the knob in frustration.

"Please, Mr. Jefferson, it's Cassandra MacGregor. Please let me in." Nothing but stony silence met her words. "For your wife's sake."

She looked at Riley, not knowing how long Jefferson would refuse to come out. "There has to be another way in."

Undoubtedly, there was, but Riley shook his head. "I can't see you climbing through windows."

"If I have to—" she began to say.

But the door opened just then. The man who stood in the

doorway, disheveled, with a reddish bristle all about his thi
face, bore little resemblance to the man Riley had met at th
party such a short while ago. Grief had hollowed out Jefferson'
features swiftly, as if it had taken a carving knife to them. Hi
eyes were red, haunted, and hardened to what and whom h
looked upon. The heart had gone out of him with Martha's las
breath.

"There's nothing you can do for her," Jefferson told Cassan
dra hoarsely, misunderstanding her meaning. "Nothing anyon
can do." He closed his eyes so that tears would not rain dow
anew. When he opened them again, his lashes shone wit
moisture. "She's gone."

Slowly, so that he seemed not to notice it at all, Cassandr
slipped her arm through Jefferson's and turned him back to th
library's interior.

"Yes," she agreed, ushering him toward the chair he favore
She saw the half-empty decanter of rum on his desk and th
glass he had hurled shattered in the fireplace. "But your daugl
ters are not gone. Your responsibilities are not."

He moved like a man who did not realize that his body wa
his own. His knees collapsed, and he sank down onto the chai

"Hang the damn responsibilities." There was a sob in h
voice, and he caught it before it erupted. But his voice quavere
"If they had not taken me away from home so often, I wou
have remained here with Martha more. Enjoyed her more.
He stared down at his wide hands as if they belonged to someor
else. As if all he had now belonged to someone else. For h
had lost everything. "Our time together was so little."

"And the girls?" she asked softly. Cassandra sank to th
floor so that she might be able to see his eyes. To know if sh
was, in some small way, reaching him. "Patsy, Polly, and Luc
Will your grieving help them any?"

One shoulder shrugged as he waved away her words. "The
are too young to understand."

"But they will not always be so." At least, she silentl
amended, two of them would not. The third, the younges
would soon follow her mother. But he had no need to he
that now. "And do not mistake yourself, sir, the very youn

iderstand far more than you think.'' She placed a comforting
ind upon his arm. ''Remember yourself? How far back does
)ur memory take you?'' She could tell by his expression that
: was not even attempting to recall. ''Events have a way of
)rming us long before we think they do.''

He raised his eyes to her face as if he were suddenly aware
iat she was there. The woman meant well, but he wanted no
:eless pap, no sympathy. He wanted what he could not have.
Iartha. The rest meant nothing.

''Cassandra, I know my wife placed great faith in you. Would
iat I had sent for you sooner—'' Guilt suddenly reared its
:ad, stabbing him.

She realized by his tone that his words had shifted from
smissing her to those of someone who was torturing himself.

''Don't blame yourself,'' she implored gently. ''There might
ive been nothing I could do.'' There never would be a way
 find out now.

Jefferson shook his head, not reassured. ''But there might
ive been.'' And that guilt he would carry with him to the end
 his days.

Cassandra rose to her knees, bringing her gaze up higher.
You can't torture yourself with what you can no longer
iange. You can only deal with the present. And the future.''

He dragged a hand through his uncombed hair. ''Don't you
iderstand? I don't want to deal with anything at all.'' *Ever
;ain,* the words whispered themselves seductively in his ear.

He rose, moving restlessly about the room. There was no
ace for him here. No place anywhere without her.

''Yes, I know.'' Cassandra rose from the floor and watched
m as he moved around. He looked the same as her da had
 the beginning. ''My father shares that problem with you.''
ie kept her emotion from her voice. ''And it has taken him
er more and more often.''

''I'd welcome oblivion,'' Jefferson told her honestly. The
hiskey had not brought it to him. Nothing seemed to. Jeffer-
n's gaze swept toward the dueling pistols that stood mounted
on his desk. ''I'd welcome it dearly.''

Cassandra moved over toward him. She could readily see

him dying by his own hand in a fit of anguish. Very carefull'
she moved the pistols farther back upon the desk. ''Marth
Jefferson would never have married a man who would hav
taken such a cowardly way out.''

A cynical smile curved his lips. ''It's not cowardly to fac
eternity, Cassandra. I thought someone like you would kno
that.''

Her eyes did not waver from his. ''It is before your time.

His hand caressed the cold metal as if it were a friend. B
even as he did it, the urge was waning. ''And where is it writte
that it would be before my time?''

Cassandra would not allow him to look away. She had
make him believe. ''It *is* written. If you should withdraw you
self now, by whatever method you choose''—her eyes flickere
over the mounted pistols—''you will do your country a gre
disservice.'' She leaned forward. ''As well as your daughters.

''My daughters,'' he whispered as if they had not just spoke
of the girls a moment ago. He visualized the tiny faces in h
mind. He had not thought of them in all this time. Only
himself and his loss. But it was their loss as well.

''They need a father. Doubly so, sir, now that they hav
been orphaned by their mother. Would you deprive them
that? Would you make them grow to womanhood wonderi
perhaps if there was not something lacking in them that the
father would not remain for their sakes?''

For the first time since she had entered, a spark of intere
alighted in his eyes. ''They will grow to womanhood?''
many of his children had died already. It was part of his wife
grief, part of the guilt that had weakened her.

''Yes.''

He looked at Cassandra closely, not knowing whether
believe or not. ''You 'see' that?''

''Yes.''

''All three?'' he pressed.

She could not lie. ''Two.''

He was silent for a moment. ''I will not ask which. I do n
want to know.'' He look a long, measured breath, steadyi
himself. ''And I? Am I to live?''

Cassandra spoke slowly. Her vision concerning Jefferson had been unusually clear in some aspect. She was not used to that. "If all things evolve as they should, you will live a long life."

The prospect did not please him. "Without Martha." He said the words stoically.

"Without Martha," Cassandra echoed. "But with your daughters, your grandchildren—and your country."

He raised a brow. It had already taken so much from him. He was not certain if he had any more to give. "That would go on without me."

"Perhaps, but not nearly so well as with you." She smiled as she added, "It has been born only recently, sir. Like a newborn, it needs you. Desperately. Your wisdom, your heart. As do your daughters. Do not abandon any of them. Martha would not have wanted you to."

She stood in silence beside him for a long time. When he finally looked down at her once more, she knew that it would be well.

Chapter Thirty-four

An hour after dawn the next day, Cassandra and Riley wer
on the road returning to Morgan's Creek. In her wake, Cassan
dra knew that she had left a great deal for Jefferson to thin
about as his broken heart began the process of healing.

And Riley had been privy to it all, standing out in the ha
just beyond the library door while she had met with Jefferso
If he had not been in awe of Cassandra's abilities before, h
truly was now.

For the first few miles of the journey, silence was their onl
company as Riley tried to come to terms with what he ha
heard. And the woman who rode next to him. Though he ha
accepted her with an open heart, her ways, he now realize
would require constant adjustment on his part.

If that's what it took, he thought philosophically, that's wh
it took. He supposed it was lucky that he had grown up wit
the sort of sister he had. Rachel, in her own, headstrong fashio
had prepared him for someone like Cassandra.

He turned toward Cassandra after a few more miles ha
passed, finally breaking the quiet.

"Was that true?" He had not been able before this to for
the words to ask. But now he had to know. "What you sai

Jefferson in the library yesterday? About the country? Did you really 'see' that, or were you merely attempting to rouse him from his malaise?''

She smiled. She had known he would listen. Perhaps had even wanted him to so that he could better understand what he was about.

"Yes, it's true," she confirmed. "He was and will continue to be a very important force in forming the way we will go. This shall be a very great nation someday, Riley."

If she could foresee so easily the path a country would take, could she not, then, see something far smaller? He drew his courage to him. To discover the future, to really know, was not quite the gift that some would think it to be.

Yet Riley had to know. "And what is it you see about us?''

She was not completely certain, if she knew, that she would tell him. One of them had to be surprised by what the future brought. But in this case, both of them would be. "That I am not allowed to see. I go each step as you do, blindly. Seeing only with my heart.''

He liked the way that sounded. "Then we shall have to make our own future, without prophesies to fulfill or guide us.''

She nodded. "Something like that.'' She did not tell him that he would be tested. Nor could she tell him how he would fare. Because she did not know. They would have to face this together.

Or separately, as might be the case.

She was being evasive, Riley thought. But he meant to do what he could to bring his own words into being. He wanted their future to be together. Forever.

Before they returned, Cassandra had some knowledge of what would greet them. Her father, praise God, was better again. She felt it an instant before she saw him. Her father was here to meet them, calling out a welcome in his hearty voice before they even dismounted. He had seen them through the front window and could hardly contain himself.

Throwing open his door, MacGregor eagerly beckoned both

his daughter and her companion to come join him. He nodde
and winked gleefully as they stepped over the threshold of h
shop.

The way his eyes danced, Cassandra knew he had a secr
to impart. She let him tell it, though she could have easi
guessed what it was that made him so happy.

MacGregor clamped a hand on each of their shoulders, ush
ering Cassandra and Riley farther into the shop. He hunche
his head forward, about to whisper a confidential matter.

"I think it's a hope chest I'll be making next," he told then
His expression fell just a fraction, not in recrimination, but i
sadness as he looked at Cassandra. "I'd thought it be for yo
but it's your sister who'll probably be needing it first."

"Brianne?" It was not a random guess on Cassandra's pa

The old man sighed dramatically and shook his head. "Yc
know the trouble with you, Cassandra?" The next momen
MacGregor grinned and winked at Riley. "There's no surpri
ing her."

That wasn't really true, and they both knew it. "Oh, yes, ther
is." She kissed her father's cheek. "And the nicest surprise
that you're better."

He patted her hand. There was an apology in the sma
gesture. It shone there in his eyes as well as MacGregor looke
upon his daughter.

"Gone awandering again, have I?"

She dismissed it with a shrug of her shoulder. "Yes, b
perhaps not again. There's much to keep you here now, an
busy as well." At least she could pray that things would l
better.

With fondness and not a little gratitude, Cassandra ran
hand over his downy cheek. The short-cropped beard he wo
was white and had been for as long as she could remember

"So tell me, what of Brianne and Christopher? Has anythir
been said?"

He knew his daughter was thinking of the matter formall
but MacGregor had another way of viewing it.

"If laughter and secret side glances are saying things, the
much has been said between those two." He chuckle

lighted, as he thought of it. "Christopher's been about the whole time you've been gone—oh, yes," he assured Cassandra as she raised a quizzical brow. "I came around just as you parted. I would have said the boy had no home if I didn't know better."

Cassandra exchanged a look with Riley. "There's more than one reason for that," she told her father.

MacGregor looked from one to the other for an explanation. "I asked him to look after the girls while Cassandra and I were away," Riley told him.

MacGregor nodded. But if Riley asked the boy to hang about, that did not place the obvious stars in his eyes.

"Did his job well, he did." MacGregor laughed with pleasure. He jerked his thumb toward the window. He had sent the two to the emporium with a list for supplies. "At least with one. Looked after her so well, I don't think they can be parted that easily anymore."

As he glanced toward the window, he saw Christopher and Brianne standing before the shop. Christopher's arms were laden down with the things Brianne had purchased at the emporium, and from the look of him, he didn't even seem to realize

MacGregor beamed. "Feel sorry for that one, I do."

"Brianne?" Riley guessed.

MacGregor laughed as he pulled out his pipe. He indulged himself in a smoke several times a day as a reward, and it was nearly time.

"Ha. It's Christopher I'm thinking of. Didn't know what hit him once she set her cap for him." He looked at Riley and gave him a warning wink. "It's a determined lot we MacGregors are when we see what we want."

Riley looked toward Cassandra. "so are the O'Roarkes." He thought that warning enough for her.

He would have gladly remained there all day, just as Christopher apparently was. But there was more than a little work waiting for him. The pages had yet to be set. Perhaps he would get himself an assistant, he mused wistfully, just until Rachel returned.

''Well, I've a paper I've neglected long enough and thing to do besides, so I shall just—''

Riley turned, about to leave, only to find his way blocke by Sam.

The man seemed to fill the entire doorway. Unlike at th tavern, Sam was unsure of himself here. And without his apro about his middle and holding a hat in his hand, Sam looke completely different.

MacGregor moved his daughter aside gently with his ha and stepped forward. ''Can I help you with anything, Sam?

''I've come about the rent, Mr. MacGregor,'' he mumble into one of his three chins.

MacGregor knew that was why the man had come, but I had hoped there was another reason. Perhaps Sam neede another table for the tavern.

At Sam's words, MacGregor spread his hands wide. ''A of course, money.''

MacGregor dug into the pouch at his side and drew out on a single bill. Because of his illness, as Cassandra called it, I had fallen behind and had no money to give Sam. He looke at him sheepishly now as he handed him the single bill.

'' 'Tis a little shy I am at the moment.''

''A lot, I'd say,'' Sam countered, regarding the single b in his hand. They owed for last month as well. ''I'm afraid I' have to—''

Riley placed his hand on Sam's arm, stopping the man befo he could say anything further. ''How much is still owed? Riley asked.

Sam looked immensely uncomfortable as he quoted a sur Though he liked earning money, playing landlord was som thing that came hard to him. He remembered his own days the other side of the collection.

An embarrassed flush creased MacGregor's cheek. ''Perhap in a week, after I've finished another piece, I'll have more f you.''

The blame was his as well as the shame, for letting thing go and letting himself drift away. It mattered not to him th he had no control over the situation. The fault was still his.

Cassandra couldn't bear the distress in her father's eyes. She turned toward Sam. "Isn't there some way we might be able to work this out for the time being?"

"I need no new clothes, Mistress MacGregor." He looked down at his clothes. "These'll probably last me until I find myself six feet under."

"I wasn't thinking of bartering my sewing." Sam didn't look like the type who was very mindful of his appearance. She licked her lower lip, unaware of just how provocative the minute action was. "I could perhaps work in your establishment in the evenings—"

Riley looked at Cassandra, appalled at the image that created in his mind. Cassandra serving ale in the midst of men hungry for affection and the press of a woman's soft body. She'd easily be eaten up alive in an establishment like that.

"No." The word was fired from Riley's mouth as quickly as it would have been shot from his musket. Cassandra looked at him in surprise. "Come with me, Sam. I've the money you need." His eyes held Cassandra's pointedly. "And I'll pay next month's as well."

Cassandra's eyes narrowed. She did not like having him take charge this way, as if she needed a keeper. She made her own settlements, not he.

"On behalf of my father, I cannot accept this," she informed Riley with more formality than he had ever heard in her voice.

Now, what had gotten into the woman? "No one is asking *you* to accept. I'm offering this to your father." He raised his eyes to take in MacGregor, who, along with Sam, had fallen silent at this exchange. Riley's look shifted back to Cassandra, this time with more than a hint of determination. "And I won't have you working at the tavern."

Cassandra fisted her hands at her waist much the way she had seen Brianne do when Brianne was being petulant. That was not what she was being, Cassandra thought peevishly. She was defending her honor, so to speak. And the right to make her own decisions.

"You've no right to order me around, Riley O'Roarke."

MacGregor fairly chuckled at the exchange. And to think he

feared that Cassandra would never meet her match. Or her equal.

"And you've no right to refuse a gift offered to your father," Riley countered. He looked at Bruce MacGregor. Riley knew what pride was, and was loath to offend the old man's. But the situation required drastic measures. "Think of it as a loan, sir."

MacGregor nodded solemnly, barely suppressing his pleased smile. It wasn't the loan that pleased him so much as it was Cassandra and Riley finally have a go at it. Some couples cooed at each other, others had to tussle a bit first. Cassandra and Riley fell into the latter category. "Just temporary, mind you."

"Of course," Riley turned toward the tavern owner. "Sam?"

The outcome was a total relief to Sam. "Don't matter to me where it comes from so long as it comes." Sam looked at MacGregor, an apology in his eyes if not actually on his lips. "I've debts of my own to pay, otherwise I wouldn't be asking so hard."

Satisfied at the resolution, he jammed his hat on his head and followed Riley outside the shop.

MacGregor accepted the understood apology. "Times are difficult now for everyone," he agreed, nodding at Sam.

There was a hail of words flying around, but Cassandra knew what was behind it. She hurried to catch up to Riley as he strode across the street. Sam lumbered on behind them. The cold air whipped Cassandra's hair about and stung her cheeks, but not as much as her indignation did. The one thing they all still had was pride, and she wouldn't let Riley interfere with that.

"I won't take charity," Cassandra insisted.

Riley was amenable to that. And had his own way around it. "Very well, you can work for me in the evenings instead of Sam."

She thought of the last time they had been in his office together. Of the way he had made love to her in the moonlight.

"Doing what?" she asked suspiciously.

He glanced at her. "You can read, can't you?"

She raised her chin defensively. "What manner of question is that? You know that I can."

"Fine." He took hold of her arm as they crossed a particularly nasty stretch of mire in the road. "You can help me with the typesetting. I love the writing, but it's the mechanics I hate, and there's more to the writing than just wisdom."

Despite herself, Cassandra laughed. "Meaning your own?"

He opened the door and looked at her over his shoulder. His grin said it all. "Who else's would I be referring to?"

She smiled, and he caught a hint of the dimple at the corner of her mouth. "Perhaps Rachel's."

"Ah, you women, you all stick together, even when you don't know each other." He opened the door and stood aside while she walked inside.

Sam looked a bit shamefaced as he entered the *Gazette*'s office. Taking off his hat once more, he ran the brim through his fingers as if he meant to rub it raw.

"It's nothing personal against your father, you understand, but I've got to make a living too," he mumbled again.

Riley unlocked a strongbox he kept in his desk. "I thought your tavern was going quite nicely."

Sam nodded. "That it is, but there are tabs unpaid, and the ale doesn't come down from heaven."

Riley made a face as he counted out the necessary bills and handed them to Sam. "I know. I've tasted it."

"Often enough," Sam chuckled as he pocketed the money. "Often enough."

Chapter Thirty-five

Soon After Martha Jefferson's death, word began to spread about Cassandra's visit at Monticello. About things that were said and things that people only imagined to be said. The tales were repeated, shrouded in mystery and almost a touch of mysticism.

There was talk of prophesies.

Some said that a blond woman gazed into crystals and foretold that Thomas Jefferson would someday be king of the United States.

Cassandra had no idea how any of this came to pass, but it did. She surmised that talk had been passed on from one plantation to the other by the slaves. She had already discovered some time ago, to her dismay, that gossip and stories had a way of following one. And only half, if that much, was true.

Little by little, Cassandra's reputation began to spread. Just as it had in its time in New York. People began coming to her slowly. They came to avail themselves of her services, not as a seamstress, but as the "other."

Word had it that Cassandra had "the touch" and could heal.

Cassandra was quick to point out to any and all who came to her with ailments that there was nothing beyond a little knowledge to her ministerings. No matter what she said to the contrary, stories concerning her abilities continued to flourish. Perhaps even *because* she protested them so vehemently.

The rumors grew, as they had in New York.

It made her uneasy. Foreboding shimmered before her, if not the future. This epoch she found herself in would not climax well. She could not foresee it, but she sensed it nonetheless.

But Cassandra could not bring herself to turn any away who sought her help. Her very nature forced her to aid whomsoever she could. Thus she became vulnerable to more stories and allowed herself to be exposed to possible public censure should something she put her hand to go awry. People were quick to revere and quicker to point a finger of blame at the very same person they had cleaved to but a day before if things did not go well.

She knew all that, had lived through it once, and still she could not change her ways.

Cassandra explained everything she did, pointing out the common herbs she used. She carefully told distraught mothers and worried grandmothers exactly what she was about when she prepared her remedies.

No one really listened to any of it. They merely praised.

And with the praise, Cassandra's unease mounted. It was as if she were waiting for something to happen, for someone to look upon the dark side and not see the good she was doing, but only accuse that she had powers that came from a nether place.

But there was one barrier she maintained as staunchly as a soldier at his post. When asked in hushed tones, accompanied by furtive glances, if she could sometimes foretell the future, Cassandra merely laughed the question away as so much nonsense. She vowed to keep her ability to herself until such time when it was not possible to do so any longer. As such a time as she needed to use it for someone else's benefit.

Until then the Sight was her guarded secret. Hers and her family's. And Riley's.

She knew little sleep. Her mornings and afternoons were taken up by her work at the widow's dressmaking shop. The

store now saw a steady stream of traffic, thanks to Cassandra'
presence.

There were still some who were intrigued by what Cassandr
could do with a needle and whispered that it was pure magi
that guided her hand and made such small stitches, such perfec
handiwork. And so swiftly too.

They marveled at how clever she was. The word *magic* mad
Cassandra doubly uncomfortable. She thought of abandonin,
her position. Or, at the very least, slowing down.

But the money she earned supplemented her father's earn
ings, and the family had need of both to maintain. And th
widow was paying her handsomely to sew. It was by the piec
that Cassandra received her money, so there was no recours
but to be swift. And make light of the comments that followec

There were some who thought her shy.

Others declared her standoffish and inclined by such behavic
to give herself airs.

For Riley there was only one word to best suit her. *Magnifi
cent.*

His spirit was only half alive each day until such time as sh
opened the door and walked into the printing shop. Cassandr
worked beside him six days a week, coming in each day whe
her work with the widow was through. This regimen sh
adhered to stubbornly, in order to repay her father's debt t
him.

Even here, at the *Gazette,* there were whispers about her.]
was as if the town could not get its fill of Cassandra, in on
way or another.

Riley took offense for her, but knew not how to combat th
rumors, except by turning a deaf ear and refusing to heed an
of the words. That had always been his way.

Yet he still worried that the words would hurt Cassandr
when she became aware of them. He knew that the threat c
unkind rumors was partially responsible for her still remainin
slightly distant with him.

It seemed like an unsolvable dilemma.

"Does it bother you?" he asked one evening after watchin
her lay down a line of type. Cassandra half turned her hea

oward him, listening while she kept an eye on her work. "That hey talk about us still?" From the very first, people in the own had paired her off with him. "About you being here with ne?"

She smiled as she picked up another letter. "I am not 'here' n the biblical sense," she replied with a laugh. " 'Tis working ve are." Then she shrugged, because there was no way to control the talk. "And people are given to talk no matter what."

Riley rose from his desk where he had been agonizing for he last half hour over an editorial concerning the council's growing influence.

"I know." He crossed to Cassandra until he was directly behind her. "I heard someone whisper the other day to his companion that the seamstress's assistant has unnatural powers."

Cassandra stiffened. Had the rumors grown to this proportion already?

The light from the lantern made her hair seem like spun gold. He sifted a strand through his fingers. His desire heated. "He was referring to your beauty and your power over men."

Cassandra turned, and in so doing her body brushed against his. The response was instant for both. Cassandra's hand tightned over the letter she held.

"I have no power over men," she denied quietly. Her eyes gently teased his as she said so.

A smile curved his mouth as he released the strand of hair he toyed with. "Oh, I do not know about that. You have awesome power, Cassandra. Over me."

Mischief rose in her eyes. " 'Tis not hard to have power over the simple-minded."

"Simple-minded, am I?"

He laughed as he swept her into his arms. Allowing himself ne moment of pure pleasure, he sampled a bit of her mouth nd savored it. The kiss deepened, but not too much for fear hat he could not stop himself. He held her at half an arm's ength and gazed at her face. Her lips were slightly mussed rom the imprint of his.

"Completely numbed is what you've made my mind, Cassandra."

He brushed his cheek against her hair. She could feel his heart beat hard against her. "I long to be with you again."

If the moment was not lightened, she knew she would give in to him. And she knew it could not be so. Not tonight. There was a dab of ink upon her fingers. Inspired, she moved back and streaked it mischievously on the tip of his nose.

He released her with a yelp of surprise.

"You already are with me." Cassandra pointed out with a gleeful laugh.

But he did not give up so easily. "Not in this fashion." He nodded about the room as he wiped the streak from his face. His eyes grew serious as his body warmed from the memory. "The other way," he said, his voice lowering to seductively entice her.

She was tempted, but now was not the time, nor the place. There was too much weighing upon her. She shook her head and there was more than a touch of regret in her eyes. "There's no time. There's too much work."

His body fairly begged for hers, for the softness that he had gotten lost in before, for the mindless exhilaration of lying with her and holding her close.

He tossed aside the rag without noting where it fell. "Then hang the work." He took her into his arms in earnest this time, ready to pleasure them both.

His mouth was but an inch from hers when she spoke. "If you kiss me now, the widow will see."

Amusement curved her mouth as Cassandra nodded discreetly toward the window.

Riley turned his head and saw the Widow Watkins boldly peering into the printing shop. She smiled, completely unflustered at being so discovered, then waved as she continued on her way to the reverend's house.

Riley sighed, releasing Cassandra. "Does your father fashion shutters?"

When he is well, she thought. "Yes." Cassandra smoothed her shirt, which had gotten rumpled against him. She could still feel the warmth of his body there. "But not soon enough to suit your ardor."

He did not care if the widow talked about them. She would anyway. Eventually, when he married Cassandra, the gossip would die away. It might even aid him in his quest for her. He'd tell her that to still the wagging tongues, they need but marry and put an end to annoying gossip.

He laid a hand on her arm. "Stay with me tonight, Cassandra."

The entreaty whispered along her skin. Desire beckoned urgently, cracking her resistance. Cassandra pressed her lips together and denied him. And herself.

"I cannot. Da's not well again, and I can't leave the burden to tending him all to my sisters."

She did too much, Riley thought, wanting to protect her even if she did not want to do so herself. "Why not? 'Tis you who are working yourself into the ground to pay for things."

Riley's words brought her own debt to mind, for she considered it hers, not her father's. "Things you have already put out money for."

He shrugged, not wanting to get into another discussion over that point. He'd thought that he had finally won that argument. Resigned to Cassandra not remaining tonight, Riley began to place more letters along the platen. Another thought came to mind.

"Consider it a dowry." He slanted a look at her face to see her reaction to his words.

She took out a letter he had set down incorrectly and replaced it with the right one. Her eyes did not meet his.

"Women bring dowries into the marriage, not men," she pointed out in a tone that said she was having a philosophical conversation with him, nothing more.

Riley spread his hands wide and gave her a guileless look. "I am a freethinker."

She pressed her lips together, eyeing him. "You are a procrastinating thinker." She pointed toward his desk. "You've an editorial to finish, have you not?"

He shook his head as he surrendered the next letter to her upturned palm. "You're as bad as Rachel."

She inserted the letter in its proper place. "Considering what you've told me of her, I will take that as a compliment."

Just like Rachel, he mused. Swift and competent and sure. Except that Rachel had never smelled like springtime. At least not to him.

"You know," Riley began thoughtfully as he sat down at the desk, "you've made things splendidly easier for me, Cassandra."

She lifted a careless shoulder at the compliment. "You are just disorganized."

Her first order of business when she began working for Riley to pay off her debt had been to restore things into order and find a place for everything.

"It wasn't such a difficult task, Riley, to set things aright."

He studied her as he twirled the quill in his fingers. "Be that as it may, with you working beside me, I have decided to take a step forward."

She stood poised over the platen, a wooden letter in her fingertips.

"And that is?" she asked cautiously.

She was afraid he was going to press her about their relationship, he thought. He felt a shaft of anger at the wariness he saw in her eyes. What was it that she was afraid of? She had trusted him with her secret and he had kept it, not sharing it even with Jason. It bothered him not at all that she had talents he could never touch. Why was there still this wall between them? It was a thin one to be sure, but he was made aware of its presence at times like these.

And it annoyed him, for he felt he had earned her trust, not her suspicions.

It would do no good to brood tonight, he told himself. The problem would have to be solved with patience, not with anger.

Instead, he thought of the news he had recently learned of just this last week. It had made him envious—and fueled his dreams.

"I thought *The Virginia Gazette* might emulate what is being done by my fellow newspaper editor, Benjamin Towne, in Philadelphia. He's begun publishing the country's very first *daily* newspaper, *The Pennsylvania Evening Post*.'' Riley watched Cassandra closely as he spoke. ''I can do it here if you continue to help.''

Relief fluttered through her. He was not going to press about them. She smiled at his request. Nothing would give her more pleasure than to help him with his work. There was a wonderful, normal feel to that.

''Then consider it done.''

It was that simple. If only the other matter were so easy, Riley thought, struggling with frustration as he once more put quill to paper. If only he knew why she still regarded him with uneasiness and did not hand him her full trust, as he had done with her.

Still, one step at a time would get him there, Riley vowed, and he was succeeding in drawing her more and more into his life.

Eventually he hoped to get her so entrenched that she would have no choice but to marry him.

Humming to himself, he began to write.

Chapter Thirty-six

The Widow Watkins eyed Cassandra as they both sat at the table in the front room of the store, working on gowns that had been requested for a party. The Reverend Edward's sister was throwing the gala affair at the end of the month. It was a party, in the widow's estimation, that attempted to be exclusive and, at the moment, succeeded only in being hurtful in its exclusions.

They had been working in almost total silence for the better part of an hour, with only the noises outside the store as distractions. In the distance the widow was certain she had heard the stagecoach rumbling by to the way station. But since she was expecting neither materials nor notions, and least of all communications, the widow simply noted it and continued with her work.

If anyone of any consequence was arriving on the coach, she would learn of it by and by. At the moment there was a pounding along her brow that had become more intense with the silence, not less so, and all her attention was devoted to it.

With a loud exhaled sigh of surrender, the widow set down the gown she was working on. She ran a hand over her eyes in frustration.

"Child, I have this dreadful aching just above my eyes. Have ɔu any remedies for that?"

Cassandra had been aware of the widow's distress for the st quarter of an hour as the woman sighed and shifted in her at almost relentlessly. She smiled at the older woman kindly.

"Rest, for one."

The widow was dissatisfied with the response. She frowned Cassandra. What good was having a healer under your roof she didn't heal? "Yes, but something faster, if you please."

Like a spell, Cassandra thought with a shake of her head.

"I've some chamomile tea in the back that might help." he kept it in a little box by the stove. They were both familiar ith it. "And a cool compress upon your brow would not ɹrt."

All these remedies would take much too much time. The idow needed relief from this pain now. Her headache made ɛr irritable.

"But I must finish this by Friday."

Cassandra recalled the pinched look upon Prudence Collins's ιce as she left strict instructions for the dress's completion in ɛr wake. The woman had been almost impossible to deal with ɹring the fittings, ordering Cassandra around as if she were mere lackey.

It was the widow who danced to the woman's attendance. assandra had remained polite but removed. So the dress had ɛcome the widow's to finish.

Cassandra picked up the peach-colored gown. "It'll be ɔne," she promised, holding in her sigh. "I'll take it home ith me and work on it tonight."

There would be little sleep for her that evening, she thought, ɹt the widow looked so woebegone, it wouldn't do to let her stress fester.

The hour had already grown late. It was time for her to leave. iley was waiting for her. "I'll just prepare the tea for you ɑd then I fear I must—"

A young boy burst into the shop without stopping to give ᵊen a perfunctory knock upon the door. She recognized him be the way station owner's youngest son, Brian.

The boy fell upon Cassandra as if she were a lost treasure. "Mistress, Mistress, my father said to bring you quickly with me."

The widow had jumped to her feet, immediately alert. Her headache became a thing of the past in the light of new excitement. She laid a steadying hand on the boy's shoulder. "But why?" she wanted to know, her eyes all but glowing with curiosity.

The boy appeared tongue-tied and took a moment to catch his breath. His head jerked from Cassandra to the widow and back again as he spoke.

"There's a lady on the coach. She's big and fat, and she's fainted dead away like my aunt Sarah used to do." With the simple trust of a child, he looked toward Cassandra. She would make all things better. He clutched her wrist in his hand. "My father's afraid something might be wrong with her and he won't touch her." His eyes implored her to come. "He wants you to."

Cassandra hesitated but for a moment. But even if she were not inclined to help, the widow all but pushed her out of the door.

"Go," she ordered. "Go, child. Help her. Do whatever it is you do."

She made it sound as if it were something supernatural, Cassandra thought. No matter how hard she tried, Cassandra thought, people continued to insist on viewing even the simplest of things she did as something extraordinary. She knew that eventually it would be to her grave disadvantage to have things arrange themselves thusly.

But she could not refuse someone in need. Not if there was a chance she could do something to help. Brian maintained his grip on her wrist and dragged her in his wake as he pumped his small legs and ran down the street toward the way station.

Riley first heard, then saw the commotion. Knowing that whatever was happening need, perforce, find its way into his *zette,* especially since it had become a daily, he followed ickly, ink stains still fresh on his hands.

He caught up to Cassandra just before she reached the coach. "What's this all about?" He glanced at Brian, who, at eight, rdly reached his waist. "Is this a new suitor bound to win ur hand?"

Brian made a funny face at Riley, but Cassandra's eyes were adly serious in face of his jest. She had no idea what was iting for her.

She nodded toward the way station. "Brian's father sent for :. The boy tells me that there's a woman on the coach who s apparently fainted."

"I think she's dead," Brian breathed importantly to Riley. : looked up at Cassandra as they reached their destination. Can you make her come back?"

"Nobody can do that," Riley told him as he ruffled the boy's ir, cutting off any more questions. He stepped between the y and Cassandra.

She flashed him a grateful smile.

There was a small crowd milling around the coach. Men were ering inside the weather-beaten vehicle, muttering among mselves. Yet no one seemed to want to make the first move. one knew the unconscious woman inside. And there had en word of an epidemic brewing farther south. All were aid to touch her.

The station owner looked relieved when he saw Cassandra proaching. He let his older son take the horses away and ter them as he quickly came to join her.

"Thank you for coming," he said with the politeness men erved for officials. But he maintained his distance, as if aid to step into the circle that protected her. His wife had rned him of such things, and she knew about these matters better than he. "The driver said that when the other passen- rs got off, the woman just leaned to the side and fell over."

One glance into the coach told Cassandra that the woman sn't "big and fat" as Brian had described her, but large th child.

" 'Tis a torturous journey for a woman in such a condition, Cassandra said.

She saw color rise to the station owner's face. Childbeari wasn't spoken of in polite society. Such enforced silence w something that Cassandra considered barbaric.

With an impatient hand, she pushed past the ring of gapi men and climbed into the coach. The young woman was obvious breeding and wasn't that much older than Cassandr She was quite pale, and despite the coolness of the day, perspir tion was beading heavily on her face and brow.

Cassandra looked out at the faces surrounding the coach. ' need someone to help me get her out.''

Riley pushed several men aside and reached into the coac his arms outstretched. "Here, Cassandra, I'll take her.''

Very gently, Cassandra eased the prone woman toward Ril until he could safely take her into his arms. Though she appear large because of her condition and the heavy clothing she wor the unconscious woman actually felt quite light.

Cassandra slipped out of the coach. Riley, holding the wom: in his arms, turned toward Cassandra, waiting for furth instructions. The others backed away, still wary that the wom: might have something that was catching.

"Just look at all this clothing she's wearing.'' Cassand shook her head. The fur coat alone was oppressively heavy. A she wore a woolen scarf besides. "No wonder she's fainted Cassandra looked for the station's owner. "Mr. Styles, we have need of your way station's facilities.''

"Of course, of course.'' He beckoned them forward, parti the hangers-on as he went. "There's a bench right inside.''

Tall, angular, and swift-moving, the way station owner l the way into the building that afforded travelers a small hav of respite while they waited for horses to be changed. The was a small kitchen in the rear where his wife prepared fo for whoever had a strong enough stomach to eat after swayi to and fro in the coach for so long.

Rebecca Styles, a subdued-looking woman with large rou eyes and body as heavyset as his was thin, looked on in silen as her husband entered. She especially watched Cassandra,

utious look in her eyes. Mrs. Styles was one of the women
ho the Widow Watkins socialized with on a regular basis and
ho claimed a myriad of superstitions as her own.

She did not care to have Cassandra anywhere near her family
· her own person. She'd said as much to the widow and been
ooh-poohed for it. But Rebecca Styles held firm to her beliefs
onetheless.

"Becky," Styles called to her. She pretended not to hear
er husband. Instead, she retreated to the kitchen, knowing
etter than to call her son to follow, even though she wanted
m to.

Riley gently placed the pregnant woman on the bench. Cas-
ndra sat down beside her. The others, travelers and curious
ike, remained outside the open door, uninvited spectators
raid to venture in, yet not wanting to be left out.

"That's all right," Cassandra assured Styles. She had no
ed for a second pair of hands getting in the way. Cassandra
uld tell that there was nothing grievously wrong. "I think
I that's required is a loosening of clothing and a little water."
e set about doing the former.

"You heard the lady, Brian," Styles snapped at his son,
ger to revive the woman. It would not do to lose a passenger,
d now that he realized it wasn't the pox or any of that which
led her, he was at his ease. "Bring some water." Styles
aced his hands on his son's back and pushed him on his way
the back, where the well was. "Get the dipper."

The boy stumbled over his own feet to comply.

Long, dark lashes fluttered as the woman on the bench
oaned, then opened her eyes. When she saw the strange faces
ound her, she started and cried out, her hand going to her
outh.

"You're among friends," Cassandra assured her gently.

Realizing she was in no danger, she seemed to calm a bit.
er eyes settled on Cassandra as she tried to draw herself up.
"What—what happened?"

Cassandra placed her hands gently but firmly on the other
oman, keeping her still. "Now, there's no sense in getting
urself agitated." She smiled encouragingly. "You've just

had a little faint 'tis all. The men around here spook easy when it comes to the delicate condition you're in.''

The woman flushed slightly at the mere mention of her present state. Gripping Cassandra's arm, she attempted to right herself in order to minimize her girth. It was evident to Cassandra that the woman was very happy to be with child, but embarrassed about the undue attention it brought.

"Thank you," she murmured. "I'm Mrs. Irving." Not knowing what else to do, the woman placed her hand in Cassandra's.

"A pleasure, I'm sure." Cassandra shook it warmly, as she had seen her father do. "I'm Cassandra MacGregor."

Mrs. Irving's eyes widened slightly with delight and surprise. "A friend to Mrs. Martha Jefferson?"

It was Cassandra's turn to be uncomfortable. Brian rushed up with the dipper, spilling half the contents as he went. She took it from him and offered it to the woman. "When she was alive, yes."

Mrs. Irving drank the cool water in three quick sips, her mind no longer on her considerable discomfort. She gave the dipper back to Cassandra. "I've heard such wonderful things of you."

Cassandra pressed the dipper into Brian's hand. She artfully changed the subject. "A lady in your condition should really not be traveling about. The hazards of the road are many."

"I know, but I'd wanted to see my family before the event. And now I'm on my way home to my husband to have this girl or boy—" Slyly, her eyes sought out Cassandra's, waiting.

Discreetly, Cassandra moved a hand to the woman's belly as she appeared to move the woman's coat aside. She knew what Mrs. Irving was asking of her and was grateful that the question was so subtly put. If Mrs. Irving had indeed been a friend of Mrs. Jefferson's, Cassandra had no doubt that Martha had told the woman of her own plea to know her future child's health.

"Boy," Cassandra told her softly.

Mrs. Irving's eyes lit up with pure joy. But she kept her voice low. "His father will be well pleased, and we shall name

m Washington, after the great man who brought us all to
dependence.''

Cassandra noted that except for Riley, the men had stepped
way, hovering at a distance as if to give the women a measure
f privacy in this delicate situation. Pleased that none had
verheard, she beckoned for Styles.

"It's all right, Mr. Styles, she's better now." Cassandra rose.
She'll be able to travel again by the time the new horses are
tched to the coach." She paused to squeeze the woman's
and. "Good luck to you."

"Thank you." And then Mrs. Irving added in a whisper,
For everything."

Scratching his head, Styles looked at the revived woman and
en at Cassandra. "What did you do?"

Cassandra gestured toward Brian, who still held the dipper
his hand. "Gave her a dipper of water, that's all."

"Mumbled over it, she did," Rebecca Styles informed her
usband after Cassandra had passed from the room. "Like as
ot, it was a spell."

Styles watched Cassandra with huge saucer eyes as she hur-
ed by the window with Riley at her side.

Chapter Thirty-seven

Riley waited until they were well away from the site of th
way station and the people there. As they walked down th
street toward the print shop, he asked Cassandra in a subdue
voice, "You saw?"

She knew he was referring to the son she had told Mr
Irving she would bear. There was a gravity to his voice tha
she wondered about.

"I saw."

He merely nodded in response to her reply.

Silence accompanied them the rest of the way to the *Gazette*'
office. Riley's expression had grown so pensive, Cassandr
couldn't help wonder what it was that he was thinking. Had
finally struck him in earnest what she could do? How differe
her gift made her from the others around them?

She stepped across the threshold as he held the door ope
for her. The chill in her bones refused to leave even thoug
the stove was still warming the room, just as Riley had left
when he saw her hurrying down the street to the way statio

Unable to deal with the silence any longer, she turned towar
him.

"Do my abilities frighten you, Riley?"

He closed the door and stared at her. "Frighten me?" He led the word over on his tongue as if he had never heard it fore.

Men were offended if you thought that they were afraid. She ghed as she removed her wrap and hung it up, then dragged hand through her hair. As ever, it hung loose about her oulders, unhampered by bonnet, combs, or pins.

Cassandra tried again. "Perhaps that is the wrong word to e—"

There was work to do, but there was *always* work to do ese days. And the more important work involved Cassandra, t his press. He needed to straighten something out with her. ley placed his hands on her shoulders and felt her tremble.

"No, that is the right word if that was the one that first curred to you." He smiled, setting her at her ease.

Frightened? How could he be frightened of anything that volved Cassandra? Except, perhaps, of her leaving him and sappearing into the night the way she had with her family en they fled New York.

"And the answer is no," he added quietly. "They don't ghten me in the least. They intrigue me, as do you."

Cassandra looked up into his eyes and knew that he spoke truth. She had not realized how much knowing that he was t troubled by her unique gift relieved her, until she felt it w through her veins.

"But I do have a question."

She lifted a brow, waiting. "Ask."

It was a little like trying to dissect magic, but he had to ow. And he wanted to know all there was to know about ssandra.

"How does it happen, Cassandra? The visions, do they sweep er you to the exclusion of everything else?" He tried to agine what it was like and couldn't.

He wasn't asking her to explain something he took to be a rlor trick of some sort. He didn't want to be entertained, he lly wanted to know, Cassandra realized. She tried her best make it simple, though it was far from that at times.

She nodded slowly. "Sometimes. At others, there is a haz glimmer."

She tried not to notice the way his hands felt on her arm lazily running up and down the sides. Warming her. It wa growing steadily more difficult to filter it out and ignore it.

"Most times, I see things in tiny pieces, a flash here, a flas there, until it comes together into a frozen moment in time. Just the way she had know a moment before he came that h would ride into her life. "Other things I can just sense."

"I see." He inhaled deeply. The fragrance of her hair swirle about his head. Slowly, he combed his fingers through her hai He knew he would never grow tired of the silky feel. "An what of us?"

The soft laugh was accompanied by the shake of her hea "You're like Brianne," Cassandra noted fondly. "I'll give yc the same answer as before. I cannot foretell everything ju because I want to. Something come to me if I concentrat Others come to me without warning or preamble." *Such e Simeon's threat growing into reality because of the tainte water.* "That is the way it usually happens."

His fingertips caressed her face. "Do you have to touch th person to see, as with Mrs. Irving?"

Her smile grew. So he had noticed. He was not a man keep in the dark easily. "You are very observant. No, not a the time."

He caught the inference in her voice. "But it helps," I guessed.

"Sometimes." It was a difficult matter to explain proper when even she didn't understand it fully at times. But it hear ened Cassandra that Riley wanted to be made to understand

She turned from him, ready to begin her work, but he car fully turned her around once more. When she looked up at hi questioningly, Riley took her hand and placed it on his che over his heart.

"And what do you see when you touch me?" Riley presse his hand over hers, sealing it to him.

Her eyes held his. The question was easy enough to answe "A part of my destiny."

She made it sound as if this were only a passing episode in
r life instead of something that was to last. "Only a part?"

She dropped her hand from his chest and lifted her shoulders,
en let them fall. "I told you I cannot really see into the future
out things concerning me. I cannot summon the vision at all.
it comes at all, it comes as it wills."

She had lost him, but he struggled to take up the trail once
ain. He meant to understand her as best he could. "But, then,
w can you say I am your destiny, even in part?"

"Some things," she told him, her voice soft as she rose up
her toes, "a woman just knows. Even a normal, simple
oman."

Riley folded his arms about her, drawing her closer to him.
That is something you will never be, Cassandra. You are as
r from simple as I am from the gods." *Except when I am
ose to you.*

He brought his mouth down to hers and took what she so
lling offered up to him.

For the second time that day, Cassandra heard a door fly
en and then bang against the opposite wall. She and Riley
mped apart as Brianne flew into the room. But Cassandra's
ir had tangled on the button of Riley's vest and she could
t draw away far.

Brianne's eyes were fairly shining. "Cassandra, you'll never
ess who—oh, I am sorry."

Brianne looked down at the floor, but then her eyes rose
ain, delighted by what she had seen and what she presumed
me before. Now that she had set her mind to Christopher
d had very nearly succeeded in bringing him to his knees
th a proposal on his lips—it was just a matter of time—she
re her sister no ill will for having Riley. Though, if truth be
own, she did think him the handsomer of the two.

But Christopher was handsome of face, and he stood to inherit
air amount of land someday. Besides, he was a McKinley, and
en she married him she would become part of the first family
the town. Things such as this pleased her immensely, and
e could afford to be generous of spirit to her sisters.

Cassandra winced a little as Riley freed her hair from his vest.

"Is it Da?" she cried. But even as she asked, she knew that it could not possibly be. Her sister was far too pleased for there to be anything wrong. Had Christopher proposed?

Brianne shook her head hard, her hair bounced about. "No but you'll never guess who just arrived in town on the stage coach."

She exchanged looks with Riley. There had been no one familiar to her when she had attended to Mrs. Irving, but then the other passengers had all moved aside to give her room.

"I was just there," Cassandra told her sister. "I didn't see anyone who could have made you so excited."

Pleased momentarily to know something Cassandra did not Brianne tossed her head. "Then you did not look closely." She took hold of her sister's hand, then belatedly looked up Riley. "Can I steal her for tonight, Riley? It's most important."

This was becoming very curious, Cassandra thought. But she was as in the dark about the person Brianne was speaking of as Riley was. Being near him had a very adverse affect on her abilities at times, she noted. Her mind became filled with him, especially when he kissed her, and nothing else could enter.

Riley spread his hands, as if he had no say in the matter. And indeed he felt he didn't. Cassandra was her own person, who didn't need anyone's support. That, he knew, would take getting used to. But he could get used to anything as long as Cassandra was part of his life.

"She is free to come and go as she pleases." He winked at Brianne, and the girl giggled. "I am a very lenient employer."

But it was Cassandra who held fast, refusing to leave. "No one is stealing me," she informed her sister, "until I know for what purpose."

Brianne gave one tug, then surrendered. Releasing Cassandra's hand, she clapped her own together. "Dennis is here."

"Dennis." There was both surprise and relief in Cassandra's voice.

"Dennis?" Riley echoed uncertainly.

He glanced at Cassandra and wondered if this was someone who was special to her. Of course it was, he upbraided himself for being a fool. If the man wasn't, she would not have looked as if the sun had just risen twice in one day.

"Dennis," Brianne repeated, and affirmed for Cassandra's sake. She leaned her head in toward her sister, excluding Riley. "And our Rose is ever so quietly beside herself with joy." Brianne's eyes danced as she clamped her hand about Cassandra's wrist once more. With her other hand she took down her sister's wrap and tossed it to her. "Oh, you must come see."

She tugged Cassandra toward the door.

"Then he is Rose's beau?" Riley asked Brianne, struggling to make sense of the situation.

Brianne rolled her eyes dramatically. "She only wishes."

The fault, of course, did not lie entirely with Rose, Brianne thought defensively. Dennis was not quick to put forth his suit, being shy himself.

"But both are as slow as molasses in making their feelings known. The rest of us know, of course," she confided with a superior nod of her head. "It's there in every look they give each other."

Cassandra's major regret in having left so abruptly was taking Rose away from Dennis before anything had come to fruition between the two. She knew Rose was too loyal to protest or even say a word. So when their father's situation made it evident that someone was going to have to help in the shop on a regular basis, Dennis had come quickly to mind.

And now Dennis was finally here, she thought with relief.

"Perhaps the separation might even spur him on to make his declaration soon," Cassandra suggested.

It would be a relief to her, she thought, to have her sisters married and taken care of, though it brought a bittersweet pang to her as well.

She freed her hands to throw her wrap about her shoulders. As she did, Cassandra looked at Riley, who was attempting to absorb this new information.

"Dennis was Da's apprentice in New York. We thought, hoped," she corrected herself, "that if he were here, helping, things would go better. Furniture that was commissioned would be assured of being finished.''

They certainly had not lacked for orders once her father's workmanship had been witnessed. But completion was now another matter. Dennis was almost as good a craftsman as her father was.

''That would be wonderful,'' Riley agreed, but there was little feeling in his voice as he thought of other consequences that might come about in the wake of this development. ''Does that mean you'll cease to work here?'' And would she use that as an excuse to drive a wedge between them?

She had taken the job only temporarily, for a number of reasons. ''Rachel will be returning,'' she reminded him.

With Cassandra there in the evenings, the print shop had ceased to be empty for him. ''I don't know when.''

She laid a hand on his. ''I shall remain until then. It would not be fair to you to leave before that.'' Cassandra would not have dreamed of abandoning him now that she had given her word to help with the daily. It was an impossible task for only one to manage. He needed her.

''And after?'' Riley pressed in a whisper as Brianne waited impatiently for her at the door, shifting from foot to foot.

She could give him no promises. ''Afterward will take care of itself.''

Cassandra knew what she wanted, and yet knew that to make plans for herself was not wise. Fate had a way of changing things with a whimsical turn of a card, and she knew that something lay ahead for both of them that would cause a strain. Whether it forced them asunder or made them stronger, she had no idea.

She knew only that she could not allow her heart to become accustomed to being Riley's alone. To loving him and only him.

And yet she felt as if she had no choice in the matter. Her feelings were urging her to make the most of the time they did have together and not dwell on what was to be, but only on what was then.

Brianne's good temper lasted only so long. She let out

ong huff as she placed an impatient hand on her hip. "Well,
re you going to come along or not?"

"I'm coming," Cassandra assured her. She took a step and
en looked over her shoulder at Riley. "Would you like to
eet him?"

Riley hesitated only a moment. If he didn't sleep tonight,
e could manage a few hours away and still complete his work.
nd since Cassandra would not be with him in his bed, there
as no reason for him to be there anyway.

He took his coat from the rack and followed her out. "Yes,
would."

Riley was more than willing to meet someone who had
nown Cassandra before he did. Who knew, there might be
ore pieces missing from the puzzle than he had initially
ought, and this man might be able to supply them.

Chapter Thirty-eight

When Brianne opened the door to her father's shop, the tall, slightly built man within flashed the smile that Cassandra had always found so endearing. He was quick to cross to her. Rose followed, fairly beaming.

He enveloped Cassandra's hand in both of his, the long artistic fingers curving over hers warmly.

"Cassandra, how wonderful to see you again. I was delighted to get your letter. I came as soon as I could." Dennis's expression sobered slightly as he looked over his shoulder toward the girl he had been reminiscing with. "Rose told me that your father's gotten worse."

Cassandra nodded, her heart heavy with the thought of it. For all the things she knew and could do, all the various portions she could mix from the herbs she gathered, she could not help her father.

"I'm afraid so. For a time it was better, but . . ." Her voice tailed off. There was nothing more to say on that subject. But she was one who always searched for something good to cleave to. "It was good of you to come."

"Good? I would have followed you before if I had known where you had all gone. The best years of my life were spen

orking for Bruce MacGregor. You were the only family I've
ver had.''

"Well, it would seem as if you have us again." Cassandra
rned toward Riley at her elbow. "Dennis Cooper, I'd like
ou to meet Mr. Riley O'Roarke. He's the editor of *The Virginia
azette*.''

"A daily," Riley added as he leaned forward to shake hands
ith the other man.

Dennis was almost boyishly handsome. Riley thought he
ther had the look of an artist about him. He hands were
elicate, not strong and powerful like MacGregor's. But Den-
s's grip had Riley amending his initial impression.

"A daily? Really?" Dennis looked clearly impressed. "That
ust take a great deal of your time." He moved back next to
ose. "It would me." The words were followed by a self-
eprecating laugh. Then, realizing that Riley did not understand
s jest, Dennis was quick to explain. "I can't read."

It was not an uncommon statement. There were still many
the county woefully lacking when it came to such skills. But
iley, whose own father had discouraged "such foolishness,"
ought that everyone should read, male and female alike. Cas-
ndra had already proudly informed him that her family did,
cluding Brianne, who had learned only because she was
rced to. Upon this Bruce MacGregor, easygoing to a fault,
d been adamant.

Riley saw a way to promote both romance and his own
siness. "Then you must teach him, Rose," he urged. "Or else
won't be given the opportunity of gaining another customer."

Rose blushed to be the center of attention, however briefly.
e blushed more deeply when Dennis turned his blue eyes on
r.

"Would you Rose? I know that it would probably be a
emendous bother, but I'd consider it a great favor if you
ould."

Rose looked as if she had all but swallowed her own tongue.
—of course, if you want me to. It wouldn't be any bother
all." The smile that came to her lips was positively dazzling.
Her parents had been right to name her Rose, Riley thought.

When a smile bloomed upon her face, she was as beautiful a
any rose he'd ever seen.

"When I was growing up," Dennis confided honestly, "ther
seemed to be no need of it. But now that there are more an
more words about to confound a man—"

"Like on the pages of a daily?" Riley supplied with a grir

"Like on the pages of a daily," Dennis agreed. "I fin
myself irritated at being lost in this maze." His gaze swe|
toward Rose once more. "It would truly be a great kindnes
if you would lead me out of it."

Before Rose could stammer out a reply, Cassandra clappe
her hands together. "Done." She knew she was sparing he
younger sister the anguish of being observed while somethin
very important to her unfolded. "Now then." Cassandra looke
at Dennis. The dust of the long journey was still on his dar
suit of clothing. "Have you eaten yet?"

"Not since morning," he admitted.

Riley's hand passed over his own stomach in sympathy.
he did not eat regularly, he became irritable and slow-witte
in his estimation.

Cassandra nodded and saw that Rose was already mental
preparing their meal.

"We would consider it an honor if you would join us f
supper. Afterward, there is a pallet in the back of the sto
where you can sleep until such time as we can make bett
arrangements for you."

Dennis shrugged, his expression affable. "I'd sleep on th
ground behind the house if necessary just to be part of all th
again. The joy seemed to ebb out of my life when you le
New York so suddenly." He made it sound as if he wei
addressing them all, but he gave himself away at the end i
he looked sideways at Rose.

Cassandra noted, pleased, that Dennis had not changed. I
never inquired after things he felt were not his business. I
had not once asked *why* they had left so abruptly. It was enoug
for him that they were reunited.

If only everyone were that way, she thought with a pan

hen she and her family would never have left. But then, if
he hadn't, she mused, she would never have met Riley.

There was a reason for everything.

"Come." Lifting her skirts, Brianne turned on her heel.
"We'll go upstairs and tell Da that you are here. He's resting,"
he explained when Dennis raised a questioning brow.

"You'll stay to supper?" Cassandra asked Riley as they
assed through the door.

"A man has to eat, why not with beautiful surroundings?"
iley tucked an arm around her shoulders as the wind picked
p.

"The blarney seems to be thick tonight," Cassandra said
ith a laugh.

But as she placed her hand on the rickety wooden banister
aat ran the length of the stairs to their living quarters, Cassandra
ad an odd premonition. It filtered in through the laughter that
as around her.

Riley saw the change in her eyes immediately. "What's the
aatter?"

She shook her head. "I don't know." Cassandra tried to
ass it off, but as she placed her hand on the latch of the door,
he started.

"Cassandra?" Riley laid a hand on her arm to steady her.

She turned her face toward his, her eyes solemn and wonder-
ag. "He's not here. Da's not here."

"Not here?" Brianne echoed incredulously. "But I brought
im upstairs myself just a while ago when he seemed tired of
tting in the shop."

Cassandra could hear the strain in Brianne's voice. "Did
ou remain with him?" This was difficult for them all.

"Of course I did," Brianne retorted. She nodded toward the
an behind her. "Until Dennis arrived and I brought him down
see Rose."

It was Rose who now polished the pieces of furniture that
ruce MacGregor completed. Rose who added the stain and
eam to it. Her young hand was steadier than her father's, and
had willingly turned over the job to her.

"He *has* to be here," Brianne insisted, throwing open the door. "Where else would he be?"

But her boldness faded as she and her sisters looked around. The light from the hearth flickered gloomily around the corners of the large room.

It was empty.

As was the bed where Brianne had last seen her father. Panic flared in her eyes as she turned to look at Cassandra. She grasped her sister's arm. "Where could he have gone to?"

"The tavern, perhaps," Riley suggested quickly. It was the first place he had met MacGregor and, though he doubted it in his heart, it was true that less likely things had come to pass. For the sake of the girls, Riley maintained a light tone. "Perhaps he was just looking for a leisurely time without the voices of women in the background," he pointed out.

But even as he said it, Riley felt he was merely grasping at straws. A man in MacGregor's condition could have wandered off anywhere. To the wood, perhaps. Or the hills beyond eventually.

Agitated, fighting back both fear and guilt, Brianne whirled on her sister. "Where is he, Cassandra?" she demanded.

For a moment there was nothing within Cassandra. No inklings, no visions. Nothing but fear. She shook her head. Dennis looked on, puzzled.

"I don't know," Cassandra whispered helplessly.

"You're supposed to know!" Brianne shouted, angry tears springing to her eyes.

Why? Why couldn't she see? Cassandra admonished herself while aloud she replied firmly, "It doesn't work that way. You know that."

Gradually she became aware that Riley's arms were around her, strong and protective. She almost wept then, but managed just barely, to hold herself in check.

His heart ached to see Cassandra's helpless anguish. Whatever powers she had were not completely hers to govern, just as she had said.

"We'll search around," Riley told her, looking at the other girls. "He's bound to be here somewhere."

"Somewhere" covered a huge amount of territory. Fear hovered above them.

"But if his mind is still cloudy—" Rose could not complete her sentence. But there was not need to. They all knew what he was thinking.

Compassion urged him on where his own desires had failed. Dennis enfolded Rose in his arms and held her to him. "He'll be found, Rose."

Cassandra closed her eyes and prayed. Riley could only hold her and give her the comfort of his presence and his heart.

When she opened her eyes once more, the filmy sheen of tears was in them. Her voice was low, measured, as she spoke again. "The constable is coming to tell us where he is."

"The constable?" Brianne echoed, her eyes wide as she looked from Cassandra to Riley.

"Why?" Rose cried, her voice cracking in fear.

Before Cassandra could answer her, there was a knock on the door behind her. Riley was the one who reached it first and opened it.

The burly man stood in the doorway, his hat in his hand. Browne looked tremendously ill at ease. He seemed relieved to see that Riley was there. It made the news a little easier to relate.

"Mistress MacGregor?" Browne inquired. It was plain that he was speaking to Cassandra.

She moved forward, her body gripped by grief that threatened to overwhelm her at any moment. She refused Riley's hand when he offered it, as if this were something she had to face alone. "Yes?"

There was no right way to say this. Browne plowed into it quickly. "I have some bad news for you. I had a man in my jail this afternoon—"

He didn't have to say any more. She knew. It flashed before her, clear as glass. Cassandra covered her mouth to stifle the gasp that rose in her throat. The man in the jail had escaped and, while fleeing from town, his horse had trampled the wandering MacGregor beneath its hooves.

"Take me to him," Cassandra ordered in a quiet voice before Browne could finish.

The constable didn't understand. He thought she was referring to the prisoner. "The man? I told you, he's escaped. I—"

"No," she interrupted. "Take me to my father."

Bruce McGregor had been carried into the jail and laid there since it was close to where the accident had happened. He lay upon the straw-filled pallet like a broken doll. Blood was still fresh about the gash on his forehead, and his blue eyes stared, unseeing, at the ceiling.

Rose covered her mouth and swayed when she saw him. Dennis caught her before she could fall. "Is he—? Is he—?"

"No," Cassandra answered as she slowly came forward. "Not yet." *But soon.*

Brianne and Rose stood about, too grief-stricken to speak. Riley held a sobbing Brianne while Dennis could only mutely comfort Rose. The constable stood back, unable to say anything more than what he had already said. That he was sorry.

Cassandra entered the small cell and knelt down beside him. "Da?"

MacGregor put out his hand, rooting about for hers. "Cassandra?" Even whispering her name hurt.

He was broken in places they could not see, she thought, aching for him.

"Aye, I'm here, Da." She grasped his hand as tightly as she dared. "I'm here."

"I was wandering again, wasn't I? I'm sorry." There was so much to say, and so little time. At the end of his road everything was so clear. So terribly clear. "I've been a foolish old man, burdening you. You deserved better."

"I had the *best,*" she said fiercely. "You've been nothing short of wonderful." Cassandra willed her tears away. Time was precious, and she couldn't waste it crying. "I won't have you saying such things against yourself." She held his hand between her own, wishing she would force life back into him.

He managed a small smile. "You always were kindhearted,

ike your mother.'' He tried to focus on her face. ''Is it to
olly I'll be going soon?''

He'd be happier that way, she knew. It was for herself and
er sisters that she was grieving.

''Yes.''

His breathing was becoming labored. ''And the boys too?
ill they be there, waiting for me?''

She nodded as she felt her heart breaking. She pressed his
and to her lips. ''They'll be waiting.''

A hiss escaped that was a sigh. ''I'll be glad of it. I've missed
em so.'' He lifted a hand to stroke her hair, but he couldn't
anage it. It fell back. ''But I hate to leave you and the girls.''

She swallowed, forcing the lump back that was growing in
er throat.

''I'll take care of them,'' she promised.

Cassandra had been a wonderful daughter. A man couldn't
ave asked for better. ''You always have. And me as well. 'Tis
orry I am that things weren't different.''

''Things were fine just as they were,'' she assured him.
Dennis is here.''

MacGregor struggled to absorb her words, but the buzzing
 his head was growing louder, voices, calling to him.

''Then Rose will be taken care of,'' he said. He was slipping
way, he felt it, and he struggled to ask, ''And Brianne will
arry Christopher?''

Cassandra was not certain of that, but this was no time to
ll him. ''Yes,'' she whispered, bending closer so that he might
ear.

''And you?'' Cassandra had always been his greatest con-
ern.

Don't leave me, Da. Please don't leave. ''I've always man-
ged.''

She had, but she needed someone. Someone to love her now
at he would not be there. ''Riley?

Riley released Brianne and moved forward. He placed a hand
er so lightly on MacGregor's shoulder to let him know that
 was there.

''Here, sir.''

The cough nearly took the last of his breath away. "Take care of her," MacGregor implored. "She needs a man to watch over her and I—" But there was no more breath left with which to finish.

His hand became limp in Cassandra's.

Bruce MacGregor was gone.

Cassandra rose to her feet slowly, giving no indication of the trembling that had seized her from within.

Her eyes were dry.

She stepped aside to give her sisters room. They fell to either side of their father and wept, their arms around his lifeless body, hugging him now that it could no longer hurt him.

Cassandra knew she could not cry before them. It would only make Rose and Brianne more frightened. More fearful.

But in her soul, where no one could hear, where no one would know, she wept.

"Good-bye, Da," she whispered.

She remained rigid even when Riley held her. If she did not, she knew she would break in two from the grief that tore at her.

Chapter Thirty-nine

The funeral to lay Bruce MacGregor in his final place of
st was arranged quickly. The attendance was small. At four
onths in town, the MacGregors were still considered to be
wcomers. The Widow Watkins attended, as did Sam and his
rls and the constable, who felt somewhat responsible for
acGregor's death. Beside them stood all the McKinleys who
d come to pay their last respects.

The funeral took place early in the day. There was no rain,
Cassandra felt there should be. None without, at any rate.
ithin her soul was another matter. She shed her tears there.
Within a few minutes the service was over. Her father was
terred into the earth, gone almost as if he never had been.
But he had, she thought mournfully. He had.

Cassandra stood looking at the grave site long after the last
t of dirt had been thrown on the mound and the undertaker
d left.

"I'm sorry, Da," she whispered so that only the wind could
:k up her words and take them to him. "So very sorry."

She didn't cry as her sisters did. Not when the reverend said
rfunctory words over the casket, nor when it was finally

lowered into the ground. Tears were for those who did not hav‹
to remain strong.

When Riley finally took her arm to lead her away, Cassandr‹
moved as if she were not there at all, as if something else fille‹
the shell of her body while her mind was somewhere else.

This is the way it was with Da, she thought suddenly. Th‹
realization frightened her and made her fight fiercely to retur‹
She could not do that to her sisters. They had need of her.

Krystyna did her best to console the grieving younger girl‹
She knew what it meant to lose a father suddenly. She'd bee‹
about their age when hers had been brutally murdered befo›
her eyes.

With Christopher on one end beside Brianne, and Denn‹
next to Rose, Krystyna placed herself between the two girls ‹
they all walked away from the small graveyard behind th‹
church.

"You will come stay with us," Krystyna urged in her tak‹
charge manner.

She included the tall blond man in her invitation. She'd bee‹
introduced to him earlier by Riley and knew that Dennis ha‹
cared for Bruce MacGregor almost as deeply as his daughte›
had. The old furniture maker had been a kind, loving man.

Krystyna laid a hand on Dennis's arm and smiled as the‹
stopped before her carriage. "All of you." Her eyes swe‹
toward Cassandra. "For as long as you would like. I wou‹
certainly welcome the company."

Cassandra nodded, grateful for Krystyna's generosity. ‹
would do the girls good to be away for a few days. They neede‹
the change, until they could come to terms with their loss.

"On behalf of my sisters and Dennis, Krystyna, I tha‹
you."

It took Krystyna less than an instant to understand Cassa‹
dra's inference. Cassandra wasn't coming. Of all of them, Kry‹
tyna was most concerned about Cassandra. There w‹
something too quiet about her grief. It did not match the di‹
traught look in her eyes.

She turned and looked at Cassandra. "And what of yo‹
behalf?

Cassandra looked away. Her gaze drifted toward the grave-
rd. Her heart quickened. "I have work to do that cannot be
t off. I have no time to go away."

Krystyna opened her mouth to comment on what she thought
that sort of servitude, but Jason for once was faster than his
fe.

"Surely the widow will release you from your duties for
few days," Jason argued, adding his voice to Krystyna's
vitation.

"Oh, come, Cass," Rose begged. "Please."

She wanted to be alone with her feelings. Cassandra pre-
nded she didn't hear her sister. Instead, she addressed herself
Jason's words. "Yes, I'm sure that she would, but I was
inking more of the work on the *Gazette*."

Riley looked at Cassandra in utter surprise. Did she actually
ink he would have her work at a time like this?

"Cassandra, I wasn't expecting—"

She turned toward him quickly. "Yes, I know, but I have
ven my word to help, and I shall." Her eyes held his. "I
ve to," she added less insistently.

Riley nodded as he realized what she was saying to him.
ere were times when work was a great healer. Its familiarity
othed. The repetitive steps helped one to place one foot in
ont of the other until the journey from a troubled place in
ne had been made.

He slipped his hand about her shoulder. "If that's your
sh."

Cassandra nodded as she drew a breath to steady herself.
That's my wish."

With very little preparation Cassandra hurried her sisters off
the McKinleys' elegant black carriage. Brianne, for once
mindful of her looks, had buried her face in Christopher's
est, weeping copiously. Sitting across from them, Dennis
ently held a numbed Rose against him. Krystyna sat beside
em while Morgan remained next to his grandson. Jason rode
s horse behind them as they began their return journey to the

plantation. Christopher's parents, Aaron and Lucinda, follow
in another carriage.

"Are you very sure?" Krystyna called back one final tim

Cassandra nodded as she waved. "I am sure."

"Very well, but the house is always open to you should yc
change your mind." Krystyna's words hung in the air as the
drove farther away.

Cassandra stood in the center of the street, watching the
go until the carriage finally turned and disappeared behind tl
way station's building.

Wearing only her shawl, she felt deeply chilled. She rac
her hands up and down her arms, trying to ward off the col

She wondered if she would ever feel warm again.

Abruptly, as the carriage disappeared from view, she turn
toward Riley. "We've a daily to see to. No use in just standir
about, getting cold."

With that, she turned and purposely started walking towa
the shop, a soldier marching to battle.

Riley followed, wondering when she was going to final
break down and into how many pieces when that event can
to pass.

Cassandra worked all day at the press, not stopping to ea
and taking only a little of the tea Riley forced on her. Seeming
tireless, she set an ocean of letters marching smartly one aft
the other in the platen. When each page was completely se
she worked the press the way Riley had taught her, settir
dampened white sheets of paper down upon freshly inked le
ters.

She pulled the lever down that brought the two sides togethe
then released it, only to begin again. Over and over the ta
was repeated. And then begun anew for the next page to l
set down and imprinted.

She managed to produce all four sides of the newspaper
an astounding amount of time.

Riley, writing the words that she recreated upon the plate

could hardly keep pace with her. He'd no sooner hand her a paragraph, than she was waiting for another to be given her.

It went on like that until the evening. He knew she was attempting to wear herself out, to come to the point where she could not think, could not feel. But that goal seemed to be a long distance away.

She had set down the last of the letters some time ago and was now endeavoring to print the fourth and final side of the *Gazette*.

Riley felt exhausted just watching her. He leaned over his desk and blew out the lamp that had provided him with light for the past two hours. There was only one other lamp in the room. The one standing by the press, guiding Cassandra's work. The fire in the black cast-iron stove was on its way to being completely extinguished.

It was time to leave.

And still she continued, working feverishly, as if possessed. Pushing back his chair, Riley rose. He crossed to Cassandra until he was standing just behind her. He wanted to hold her, to comfort her, but he knew not how. She would not let him.

"You're working faster than I can write. Slow down, Cassandra," he urged softly.

She didn't turn to look at him. Her hands flew from one thing to another like magic. "I'm almost finished."

As far as he was concerned, she *was* finished. Only a few more pages remained to be imprinted.

"The last few can be done tomorrow," he coaxed. "It's late."

She pulled hard on the lever, then released it. With fingertips that felt numb, she peeled off the page. If only her soul would feel the same way, she thought in despair. Numb. She'd welcome that. But it wasn't numb. It bled and ached until she thought she'd been driven to distraction by it.

So she worked and prayed it would ease.

"The last few can be done now," she told him doggedly as he reached for the next sheet.

Very gently, Riley took the paper from her fingers and then turned her around so that she faced him. "You need to eat."

She lifted her chin. "I'm not hungry." Her stomach felt too sick to have any use for food.

"To rest," he amended patiently.

But she shook her head, her mouth firm. "I'm not tired."

Riley held her by her shoulders and looked into her eyes. "To cry."

This time she did look at him. Directly at him. Her eyes were flat, fathomless, where once they had been endless. "I don't want to."

She was lying. He could feel it.

"Why? It's all right to cry, Cassandra." He released her when she withdrew from him, but what he really wanted to do was shake her. Why was she being so stubborn? "He was your father."

"You don't have to tell me what he was," she snapped at him. "I know."

Though she knew she was behaving irrationally for perhaps the first time in her life, Cassandra could not help herself. An apology hovered on her tongue, but she swallowed it. Instead, she grabbed the wrap she had carelessly hung upon the rack by the door and fled into the night. The door hung open in her wake.

She did not stop running until she had raced up the stairs to her home and closed the door behind her. The emptiness enshrouded her like a mourning robe. There was not even the customary warm glow of a fire in the hearth. There had been no one to make one today.

She felt inclined to do nothing save sit there, but she forced herself to make a small fire. It felt unnaturally cold, and she could not allow herself to become ill. There were the girls to think of. At least, until such time as they were married.

After that, she did not know.

Once the fire had taken, Cassandra sat down on the floor on the woven rug her father had brought with them all the way from Scotland, the rug that had lain on the floor before his marriage bed. Tucking her legs to her breast and resting her chin on her knees, Cassandra stared into the flames.

And berated herself all over again.

Why hadn't she known? Why hadn't she sensed something as wrong? She was a seer, why hadn't she seen? She should ave been able to find her father before any of this had come ♦ pass. More than that, she should have known he was off and andering before it had been discovered.

Ashamed, bereft, she hid her face in her hands.

All these years, the power had been there in her to aid others. Vhy not her own? Why hadn't it warned her that her father ould be in danger?

The door behind her opened, but she didn't bother to turn ound.

The door had given when he tried it. She had left it unlatched. iley slipped into the room.

By his own reckoning, he had given her a little time to be one. But then his concern had urged him to come after her. e knew that there would only be one place where she could .

Though she attempted to be so resilient, so independent, iley knew that Cassandra needed someone. But now that he as there, he found himself groping for words when confronted ith her stiff, ramrod-straight back. She didn't want him there.

He pointed toward the hearth. "That's not a proper fire."

She lifted a disinterested shoulder and then let it fall. "It'll ."

Needing to do something with his hands, Riley bent over d began stoking the fire, adding twigs and then a log. It was e last of the pile.

He dusted his hands as he joined her. "I'll cut firewood for u tomorrow."

Cassandra continued staring into the fire, her voice numb, moved. "Don't bother yourself."

He couldn't stand to hear her this way. He dropped down his knees beside her. "Cassandra, get hold of yourself."

Her head jerked up then. There was a warning in her eyes. he wanted to be left alone. "I am in perfect control."

Riley refused to back away, though everything in her manner ld him to. "That's just it. *No one* is in such control. For

God's sake, Cassandra, you're not made of stone. It's all righ
to cry.''

Her mouth twisted as bitterness nipped her. ''And what goo
would my tears do him? What good would that do Da now?''
she demanded hoarsely, her voice almost breaking. ''He's gone
And it's my fault.'' She pressed her hand to her mouth as i
to stop the flood of words. They came anyway. ''My fault,'
she whispered against her palm.

Riley took her by the shoulders as if to shake the notio
from her head. He struggled with the temptation to do just that
He'd never heard such nonsense before.

''How, dammit, how is it your fault?''

She jerked away from him, then rose, restlessly movin
around a room that had no place for her any longer.

''I should have known something was wrong. Instead o
standing there, kissing you, I should have known.'' Cassandr
dragged her hand through her hair as her breath hitched.

Riley was quick to jump to his feet. She couldn't be serious
''You said yourself that your powers come at will. Theirs, no
yours.''

''Yes, but''—she gestured helplessly—''being with yo
clouds everything.''

There was a compliment in that, but he had no time to savo
it. It was more important to show her the error of her thinking

''You still did not know anything was amiss when your siste
came for you. And it was then, not before, that your father lef
the house,'' he pointed out. ''Besides, that's all done with
Why berate yourself for what you cannot change?''

She lifted her shoulders again and then, helpless, let ther
drop. He heard the slight catch in her breath. There was logi
to his words, but they gave her no comfort. She did not lik
dealing in logic.

''Oh, Riley it's my fault, all mine.''

''No, it's not. And someday you'll come to realize that.''

He took her into his arms. Cassandra struggled to pull away
She wanted no pity, no sympathy, no mercy.

Riley held tight until she surrendered to the strength h

fered. Unable to fight him any longer, she cried, sobbing her
rrow, her grief, and her guilt against his chest. He did naught
t hold her, stroking her hair and rocking her against him.
And waited until she was through.

Chapter Forty

Cassandra looked up at Riley after what seemed to be an eternity later. She felt completely drained and, as Riley had predicted, somewhat better. Aware of what she must look like with swollen eyes and tracks of tears coursing down her cheeks, she wiped the back of her hand against her tear-stained face.

She didn't want him to see her like this, but found herself unable to draw away from the comfort of his arms. "I'm sorry."

"For what?" Riley wanted to know. "For being human? I've known that about you all along, Cassandra." He looked down into her eyes. "No matter what has been granted to you, you're a woman first, and it's the woman whom I've come to love, not the seer or the healer."

There was no longer any resistance left within her. His words were exactly what she needed to hear. What she wanted. Her eyes fluttered shut for a moment as he caressed her face.

Her fingers wove into the vest he wore as she held on tightly.

"Hold me, Riley," she murmured urgently, her words rippling along his skin. "Hold me as if there is never going to be a tomorrow."

She sounded frightened of something, but he didn't ask. He knew better. If she wanted him to know, she would tell him

her own good time. And perhaps it was nothing at all, only
the words of a grieving, bereft woman who had lost the father
she adored.

Softly, he ran his fingers along her long, shining hair. He
was prepared to remain like this for as long as she needed him.
Longer.

"I'll stay the night, Cassandra," he whispered into her hair.

"I know," she replied quietly, then looked up into his face.
"I want you to."

There was no more that needed to be said.

This time, as he began to make love to her, the passion that
slammed between them was of a different nature. It was formed
not of heat and light, but of love. Of compassion and understanding that underlined the basic need that stirred between a man
and woman.

Riley wanted nothing more than to ease her aching heart, to
make Cassandra forget, however briefly, the grief she harbored
within her.

Though he had never wanted her so fiercely before, he somehow managed to maintain all that under strict control. All that
he felt, wanted, desired, took second place to her needs, to her
wants.

To her.

With hands that were sure and familiar about their task, they
undressed each other, not with wild, hungry abandonment, but
with restraint and tenderness, knowing what there was waiting
for them in a heartbeat. Their eyes upon each other, they
divested each other of everything.

"I've a robe of bearhide that will keep us warm," she offered.
She trembled as his touch skimmed lightly upon her limbs.

"You, Cassandra," Riley murmured, his lips kissing first
the corner of her lips, then the other, "you will keep me
warm."

Ever so gently he cracked the icy wall newly constructed
about her heart, about her feelings.

With the firelight bathing them in golden hues, Riley lay
with Cassandra upon the rug her father had cherished so. It
was as if Bruce MacGregor were giving them his final blessing.

Riley touched her body reverently. His movements were :
gentle, it was as if he thought she were made of the finest chi-
and would shatter in his hands if he were not careful.

The kindness touched her.

She smiled into his eyes as he hovered, his body over her
touching but not yet one.

"I won't break, Riley," she whispered against his should
as their bodies entwined. The purging heat began to filt
through her, freeing her heart for him. "I promise."

It was as if Cassandra had lit a match to him. Her wor
ignited the desire he had, until that moment, successfully ma
aged to rein in. Riley swathed her body in heated, passiona
kisses that set her soul aflame.

Over and over his hands touched, his mouth teased.

Her breath catching in her throat, her hands eager upon h
body, Cassandra raced breathlessly to the soul-saving mindles
ness that waited for her, calling to it as to an old friend.

"Take me, Riley," she begged. "Take me now."

"Now," he told her, his mouth finding hers again, just .
his body was sealed with hers, "and always."

As the wind howled outside her window, mourning the pas
ing of a gentle man, Cassandra lost herself in Riley and tl
love he had for her.

Whatever tomorrow brought, she swore to herself, she wou
always have tonight.

Riley passed the reins of his horse from one hand to tl
other as he stood in front of Cassandra, unable to banish tl
unease he felt. Jason sat astride his own horse, not the leng
of a man away from him, patiently waiting for the leave-taki-
to be over and done with.

As far as Riley was concerned, he didn't want it to be ove

"I don't like leaving you like this," he told Cassandra.

They stood before the *Gazette*'s office. It had only been
week since MacGregor had died. In his heart Riley felt that
was too soon to leave her alone, even for a few days, no matt
what she said to the contrary.

He had remained with her each night until Rose and Dennis ad returned from the McKinley plantation. He would slip into er home long after dusk had fallen and the good people of Morgan's Creek were safe in their beds, away from their windows. He cherished those long, passionate nights and longed or her to be his forever.

But she had let him know in subtle ways that it was too soon speak of marriage. If he did broach it, Riley knew Cassandra ould say no.

And now he had to be leaving her.

It didn't feel right.

"I'll be fine, Riley," Cassandra insisted. She smiled at him ad placed the reins firmly into his hands to stop his fidgeting. And 'tis very proud of you I am. 'Tisn't everyone who was osen to represent us at something so impressive as an official uncil meeting in North Fork."

As if to erase the argument she knew was brewing on his ngue, Cassandra rose up on her toes and brushed a kiss on s cheek.

She turned toward Jason. "You'll take care of him?"

Jason laughed as he urged his horse forward. He tipped the rner of his hat. "Count on it, Cassandra."

Riley scowled at the exchange. He might not be as experi-ced in some matters as the others, or as well-to-do, but he d experience of a different nature, and that counted far more an money or land.

"I'm not a child, Cassandra, to be watched over."

Cassandra crossed her arms before her, tucking in the ends the heavy shawl she wore against the September winds. And neither am I." Her eyes, amused, flickered over Jason. en back to Riley, her point made. She tilted her head to one le, studying Riley's expression. "There, how do you like ""

He suppressed a smile. It wouldn't do to let her know that e had tickled him. "I see your meaning."

"Good." She nodded, content. "And I'll see to your daily. ith all the work I'm to be faced with, I'd best get started, so I thank you to be off."

Cassandra shooed him to his horse. When he mounted, sh placed a hand on the animal, detaining him a moment longe "Don't forget to take notes on the meeting. We'll need it fo the *Gazette* when you get back."

Riley laughed, shaking his head. In such a small amount o time, she had taken over completely. He lifted a bemused brov

"And just who is running the paper?"

"I am," she answered simply, "in your absence."

There was no quarrel with that. She, with her velvet-glov touch, ran everything. Him included, whether she admitted or not.

"She has you there," Jason pointed out.

"Aye, that she has," Riley admitted.

But he still didn't like leaving her, though the council meetin in North Fork promised to be important. Riley knew how mee ings like that could be, with men gathered to exchange ideolo gies. Time dragged and then disappeared entirely withou anything being resolved.

But there was no better method to turn to. And he had t accompany Jason. Aaron and the reverend were going as wel and Riley knew his voice was needed to balance things out.

His eyes held Cassandra's for a moment as an odd feelin passed over him. "Take care of yourself."

Cassandra smiled. "I always have. Good-bye, Riley, Jason. She nodded. "Godspeed."

As he rode away, Riley could not shake the persistent feelin that he should remain. That Cassandra needed him. Or woul

Perhaps her ways were rubbing off on him, he thought a he turned to wave at her one last time.

"Keep turning like that, and you'll fall off your horse, Jason admonished with a laugh.

Riley frowned as he faced forward again. "I suppose you'v never been in love."

"Yes, my friend, and a more glorious hell a man could n commit his soul to. Let's ride." Jason pressed his thighs again his horse, urging it on faster. "We've miles to go before dark.

Cassandra watched Riley until he and Jason were but tir specks on the horizon.

Feeling uncustomarily lonely, she stopped for a moment at the furniture shop. As the eldest, her father had left it to her, as well as the monthly payments on it. Dennis worked for her now, happy to be of help.

Dennis was within the shop, working with Rose at his side. Things had returned to the way they were, or should have been, Cassandra thought as she watched the two of them together, whispering, enjoying each other's company. She felt a little like an intruder.

Brianne was still at the McKinley plantation with Krystyna and Christopher, Cassandra thought with a smile. She would not be returning for another week. If Cassandra knew her sister, Brianne would return with a proposal under her belt.

That meant that both her sisters would be gone soon, on their own. Cassandra knew that the thought should have made her happy, but there was a note of sadness associated with it which she could not seem to erase.

After spending a few minutes talking to Dennis and inquiring how work was progressing, Cassandra left again, heartened. Wherever they went, her family would still remain her family.

She eased the door shut behind her, leaving Dennis and Rose to get back to work. As should she. There was much to do at the Gazette and no one to do it but her. Riley had contemplated shutting down for the duration of his absence, but Cassandra had insisted that she could keep the paper going for that time. She had learned enough about both printing and writing to produce a fairly good periodical. Or so she hoped.

It filled her with pride to be able to help him in this manner. The Gazette was an important part of Riley's life, and if she wanted to be part of that life, however briefly fate allowed her, she had to learn all about it.

As Cassandra walked toward the print shop once more, a movement attracted her attention. From the corner of her eye she thought she saw a man in the distance, riding astride on a apple gray horse.

Her heart froze.

But when she turned to get a better look, there was no

horseman there. There was only a wagon being driven by a man she knew by sight only.

She was letting her imagination get carried away, she admonished herself as she hurried on. The last week had been a difficult one for her as she had gone about reorganizing her life. It was only natural that, tired, her mind played tricks on her.

There was no reason to believe that he was here, after all this time.

And even if he were here, what of it? What could he do to her?

She was slowly becoming entrenched in the social structure of the town and had good friends in the McKinleys, as well as in the Widow Watkins, for all her loose talk and gossip.

Cassandra smiled to herself as the cool air nipped her cheeks. She knew the woman regarded her as the daughter she had never been blessed with. The widow had given Cassandra all the time she might need to gather herself together and had offered both her home and her comfort to Cassandra should she had need of either.

These were good people here, kind people, Cassandra insisted silently to herself. They would not turn on her, despite the way a few looked at her when she passed by. She had done nothing but good here.

She had done nothing but good in New York too, a small voice whispered in her mind.

Anticipation and foreboding vibrated through her, a coiled snake about to strike.

With determination, she pushed the feeling aside. Pressing her lips together, she opened the door to the shop, then stopped before she had even crossed the threshold. A shadow seemed to fall over her shoulder, spilling into the print shop ahead of her.

Her heart in her throat, Cassandra turned and looked up into the face of the man who had haunted her dreams these last months.

Exercising extreme control, she kept her thoughts, her real

on, from her face. No emotion seeped through at all as she
looked at him.

"Simeon." The name was synonymous with a curse on her
lips.

The tall, good-looking man removed the cigar from his mouth
and smiled broadly. "Hello, Cassandra, you're looking well."
His eyes slid over her as if he already possessed what he
had always coveted.

Chapter Forty-one

Cassandra grasped the side of the door for support as s‹ backed away from Simeon. Her body blocked his access in the print shop. Under no circumstances did she want him insi‹ Riley's store. To have Simeon step foot into it would be somehow defile everything that she and Riley had betwe‹ each other.

She struggled to think clearly. Having Simeon here, standi‹ before her, when she thought he was finally out of her life w‹ like suddenly being drawn into a bad dream.

With effort she managed to speak again, though she felt t‹ very air had been drawn from her lungs. "How did you fi‹ me?"

Things like that were pitifully easy, when one had t‹ resources to indulge oneself. He smiled, and it only enhanc‹ his malevolent expression.

"I had Dennis watched. I knew that he would lead me‹ you eventually. It was only a matter of time."

Simeon's lips curved contemptuously at the mention of t‹ apprentice. It had cost him dearly to have Dawson watch a‹ then follow Cooper once he left New York. But it had be‹ worth the money. Now he could make Cassandra pay for h‹

nsgression. No one turned a back on him, Simeon thought.
) one.

"He's like a puppy, eager to follow and serve his master."
meon turned up the collar of his stylish coat against the wind.
Curious, he peered over her shoulder into the shop. Was this
aat she preferred, when he had offered her riches and the
nor of sharing his name?

"What a queer place you've ended up in, Cassandra." Velvet
)wn eyes turned to look at her expectantly. "Aren't you
ing to ask me in?"

He fairly purred the request, but Cassandra was not fooled.
)liteness and manners melted away when Simeon did not get
1at he wanted.

"No." She remained steadfast in the doorway, defying his
trance.

Dark amusement lifted the corners of his mouth. His eyes
ire cold and hard, she thought. "Would you prefer that the
od people of Morgan's Creek overhear our conversation?"

He was trying to intimidate her. It only made her all the
)re steadfast in her position. "I have nothing to hide."

The velvet eyes swept over her knowingly, mocking her.
)on't you?"

Cassandra felt her throat tighten as she clung to the truth.
Jo."

The smile slowly transformed into a devilish smirk. "What
out all those people who died?"

This was the crux if it, the crux of his threat, this lie he
)uld build on.

"That wasn't my fault. The water they drank was tainted."
: knew that as well as she. It had been water from the stream
it ran through his property. The stream where the diseased
imals had been found floating dead.

Simeon shrugged, his shoulders barely moving. "Possibly,
t it was so much more creative and exciting to think that a
tch had done that to them." His eyes grew wide with sardonic
light. He wanted to frighten her, to make her pay for the
ibarrassment he had suffered when she had left so abruptly.
n retaliation for their ostracizing her."

She stared at him, wide-eyed. No one had ostracized her There had been a few harsh words, nothing more. Fear for he family had made her flee then, before anything could falsely be made of the deaths. She had not wanted her father to be subjected to the pain of watching her vilified. But her father was gone and there was no reason to run any longer.

"Lies," she retorted, her voice calm. "All lies. None of tha ever happened."

Though the people had died, the rest was but a fabrication of his deluded, narcissistic mind. She had been the first, proba bly the only one, to have ever spurned Simeon.

The wicked smile intensified. "Ah, but who's to know the are? If you protest—" He paused, attempting to remember passage he had read. "What was it that Shakespeare wrote? was about that murderess, I think. 'The lady doth protest to much.' They'll be certain you did it, then."

Simeon looked at her pointedly. She was trapped and the was only one way out. One way to save herself. This time h wouldn't let her flee. He had other ways to repay her for th insult she had dealt him.

To even remember the episode caused her great pain. Cassan dra had stayed up long nights, nursing her neighbors, heartsic each time another case was reported. Heartsick each tin another died. There had been twelve of them in all.

"Those people died. I couldn't help them. I didn't *mak* them die."

He waved a careless hand at her denial, enjoying the gam Simeon relished toying with her. Relished torturing her.

"A mere detail no one wants to hear." He spoke the trut and she knew it, he thought.

He knew a great deal more of human nature than she di She was naive and believed in basic goodness, which was lot of rot. But she had some sort of magic at her disposal, a he wanted it. Power meant money and money meant mo power. Simeon loved power.

"They much prefer to believe the worst. To be frightened He loomed close to Cassandra. Far too close for her likir

Why do you think ghost stories are told late at night when e moon is full?''

She set her mouth hard. Why was he doing this to her? Why uldn't he just go away and forget all that ever happened? It as not as if she had broken a promise to him. She had never d him to believe that there was anything between them except e most civil of courtesy. She certainly hadn't allowed him believe that she returned any sort of affection.

''I don't know and I don't care.''

Simeon wound a long, soft strand of her hair about his finger, ying with it as he watched her eyes, her incredible blue eyes at saw far more than he could ever hope to.

''You can still come away with me, Cassandra. I still fancy u.'' His mouth hovered close to hers. ''Still want you.''

She pushed him back with both hands, her eyes aflame with ger. '' 'Tis only because I said no that you want me. Has ere never been anyone to say no to you?''

His smile chilled her. She had a premonition that something ful lay ahead. ''No.''

Cassandra summoned her courage to her, as if it were an my that had become lax in their duties. ''Well, I did, and I ll again. Get out, Simeon. You've nothing to base your lies and no fertile ground to plant them in here.''

People were the same everywhere. Willing to believe the orst before the best. The man he had sent to follow Dennis d told him some interesting things about the townspeople d Cassandra.

Simeon's expression was a portrait of innocence as he looked her. ''No?''

''No.''

Giving way to temper, Cassandra slammed the door in his ce, then quickly latched it. She leaned against the wooden or, her heart hammering. She fully expected to hear a display rage, to hear pounding on the door at her back. Instead, there as only soft, confident laughter. And then silence.

That frightened her more.

When her breathing had steadied, Cassandra ventured to look t the window that faced the main street.

Simeon was gone.

For now, she thought. Temporary relief flowed through he
But she knew that he would not be gone for long. A man lil
Simeon did not go through the trouble of having her found a
then disappear after a few words had been exchanged. He mea
to do something awful.

But she had no idea what, no matter how deeply she conce
trated.

Cassandra lived in daily fear of her next encounter wi
Simeon. She knew in her heart that when it came, somethir
dreadful would come to pass.

But the days slipped by, one after the other, and nothir
happened. If she had not known better, she would have sa
that she had imagined the entire episode involving the ma
There seemed to be no trace of him anywhere. She never pass
him on the street, and no one mentioned a newcomer in tow

Afraid of worrying Rose so soon after their father's deat
Cassandra said nothing to her about Simeon. Instead, she to
heart at the happiness that was blooming in her sister's ey
It was clear that Rose was deeply in love with Dennis and I
with her. All that was required now were the words. And th
would come, Cassandra thought, sensing it, soon.

That left Brianne, and she was Christopher's as surely as tl
sun rose in the morning. Things were going very well, almc
too well.

Perhaps, Cassandra began to consider, she had not se
Simeon at all. Perhaps it had all been a hallucination, a visi
so powerful, she could not differentiate it from reality. H
father's death had indeed left her overwrought.

The answer lay in that, she decided. If she really had se
Simeon, he would have surely approached her again. Instea
almost two weeks had passed since she had seen him.

And almost two weeks since Riley had left.

She counted the days until Riley would return, praying
would be soon. She missed him more fiercely than she h

er missed anyone in her life. And ached for his touch as
ght wrapped a dark robe about dusk.

To ward off her loneliness and the tiny, gnawing fear that
ill remained, Cassandra kept herself incessantly busy. She
orked on the *Gazette*, laboring on it way into the night. Each
y she asked Sam for the latest news that he had heard at the
vern the evening before. And the Widow Watkins was a
luable source of stories.

If she found herself with any time to spare, Cassandra would
end a while at the shop with the widow. To keep her hand
, she would work on a dress as she passed the time.

And all the while, she waited.

Something was coming. Something ominous. Something that
ould change her life.

And still there was no Simeon.

It was at the dressmaker's shop that the skeins of her life as
e knew it began to unravel. The afternoon Cassandra entered,
hausted from spending the past ten hours over the press, she
und Rebecca Styles sitting with the widow.

The heavyset woman didn't seem to notice her presence at
st. She sat, wringing her hands, and sobbing pitifully. "He's
ch a little boy. I just don't know where he's gone off to."

It was then that she heard Cassandra close the door behind
r. Rebecca sat up ramrod straight, clamping her mouth shut.

The widow laid a gentling hand on her friend's arm as she
oked up at Cassandra and smiled her welcome. "Perhaps
assandra can be of help."

"No." The word snapped out with the viciousness that came
om cornered fear. Rebecca's small eyes slanted toward Cas-
ndra, filled with dread and dislike.

Cassandra pretended not to notice. From the first, Mrs. Styles
d never seemed to like her. "Help with what?" She looked
the widow for an explanation. "Is someone ill?"

The widow shook her head, her hand tightening on Rebecca's
m, preventing her from leaving. "No, Brian is missing."

The little boy who had come running for her, Cassandra
membered, when Mrs. Irving had fainted on the coach. Instantly she felt compassion for his mother.

Cassandra sat down on the chair next to the woman an
touched Mrs. Styles's shoulder. The woman jerked away, nc
wanting any physical contact between them.

Eerily, as she touched the distraught woman, Cassandra fel
that she was taking the first step on a path from which ther
was no return. With effort, she shrugged it off.

Instead, her eyes were on Rebecca. "How long has he bee
gone?"

Rebecca wadded her handkerchief in her lap. She looked &
it rather than at Cassandra. "Since yesterday morning. I tol
him not to go running off," she sniffed. "But he never listen
to me."

"Where does he normally go to play?" Cassandra persistec

"It varies." It was apparent to both women that Rebecc
did not want to speak to Cassandra, to even be in the sam
room with her. But her concern for her son was even greate
than her fear of Cassandra. "My husband and older boy looke
for him yesterday until it was too dark to see. They came hom
without him." Her voice rang so hollow, Cassandra ached fc
her.

The Widow Watkins looked at Cassandra with a long, stead
gaze. Cassandra realized that the woman somehow knew wh
she was, at times, able to do.

"Can you help?" the widow asked her pointedly.

"No." Cassandra didn't want to admit so openly what
was that she could do. If people knew she was a seer, mo
would look at her with Rebecca Styles's eyes, filled with appre
hension. It was too great a step, too much to ask of her. Sh
wanted only anonymity.

The widow leaned over to place a hand over Cassandra'
Her eyes entreated her.

"Cassandra, it's a boy," the widow urged. "A little bo
Lost."

Cassandra sought to hide behind vague details. "I can hel
you look for him." She rose to her feet. "If you'll just giv
me a moment to gather my things."

And then she stopped.

She felt an urgency in her chest, as if something horrid wer

going to pass. Whether it involved her or the boy she was
now thinking of, Cassandra didn't know.

The next moment it burst upon her, white hot and blazing.
A vision as clear as air.

Cassandra clutched the back of the chair to keep from stum-
bling.

"The stream," she said in a hushed whisper, perspiration
dripping from her.

Stunned, the two women looked at her. The widow rose
quickly to her feet and came to Cassandra's side, to hold her
as she swayed.

"What?" she breathed, hoping to coax more from the girl.

Cassandra saw it all. Tears froze in her throat.

"The stream. Hurry."

It was all Cassandra could manage to say.

gaine to pull it together, to find the dull ache she had was more than just the weather's doing, so...

Cassandra wished it had rained harder. That the river had flowed to their waists.

Cassandra shook her head, mentally pulling herself from these thoughts.

The constable, meanwhile, had noticed her staring into the fire like that.

Rebecca, the poor woman, looked at him. The widow told him to let her say goodbye to Cassandra's son, to hold her.

"Yes," the constable began, wanting to say that he'd...

Cassandra shook all Tessa's love in her things.

"Come here, Tessa,"

It was all too much. Could manage things.

Chapter Forty-two

"My baby, my poor, poor baby."

Rebecca sobbed piteously as her husband and two other men pulled the small, wet body from the stream. She stood, watching on the bank, shaking, as the widow draped an arm around her shoulders.

The search party, along with the constable, stood on the bank next to them. Cassandra stood apart, having directed the men where they could find Brian.

The little boy was dead. She knew that, and yet Cassandra hoped with all her heart that for once she was mistaken.

"Move aside," she ordered as the men brought Brian out and laid him on the ground.

Quickly, she wrapped the fragile body in a blanket one of the men had thought to bring.

In the blink of an eye at the dressmaker's shop, Cassandra had seen how it had happened. The boy had been trying to cross the shallow part of the stream by balancing himself on a log. He slipped and fell in, hitting his head on the log. The boy had drowned in water that had scarcely come up to his knee.

Cassandra held Brian's lifeless body in her arms. There was
othing she could do to bring him back. No medicine she could
ix, no cures she could proposed.

He was dead.

Cassandra looked up, agony and tears shimmering in her
yes as she sought out Brian's mother in the small cluster of
eople on the bank.

Her throat was thick with emotion. "I'm sorry. He's gone."

Bereft, beside herself, Rebecca took the lifeless form from
assandra's arms. Her eyes burned like hot coals as she looked
t the younger woman.

"You killed him," Rebecca shrieked. "You killed my
aby."

Embarrassed, grieving, Matthew Styles awkwardly tried to
lace his arms about his wife. "Hush, Becky."

She shrugged him off, her mouth twisted in hatred that had
orn free.

"She did. She did," she insisted, almost babbling the words.
"She's evil." Rebecca swung her head around, looking at the
en in the search party. "How would she have known where
find him if she didn't kill my boy?"

The constable moved forward, attempting to calm down the
rational woman. He could see that Styles was having no luck
ith his wife. "Why would she have brought you here if she
as guilty of doing the boy harm?"

"Harm?" Rebecca echoed incredulously. "Harm? He's
ead, not harmed."

"Perhaps I can answer that question for you, Constable."
he others turned as Simeon stepped forward. Preoccupied with
e tragedy before them, no one had seen Simeon approach.

He smiled, enjoying the moment of drama. And he knew
xactly how to use it to his benefit. His eyes locked with
assandra's in triumph.

"Because she wanted you all to know the extent of her
owers."

Staying at Sam's Tavern, Simeon had bided his time. When
e young boy had gone off by himself, he knew he had found

his opportunity and had followed Brian to assure himself that things went his way.

The others looked at him, confusion in their simple, open faces.

It was almost too easy, Simeon thought. When the boy had fallen into the water, Simeon had made certain that he remained that way until he was dead. It seemed a small price for his ultimate revenge. The blame all lay with Cassandra. Had she not refused him, the boy might still be alive.

"Powers? What powers?" the constable demanded.

For the moment, Simeon ignored the question, continuing with his own scenario.

"She wanted to show you so that you would not defy her in the future. She did not 'bring' the boy here in the usual sense." He walked among them now, talking to each man individually. "She lured him here. With her powers." He turned and looked squarely at Cassandra. "While she sat safely in town."

"What nonsense is this?" Browne demanded. He had been around too long to believe in things he couldn't see or touch.

Simeon turned on his heel and faced Browne directly, his own elegant appearance a direct contrast to the rough-hewn garb worn by the constable.

"Not nonsense, truth. Look to your history, good people." His gaze swept over all of them at once. "Did not witches once roam about Salem?"

The man directly behind Simeon snorted and laughed as if he thought the stranger to be mad. "This here ain't Salem, Mister."

Simeon turned on him, his eyes dark and hypnotic. Cassandra had seen him all but suck the confidence away from greater men. "You think they stayed in one place?"

The man wavered and looked down at the ground. "Ain't no such thing."

Simeon smiled to himself. He *had* them. He knew it. Just a few more words would surely send them over the edge in their confusion and unease.

"No?" he asked innocently. He pointed to Cassandra. "Then
w did she know where your son was, madam?" His eyes
rned toward Rebecca, who was more than willing to believe
hat he was saying. He could see that, and he played to her.
Or that the blacksmith was the man responsible for the raid
the *Gazette?*"

Cassandra looked at Simeon sharply. How had he known of
at?

And then it came to her. The man who had followed Dennis
ust have remained in town to ask as many questions as he
uld. Perhaps he had even read of events in the *Gazette* and
eced them together for Simeon.

Dear God, but he was clever.

The panic, fed by the premonition and filtering through her
nbs, grew.

She could almost see Simeon weave the tangible web of fear
ound the people as he spoke and moved among them.

"Have other things not occurred recently that struck you
od people as being odd?" Simeon's glance shifted from one
rson to another. "Think," he urged them softly, seductively.

Browne was in no mood for what the stranger was suggesting.
"ust who the hell are you?"

The constable noted that the widow and Styles's wife looked
hast at his language, but he didn't feel inclined to curb it.
e didn't like the stranger on principle. Anyone who tried to
eate trouble in his town would very quickly be shown the
th out once more.

"Simeon Radcliffe." He took off his hat and bowed toward
e constable, then toward the two other women. "Someone
om Mistress MacGregor's past." He replaced his hat again.
"Someone who witnessed the witchcraft she is capable of."
e said the words as simply as if he were discussing last
ason's harvest. "Ask her if a dozen people did not die just
fore she left New York." His eyes seemed to hypnotize the
ople around him as his voice rang with sincerity. "Ask."
e order shimmered before them.

Browne looked at Cassandra. What Simeon suggested was

ridiculous, but there might be something more to his words. Perhaps she was a murderess.

"Well?"

Cassandra felt her mouth become dry. Had the constable been turned against her as well? She lifted her head high.

"There was an epidemic," she began to explain.

Simeon was not about to allow her to say more than he wanted her to. She wasn't going to be given the chance to defend herself, to undo what he was masterfully piecing together.

His mouth curved with an ironic smile. "*Epidemic.* What a convenient word for a tragedy befalling people who displeased you."

He inclined his head toward her, though he maintained his distance. "How did the boy displease you, Mistress MacGregor?" His eyes widened as if an idea had come to him. "Or was it his father who incurred your wrath? Or his mother? Or was it just a whim on your part?"

His words were rousing the response he wanted. Rebecca Styles listened and felt her heart constrict. In her blinding grief she lunged at Cassandra, her hands extended like claws, ready to draw blood.

Cassandra quickly backed away, raising her hands before her to protect her face. She took no other measure to ward off the blows.

"No, no, Madam, you cannot overpower her with mere physical blows," Simeon informed Rebecca as her husband clutched her around her waist, holding her back. "That will not harm her in any fashion. The only way to avenge your son and rid yourself of a witch's curse is to burn her," he said quietly. His voice was soft. "The way your forefathers did before you."

Browne pushed his bulk in between Simeon and Cassandra, warning others by his stance to keep back. "There will be no burning of anyone in my town."

Simeon was not intimidated by the man. He had bought and sold men of greater moral fiber than this country bumpkin.

"Is it yours, sir?" He looked from Browne to Cassandra. "Or hers? To toy with as she will."

The widow raised her voice in protest, though she remained

here she was. She could feel the shift in mood within the
small search party. And the mood was ugly. "Cassandra's done
no harm."

Simeon pointed to the lifeless body on the ground, focusing
everyone's attention to it.

"The boy is dead."

Cassandra could feel the ill will against her rising. "Brian
slipped from the log and hit his head," she insisted.

Amusement flickered through Simeon's eyes, as if her very
words had damned her.

"How do you know that? Did you see it? Or cause it to
happen?"

He knew she was too kindhearted to ever think another
human being would have a hand in the boy's demise, or that
he had been there and made certain that the opportunity which
presented itself to him was not lost. That he had held the boy
under until he was dead.

The men began to murmur among themselves. The constable
knew that the mood was turning ugly, dangerous. He'd been
in too many bad situations himself not to recognize the signs
of mob justice in the making. Browne drew his pistol and
brandished it before him as he scanned the group of men before
him.

"Get back, all of you," he ordered.

But then, the next moment, the pistol fell from his hand as
Browne crumpled, unconscious, to the ground.

Simeon threw aside the rock he had used. The men in the
crowd looked at him uncertainly. He smiled at them, the soul
of benevolence.

"Do not let a fool stop you from doing what is right."

Surging forward, the men circled around Cassandra as she
gasped. Someone grabbed her hands from behind. The widow
protested, but no one paid any attention.

Cassandra looked at Simeon as panic clawed at her throat,
almost closing it off.

"Why?"

His nostrils flared a little as he looked down at her in sweet

triumph. "You know the answer to that. I told you onc
before."

If I cannot have you, you will not live.

The threat echoed in her head like a prophesy of doom, ju:
the way it had that day she refused his proposal. She had n
known then what lengths he would go to to avenge himsel
but she had had a dreadful feeling.

She had not been mistaken.

"You can't do this!" the widow cried.

But someone within the group caught her and held her bac
before she could come to Cassandra's aid.

Simeon looked completely unruffled. "On the contrary, the
must, if the town is to survive." He measured each wor
carefully tipping the scale in his favor. "Release her now an
her fury will be great. Do you want to take a chance on tha
To suffer her wrath and become a broken shell like that poo
defenseless boy?"

Cries of "No," "Kill her now," "Burn the witch" ricc
cheted off one another, mingling until they all merged and non
of it made any sense.

Cassandra's head began to swirl, and she felt herself on th
very verge of fainting. She dug her nails into her palms, fightin
to remain conscious.

"I didn't have anything to do with that. I'm not a witch,
Cassandra cried, looking from one face to another. She didn
know any of these men. They were no longer her neighbor
they were a mob out for revenge. "I am a seer."

"A seer?" one of the men repeated, bewildered.

Simeon broke in smoothly. "Another word, in her worl
for wizard. Witch." His tongue curved around the word, makin
it a curse, a threat, in a single breath.

He turned toward Rebecca and her husband. He placed
hand on either of them, forming a bond against Cassandr
"Avenge yourself, madam, and you, sir, before it is too late.

Dropping his hands, Simeon stepped back to watch what h
words wrought.

Rebecca looked down at her son. Such a pretty boy he ha
been. Such a joy. She dropped to her knees to cradle him on

ore to her breast. When she looked up, there was nothing but
eer hatred in her eyes.

"I say kill her now. Burn her right here. Now." She nodded
ward Simeon, tears streaming from her eyes. "Like he said,
fore it's too late." Rebecca looked accusingly at her husband.
I told you she was evil. I told you. I had the feeling. But you
ouldn't listen, and now Brian's dead."

She glared at Cassandra as she stumbled up to her feet. "Did
to spite me, didn't you?" Grief almost tore her mother's
art in half. "Took my boy because I saw you for what you
ere."

Cassandra felt it was useless to try to reason with Mrs. Styles.
e woman wouldn't listen to her. But perhaps some of the
hers still might. "No, you have to believe me. I saw what
as happening, only saw it."

Rebecca had no knowledge of seers. The word *witch*, she
derstood.

"If you only saw it, like you claim, then why didn't you
p it?" she demanded.

Cassandra felt the trembling begin within and fought to stop
"Because it was too late. Because I was not here."

Rebecca didn't hear Cassandra's explanation. She was deaf
everything but the cry to avenge her son's death that echoed
her brain. "You drowned him, you did. And nothing's going
change that."

She felt the hold on her arms tighten, pinning them in place.
e looked about her at the men.

"Have you all lost your minds?" Cassandra cried. "I've
ne nothing, nothing for you to treat me this way. Nothing
make you believe the lies he's telling."

Simeon had stood back, content to watch the crowd become
enzied. He posed a simple question to fuel them on. He knew
at at this point, anything would.

"How do you account for all those healings?" he asked
ssandra.

"Yes, what about them?" someone behind Cassandra
dded.

"Herbs, common herbs," she told them, knowing it did n[o] good. "There's no magic there."

But the search party was far too worked up by Simeon['] words to pay Cassandra's any heed.

Chapter Forty-three

It was a nightmare, just a nightmare, Cassandra desperately repeated to herself over and over again. Any moment she would waken and all this would be gone. The angry faces, the hateful words, all gone.

And Simeon, he would be gone as well.

But it didn't go away. It became worse.

Rough, grasping hands dragged her over to the tall shrubbery that ran along one side of the stream. Thrusting her hands behind her, they tied her there.

Her heart hammered madly as Cassandra looked at the faces of men who did not seem to see her as she was at all, but as something vile and horrid. A child murderess. They saw her as an illusion that Simeon had created.

This was here Riley had first made love to her.

The memory shot through her mind.

And here was where she was to die.

It was useless to plead. Her words would only fall on ears that were deaf, on hearts that were closed. Simeon had made good his promise and would exact his revenge.

Fear vibrated wildly in her heart. Cassandra struggled not to let it free. If she was going to die, it was going to be with as

much dignity as only she alone could afford herself. Simeo⟩
would not strip her of that. She would not give him the satisfa⟩
tion of seeing her plead.

Bits of twigs and dried leaves were hurriedly gathered a⟩
placed at her feet as Simeon's voice urged them on in t⟩
background, instructing, fueling. Sealing her fate. Cassand⟩
could hear the widow sobbing and pleading on her behalf.

But it was to the voice of Rebecca Styles that the men ⟩
the search party listened in their primitive fear. Rebecca a⟩
Simeon. And Simeon had branded her a devil, a witch. S⟩
was "evil in a comely form" that they need rid themselves ⟩
to insure that all their children would be safe in their be⟩
tonight and all the nights that were to come.

The only man who could help her, Browne, lay unconscio⟩
on the ground, guarded by one of the men.

It was over.

Simeon fashioned a torch from a branch and his own ve⟩
The sizzle she heard as it was lit cut through all the oth⟩
sounds. Cassandra bit her lip to keep from crying out. H⟩
breath grew short and he head began to spin.

Cassandra held her head up high and prayed for a qui⟩
release.

"I believe the honor of lighting the pyre should go to yo⟩
Madam, for what she has done to you." With a flourish Sime⟩
handed the torch to Rebecca.

But his eyes were on Cassandra. On her eyes. Even the⟩
she realized, if she begged him, he would find a way to sa⟩
her.

She had but to ask.

And then she would forever belong to him.

Cassandra closed her eyes and prepared to die a horri⟩
death. It was preferable, she told herself, to the living hell s⟩
would be forced to endure as his wife.

Oh, Da, please don't let it be long. I'm not brave.

Cassandra's eyes flew open again at the crack of a mus⟩
being fired. She was still alive and the fire was unlit.

She sagged against the tall bush, relief dissolving the stren⟩
in her limbs. Sheer will forced her back up. She stared, asto⟩

hed, at the man who fired, certain that in some way she had
onjured him up from the depths of her mind.

Riley.

Riley and Jason rode quickly into the midst of the macabre
cene. The men on either side of them stepped back, out of
eir way, their movements like those of people waking from
bizarre dream.

"You were right," Jason cried in amazement. "By God,
ou were right."

Riley had woken in the middle of the night, shaken and
onfused by a dream. Like a man possessed, he immediately
egan to dress, telling a startled Jason that he had to return.
hat he had dreamed of Cassandra's father begging him to
ave his daughter's life. It had been too real for Riley to ignore,
espite Jason's entreaties to remain.

Though he knew it sounded foolish, Riley had heeded the
arning, afraid to ignore a feeling so strong. Unable to convince
m to stay, Jason had thrown up his hands and accompanied
m. He was concerned that some sort of madness or malady
ad seized his friend. If Riley went alone, something dire could
eset him on the road. Jason believed him to be ill, and, as
ich, could easily fall from his horse.

Now it seemed that Riley had been right in heeding his
remonition.

"What the hell is going on here?" Riley demanded, unable
comprehend the scene. It seemed too bizarre to possibly be
al.

The torch had flown out of Simeon's hand when Riley had
red and nicked his hand. Simeon clutched it against him now
stem the flow of blood. More determined than ever, he picked
the torch in his bloodied hand, eager to apply its flame to
e pyre.

"We're ridding ourselves of a threat."

Jason, still astride, raised his musket and aimed it at Simeon,
s silent warning clear.

Riley quickly slid off his horse and hurried to Cassandra.
Cassandra is not a threat to anyone." Had everyone all gone
azy? What in the bloody hell was happening here?

"She killed my son," Rebecca insisted, her eyes burnin with an unnatural glow.

"Cassandra is no more capable of killing than she is (lying," Riley insisted.

"Witchcraft," Simeon clarified. He gritted his teeth again: the pain searing through his hand and indicated Cassandra wit his eyes. "She lured the boy here in retaliation for the slight she's borne from his mother. Just as she killed twelve peopl in New York." He paused for a moment to let the informatio be absorbed. "some of them children, like the boy she murdere today."

The horror, the fear, would not leave Cassandra's breas Her voice was breathless as she told Riley, "They all dran from tainted water. Water from his property." She looked : Simeon, her eyes dark and accusing. "I had nothing to do wit it." Her chest heaved as she suppressed a sob. "I tried to sav them."

Simeon looked like a man possessed. "The only one she' trying to save is herself. She's lying, I tell you. Lying. I wa there. I saw what she did. She cast spells. She's a witch!"

Cassandra strained against the ropes that bound her to th bush. This, she suddenly knew, was the test she had bee fearing, the one that would drive Riley from her. The one tha would cause him to see the way others saw her.

Fear was a powerful emotion, and it was heavy here in th valley.

Riley pulled the torch away from Simeon and flung it int the stream. A white plume hovered above the water as the torc sank. His eyes were fierce as they washed over the strange This, he knew, was the man Cassandra had feared. The ma who stood between them somehow.

"The only one who's trying to cast spells around here you," Riley retorted. He turned his back on Simeon and beg: to untie Cassandra.

With an angry snarl Simeon pulled out a knife from his lon elegant black boot. Raising it, he lunged at Cassandra.

She shrieked a warning to Riley. He swung around just

ne deflect the blow. The two men fell to the ground, grappling
r possession of the knife.

Paralyzed, Cassandra held her breath as she watched. Jason
rriedly finished untying her. He looked at the numbed, blank
ces of the men around him and swore under his breath. "I
ould have never believed this of all of you." He threw the
pes aside.

Cassandra mumbled her thanks as she rubbed her wrists. Her
es were fixed on the two men fighting before her. Because
her.

The fight was over quickly. Simeon's prowess was in his
ngue, not his brawn. Accustomed to holding his own, Riley
sily wrestled the knife away from Simeon. Rising to his feet,
ley looked at the hilt.

"Rather a fancy thing for a blackguard to be using. I expect
e constable will have plenty of room for you in his jail."
ley looked just beyond the small circle and saw that Browne
as coming to. "Till then I'll just hang on to this." He turned
ward Cassandra to see if she had been harmed.

The pistol that Browne had dropped when Simeon struck
m was on the ground, not far from Simeon. Battered and that
uch more enraged because of his defeat, Simeon flung himself
the weapon. He scrambled to his feet, aiming the pistol at
ley's back.

"No!" Cassandra shouted, seeing it all flash before her eyes
moment before it was to happen. She threw her body against
ley, and they both fell, out of the direct line of fire.

The next moment there was another crack. Jason had fired
musket at Simeon. With a shocked expression, Simeon
pped at the blood spurting from his forehead and fell to the
ound, dead.

Shaken to the very bone, Cassandra struggled to compose
rself. She clutched Riley's arms as he helped her to her feet.
r a moment she could only lean against him, completely
ained.

Her eyes were drawn to Simeon's prone form. She could
t make herself believe that he was finally dead, even though
e knew he was. She had no need to touch him to know.

"Who was he, Cassandra?" Riley asked gently as Jase bent over the body.

It was over. Finally over.

"A man who wanted me to marry him. A very rich, powerf man who didn't understand that he could be refused." Sl leaned her cheek against Riley's chest, taking comfort in tl warmth she found there. In each breath he took. "Simeon ha me followed and threatened to do here what he had threaten to do in New York when I refused him."

She raised her head to look into Riley's eyes. "He said I could make people believe that I was something I was no And kill me for it. It was his way of punishing me for n doing what he wanted. Before me," she added, her mou curving sadly, "Simeon always got his way. He became accu tomed to it."

The shame and horror of what they had almost done beg to filter through to the men standing around her. Wordless they hung their heads and drifted away, hoping someday to forgiven. And to someday understand why they had been moved, so caught up in a moment's furor created by a strang with a silver tongue.

Matthew Styles raised the lifeless body of his young s from the ground and turned slowly to leave, his burden heavi than the weight in his arms.

Cassandra stopped him for a moment, her hand upon I arm. "I am sorry about your son." Nothing but compassi shone in her eyes.

He nodded stoically, his own shame there for her to se "And I'm sorry about the madness that overtook us, Mistre I'll do what I can to make amends." Though for the life him, he had no idea how to go about it, or even how to beg

Cassandra wanted nothing more than to put this all behi her and be allowed to live unhampered, unharmed. She nodd toward Rebecca, who stood staring, glassy-eyed, at nothi "See to your wife, sir. She's the one who needs you, not I

"All right if I use your horse?" Browne asked Jason as t bereft couple walked away. "I've got to get the misera bastard—begging your pardon, Mistress"—he nodded towa

Cassandra—"to the undertaker, and he's too heavy to carry."
Browne looked down at the body. "Though maybe I should
just leave him here."

"No," Cassandra retorted with passion, "not here." She
would come here often, in the years that were ahead, to gather
her herbs. She did not want to pass here, knowing that Simeon's
remains lay rotting and mingling with the soil.

Jason nodded. "Take him." He handed the reins to Browne.
"I'll be in town soon to claim him." He followed Browne to
help him position the body over the saddle.

In all the excitement, Riley hadn't had an opportunity to ask
Cassandra how she was. He stroked her head and quickly studied her face for signs of injury. "Are you all right?"

She took a deep breath before replying. "Yes, now that
you're here."

He held her close to him. He couldn't bring himself to dwell
on how near he had come to losing her. Later, when the memory
became distant, he could think about it, but not then. "And I
always will be."

It seemed too much of a coincidence to her that he appeared
now, just as she had need of him. "How did you know?"

He smiled and laughed. It did seem extraordinary. "Your
father warned me."

She could only stare at him. "Da?"

Riley nodded, feathering his fingers through her hair as he
spoke. "In a dream. It was so vivid, I couldn't shake loose of
when I awoke. It seemed urgent that I return." He looked
to her face, his smile softening. "Perhaps I have a bit of the
power as well."

Cassandra's mouth curved into a gentle, loving smile. "Perhaps." She had no doubts that somehow her father *had* warned
Riley. There was too much of the Highlands in her not to
believe.

Riley let his hands travel through her hair and trail down
along her back. She was real and she was his. "And do you
know what my next vision is about?"

"No, what?"

"Us." He whispered the word as if it had always been this

way, since the beginning of time. *Us.* It had a beautiful sou~
to it. "You and I. We'll be together, Cassandra, as man a~
wife." His expression lost its playfulness as it grew seriou~
"I'll not take no for an answer."

"Then I'll not give it to you," she replied simply. Yes, th~
was right. This was as it should be. The words sang throug~
her heart.

Riley couldn't believe what he was hearing. He held h~
away from him for a moment, studying her face. "Then it
yes?"

She almost laughed to see his expression. It was such a j~
to feel again, in the wake of what had almost been. "Yes."

She was finally his. It seemed incredible. "When?" he ask~
suspiciously.

Cassandra lifted a shoulder, then let it drop. "As soon
you want. I've been yours since the very first moment you ro~
in."

It didn't quite make sense to him. He narrowed his brow~
"If you knew that, then why—?"

She wove her fingers into his shirt, burrowing into the fol~
of his warm coat. "Because I could not burden you with n~
life, my troubles. It wouldn't have been fair to do that to you
Her lips spread into a wider smile. "But you came and sav~
me anyway. It seems that I need a protector to watch over n~
after all."

They were going to get married, he decided, as soon as
could make the arrangements. Tonight if possible. "I acce~
the position." He feathered his fingers along her cheek, cuppi~
it. "And you, Cassandra. I've always accepted you."

He had, she thought, for what she was to others. And wh~
she was to him. There was nothing more to ask of him.
realize that now."

"Well, kiss her and be done with it," Jason prodded. Th~
turned to see him watching as he stood with Riley's horse. T~
grin on his face was wide. "We have to get back before da~
The wind's picked up again."

But neither one heard his complaint. For Riley was doi~
just as Jason had advised.

ROMANCE FROM JANELLE TAYLOR

NYTHING FOR LOVE	(0-8217-4992-7, $5.99)
STINY MINE	(0-8217-5185-9, $5.99)
ASE THE WIND	(0-8217-4740-1, $5.99)
DNIGHT SECRETS	(0-8217-5280-4, $5.99)
OONBEAMS AND MAGIC	(0-8217-0184-4, $5.99)
EET SAVAGE HEART	(0-8217-5276-6, $5.99)

ROMANCE FROM FERN MICHAELS

DEAR EMILY   (0-8217-4952-8, $5.9

WISH LIST   (0-8217-5228-6, $6.9

AND IN HARDCOVER:

VEGAS RICH   (1-57566-057-1, $25.0